Billiards at Half-past Nine

BOOKS BY HEINRICH BÖLL

Acquainted with the Night
Adam, Where Art Thou?
The Train Was on Time
Tomorrow and Yesterday
Billiards at Half-past Nine
The Clown
Absent Without Leave
18 Stories
Irish Journal
End of a Mission
Children Are Civilians Too
Adam and The Train
Group Portrait with Lady

Billiards at Half=past Nine

HEINRICH BÖLL

Translated from the German

McGraw-Hill Book Company

New York • St. Louis • San Francisco • Düsseldorf
Mexico • Montreal • Panama • São Paulo • Toronto

billiards at half-past nine

Library of Congress Catalog Card Number: 62-15141
07-006401-6

1 2 3 4 5 6 7 8 9 MU MU 7 9 8 7 6 5 4 3

Billiards at Half-past Nine

[handwritten annotations: Leonora's perspective; organizing principles of contradicting realms; Neat offices, billiards, vs. "Trucks, Apprentices, and Nuns"; outside world; Violence? Religion; Bleedinghum — what does it mean?]

This morning, for the first time ever, Faehmel was curt with her, almost rude. He called about half-past eleven and the very sound of his voice over the phone spelt trouble. The tone was new to her, and frightening, precisely because everything he said was, in fact, as irreproachable as always. But in this new voice all courtesy had been reduced to mere formula, as if he were suddenly offering her a glass of H_2O instead of water.

"If you please," he said, "look in your desk and get that little red card I gave you four years ago." She pulled out the drawer, pushed aside a chocolate bar, some cleaning cloths, the metal polish and took out the red card. "Now, be so kind as to read what it says on the card."

Voice trembling, she read: "Available at any time to my mother, my father, my daughter, my son or Mr. Schrella. Otherwise to no one."

"Repeat the last sentence, please." She did—"Otherwise to no one." "And by the way, how did you find out that phone number I gave you was the Prince Heinrich Hotel?" She said not a word. "I want to stress the fact you're to follow my instructions even when they date back four years . . . if you please."

Not a peep out of her.

"Stupid thing . . . !" The inevitable "if you please," had he forgotten it?

She heard muttering, then a voice calling, "Taxi, taxi," after which the connection was cut off. She laid down the receiver, shoved the little red card into the center of the desk and felt a kind of relief. His rudeness, the first in four years, was almost like a caress.

When she was at sixes and sevens, or fed up with the extremely routine nature of her work, she would go out of doors and polish the brass nameplate: "Dr. Robert Faehmel. Architectural Estimates. Closed Afternoons." Train smoke, street dust, smog gave her a daily excuse to use the cloths and metal polish, and she liked to stretch out the chore to a quarter, a half-hour. Now, across the way, she could see the printing presses stamping away, tirelessly impressing edification on white paper. She felt their vibration, imagined herself on a ship about to get under way, or already out at sea. Trucks, apprentices, nuns. Life in the streets, crates in front of the grocer's, oranges, tomatoes, cabbages. Next door, in front of Gretz' shop, two butcherboys were hanging up the wild boar, as they did every day. Dark boar's blood was dripping onto the asphalt. Defiance welled up in her. She thought what it would be like to give notice and go to work in some grimy, backyard hole-in-the-wall where electric cable or spices or onions were sold, where sloppily suspendered middle-aged foremen had ideas, thus providing the satisfaction of giving them the brush-off. Places where you had to put up a battle to get that extra hour to spend waiting at the dentist's. Where a collection was taken up when one of the girls got engaged, or had a stork shower. Or to buy a book on love. Where your fellow-workers' dirty jokes kept you alive to the fact that you, yourself, were a virgin. Life. Quite different from this perfect order, this flawlessly dressed and unfailingly polite employer

2

who gave you the creeps. There was contempt, you could sense, behind the politeness he handed out to everyone he came in contact with. Yet who, actually, who outside herself did he have anything to do with? As far back as she could remember, she'd never seen him talking to anyone, except his father, son or daughter. His mother she'd never laid eyes on. She was off in a mental hospital somewhere. Nor had that Mr. Schrella, also on the red card, ever set foot in the office. Faehmel meanwhile held no office consultations. Clients who phoned for an appointment were asked to state their business in writing.

When he caught her making a mistake, he merely passed it off with a wave of his hand, and said, "All right, now do it over, please." As a matter of fact this seldom happened; the few errors that crept in she usually discovered first herself. In all events, that "please" of his he never forgot. When she asked him for time off, he gave it to her, hours, days. The time her mother died, he said, "We'll close the office for four days. Or would you rather have a week?" But she hadn't wanted a week, not even four days. Only three, and even that was too long in the empty apartment. Needless to say, he showed up for the funeral and graveside services, and his father, his son and daughter also put in an appearance, all of them bringing enormous wreaths which they laid on the grave themselves. They listened closely to the liturgy, and the old father, whom she liked, whispered to her, "We Faehmels know death very well. We're on a solid footing with that fellow, my dear child."

Every favor she wanted was granted without demur and as a result she found it harder and harder, as the years slipped by, to make any requests at all. He had progressively cut down her working hours. During the first year she had worked from eight till four. But for the past two years her work had become so organized she could easily get it done between eight and one. Even so she had time to be bored, to drag out the cleaning chore to a half-hour. And now not as much as a single cloudy spot left on the brass sign! She screwed the cap of the metal polish back on, folded the rags and heaved a sigh. The printing presses were still pounding away, tirelessly impressing edification on white paper, the boar carcass was still dripping blood. Apprentices, trucks, nuns. Life in the streets.

There it lay on the desk, the red card with "Otherwise to no one" in the flawless architect's writing. There, too, was the phone number which, having time on her hands, blushing at her own curiosity, she had identified as the Prince Heinrich Hotel's. The name had provided fresh scent for her nose to follow. What did he do in the Prince Heinrich Hotel every morning between half-past nine and eleven? That icy voice on the phone, saying, "Stupid thing." And without any "please" after it! The departure from style cheered her up, reconciled her with a job any automaton could manage.

Among the carbon copies left behind by her predecessor she had found two form letters, both of which had continued in use unchanged during the years of her regime. One was for clients who had placed a commission: "Thank you for your confidence, which we shall try to justify by speedy and accurate fulfillment of your assignment. Respectfully yours. . . ." The other was used when stress and strain data and the like were delivered to clients: "Herewith the desired information concerning construction project X. Kindly credit the fee, in the amount of Y, to our bank account. Respectfully yours. . . ." Certain variations, of course, were left to her. For X she might insert "Publisher's house at the edge of the forest," "Teacher's house on riverbank," "Holleben Street railway bridge." The fee entered at Y, too, she figured out herself, according to a simple scale.

Beyond this there was the correspondence with his three associates, Kanders, Schrit and Hochbret, to whom she had to forward the commissions in turn as they came in. "This way," Faehmel had said, "justice automatically runs its course and the odds are even for a lucky break." When the data came back, Schrit had to go over Kanders' figures, Kanders over Hochbret's, Hochbret over Schrit's. There were also card indexes to be kept, bills for expenses to be entered in a ledger, drawings to photocopy and double postcard-size extra photocopies to be made for his private records. But mostly her work consisted of getting letters ready to mail, again and again drawing the sticky side of green, red or blue stamps with President Heuss' picture on them across the little sponge and pasting them on neatly at the upper right-hand corner of the yellow envelopes. From time to time the Heusses needed were brown, violet or yellow, and even that much was a welcome change.

Faehmel had made it a rule never to spend more than an hour a day in the office. He wrote his name under "Respectfully yours," under itemized billings. If more commissions came in than he could handle in an hour a day, he turned them down. For such cases there was a mimeographed form letter, the text of which read: "We regret to inform you that owing to the pressure of work we must forego the privilege of handling your esteemed commission. Signed, F."

Not once, while sitting opposite him mornings between half-past eight and half-past nine, had she ever seen him doing anything that was human and intimate, such as eating or drinking. She'd never even seen him have a head cold. She blushed, thinking of things more intimate than these. The fact that he smoked didn't make up for all the other things she missed. The snow-white cigarette was too perfect, only ashes and butt in the ash tray for consolation. Still, that much at least was waste, evidence that something had been used up. She had worked for mighty bosses before, men whose desks were like a captain's bridge, whose physiognomy inspired dread. Yet even these big shots had drunk a cup of tea or coffee now and then, or eaten a sandwich, and the sight of tycoons eating and drinking had always been a source of excitement. Bread crumbled, sausage skins and fatty ham rind were left over. Hands had to be washed, handkerchiefs taken out. Mouths were wiped on granite visages that, one day, would be cast in bronze, from pedestaled monuments to give notice of their greatness to future generations. But Faehmel, when he arrived from the rear premises at half-past eight, brought no whiff of breakfast with him. Nor, as you might expect of a boss, was he ever either nervous or carefully poised for action. Even when he had to write his name forty times under "Respectfully yours," his signature stayed fine and readable. He smoked, he signed, once in a great while gave a drawing a glance, at half-past nine took his hat and coat, said, "See you tomorrow," and vanished. From half-past nine till eleven he was at the Prince Heinrich Hotel, from eleven to noon in the Cafe Zons, all this while available only to his "mother, father, daughter, son and Mr. Schrella." At noon he went out for a walk, then at one o'clock met his daughter for lunch at The Lion. How he spent his afternoons and evenings she had no idea. She only knew that he went to Mass every morning at seven, was with his daughter from half-past seven till eight, from eight till half-past eight breakfasted alone.

She never got over being surprised by the pleasure he showed when his son came to pay him a visit. Again and again, at the office, he would open the window and look down the street as far as the Modest Gate. He had flowers sent to the house, engaged a housekeeper for the length of the visit. The little scar on the bridge of his nose turned red with excitement, the gloomy back part of the house teemed with cleaning women as daily they brought out empty wine bottles and left them in the hall for the rubbish man. More and more bottles accumulated, first in rows of five, then of ten, until the whole length of the back entry was taken up by a stiff, dark green forest stockade of bottles, the tips of which she counted, blushing at her nosiness. Two hundred and ten bottles emptied between the beginning of May and the last of August. More than one bottle a day.

Yet he never smelled of alcohol, his hands never shook. The

stiff, dark green forest became unreal. Had she actually seen it? Or was it only a dream? Schrit, Hochbret or Kanders certainly she had never seen, each being buried as he was in his own little hideout far away from the others.

Only twice had any one of them caught another making a mistake. Once was when Schrit had miscalculated the foundation for the municipal swimming pool—this detected by Hochbret. It had been all very upsetting, but Faehmel had merely asked her to identify the notes penciled in red on the margin of the drawing as belonging respectively to Schrit and Hochbret. For the first time it dawned on her that Faehmel really knew his business. Half an hour he sat at his desk with slide rule, reference tables and sharpened pencils, then said, "Hochbret is right. The swimming pool would have caved in after three months." Meanwhile not a word of blame for Schrit, of praise for Hochbret. Just this once—as he signed the revised estimate—he laughed, and his laugh was as eerie as his politeness.

The second mistake had been made by Hochbret, when he worked out a statics analysis for the Wilhelmskuhle railway overpass. That time the error was discovered by Kanders. Once again she watched Faehmel—for the second time in four years—sit down at his desk and calculate. Once again she had to identify Hochbret's and Kanders' red-penciled notes. It was this incident that gave him the idea of prescribing different colored pencils for his different associates: Kanders red, Hochbret green, Schrit yellow.

Slowly, a piece of chocolate melting in her mouth, she wrote, "Weekend house for film actress," then, "Annex for Co-operative Welfare Society" as a second piece dissolved. At least clients did have names and addresses to tell them apart by, and the enclosed drawings likewise made her feel she was involved in something real. Building stone and sheets of plastic, iron girders, glass bricks and bags of cement, all of these could be visualized, whereas Kanders, Schrit and Hochbret, though

7

she wrote their addresses every day, could not. They sent in their totals and estimates without comment. "Why letters?" Faehmel had said. "We're not in the business here of collecting confessions, are we?"

Sometimes she took down the encyclopedia from the bookshelf and looked up the places to which her daily envelopes were addressed. "Schilgenauel, pop. 87, of which 83 Rom. Cath., famous 12th cent. parish church w. Schilgenauel altar." Kanders lived there. And his insurance card revealed the following information: "Age 37, bachelor, Rom. Cath." Schrit lived way up north, in "Gludum, pop. 1988, of which 1812 Prot., 176 Rom. Cath., pickle factories, mission school." Schrit was "48, married, Prot., 2 children, of which 1 over 18." She didn't need to look up Hochbret's home town. He lived in Blessenfeld, out in the suburbs, only a thirty-five-minute bus ride away. The crazy idea often popped into her head of looking up Hochbret, of making sure he was real by hearing his voice, seeing him in the flesh, feeling his handshake. But his youth—he was just thirty-two—and the fact he was a bachelor held her back. Although the encyclopedia described Kanders' and Schrit's home towns with the exactness of an identification card, and although she knew Blessenfeld very well, still all three of them remained beyond her power to visualize, even when she made out their monthly insurance premiums, filled in postal orders for them, sent them schedules and periodicals. They remained as unreal as that Mr. Schrella, named on the red card, to whom Faehmel was always available, though in four years not once had Schrella ever asked to see him.

She let the red card, cause of his first rudeness to her, lie on the desk. What was the name of that gentleman, the one who had come into the office about ten and urgently, urgently, very urgently asked to speak with Faehmel? A big, gray-haired man with a rather ruddy face, he smelled of exquisite expense-account meals and wore a suit reeking of class. He had combined power, dignity and masterful charm in an utterly irresistible way. His title, vaguely, smilingly murmured, had something to do with minister—ministerial councillor, director, manager—something like that. When she'd said she hadn't any idea where Faehmel was at the moment, suddenly, shooting out a hand, laying it on her shoulder, he said, "Come on now, sweetie, out with it. Where can I find him?" And she had given in to him, not knowing just how it happened. She gave away the deep-down secret, the scent of which had so keenly led her on: "Prince Heinrich Hotel." Whereupon he had murmured something about being an old school friend, about an urgent, a very pressing matter, something about defense, weapons. Behind him he left the aroma of a cigar which, when he smelled it an hour later, set Faehmel's father excitedly sniffing.

"Good heavens, good heavens, what a weed that must have been, what a weed!" The old man snuffed along the walls, poked his nose down close to the desk, put on his hat and a couple of minutes later was back with the tobacconist whose customer he'd been for the past fifty years. The two of them stood for a bit in the doorway sniffing, then dashed about the office like agitated dogs. The tobacconist crawled under the desk where a whole cloud of cigar smoke had lingered intact. He clapped his hands, gave a triumphant laugh and said, "Yes, Your Excellency, it was a Partagas Eminentes."

"And you can get them for me?"

"Absolutely. I keep them in stock."

"God help you if the aroma isn't exactly the same!"

Once more the tobacconist sniffed and said, "Partagas Eminentes, I'll bet my neck on it, Excellency. Four marks apiece. Would you like some?"

"One, my dear Kolbe, just one. My grandfather earned four marks a week, and I respect the dead. I have my sentimentalities, as you know. Good Lord, my son has smoked twenty thousand cigarettes in here, and that weed knocks them all for a loop!"

She felt highly honored, having the old fellow smoke his cigar in her company, leaning back in his son's easy chair.

The chair was too big for him, and so she eased a cushion behind his back, then listened, while she went on with that most impeccable of occupations, sticking on stamps. Slowly she drew the backs of a green, red, blue Heuss across the sponge, and stuck them neatly on at the upper right-hand corner of envelopes that would travel to Schilgenauel, Gludum and Blessenfeld. Just so, while the old boy gave himself up to a pleasure it seemed he must have been vainly seeking for the past fifty years.

"Good heavens," he said, "at last I know what a good cigar is. Had to wait all this time for it, dear child, until my eightieth birthday. No, no, don't make any fuss, don't get excited. Of course I'm eighty today! Wasn't it you who ordered flowers for me from my son? Beautiful, thank you. We'll get to my birthday later, all right? You have a cordial invitation to my party tonight at the Cafe Kroner. But tell me something, my dear Leonore, why in all the fifty years—fifty-one, to be precise—I've been a customer there didn't anyone try to sell me a cigar like this? Am I stingy, perhaps? Never have been. You know I haven't. Used to smoke ten-cent cigars when I was young, then twenty-centers when I was earning a little more money, and then sixty-centers, year after year. Tell me, dear girl, what do you suppose they're like, people who walk around with a dollar corona stuck in their mouth? Fellows who pop in and out of offices with it as if it were a nickel stogey? I wonder what they're like, people who smoke up three times my grandfather's weekly wage between breakfast and lunch. Mmm, making an old codger like me go dry in the mouth and crawl round his son's office like a beagle in a hedge. How's that? One of Robert's schoolmates? Ministerial councillor, you say, director, manager? Even a cabinet minister! Then I must certainly know the chap. Defense department? Weapons?"

Suddenly mist came into his eyes. A trap door slammed shut. The old man was drifting back in time, sinking back into the first, the third, the sixth decade of his life. He was burying one of his children again. Which one could it be? Johanna? Heinrich? Over whose white coffin was he scattering a handful of earth, strewing flowers? Were the tears in his eyes the tears of 1942, when he got the news of Otto's death? Was he weeping at the asylum door behind which his wife had vanished? The tears, while his cigar, forgotten on the ash tray, went up in delicate wreaths of smoke, were from 1902. He was burying his sister Charlotte, for whom he had saved and saved, gold coin by coin, so that things might go better for her. The coffin slid down, held by creaking ropes, while the schoolchildren sang, 'Watchman, whither has the swallow flown?' Chirpy children's voices intruded into the perfectly appointed office; the aged voice sang back over half a century. Now only that October morning in 1902 was real. Fog on the Lower Rhine. Damp fog, coiling in sarabande across the wet beetfields, the crows in the willow trees scrawking like Mardi Gras noisemakers. While Leonore drew a red Heuss over the damp sponge. Thirty years before she was born peasant children had sung, 'Watchman, whither has the swallow flown?' Now a green Heuss, drawn across the little sponge. Careful. Letters to Hochbret went at local rates.

When this mood came over him, the old man had a blind look. She would have liked then and there to rush off to the florist's and buy him a lovely bouquet. But she was afraid to leave him alone. He stretched out his hands; cautiously she pushed the ash tray toward him. He took up his cigar, put it in his mouth, looked at Leonore, and gently said, "You mustn't think I'm crazy, child."

Yes, she was fond of him. Regularly, on her afternoons off, he came to the office to pick her up, so she could take pity on his carelessly kept books, over there on the other side of the street, high above the printing works, where he lived in a "studio" dating back to his salad days. There he kept documents checked and approved by income tax officials whose modest gravestones had already toppled over before she had learned to write. Credits in English pounds, dollar holdings, plantation shares in El Salvador. Up there she rummaged through account settlements, deciphered handwritten statements from banks long since failed, read old wills bequeathing legacies to children by now outlived forty years. 'And to my son Heinrich exclusively I leave the two estates of Stehlinger's Grotto and Goerlinger's Lodge, having noted in his nature that air of repose, I may even say that delight in seeing things grow, which I take to be the prerequisite of a farmer's life. . . .'

"Here," the old man cried, brandishing his cigar, "right here in this very office, I dictated a will to my father-in-law the night before I had to leave for the army. While I was dictating it the youngster was sleeping up there. Next morning he came with me to the station, kissed me on the cheek with his soft child's lips. He was only seven then. But none of them, Leonore, not one ever got what I gave. It all came back to me, properties and bank accounts, dividends and rents. I was never able to give anything away. It took my wife to do that. People actually got what she gave away. And nights, when I lay beside her, I often used to hear her muttering—long and soft, hours on end, like water purling from her mouth— '*whywhywhy?*' "

Again the old man wept. He was in uniform this time, a captain in the Engineer Reserves, Privy Councillor Heinrich Faehmel, home on compassionate leave to bury his son, age seven. The Kilbian vault closed round the white coffin. Damp, gloomy masonry, yet bright as the sun's rays the golden figures marking the year of his death: 1917. Robert, dressed in black velvet, waited out in the carriage.

Leonore let the stamp fall, a violet one, not trusting herself to stick it on Schrit's letter. The carriage horses were snorting outside the cemetery gate, while Robert Faehmel, age two, was allowed to hold the reins. Black leather cracked at the edges and the figures, 1917, freshly gilt, shining brighter than sunshine. . . .

"What's he up to? What does he do with himself, my son, the only one I have left, Leonore? What does he do in the Prince Heinrich Hotel every morning from nine-thirty to eleven? I remember how we used to let him watch the way they tied the nosebags onto the horses. What's he up to? Can you tell me that, Leonore?"

Hesitantly she picked up the violet stamp and softly said, "I don't know what he does there, I really don't."

The old fellow put the cigar in his mouth and leaned back in the armchair, smiling—as if nothing at all had passed between them. "What do you say, Leonore, to working for me regularly afternoons? I'll come and pick you up. We can have lunch together at noon, then from two to four or five, if you want, you can help get me straightened out up there. What do you say to that, my dear?"

She nodded, said "Yes." She still didn't trust herself to draw the violet Heuss across the sponge and stick it on Schrit's letter. Someone in the post office would take the letter out of the box and the machine would stamp "Sept. 6, 1958, 1 P.M." on it. And there sat the old man, come to the end of his seventies, starting his eighties.

"Yes, yes," she said.

"Then it's a date?"

"Yes."

She looked into his thin face, the face in which for years she had vainly sought a likeness to his son. Politeness, it seemed, was the only trait common to the Faehmels. But with the old man it was more ceremonious, decorative, the courtesy of the old school, almost a *grandezza*. Nothing mathematical in it like the politeness of his son, who made a point of dryness and only by the glimmer in his gray eyes indicated he might be capable of more warmth.

The old man, now, he actually blew his nose, chewed his cigar and sometimes complimented her on her hairdo, her complexion. His suit at least showed some sign of wear and tear, his tie was always a little crooked, on his fingers ink stains, on his lapels eraser rubbings. He carried pencils soft and hard in his vest pocket and occasionally he would take a sheet of paper from his son's desk, sketch an angel on it, an *Agnus Dei,* a tree, the portrait of one of his contemporaries, hurrying by outside. And sometimes he gave her money to go and buy cake, asked her to make a second cup of coffee, making her happy that for once she could plug in the electric percolator for someone beside herself. That was the kind of office life she was used to, making coffee, buying cakes and being told stories with a proper beginning and end. Stories about the life lived back there in the apartment wing of the building, about the dead who had died there. Back there for centuries the Kilbs had tried their hand at vice and virtue, sin and salvation, had been city treasurers, notaries, mayors and cathedral canons. Back there in the air still lingered some intimation of the acrid prayers of would-be prelates, of the melancholy sins of Kilbian spinsters and the penances of pious Kilbian youths. All in that gloomy part of the house back there, where now, on quiet afternoons, a pale, dark-haired girl did her homework and waited for her father to come home. Or was he at home afternoons? Two hundred and ten bottles of wine emptied between the beginning of May and the last of August. Did he drink them all by himself? With his daughter? With ghosts? All of it unreal, less real than the ash-blond hair of the office girl who fifty years ago had sat there in her place, keeping watch over legal secrets.

"Yes, she sat right there, my dear Leonore, on exactly the same spot where you're sitting now. Her name was Josephine." Had the old man said nice things about her hair, too, and her complexion?

The old man laughed and pointed to the proverb hanging up on the wall above his son's desk, solitary relic from times past, painted in white letters on mahogany. "Their right hand is full of bribes," it said. A motto of Kilbian as well as Faehmel incorruptibility.

"My two brothers-in-law, point of fact, didn't go much for the law. Last male descendants of the line. One chose the Uhlans, with their lances and fancy uniforms, the other just liked to kill time. But both of them, the officer and the loafer, were in the same regiment, and fell in the same attack on the same day. They rode into machine-gun fire at Erby-le-Huette, and there went the name of Kilb. And took their vices with them into the grave, the void. Like so many scarlet flowers, at Erby-le-Huette."

The old man was happy when he got white mason's mortar on his pants and could ask her to brush him off. Often he carried fat rolls of drawings under his arm, and whether he had taken them from the files or was actually working on an assignment, she never knew.

He sipped at his coffee, said how nice it was, pushed the cake dish over to her, dragged on his cigar. The reverential look came back on his face. "One of Robert's schoolmates? I really should know him. You're sure his name wasn't Schrella? Positive? No, no, ridiculous, he'd never smoke cigars like this. Never. And you sent him to the Prince Heinrich? That'll make trouble, my dear Leonore, there'll be a row. He doesn't like it, my son Robert, when people upset his routine. He was like that even as a boy. Perfectly nice, intelligent, polite, everything just so. But if you overstepped a certain mark, he blew up. Quite capable of committing murder. I was always a little scared of him. You, too? Oh, he won't do anything to you, girl, not for what you did. Be sensible. Come on, now, let's go and eat. We'll celebrate your new job and my birthday. Don't do anything foolish. If he's already raised the deuce over the phone, then it's over and done with. Pity you can't remember that fellow's name. I had no idea he still kept up with his old school chums. Let's go. Come on. Today's Saturday, and he won't mind if you close a bit early. Leave that to me."

St. Severin's was striking twelve. She counted the envelopes quickly, twenty-three, gathered them up, got a good hold on them. Had the old man really been there only half an hour? The tenth chime of the twelve was ringing.

"No, thank you," she said. "I won't bother to put on my coat. And please, not to The Lion."

Only half an hour. The presses had stopped their stamping. But the wild boar bled on.

two

By now it had become a habit with the desk clerk, almost a ritual, second nature, every morning at half-past nine sharp to take down the key from the board, to feel the light touch of the dry, well-kept hand as it took the key from his, to glance at the pale, severe face with the red scar on the bridge of the nose. And then, with a hint of a smile only his own wife might have noticed, to look thoughtfully after Faehmel as he ignored the elevator boy's beckoned invitation, walked upstairs, lightly running the billiard room key across the brass balusters. Five, six, seven times the key made a ringing sound like a xylophone with only one tone. Then, half a minute later, Hugo, older of the two bellboys, came along and asked, "The usual?" Whereupon the desk clerk nodded, knowing that Hugo would now go to the restaurant, get a double cognac and a carafe of water, and disappear into the billiard room upstairs until eleven o'clock.

The desk clerk sensed something ominous in this habit of playing billiards every morning from half-past nine till eleven, always in the same bellhop's company. Disaster or vice.

Against vice there was a safeguard. Discretion. Discretion went with the room when you hired it. Discretion and money went together, abscissa and ordinate. Eyes that looked yet did not see, ears that heard yet did not hearken. Against disaster, however, no protection existed. Not all potential suicides could be spotted at the door. Indeed, were they not all potential suicides? It came, disaster, in with the suntanned actor and his seven pieces of luggage. Took the room key with a laugh. As soon as the bags were stacked, slid the pistol from his overcoat pocket, safety catch already off, and blew his brains out. Disaster came sneaking in like something from the grave, in golden shoes, with golden hair and golden teeth, grinning like a skeleton. With ghosts in vain pursuit of pleasure, who left an order for breakfast in their room at half-past ten, hung a 'Please Do Not Disturb' card on the outer knob, inside piled suitcases high against the door, swallowed poison pills. And long before the shocked room-service girl dropped the breakfast tray, already it was rumored through the hotel that 'There's a body up in Room 12.' Rumors even spread at night, when late drinkers were slinking from the bar to their rooms and at Room 12 sensed foreboding behind the door. There were even some who could tell the silence of sleep from death's silence. Disaster. He felt it in the air when he saw Hugo going up to the billiard room at a minute after half-past nine with a double cognac and the water carafe.

Around this time of day, too, he could ill spare the boy. A tangle of hands formed at his desk, demanding bills, grabbing an assortment of travel folders. At this time of day again and again he caught himself—a few minutes after half-past nine—getting impolite. Right now, to this schoolteacher, of all people, the ninth or tenth person to ask him how to get to the graves of the Roman children. The teacher's reddish complexion disclosed the fact that she came from the country, her coat and gloves that she lacked the income presumptive in Prince Heinrich guests. He wondered how she happened to be regimented along with these other agitated old biddies, not one of whom felt obliged to inquire after the price of her room. Would she, now tugging self-consciously at her gloves, would she consummate the all-German miracle, against which old Jochen had bet ten marks? 'Show me a German who ever asks how much anything costs before he buys and I'll give you ten marks.' No, even she wasn't going to win him the prize. He calmed himself with an effort, pleasantly explained how to get to the graves of the Roman children.

Most of them asked straight off for the boy now slated to be in the billiard room for an hour and a half. It was he all of them wanted, to bring their luggage to the foyer, to take it to the airlines coach, to the taxi, to the railroad station. Ill-tempered globetrotters waiting in the foyer for their bills, discussing plane arrivals and departures, all of them wanted ice for their whiskey from Hugo, him alone to strike a match for the cigarette dangling unlit in their mouth, just to see how well trained he was. Hugo alone they wished to thank with a wave of languid hand. Only when Hugo was on the scene did their faces quiver in mysterious spasms, impatient faces, whose owners could hardly wait to rush, carrying their nasty tempers with them, to distant corners of the earth. They were champing at the bit, longing to ascertain in the mirrors of Persian or Upper Bavarian hotels the exact shade of their tan. Shrill female voices were calling for lost articles. It was 'Hugo, my ring,' 'Hugo, my handbag,' 'Hugo, my lipstick.' All of them expected Hugo to dash to the elevator, noiselessly ascend to Room 19, Room 32, Room 46 to search for ring, handbag and lipstick. And there was old Madame Musch, leading in her mongrel, which, after lapping up milk, gorging on honey and turning up his nose at fried eggs, would have to be taken out for a walk, so he might relieve his doggy needs, and revive his fading sense of smell, on kiosks, parked cars and waiting buses. Obviously only Hugo could cater to this dog's spiritual needs. Then there was Oma Blessieck, who spent a month every year at the Prince Heinrich, while she visited her children and ever-more-numerous grandchildren. Though she had hardly set foot in the place, already she was after Hugo.

"Is he still here, that nice little young one who looks like an altar boy? The thin one with the auburn hair who's so pale and always looks so serious?" The idea was to have Hugo read the local newspaper to her while she ate her breakfast, while she licked honey, drank her milk and did not turn up her nose at fried eggs. As he read, the old girl, hearing the names of streets familiar from her childhood, would look up ecstatically. Accident near Memorial Field. Robbery on Frisian Street. "I had pigtails this long when I used to go roller-skating there— this long, Hugo." The old girl was frail, but tough. Was it for Hugo's sake she had flown across the great ocean? "What?" she said, disappointed. "Hugo won't be free till eleven?"

The driver of the airlines coach was standing at the revolving door, hand lifted in warning, even while complicated breakfast bills were still being added up. There sat the man who had ordered half a fried egg, indignantly rejecting the bill on which he'd been charged for a whole one. And even more indignantly rejecting the manager's offer to cross off the item altogether, instead demanding a new bill, on which he was charged for only half a one. "I insist on it." No doubt he traveled the world round just to collect restaurant bills charging him for half a fried egg.

"Yes, Madam," the desk clerk said, "first left, second right, then third left again, and you'll see the sign: 'To the Roman Children's Graves.' "

At last the driver for the bus crowd had assembled all his passengers, all the teachers had been given the right directions, all the fat pet dogs taken out to pee. But the gentleman in Room 11 was still fast asleep, had been for the past sixteen hours with a 'Please Do Not Disturb' card hanging outside his door. Disaster, either in Room 11 or in the billiard room. It stuck in your mind, that ceremony right in the middle of the foolish bustle of departure, key taken down from the board, faint brushing of hands, glance at the pale face, the red scar on the bridge of the nose, Hugo's "The usual?", your nod. Billiards from half-past nine till eleven. But the hotel underground as yet had reported nothing out of the way, either disastrous or corrupt. That fellow up there actually did play billiards from half-past nine till eleven. No partner, just himself, sipping at his cognac, at his glass of water, telling Hugo stories from way back, having Hugo tell him stories about when he was a kid. Not saying a word when the chambermaids or cleaning women stopped at the open door on their way to the laundry elevator to watch him, looking up at them from his game with a smile. No, no, that guy's harmless.

Jochen hobbled out of the elevator with a letter in his hand, held it up, shaking his head. Jochen lived high up, under the pigeon loft, near feathered friends who brought messages from Paris and Rome, Warsaw and Copenhagen. Jochen in his made-up uniform, something between a crown prince and a noncommissioned officer, defied classification. A bit of a factotum, a bit of a gray eminence, everybody's confidant, not a room clerk, not a waiter, but a little of all these, and something of a cook to boot. It was he who was responsible for the saying around the hotel always used to counter moral aspersions on the guests: "What would be the point in having a reputation for discretion, if everybody's morals were above suspicion? What good is discretion when there is nothing left to be discreet about?" Something of a father-confessor, of a confidential secretary, of a pimp. Jochen, with twisted arthritic fingers opened the letter and grinned.

"You might have saved yourself the ten marks, I could have told a thousand times more—and all for free—than that little con man. Argus Information Bureau. 'Herewith the information requested concerning Dr. Robert Faehmel, architect, resident at 7 Modest Street. Dr. Faehmel is 42 years old, a widower, two children: a son, 22, architect, not living here; a daughter, 19, at college. Dr. F.'s assests: considerable. Related on his mother's side to the Kilbs. Nothing negative to report.' " Jochen chuckled. " 'Nothing negative to report'! As if there ever had been anything out of the way about young Faehmel. And with him there never will be. One of the few people I'd stick my hand in the fire for any time, any old time of the day. Get me? This rotten arthritic old hand, right square in the fire! You don't have to worry about leaving that kid up there alone with him. He's not that kind. And if he was, so what? They allow queers in the government, don't they? But he's not that kind. He already had a child when he was twenty, by the daughter of one of my friends. Maybe you remember the girl's father, Schrella. He worked right here once, for a year. No? You weren't here at the time? Then take my word for it, just let young Faehmel play his billiards in peace. A fine family. Really is. Class. I knew his grandmother, his grandfather, his mother and his uncle. They used to play billiards here themselves, fifty years ago. You wouldn't know, of course, but the Kilbs have lived on Modest Street for three hundred years. That is, they always did—there aren't any left any more. His mother went off the beam, lost two brothers and three of her children died. Never got over it. Fine woman. The quiet kind, if you know what I mean. Never ate a crumb more than the ration card allowed her, not an ounce more, and her children didn't get more than was coming to them, either, not from her. Crazy, of course. Whatever she got extra, she'd just give it all away. And she always got plenty: they owned big farms, and the Abbot of St. Anthony's, down there in the Kissa Valley, he sent her tubs of butter, jars of honey, bread and so on. But she never ate any of it, or gave any of it to her children. They had to eat that sawdust bread with artificially colored marmalade, while their mother gave all the other stuff away. She even gave away money. Seen her do it myself. Must have been in '16 or '17—used to see her coming out the front door with the bread and the jars of honey. 1917! Can you imagine what it was like then? But none of you can remember. You can't imagine what it meant, honey in 1917, or in the winter of '41–'42. Or the way she went down to the freight yard and tried to go along in the cars with the Jews. Screwball, they said. They locked her up in the looney bin, but for my money she wasn't crazy at all. She was the kind of woman you only see in the old pictures in the museums. I'd go right down the line for her son, and if he doesn't get first-class, number one service, things are going to hum around this joint. I don't care if ninety-nine old women are asking for Hugo. If Herr Faehmel wants the kid with him, then he's going to get him and don't you forget it. Argus Information Bureau! Just imagine paying those fakers ten marks! Now I suppose you're going to tell me you don't know his father, old man Faehmel? Good! You do know him. But I bet you never thought he might be the father of the one playing billiards up there. Sure, everybody and his brother knows old man Faehmel. Came here fifty years ago in one of his uncle's hand-me-down suits with a couple of bucks in his pocket. He used to play billiards right here, too, at that time, here in the Prince Heinrich, before you even knew what a hotel was. Some desk-clerk you are! Leave that one upstairs be, then. He'll never do anything foolish or cause any harm. Worst he might do is get teed off in a nice quiet way. He was the best man at the plate and the best hundred-meter-dash man this old town's ever had. He was tough, and if he had to be hard, he was hard, all right. He just couldn't stand seeing some people giving other people a rough time. And if you can't stand that kind of stuff, first thing you know you're mixed up in politics. He was in politics when he was nineteen years old. They'd have cut his head off or locked him up for twenty years if he hadn't fooled them and taken off. That's right, you don't need to look so surprised. He got away and stayed away for three or four years. I don't know exactly what went wrong, I never heard. All I know is that old Schrella was mixed up in it, and the daughter, too, the one young Faehmel had the baby by later on. Well, he came back and they didn't lay a finger on him. Went into the army, the Engineers. I can see him now, home on leave in his uniform with the black piping on it. Don't gawk at me with that dumb look on your face. Was he a Communist? How should I know whether he was or he wasn't. And supposing he was, every decent man's been one sometime or other. Go on and have breakfast; I'll be able to manage the old hens."

Disaster or vice, they hung in the air, but Jochen had always been too harmless himself to foresense suicide, to believe agitated guests able to tell the difference between the silence of sleep and death's silence behind closed doors. He pretended to be cunning and corrupt, but all the while he believed in people.

"Well, there you are," said the desk clerk. "I'm going to get my breakfast. Just don't let anyone barge in on him, will you, he's very fussy about it." He put the red card on the counter for Jochen. "Available only to my mother, my father, my daughter, my son and Mr. Schrella. Otherwise to no one."

Schrella! Was he still alive? The thought startled Jochen. But surely they must have done away with him. Or did he have a son?

It knocked for a loop, this aroma, everything that had been smoked in the foyer for the past couple of weeks. It was a fragrance you carried ahead of you like a banner. Here I come, Mr. Big, conquering hero whom none can resist. Six feet two, gray-haired, middle forties, suit of board-chairman quality; salesmen, storekeepers, artists never clad thus. This was official elegance, Jochen could smell it. Here was a minister of state, perhaps an ambassador, exuding importance and fat with signatures of almost law-making dominion, breezing through padded, steely, triple-plated antechamber doors, sweeping aside all opposition with snowplow shoulders, all the while radiating kindly courtesy, which you knew was a veneer, even as he made way for Oma to let her retrieve that repulsive doggy of hers from the second boy, Erich. He even helped the old bag of bones reach for and take hold of the stair railing. "Don't mention it, Madam."

"Nettlinger."

"Can I help you, sir?"

"I have to speak to Dr. Faehmel. It's urgent. At once. Official business."

Shake of the head, soft demur, as he toyed with the red

card. Mother, father, son, daughter, Schrella. Nettlinger not wanted.

"But I know he's here."

Nettlinger? Haven't I heard that name somewhere before? It's the kind of face that must have made some sort of impression I wouldn't want to forget. I've heard that name before, many years ago, and I said to myself at the time, make a note of that boy, don't forget him. But now I can't remember what it was about him I wasn't supposed to forget. Anyway—watch out! If I knew all the things he's done, no doubt I'd be sick to my stomach. If I had to sit and watch the film of his life they're going to run off for that bastard's benefit on Doomsday, I'd puke myself into a puddle. He's the type that has the gold teeth ripped out of corpses, that orders kids' heads shaved. Catastrophe? Vice? No, murder in the air.

And characters like that never know when and when not to tip. That's all you need, to tell class. Now, for instance, might be the right moment for a cigar. But not for a tip, and never for such a big one as that twenty-mark bill which he's pushing across the counter with a grin. How stupid can you get? People like that don't even begin to know how to act, haven't the faintest idea how to handle a hotel clerk. As if secrets were for sale at the Prince Heinrich! As if a guest who paid forty or sixty marks for his room could be had for one green twenty. Twenty marks from a stranger whose only reference was his expensive cigar and his fancy suit. And that was the type, mind you, that got to be a cabinet minister, a diplomat, even, and yet didn't even know how to grease a palm, most ticklish of all arts. Gloomily Jochen shook his head, left the green bill untouched. *Their right hand is full of bribes.*

Can you beat it! A blue bank note was being added to the green one, raising the bid to thirty; a dense cloud of Partagas Eminentes was puffed into Jochen's face.

Blow away, pal, blow your four-mark cigar smoke in my face, and cough up another bill, a violet one, if you want to.

24

Jochen's not for sale. Not for you and not for three thousand in
bills. I haven't cottoned to many people in my life, but I happen
to like that young fellow up there. Tough luck, pal, you and
your important face and that hand of yours always itching to
sign something, tough luck, but you got here a minute and a
half too late. You ought to know that folding money isn't
down my alley. In case you don't realize it, I've got a notarized
contract right in my pocket, which says that the rest of my life
I can live in my little room up under the roof and keep pigeons.
For breakfast and lunch I have the choice of the menu, on top
of that a hundred and fifty marks cash every month, three
times more than I really need for my kind of tobacco. I have
friends, too, in Copenhagen, Paris, Warsaw and Rome. If you
only knew how carrier-pigeon people stick together! But of
course you don't. All you think you know is that money is everything. That's what you and your kind tell each other. Naturally,
you think, naturally a hotel clerk will do anything for money;
he'd sell his grandmother down the river for a fifty-mark note.
There's only one thing I'm not allowed to do, my friend, one
single curb on my freedom. When I'm down here working the
desk I can't smoke my pipe. And this exception I regret for the
first time today. But for that I'd show you and your Partagas
Eminentes a cloud or two of smoke; I'd turn you into a herring.
To make it plain and simple, you can kiss my arse a hundred
and twenty-seven times. Faehmel's not for sale to you, friend.
He'll play billiards up there without being bothered from half-
past nine till eleven. Not that I can't think of something better
for him to be doing, namely sitting in your place in the min-
istry. Or, even better, throwing a few bombs the way he did
as a young fellow, to put the fear of God into bags of crap like
you. If you don't mind, my friend, when he feels like playing
billiards from half-past nine till eleven, then billiards he's going
to play. You can put your cabbage back in your pocket and
call it a day, and if you flash another bill in my face, I won't
be responsible for what happens. I've had to swallow tactless-
ness by the gallon, put up with bad taste by the ton and not
say a word. I've written down adulterers and queers by the

dozen on the register, guys wearing the horns and wives on the warpath. But don't ever get the idea that was all in the cards when I was born. I was always a good boy, used to serve Mass, as no doubt you did yourself, and sang the songs of Father Kolping and St. Aloysius in the Kolping Glee Club. Pretty soon I was twenty, with six years' service in this fleabag behind me. And if I haven't lost all faith entirely in humanity since then, it's only because of people like young Faehmel up there and his mother. Put your money in your pocket, take that cigar out of your mouth and bow down, then, before an old man who's wrung more dirty water out of his mittens than you ever knew existed. Then let the boy back there open the door for you, and scram.

"Have I got it right? You want to talk with the manager, sonny?"

First he went red, then quite blue with rage. Damn it all, there I go, thinking out loud again. Did I get too palsy with him? Hope not, that would be an awful mistake, never forgive myself for it. For it'll be a long day when I get palsy with the likes of him.

Where do I get my nerve? I'm an old man, nearly seventy, I was thinking out loud. I'm a bit soft in the head, I'm slipping upstairs, a fit subject for protection under the mental incompetence act and social security, such as it is.

Department of Defense and Armament? That's all I need! Round there to the left for the manager, please, then second door to the right, you'll see the complaint book bound in morocco. And if you ever order fried eggs in this place, and if I happen to be in the kitchen when the order comes through, it'll be my pleasure in person to spit a gob into the frying pan for you. A kiss for you, in with the melted butter. And don't mention it, sir.

"I told you once, sir. Left that way, second door on the right, manager's office. Complaint book bound in morocco. You'd like me to tell him you're coming? Certainly. Operator. Manager, please, desk clerk speaking. Yes, sir, a gentleman— what's the name? Nettlinger, excuse me, Doctor Nettlinger wishes to speak to you at once. About what? To complain about me. That's right. Thank you. The manager's waiting for you, sir. Madam? Yes, Madam, parade and fireworks this evening, first street on the left, then second right, third left again, and you see the sign: 'To the Roman Children's Graves.' No trouble at all, don't mention it. Thank you very much." One mark's not to be despised from a good old girl of a schoolteacher like that. Yes, just look at me, taking little tips with a smile, and turning down the big ones. Roman children's graves, there you have something clear and simple. You'll never see me turn up my nose at the widow's mite. And tips are a bellhop's very life and soul. "Yes, just around the corner— absolutely right."

I can tell if they're out for a shack job even before they step out of the taxi, I can smell it a mile away. I know all the angles cold. The timid ones, for instance, it's written all over them so plain I feel like telling them, it's not as bad as that, children, it's all happened before, I've spent fifty years in the hotel game, rely on me to make it easy. Fifty-nine marks eighty, tips included, for a double room. You've got a little consideration coming for that kind of money. However, eager as you may be, just don't start doing it in the elevator. Making love in the Prince Heinrich takes place behind double doors. Don't be so bashful, folks, don't be so timid. If you only knew. I mean, how many people have hauled their ashes in these rooms, made sacred by high prices. Religious ones and unreligious, good ones and bad. Double room with bath, bottle of champagne, room service. Cigarettes. Breakfast at half-past ten. Very good, sir. Sign here, please, no here, sir—and I hope you're not so stupid as to sign your right name. This thing really does go to the police, then it's stamped, it becomes a document and can be used as evidence. Don't gamble on the powers that be, young fellow. The more there are of them, the more pinches they need to keep them busy. Maybe you were a Communist once yourself, in which case keep your eye peeled extra sharp. I used to be one. And a Catholic, too. Sort of stuff that doesn't come out in the wash. Even today there are certain people

I just can't stand hearing run down. Whoever makes a crack about the Virgin Mary or Father Kolping better watch his step. Boy, Room 42. That way to the elevator, sir.

There they are, just the ones I was expecting, a pair of them on the loose, bold as brass, nothing to hide, making sure the world knows how free and easy they are. Why do you have to make such a production out of it, why lay on that I've-got-nothing-to-hide stuff with a trowel? If you really haven't got anything to hide, then you don't need to hide it. Sign here, please, sir, no here. With this dumb babe you've got in tow, I certainly wouldn't want to have anything to hide. Not with this one. Love is like tipping. Pure matter of instinct. You can tell by looking at a woman whether it's worthwhile to have something to hide with her. With this one it isn't, believe me, my boy. Sixty marks for the night, plus champagne in the room plus tips plus breakfast plus everything else you have to give her: just not worth it. You could get a better deal from a good honest whore who knows her business. Boy, show the lady and gentleman to Room 43. Dear God, how stupid can you get! "The manager? Yes sir, coming sir, yes sir."

Of course people like you are practically born to be hotel managers. It's like women having certain organs removed. No more problems then. But what's love without problems? And if a man has his conscience out, not even a cynic is left. Take trouble away, and you're human no longer. I trained you as a bellboy, you spent four years under my wing. Then you took a look around the world, went to different schools, learned languages. In officers' clubs, Allied and un-allied, you sweated out a fearful hosing from conquerors and conquered. Then you came back here on the double, and the first question that crossed your lips when you arrived, so sleek and plump and conscienceless, was, 'Is old Jochen still around?' And here he is, the same old potato, my boy.
"You've insulted this gentleman, Kuhlgamme."
"Not on purpose, sir. In fact, it wasn't an insult at all. I

could name you a hundred people who would be proud to have me call them sonny."

The crowning impertinence. Incredible.

"It just slipped out, Dr. Nettlinger, sir. I'm an old man, you might say I'm half covered by Paragraph 51."

"The gentleman demands an apology."

"And right away. It's carrying things pretty far, if I may say so, to be talked to like that by a bellhop."

"Apologize to the gentleman."

"Beg your pardon, sir."

"Not in that tone."

"Which tone would you like? Beg your pardon, sir, beg your pardon, sir, beg your pardon, sir. Those are the only three tones I have to pick and choose from. So, if you don't mind, select the one that suits you. Look here, I don't mind being used for a doormat. I'll kneel right down here on the carpet quick as a wink and kiss the man's boots, old as I am, even if I have an apology coming to me, too. Attempted bribery, sir. The honor of our old and famous hotel is at stake. A trade secret for thirty lousy marks? I'm the one who feels insulted. And the hotel's been insulted, the place where I've worked for more than fifty years. Fifty-six, to be exact."

"I demand you put an end to this ridiculous and painful scene."

"Show the gentleman to the billiard room at once, Kuhlgamme."

"No."

"You will show the gentleman to the billiard room."

"No."

"I'd hate to see all the years you've given to this hotel, Kuhlgamme, go down the drain for not carrying out a simple order."

"In this hotel, sir, when a guest says he doesn't want to be disturbed, that's an order, and it's never been broken once. Except, naturally, if it's a Higher Power. Secret police. Then our hands would be tied."

"Consider me a Higher Power."

"You mean you're from the secret police?"

"I'm not going to put up with this kind of talk."

"Show the gentleman to the billiard room, Kuhlgamme."

"Do you want to be the first, sir, to smirch the banner of discretion?"

"Then I'll take you to the billiard room myself, Doctor."

"Over my dead body, sir."

You have to be as old and corrupt as I am to know that certain things are not for sale. Vice stops being vice when there's no virtue. And what virtue is you can never know, until you realize that even a whore will turn down some clients. But I should have known you were a bastard. Up there in my room I spent week after week with you, teaching you how to accept tips discreetly, practising with coins, groschen and marks and folding money, too. It's something one must know, how to take money discreetly, for tips are the life and soul of our profession. I tried to hammer it into your thick skull, no easy job. Even then you tried to gyp me. Pulling a fast one like trying to make me think we had used only three marks instead of four when we were practising! You've always been a bastard. You never learned some things just aren't done. And now you're at it again. Not that meanwhile you haven't learned to rake in the tips, but I bet these here were not even thirty pieces of silver.

"Get back to the reception desk at once, Kuhlgamme, I'll take care of this matter myself. Step aside. Or else."

Only over my dead body, and just look, it's ten to eleven already. In ten minutes he'll be coming down the staircase anyway. If you had any sense we could have skipped the whole production. But even ten minutes—only over my dead body. You've never learned what honor is because you've never known dishonor. Here I take my stand, Jochen, corrupt and jam-packed with rottenness from head to toe. But only over my dead body will you ever get into that billiard room.

three

For some time now he had given up playing according to the rules, trying for runs, racking up points. Now gently, now hard he played the ball, seemingly at random, and each time, as it caromed off the other two, for him brought forth a new geometric pattern from the green void, making a starry heaven. Cue ball kissing white ball over green felt, red ball over green felt, bringing tracks into being at once to be extinguished. Delicate clicks defined the rhythm of the figure formed, five times, six times, when the struck ball caromed off the cushion or the other balls. Only a few tones, light or dark, emerged from the monotone. And the swirl of lines was all angularly bound by geometric law and physics. Energy of the blow imparted to the ball by cue, plus a little friction, question of degree, the brain taking note of it, and behold, impulse was converted into momentary figures. No abiding forms, nothing lasting, all fleeting, force expended in a mere rolling of spheres. Often he played for as long as a half-hour with only one ball, white over the green surface, a solitary star in the sky. Light, faint music without melody, painting without likeness. Hardly any color. Mere formula.

The pale youth guarding the door leaned against the white lacquered wood, hands behind his back, legs crossed, wearing the violet uniform of the Prince Heinrich.

"No stories today, Doctor?"

He looked up, put down his cue, took a cigarette, lit it and looked off down into the street, now in the shadow of St. Severin's. Apprentices, trucks, nuns. Life in the street. Across the courtyard gray autumn light came reflected almost silver from the violet drapes of the dining room. Framed in these velvety hangings guests were eating belated breakfast. Even their soft-boiled eggs looked ominous in that light. Respectable matronly faces took on a depraved look. Frock-coated waiters with knowing eyes looked like so many Beelzebubs, emissaries from Asmodeus, though actually they were nothing but harmless members of the waiters' guild, who went home after work and diligently read the lead article in the union paper. Yet now they seemed to be concealing cloven hooves inside cleverly constructed orthopedic shoes. Were not elegant little horns growing out of their white, red, yellow foreheads? The sugar in the gilt bowls had lost its sugary look. Wine was not wine, bread not bread, both aglow like ingredients of some secret vice. A celebration was in progress here, and the godhead's name was not to be uttered, only thought.

"Stories? What stories, boy?"

His memories had never hinged on words and pictures, only on movement. Father was Father's gait, the spritely curve described, each step, by his right trouser leg, for a brief instant exposing the dark blue inner lining of the cuff, this while Father was on his way mornings past Gretz' shop to the Cafe Kroner to eat breakfast. Mother, she was the complicated-humble gesture described by her hands when she folded them over her breast, the sign she was about to say some foolishness. How bad the world was, how few the pure in heart. Her hands wrote it in the air before she put it into words. Otto, he was marching legs, when he went out through the hall in jackboots, and off down the street. Hostility, -tility, -tility went the ring of his heels on the flags, heels which before had marched to a different beat of brother, brother, brother. Grandmother: a gesture she had made for seventy years, mimicked many times daily by his daughter as he watched. A movement centuries old, a heritage running in the family that never failed to startle him. His daughter, Ruth, had never seen her great-grandmother. Where, then, had she got that gesture? Unaware, she brushed her hair back from her brow as her great-grandmother had done.

And he saw himself, playing rounders, bending over the bats to pick out his own, saw how he rolled the ball back and forth in his left hand, back and forth until he had the heft of it just right to toss in the air at the critical moment exactly where he wanted it, just high enough to give him time to get both hands set on the bat handle and lash at the ball with all his might, sending it flying to the farthest outfield.

He saw himself in riverside fields, in the park, in the garden, bending down, straightening up, hitting the ball. All was timing. The others were fools who did not know you could figure how long it took for the ball to fall when you tossed it up to knock out a fly, or that with the same stopwatch you could also find out how long it took to get your grip set on the bat. And that everything else was only a question of co-ordination and practice, whole afternoons spent practicing in the fields, the park, the garden. They did not know there were formulas you could use, scales on which to weigh the balls. Just a little physics, a little mathematics and practice. But they turned their backs on both these subjects, on which the whole business hinged. They had no use for training, cheated their way through, at school for weeks at a time learned boneless maxims by rote, foundered in nebulous nonsense, even misconceived the poet Hölderlin. Even a word like 'plummet,' when they said it, became pulpy nonsense. Something as clear as 'plummet.' A line, a piece of lead, you threw it into the water, felt when the line hit bottom, drew out the line, by it measured the water's depth. Yet when they said 'plummet' it sounded like bad organ music. They could neither play rounders nor read Hölderlin. *Firm in compassion the eternal heart.*

They were talking it up in the field, to distract him at the plate, hollering, 'Come on, Faehmel, let's get going!' The outfielders were roaming the outfield, two of them playing very deep where he usually hit the ball, long flies much dreaded by the opposition. Mostly they landed right out in the street, where, on this Saturday in the summer of 1935, steaming chestnut horses were coming out the brewery gate. Beyond, the railway embankment, where a shunting engine was puffing up silly white clouds into the afternoon sky. From the right, near the bridge, came the hissing of shipyard arc-welders, as sweating workmen, toiling overtime, welded together a Strength-through-Joy river steamer. Bluish, silvery sparks hissed and riveting hammers—tak, tak, tak—kept time. In nearby municipal garden plots newly erected scarecrows in vain were trying to scare off invading sparrows, and pale old fellows on Old Age, no tobacco for their pipes, waited longingly for the first of the month. And it was only the memory of his body's movements at that time, nothing else, which brought back images, words and colors. All hidden behind formulas was 'Get going, Faehmel, get going!' He had taken the ball and was letting it lie just right in the cup of his hand, lightly held between fingers and palm, so as to have it meet the least possible resistance when tossed into the air. He had his bat ready in his other hand, longest one of all (no one bothered with the laws of leverage), fat of the bat covered with adhesive tape. Quickly he glanced at his wristwatch. Three minutes and fifteen seconds until the athletic instructor would whistle the end of the game—and still no answer to the question why the Prince Otto Gymnasium outfit had raised no objection about having the coach of Ludwig College, his side, umpire the decisive game. His name was Bernhard Vacano, but they called him Old Wobbly. He had a melancholy air, a plumpish sort with a platonic liking for little boys. He was also very fond of cream puffs and sweetishly dreamy movies in which strong blond youths swam across rivers, then lay in meadows, blade of grass in their mouth, waiting for adventures. Most of all Old Wobbly liked his plaster reproduction of the head of Antinous, which, at home among his rubber plants and shelves of physical culture books, he fondled, on the excuse of dusting it. Old Wobbly, who called his favorites 'junior' and the others 'bums.'

'Okay there, bum, come out of your trance,' he said, running sweat, belly wobbling, whistle in his mouth.

But there were still three minutes and three seconds to the final whistle, thirteen seconds too many. If he took his cut at the ball now, the next man would come to bat, and Schrella, waiting at base, would have to run again, giving the fielders another chance to throw the ball as hard as they could, as he sped for the next base, into his face, at his legs, into the small of his back. Three times he had seen how they pulled it. Someone from the other side would hit Schrella, whereupon Nettlinger, who actually played on his and Schrella's side, tagged the opposing player by simply throwing the ball back to him. Then again the player caught Schrella, making him double up with pain. And again Nettlinger, in retrieving the ball, simply threw it to the opposing player, who this time hit Schrella in the face with it—while Old Wobbly stood by, whistled time when Schrella was hit, whistled again when Nettlinger simply tossed the ball to the opposing fielder, whistled again when Schrella tried to limp out of the way. It all went very fast, balls flying back and forth. Had he, waiting at the plate, been the only one to see it? Not one among all the spectators, tensely waiting with their little colored pennants and caps for the end of the game? Two minutes and fifty seconds before the game was over, score 34-29, Prince Otto. Could it be this, this that he alone had seen, that was the reason they had accepted Old Wobbly, his side's athletic coach, as umpire?

'Come on, bum, the game's over in two minutes.'

'Correction, please. Two minutes, fifty seconds left.' Saying this, he tossed the ball high into the air, took a lightning grip and leaned into it as it came down. He could feel it from the weight of the blow, the elastic give of the wood—another one of his fabulous hits. He looked to see the ball take off, couldn't find it, heard the 'ah' of the crowd, a great 'ah' spreading out like a cloud, growing louder. He saw Schrella making it slowly home, bent and hobbling, a smear of blood near his nose. The scorers counted: seven, eight, nine. With maddening slowness the rest of the opposing team came trooping in past Old Wobbly, who was fit to be tied. The game was won, clearly won, even though he had forgotten to run around the bases and score yet another, tenth point. The Ottonians were still out looking for the winning ball, out beyond the street, crawling about in the grass near the brewery wall. Anger was plainly audible in Old Wobbly's final shrill on the whistle. The final score was announced: 37-34, Ludwig College. The 'ah' swelled into a great 'hoo-ray,' surged on over the field, while he was taking his bat, digging the handle into the ground, raising the handle a little, lowering it again until he seemed to have hit on the right angle. Then he brought his foot down on the bat's weakest point, where the handle tapered. Schoolchildren gathered round him, wondering, dumbstruck. Something big was happening, they sensed. Faehmel's famous bat was being smashed. Where the wood split the splinters were dead white. Already the kids were scrambling for souvenirs, fighting like little fiends for bits of wood, snatching scraps of adhesive tape from each others' fingers. Shocked, he stared into the heated, foolish faces, into wondering eyes shining with excitement, and felt the cheap bitterness of fame, on a summer evening on July 14, 1935, at the edge of the suburbs, on the trampled playing field across which Old Wobbly, that moment, was chasing out the sixth form of Ludwig's to collect the little out-of-bounds markers. Far beyond the street, by the brewery wall, blue and yellow jerseys were still visible. Ottonians were still looking for the ball. Presently they came straggling back across the street, drew up in a double row in the middle of the diamond, and waited for him, the team captain, to lead the game-ending cheer. Slowly he walked over to the two lines. Schrella and Nettlinger were in the same row, next to each other. Nothing seemed to have happened between them, nothing at all. Behind him the younger school kids were still wrestling over the souvenirs. He walked to his place, the spectators' admiration physically nauseating to him, and three times called out 'Hip, hip, hurrah!' Like beaten dogs the Ottonians slunk back to search for the missing ball. Not to find it would be an irredeemable disgrace.

"And yet I knew, Hugo, how much Nettlinger had his mind set on winning. Win no matter what it costs, he said, yet that's what he did, risked our losing the game just so somebody on the other side could peg Schrella again and again with the ball. And Old Wobbly must have been in cahoots with him. I was the only one who saw through it. The only one."

He had been afraid, going to the dressing room, afraid of Schrella and of what Schrella would say to him. The air had suddenly grown cool. Evening mist was rising from the fields, coming from the river and flowing, like layered wadding, around the building where the dressing room was located. Why, why had they done that to Schrella, and why did they trip him up on the steps during recess? He had struck his head on the steel edge of the steps, driving the steel bow of his spectacles into an ear lobe. Old Wobbly had come out of the classroom with the first-aid kit far too leisurely. Nettlinger, scorn on his face, had held the adhesive plaster taut so Wobbly could snip a piece off. On the way home they ganged up on Schrella, dragged him from one doorway to the next, beat him up among ash cans and parked baby carriages, and finally pushed him down some steps leading to a dark cellar, where he had lain a long while with his arm broken, amid the smell of cabbages and sprouting potatoes, staring at dusty preserving jars, until a boy sent down to get apples had discovered him and alerted

the occupants of the house. Only a few hadn't joined in—
Enders, Drischka, Schweugel and Holten.

He had once been friends with Schrella, years before this.
They'd always gone to visit Trischler together, who lived down
at the Lower Harbor. Trischler's father ran a bar and Schrella's
father worked for him as a waiter. They played on the old
barges and abandoned pontoons, and fished off the boats.

Now he stopped in front of the dressing room, listening to
the medley of voices within, hoarse with the excitement of
youthful myth-making as they talked about his already-legend-
ary home run. As if the ball had gone right out of sight onto
Olympian heights.

'I saw it go. How it traveled! Why, it went like a bullet!'

I saw it, the ball Robert hit.

I heard it, the ball Robert hit.

They'll never find it, the ball Robert hit.

Talk stopped when he came in. Fear lay in the sudden silence, for they were in almost deadly awe of him, he had done
what no one would have believed possible, something out of
this world unless you'd seen it. Who would have the honor of
bearing witness to a home run of such magnitude?

Quickly, barefoot, towels slung around their shoulders, they
went into the showers. Only Schrella stayed behind. He had
put his clothes on without taking a shower. For the first time
it struck Robert that Schrella never took a shower after a game,
never took off his jersey in front of the rest. He was sitting
there on a stool, blue and yellow contusions on his face and
still wet around the mouth where he had washed away dried
blood. The skin on his upper arms was discolored where he had
been struck by the ball, the one the Ottonians were still looking
for. He sat there, rolled down the sleeves of his faded shirt, put
on his jacket, took a book out of his pocket and read: *At evening when the bells ring peace.*

It was awkward to be alone with Schrella, to be thanked by
the cool eyes, too cool even to hate. A barely perceptible

flicker of the lashes, no more, a fleeting smile of thanks to the savior who had hit the ball. He smiled back at Schrella, an equally small smile, as he turned to the metal locker and took out his clothes, himself wanting to get out of there as quickly as he could without bothering with a shower. On the wall over his locker someone had scratched: 'Faehmel's Home Run, July 14, 1935.'

The place smelled strong of leather gear, of dried earth crumbled from soccer balls, handballs, footballs, and caught in the cracks of the concrete floor. Dirty little green and white marker flags were stacked in the corner, soccer nets were hanging up to dry. There was a splintered oar and, framed behind cracked glass, a yellowed certificate, 'Awarded to the Pioneers of Soccer, Ludwig College, Lower Sixth Form, 1903, by the Regional Chairman.' A laurel wreath was printed around the group photo. Hard-muscled eighteen-year-olds of the 1885 military class, wearing little mustaches, stared out of the picture at him, looking with animal optimism toward the fate which the future held in store for them. To rot at Verdun, to bleed to death in the quagmires of the Somme. Or, fifty years later, in a military cemetery at Chateau Thierry, to provide occasion for tourists, en route to Paris and overcome by the mood of the place, in the rain-spattered visitors' book to inscribe conciliatory sentiments. The dressing room smelled of iron, of incipient manhood. A damp mist was coming in from outdoors, drifting in mild clouds across the river meadows. Out of the tavern upstairs in the same building came the sonorous rumble of men off work for the weekend and hoisting a few, the giggling of barmaids, clinking of beer glasses. At the end of the hall upstairs skittle players were already at work, making the skittles tumble. Whereupon a triumphant or a disappointed 'ah' echoed down the stairs and into the dressing room.

Blinking in the twilight, shivering shoulders hunched, Schrella crouched there. The moment of departure could be held off no longer. One last time he straightened his tie and smoothed out the last fold in the collar of his sports shirt—oh yes, just so, always just right—once again adjusted his shoelaces and counted the money in his wallet for the journey home. The others were starting back from the showers, still talking about 'the ball Robert hit.'

'Want to go together?'

'Why not.'

They ascended worn concrete steps, still strewn with springtime litter, candy wrappings and empty cigarette packages. Then they went up onto the overpass, where sweating oarsmen were heaving a boat up the long ramp. Side by side, not saying a word, they crossed the viaduct, running away across lowlying layers of mist as over a river. Ships' hooters, red lights and green on deckhouses. In the shipyard red sparks were shooting up, describing figures in the grayness. Silently they went as far as the bridge, climbed the dark stairs, where, scratched in red sandstone, youths on the way back from a swim had eternalized their longings. A freight train rumbling over the bridge, carrying slaggy waste to the western bank, for further minutes relieved them of the need to speak. A shunting engine's lights swung about, warbly whistles directed the train as it was shoved backward onto the right-hand track. Down below in the fog, boats were gliding northward. Ships' horns wailed warnings of mortal danger, bellowed mournfully over the water, a tumult providentially making talk impossible.

"I came to a stop, Hugo, leaned over the parapet facing the river, took cigarettes from my pocket, offered them to Schrella, who struck a light for me. We smoked quietly while the train rumbled away and off the bridge. A line of barges moved along below us, we could just hear their gliding underneath the blanket of mist. All we could see were a few sparks coming up every once in a while from a galley stovepipe. It was quiet for minutes at a time, until the next string of barges came sliding quietly under the bridge, moving north, northwards to North Sea fogs. And I was scared, Hugo, for now I had to ask him, and if once I did, I would be involved, there would be no turning back. It must have been a terrible secret, if Nettlinger gambled on losing the game for it, and the Ottonians were willing to take Old Wobbly as umpire. Now it was almost dead still, and that gave a great weight to my impending question. It burdened it with eternity, you might say. I was cutting loose, Hugo, although I did not as yet know from what or wherefore, I was saying goodbye to St. Severin's dark tower, rising up out of flatly layered mist, to my parents' house not far from the tower, where my mother, right at the moment, was putting the finishing touches on the supper table, straightening the knives and forks, arranging flowers in little vases, tasting the wine. Was the white wine cool enough, the red not too cool? It was Saturday night, a religious time with us. Had she opened her missal yet, from which she would read the Sunday responses in her gentle voice? My room at the back looked out over the garden, where the old, old trees were in full leaf, where I used to lose myself passionately in mathematical formulas, in the severe curves of geometric figures, in the stark, wintry-clear branches of spheric arcs sprung from my drafting compass and pen. Up there I used to draw the churches I planned to build some day. Well, Schrella flicked his cigarette butt down into the sheet of fog; the glowing tip made airy spirals as it fell. Schrella turned to me, smiling, waiting for the question I still hadn't asked, shaking his head.

The chain of lamps running all the way to the other shore stood out sharply in the murk.

'Let's go,' said Schrella. 'There they are, can't you hear them?' I could hear them. The bridge stairs had already begun to resound under their tread. They were talking about the summer places they'd soon be going off to, Allgäu, Westerwald, Bad Gastein, the North Sea. And about the ball Robert hit. It was easier to ask my question walking.

'Why did they do it?' I asked. 'I don't get it. Are you Jewish?'
'No, I'm not.'
'What are you, then?'

'We're Lambs,' said Schrella. 'We've sworn never to put the *Host of the Beast* to our lips.'

'Lambs?' The word chilled me, I was afraid of it. 'A religious sect?' I asked.

'Perhaps.'

'Not a political party?'

'No.'

'Not for me,' I said. 'I can't be a lamb!'

'You want to make Communion with the *Host of the Beast?*'

'No, I don't,' I said.

'Shepherds,' he said, 'there are some shepherds who don't forsake the flock.'

'Quick,' I said. 'Hurry up, they're catching up with us.'

We went down the dark bridge steps at the western end, and as we reached the street I hesitated an instant. My way home was to the right, Schrella's to the left. But I did it. I followed him to the left, where the road wound toward the town, through lumber yards, coal bunkers and allotment gardens. Once beyond the first bend, now deep in the low mist, we stopped and watched the shadowy forms of the other students moving across the bridge. We could see them silhouetted above the parapet, we listened to the sound of their footsteps and their voices as they came down the flight of steps; we heard the echoing ring of their heavy hobnailed boots. We heard a voice calling, 'Nettlinger . . . Nettlinger . . . wait, wait!' And Nettlinger's own loud voice came wildly bouncing back from across the river, broken by the columns of the bridge, to lose itself behind us among the garden plots and warehouses. Nettlinger, crying out, 'Where's our lamby-boy and his shepherd?' Splintered fragments of laughter fell about us.

'You heard that?' Schrella asked.

'I heard it. Lamb and shepherd.'

We looked up at stragglers' shadows coming across the foot-path of the bridge. Their voices, which had been muffled as they crossed, grew clearer as they came down into the street, then were broken by the arches of the bridge. 'The ball Robert hit,' we heard them say.

'Tell me more,' I said to Schrella. 'I've got to know the details.'

'I'll show you the details,' he said. 'Come with me.' We groped our way through the murk along barbed-wire fences, and came to a wooden fence still smelling of fresh yellow paint that glowed in the dark. Over a locked door was an enamelled sign lit up by a naked electric bulb. The sign said: 'Michaelis, Coal, Coke, Briquettes.'

'You still know the way?' Schrella asked.

'Yes,' I said. 'We came this way together many a time, seven years ago, when we used to play down at Trischler's. What's happened to Alois?'

'He's a bargeman, like his father.'

'And is your father still a waiter down there in the tavern where the rivermen go?'

'No, he's at the Upper Harbor now.'

'What about those details?'

Schrella took the cigarette out of his mouth, pulled off his jacket, pushed his suspenders off his shoulders, pulled up his shirt and turned his back toward the dim electric light. His back was covered—peppered, more like it, I thought—with small, reddish-blue scars, the size of peas.

'My God,' I said. 'How did that happen?'

'Nettlinger,' he said. 'They do it to you down there in the old barracks near Williams' Pit. Old Wobbly and Nettlinger. They call themselves auxiliary police. They grabbed me in a raid they were making on beggars down by the docks. They arrested thirty-eight beggars in one day, and I was one of them. They questioned us, using barbed-wire whips. They said, "Admit you're a beggar." And I said, "That's right, I'm a beggar." '

Some of the guests were still eating a late breakfast, imbibing poisonous-looking orange juice. The pale young man was leaning against the door like a statue; the violet-colored velvet of his uniform made his face appear almost green.

"Hugo, are you listening to what I'm saying . . . Hugo?"

"Certainly, Doctor, I'm listening to every word."

"Get me a cognac, please . . . a double."

"Yes, Doctor."

Time glared at Hugo as he started down the stairs to the dining room, the great calendar he had to set mornings, turning the big pasteboard number under month and year. Today: September 6, 1958. It made his head swim, all that had happened long before he was born. Decades, half-centuries ago, 1935, 1903, 1885—yet it was all there, hidden far back in time. The echo of the past had been in Faehmel's voice when he was leaning against the billiard table and looking down into the square in front of St. Severin's. Hugo took a firm grip on the banister, drew in a deep breath like someone coming up for air, then opened his eyes and promptly ducked behind the great pillar.

The sheep-lady was coming down the stairs, barefoot and dressed like a shepherdess, the hip-length, capelike garment she had on exuding the odor of sheep dung. She was on her way to eat her millet gruel, with it black bread, a few nuts and sheep's milk kept fresh for her in the refrigerator. She brought the milk with her in thermos bottles and her sheep turds in little boxes. The turds she used to perfume her coarsely woven underwear of unbleached wool. After breakfast she sat for hours down there in the public room, knitting, knitting, going to the bar now and then to get a glass of water, smoking her short-stemmed pipe, sitting on the couch with her bare legs crossed and showing the dirty callouses on her feet. Meanwhile she held audience for disciples of both sexes, dressed like her, legs crossed, knitting, every now and then opening the little boxes of sheep dung supplied them by their mistress to sniff, as if the contents were expensive scent. At regular intervals the sheep-lady cleared her throat and from her perch asked in a girlish voice, "How shall we redeem the world?" To this all her followers, men and women, responded, "Through sheep's wool, sheep's leather, sheep's milk—and through knitting." Needles clicked away. Then silence. A youthful acolyte leaped up, went to the bar, brought the sheep-lady a glass of water and again the girlish voice threw out a question from the couch: "Where does the world's salvation lie concealed?" "In the sheep." Little boxes were opened, turds rapturously sniffed, while flash bulbs exploded and reporters' pencils raced over pages of stenographic notebooks.

Slowly Hugo moved farther back as she passed the pillar to the dining room. He was afraid of her. Only too often he had seen her soft eyes go hard, when she was alone with him, or when she caught him on the stairs and had him bring milk to her room, where he would come upon her with a cigarette stuck in her mouth. She would snatch the glass from him, laugh, drain it in a draft, serve herself a cognac, and move, glass in hand, toward him as he slowly retreated backwards to the door. "Has no one ever told you your face is worth a fortune, pure gold, you stupid boy? Why won't you be the Lamb of God in my new religion? I'll make you famous, rich. They'll get down on their knees to you in a lot finer hotels than this. Haven't you been around long enough to know that only a new religion can cure their boredom? And the more stupid it is, the better. Oh, go away, you're too stupid."

He stared after her as she waited, her face a mask, for the waiter to open the dining room door. His heart was still pounding when he came out from behind the pillar, and went slowly down to the restaurant.

"A cognac for the Doctor upstairs, a double."

"Your doctor's just caused a hell of a stink."

"What do you mean, stink?"

"I don't know. I think someone wants to see him on the double—your doctor. Here, take your cognac and get lost. There must be seventeen women of all ages on your trail. Come on, scram, there's another one coming down the stairs."

She looked as if she had drunk pure gall for breakfast, the one in the golden gown and golden shoes with lion-skin hat and muff. She evoked aversion whenever she appeared. Some superstitious guests screened their faces when they saw her coming in. Chambermaids gave notice because of her, waiters refused to serve her. But he, when she caught him, had to play canasta with her for hours on end. Her fingers were like chicken claws, the only human thing about her was the cigarette in her mouth. "Love, my boy, never known what it is. Not a soul who doesn't make it clear to me that I disgust him. My mother used to curse me out seven times a day, scream her loathing in my face. My mother was young and pretty, my father young and good-looking, and so were my brothers and sisters. They'd have poisoned me if only they'd had the courage. They said, *a thing like that should never have been born.* We used to live in a yellow villa above the steel works. Thousands of workers left the mill at night, and women and girls, all of them laughing, were waiting for them. They'd all go down those dirty streets together, laughing. I can see, hear, feel and smell like any other human being. I can read, write, count and taste—yet you're the first human being to stick it out with me more than half an hour, first one, you hear?"

She left a trail of dread behind her, the breath of disaster, throwing her room key on the desk, shrieking into the face of the boy replacing Jochen, "Hugo, where's Hugo?" When the boy shrugged his shoulders, she walked on to the revolving door, and the waiter who started it turning for her looked down at the floor. Then, the moment she was outside, she drew down her veil over her face.

"I don't wear it inside, boy. Let them see something for their money, and look at me for mine. But the people outside haven't earned it."

"Here's your cognac, Doctor."
"Thanks, Hugo."
He liked Faehmel. Faehmel came every morning at half-past

nine, gave him a reprieve till eleven, had already endowed him with a sense of eternity. Had it not always been like this? Had he not been standing at this same whitely lacquered door for centuries, hands folded behind his back, watching the quiet game, listening to words that sent him now sixty years back, now twenty ahead, then ten back again, only suddenly to fling him into the calendar-card reality outside the billiard room? White-green, red-green, red-white, always inside billiard cushions enclosing no more than two square meters of green felt. It was all clean, dry, precise. Between half-past nine and eleven. Downstairs to fetch the double cognac twice, maybe three times. Time here ceased to be a dimension making things measurable. Time was blotted out by that green rectangle of blotting paper. In vain hours chimed, hands moved in vain, in vain ran away from each other in senseless haste. When Faehmel showed up it was drop everything—and just at the one time when there was most to do, old guests leaving, new ones arriving. Yet he had to stand there until St. Severin's struck eleven. But when—when would that be? Airless rooms, timeless clocks, and he submerged here, moving swiftly under oceans, reality not penetrating, its nose pressed against glass outside, as against shop or aquarium window, dimensions lost, except flatness, the flatness of children's cutouts. Here people's clothes were provisionally draped upon their bodies, so many paper dolls. Helplessly they kicked against time's walls, thicker than centuries made of glass. St. Severin's shadow was far away, farther still the railroad station, the trains not real, through, freight, express, fast and slow, with them carrying trunks to customs stations. Only the three billiard balls, rolling over green blotting paper, forming ever-new figurations, were real. Infinity in a thousand formulas, all contained within two square meters. He struck them forth, his cue a wand, while his voice lost itself in eons of time.

"Is there any more to the story, Doctor?"

"You want to hear it?"

"I'd like to."

Faehmel laughed, sipped at his glass of cognac, lit himself a fresh cigarette, took up the cue and played the red ball. Red-white rolled over the table's green.

"A week after that, Hugo. . . ."

"After what?"

Again Faehmel laughed. "After that rounders game, that fourteenth of July in 1935 they scratched into the plaster above the locker—a week after that, I was glad that Schrella had reminded me of the road leading to Trischler's house. I was standing at the railing of the old weighhouse in the Lower Harbor. From there I had a good view of the road. It went past woodyards, coalyards, ran down to a place where building materials were sold, from there went to the basin, closed off by a rusty iron fence and now used only as a ship-breaking yard for condemned vessels. The last time I'd been there was seven years before, with Schrella, when we went to visit Trischler. But it could have been fifty. I was thirteen when I first went there. In the evening long trains of barges lay moored at the embankment. Barge-women with their market baskets walked ashore up swaying gangplanks. The women had red faces and a steady eye. Men came after the women, out to get beer or a newspaper. Trischler's mother, all in a flutter, looked over her wares—tomatoes and cabbages and bunches of silvery onions hanging on the wall. Outside a drover was giving his dog short, sharp commands, getting them to drive the sheep into a pen. Across the river—on the side where we are now, Hugo—the gaslamps were being turned on, yellowish light filling the white globes. A great line of them ran north, propagating infinity. Trischler's father snapped on the lights in his beer garden, and Schrella's father, a napkin over his arm, came down to the two-boat house out back, where we—Trischler, young Schrella and I—were chipping ice and throwing it over the beer cases.

But now, seven years later, Hugo, on this twenty-first of July in 1935, the paint had peeled off all the fences, and the only new thing in sight was the door at Michaelis' coalyard.

On the other side of the fence a big pile of briquettes lay crumbling apart. At every turn in the road I looked back to make sure I wasn't being followed. I was exhausted, I could feel the wounds on my back. The pain began to throb like a pulse. For ten minutes there hadn't been a soul on the road. I looked along the narrow stretch of clear, ruffled water joining the Lower to the Upper Harbor. Not a boat in sight. I looked up at the sky. Not a plane, either, and I thought, you must take yourself pretty seriously if you think they'll send planes out looking for you.

You see, I'd done it, Hugo, I'd gone with Schrella to the little Cafe Zons on Boisserée Street, where the Lambs had their meetings. I'd mumbled the password to the proprietor: 'Feed my lambs.' And I had sworn to a young girl called Edith, and I looked right into her eyes as I did it, that I would never make oblation to the *Host of the Beast.* In that same dark back room I had made a speech, in it using unlamblike words smacking of blood and rioting and revenge, revenge for Ferdi Progulske whom they'd executed only that morning. The ones sitting around the table listening themselves looked as if they had just had their heads chopped off. They were frightened, they realized that a boy's seriousness is as serious as an adult's. Fear lay on them, and the knowledge that Ferdi was really dead. He was seventeen years old, a hundred-meter runner, a carpenter's apprentice. I'd only seen him four times all told, twice in the Cafe Zons and twice in my own house, yet I'd never forget him as long as I lived. Ferdi had sneaked into Old Wobbly's apartment and thrown a bomb at Wobbly's feet as he came out of the bedroom. Old Wobbly got out of it with burns on his feet, a shattered bureau mirror and a smell of cordite in the place. Madness, Hugo, adolescent high-mindedness. You hear? Are you really listening?"

"I hear, all right."

"I'd read Hölderlin: *Firm in compassion the eternal heart.* But Ferdi only read Karl May, who seemed to preach the same high-mindedness. All foolishness, paid for under the executioner's ax in the gray of the morning, while church bells were tolling for matins and baker boys counted warm rolls into their string bags, and here in the Prince Heinrich Hotel the first guests were having breakfast served, while the birds were twittering, milkmaids stealing in and out of quiet doorways on rubber-soled shoes leaving bottles of milk on clean coco mats. Meanwhile men from newspaper promotion departments were racing around the city plastering billboards with red-bordered bulletins, saying: 'Execution! The Apprentice, Ferdinand Progulske . . . !' So all early risers could read them, the streetcar motormen, the school kids, the teachers and everyone else hurrying to catch the morning trolley, sandwiches in their pockets, and carrying the local paper, as yet unfolded, with a headline announcing 'An Example Set.' And for me to read, too, Hugo, as I was getting into No. 7, right out in front of here at the corner.

Ferdi's voice on the phone—had I heard it yesterday or the day before? 'You'll be at the Cafe Zons as we agreed?' A pause. 'Are you coming, or aren't you?' 'I'll be there.' Enders even tried to catch hold of my sleeve and pull me into the streetcar that morning when the news broke, but I pulled loose and waited until the streetcar had disappeared around the corner. Then I went to the trolley stop on the other side of the street, where you still catch No. 16, and rode through peaceful suburbs to the Rhine, then away from the Rhine again until the car finally swung into the loop at the end of the line between gravel pits and army barracks. By rights, I thought at the time, it should be winter. Winter, cold, rainy, sky overcast—that would make it more bearable. But it was not. For hours I wandered around among prosy allotment gardens, looking at peas and apricots, tomatoes and cabbages, listening to the clink of beer bottles and the ice cream man's bell. There he stood at a crossing, dipping ice cream into crumbly cones. How can they do it, I thought, how can they eat ice cream, drink beer, sample apricots while Ferdi. . . . Around noontime I fed my sandwiches to some morose chickens scratching out geometric figures in the muck of a junkyard. Out of a window came a woman's voice, saying, 'Did you read about that kid, the one they. . . .' And a man's voice answered, 'Shut up, goddamn it, I know all about it. . . .' I threw my sandwiches to the chickens, continued on and got lost down among railroad cuts and culverts. Finally I reached another terminus somewhere and rode through a series of strange suburbs. I got off and turned my pockets inside out. Black gunpowder trickled onto the gray pavement. I started to run, past more railroad embankments, storage dumps, garden plots, houses. Finally, a movie theater, where the woman in the box office was just pushing up her window. Three o'clock? Three exactly. Fifty pfennigs. I was the only one in the audience. Heat hung over the corrugated iron roof. Love, blood, a betrayed lover drew his dagger. I fell asleep and didn't wake up until the movie-goers for the six o'clock show came barging into the theater. I staggered outside. Where was my school bag? Back inside the movie? By the gravel pit, where I'd sat for a long while watching the trucks being piled full, so high the load spilled over? Or was it back at that other place, where I had thrown my bread to the sullen fowl? Ferdi's voice on the phone, was it yesterday or the day before? 'You'll be at the Cafe Zons as we agreed?' Pause. 'Will you be there or won't you?' 'I'll be there.'

A rendezvous with a headless boy. A piece of folly already precious to me, the price of it having been so high. Meanwhile I had had my turn with Nettlinger. He'd lain in wait for me in front of the Cafe Zons. They took me to Williams' Pit and beat me with the barbed-wire whip. The barbs tore up my back. Through the rusty window bars I could see the banking where I had played as a child. Time and again our ball had rolled downhill on us, and time and again I had climbed down helter-skelter to bring it back, always having a quick, scared look at the rusty bars, sensing something evil behind the dirty windowpanes. Nettlinger laid on.

In the cell I tried to take my shirt off, but shirt and skin were all chewed up together, so that when I pulled at my collar or sleeve, it felt as if I were pulling my skin over my head.

There were other bad moments, too. When I stood at the weighhouse railing, at the end of my tether, the pain was greater than the pride I took in my wounds. My head sank to the railing, my mouth pressed to it, and the bitterness of the weather-pitted iron felt good in my mouth. Another minute and I would be at Trischler's house, and then I would know whether they had got there first and were waiting for me. I got a terrible start. A workman with his lunch box under his arm came up the street and disappeared into the place where building materials were sold. As I went down the steps I held to the handrail so hard that my sliding hand peeled off flakes of rust. The rhythms of the riveting hammers that had sounded so cheerful seven years before were gone, nothing left but a weary echo of them now. One old man with a sledge hammer, working from a raft, breaking up a ferry boat. Nuts and bolts rattled into a box. When the ferry timbers fell, the thud they made told just how badly rotted they were. The old man kept tapping at the boat's engine and listening to the sound as if he were sounding the heart of someone very dear to him. He bent down deep into the bilge of the boat and fished out all sorts of parts: screws, the engine head, injection nozzles, cylinders. He held them up to have a look at them, sniffed them before throwing them into the box with the nuts and bolts. At the stern of the boat was an old winch, hanging on it the remains of an old cable, rusty rotten as an old stocking.

With me memories of people and events have always been linked memories of movement, which stick in my mind as patterns. The way I leaned over the railing, lifting my head, letting it fall, lifting it, letting it fall lower to watch the street—the memory attached to this movement brought words and colors, images and moods back into my consciousness. I didn't remember how Ferdi had looked, but instead how he'd lit a match, how he'd raised his head a little when he said, yes yes, no no. I remembered how Schrella wrinkled his forehead, the way he moved his shoulders, Father's walk, Mother's gestures, the way Grandmother moved her hand when she brushed the hair away from her brow. . . . And the old man down below, the one I could see from the top of the banking, and who just then was knocking punky wood loose from a big screw—that was Trischler's father. For the hand was making movements no other hand but his could make. I'd watched the same hand opening boxes, renailing them shut. Stuff smuggled across the frontier in dark ships' holds. Rum and raisins, chocolate and cigarettes. In the tow-boat house in back of the beer garden I'd seen that hand make movements peculiar to it and none other. The old man looked up, blinked at me, and said, 'Hey, sonny, that road up there doesn't go anywhere.'

'It goes to your house,' I said.

'Anybody who comes to my house comes by water, even the police. Even my son comes by boat, when he comes at all, which isn't often.'

'Are the police there now?'

'What do you want to know that for, sonny?'

'Because they're looking for me.'

'Been stealing?'

'No,' I said, 'I just refused the *Host of the Beast.*'

Ships, I was thinking, ships with dark holds, and captains with a lot of practice fooling customs men. I won't take up much room, no more than a rolled-up carpet. I would get across the border stowed in a rolled-up sail.

'Come down here,' said Trischler. 'They can see you up there from the other side of the river.'

I turned around and let myself slowly slide down the embankment toward Trischler, grabbing at bunches of grass as I went.

'Oh, it's you,' the old man said. 'I know your face, but I've forgotten your name.'

'Faehmel,' I said.

'Of course. They're after you, it came over on the early

morning news. I might have known it when they described you. Red scar on the bridge of the nose. That was when we rowed across at high tide and ran into the bridge piles when I misfigured the current. You banged your head on the iron gunwale.'

'Yes, and I wasn't allowed to come over here again.'

'But you did come again.'

'Not for long—until I got on the outs with Alois.'

'Come on. And duck when we go under the swing bridge or you'll get a dent in your head—and they won't be letting you come here again. How did you get away from them?'

'Nettlinger came into my cell at sun-up. He took me out the back way, where the underground passages lead to the railroad cut, by Williams' Pit. He said, "Get lost, start running. All I can give you is an hour's lead; after that I'll have to report it to the police. As it is I've had to go right around the city to make it here." '

'So that's it,' the old man said. 'That's what you get when you start throwing bombs! You would go and take an oath and—anyway, yesterday I packed up one of your boys and shipped him across the frontier.'

'Yesterday?' I asked. 'Who was it?'

'Schrella,' he said. 'He holed up here and I had to make him leave on the *Anna Katharina*.'

'Alois always wanted to be mate and steer the *Anna Katharina!*'

'He is mate on the *Katharina*. Come on, now.'

I began to stagger as we went toward Trischler's house along the slant-topped wall at the foot of the embankment. I got to my feet, fell again, again got up, and doing this jerked skin and shirt apart, stuck them together, pulled them apart, over and over, and the pain, like thorns being stuck in my back again and again, made me half lose consciousness. Movements, colors, smells from a thousand memories became all mixed up, piled one on top of the other. All sorts of numbers floated through my mind, changing color, taking on different angles and directions, generated out of me by the pain.

High tide, I thought, high tide, as again a desire came over me to throw myself in and be carried away to the gray horizon.

In my dreamlike state I was troubled by the question whether a barbed-wire whip could be hidden in a lunch box. Movements remembered changed into lines, which joined into figures, green, black and red ones, representing, like a cardiogram, a particular person's rhythms. The way Alois Trischler jerked his line to set the hook when we were fishing in the Old Harbor, the way he cast his lure out into the water, the way his arm traveled as he held his rod against the pull of the current, thus indicating its speed. Also, the way Nettlinger raised his arm to throw the ball into Schrella's face, the trembling of his lips, the twitching of his nostrils, these changed into a gray design like a dead spider. Like so much information coming over a teletype from somewhere I couldn't place, people unfolded out of my memory, so many stigmata. Edith, the Edith of that evening after the rounders game when I went home with Schrella. Edith's face out in the park at Blessenfeld, when she lay under me on the grass, all wet from the summer rain. Raindrops glistened on her blond hair, rolled along her eyebrows, a garland of silver drops on Edith's face which rose and fell with her breathing. This garland was fixed in my memory in a form suggesting the skeleton of some sea creature found on a rust-colored beach, its constituent drops multiplied into countless little clouds of the same size. Then there was the line of her mouth as she said to me, 'They'll kill you.' That was Edith.

I was tormented in the dream by having lost my school bag —I had always been meticulous about everything—and I found myself tearing my gray-green copy of Ovid from a scrawny chicken's beak. I haggled with the usherette in the movie house over the Hölderlin poem she had ripped out of my anthology because she found it so beautiful: *Firm in compassion the eternal heart.*

When I came to it was suppertime, with Frau Trischler bringing in the meal, milk, an egg, bread, an apple. Her hands became young when she bathed my flayed back in wine. Pain flamed through me when she squeezed wine from the sponge and let it flow into the furrows on my back. Afterwards she poured oil over me, and I asked her where she had learned to do it like that.

'It tells you how in the Bible,' she said. 'And I've done it once before, on your friend Schrella! Alois will be here the day after tomorrow and leave Ruhrort Sunday for Rotterdam. You needn't be afraid,' she said. 'They'll get you through. On the river people know each other, as if they lived on the same street. More milk, young man?'

'No, thanks.'

'Don't worry. Monday or Tuesday you'll be in Rotterdam. Now what is it? What's the matter?'

Nothing. Nothing. The all-points bulletin was still out: red scar on bridge of nose. The father, the mother, Edith—I felt no desire to calculate the differential of their kindnesses, to count off the rosary of my pain. The river was bright and cheerful, with white excursion boats flying gaily colored pennants, freight carriers painted red, green and blue, carrying coal and wood back and forth, from here to there. On the other side of the river ran the green boulevard, the terrace outside the Cafe Bellevue was snow-white. Beyond, the tower of St. Severin's, the sharp red light running up the corner of the Prince Heinrich Hotel, and my parents' house only a hundred steps more. They would be sitting down to dinner now, a full-dress meal with my father presiding over it like a patriarch. Saturday, celebrated with sabbatical formality. Was the red wine too cool? The white cool enough?

'More milk, young man?'

'No thanks, Frau Trischler, really. . . .'

. . . The men on motorcycles went racing through the city from billboard to billboard with their red-bordered bulletins: 'Execution! The Student, Robert Faehmel. . . .' Father would be saying a prayer at the supper table: *He who has been scourged for us.* Mother's hand would describe a pattern of humility at her breast, before saying: 'It's a wicked world, not many are pure in heart.' And Otto's resonant heels would be beating out brother, brother, on the floor of our house, on the flagstones outside, on down the street to the Modest Gate. . . . That hooting outside was the *Stilte,* the clear notes cutting into the evening sky, white lightning furrows in dark blue. Now I was stretched out on a tarpaulin, like someone being prepared for burial at sea. Alois lifted up one side of the canvas to wrap me in, and, woven white on gray, I could clearly read: 'Morrien. Ijmuiden.' Frau Trischler bent over me, weeping, and kissed me, and Alois slowly rolled me in as if I were a particularly valuable corpse, and took me up in his arms.

'Boy!' the old man called after me, 'don't forget us, boy!'

Evening breeze, the *Stilte* giving another hoot of friendly warning. The sheep were bleating in their pen, the ice cream man was shouting 'Ice cream, ice cream!' then stopped, which no doubt meant he was filling crumbly cones with vanilla ice cream. The plank swayed when Alois carried me aboard. A low voice asked, 'Is that him?' and Alois answered, in the same low way, 'It's him.' Leaving, he murmured to me, 'Remember, by Tuesday night you'll be in the harbor of Rotterdam.' Other arms carried me below decks down a companionway. It smelled below first of oil, then of coal, and finally of wood, the hooting now seemed far away, the *Stilte* shuddered, a deep rumbling sound grew stronger. I could feel we were moving, on down the Rhine, always farther away from St. Severin's."

St. Severin's shadow had drawn nearer. Already it filled the left-hand billiard room window, and was closing in on the one to the right. Pushed forward by the sun, time drew closer like a threat, filling up the great clock which would soon spew it out in terrible chimes. The billiard balls rolled on, white-green, red-green. Years were cut into pieces, seconds, seconds drawn out into eternities by the clock's calm voice. If only he wouldn't have to fetch more cognac, anticipate calendar and clock, put up with the sheep-lady and *a thing like that should never have been born.* Better just to hear the *Feed my lambs* saying again, hear about the woman who had lain in the grass in the summer rain, about the boats coming to anchor, the women walking up gangways, the ball that Robert hit, Robert who had never taken the *Host of the Beast,* who played on wordlessly, always making new patterns with cue and ball on two square meters of green table.

"How about you, Hugo?" he quietly said. "Aren't you going to tell me any stories today?"

"I don't know how long it went on, but it seemed forever to me. Every day, after school, they beat me up. Sometimes I stayed put until I was sure they'd all gone home to eat, until the cleaning woman arrived, down in the hallway where I was waiting, and asked me, 'Why are you still hanging around, boy? Your mother must be looking for you.'

But I was afraid, I even used to wait until the cleaning woman had gone, and get myself locked in the school. I didn't always get away with it; most of the time the cleaning woman threw me out before she locked up. But when I managed to get locked in, I was glad. Then I scrounged food in the desks and garbage pails which the cleaning woman had put out in the hall for the collector, plenty of sandwiches, apples and left-over cake. That way I was all alone in the school and they couldn't do anything to me. I hid in the teachers' clothes closet behind the cellar stairwell, because I was afraid they might look in through the window and find me. But it was a long time before they found out how I used to hide out in the school. I squatted there often for hours, waiting until it was nighttime and I could open a window and get out. Lots of times I would just stare and stare at the empty schoolyard. Can anything be emptier than a schoolyard, late in the afternoon? It was fun, until they discovered how I was getting myself locked in the school. I scrunched up there in the teachers' closet or underneath the window ledge and waited to see if I could feel something I only knew by name—hatred. I wanted to hate them real bad, Doctor, but I couldn't. I was just plain afraid. Some days I waited only till three or four o'clock, thinking they'd be all gone by then and I might run across the street quick, past Meid's stable, round the churchyard and then home, where I could lock myself in. But they took turns going home to eat—that was one thing they couldn't do, go without food—and when they jumped me I could smell what they'd been eating, even before they got real close, potatoes and gravy, roast meat, ham and cabbage. And while they were working me over I used to think, why did Christ die, anyway? What good did it ever do me? What do I care if they pray every morning, take Communion every Sunday and hang a big crucifix in the kitchen, over the tables where they eat their potatoes and gravy, roast meat, ham and cabbage? Nothing, that's how much I care. What's it all amount to, if they lie in wait every day and beat me up? It's been going on like this for five or six hundred years. Yet they're always shooting off about how old their church is, and they've been burying their ancestors in the churchyard for a thousand years, for a thousand years they've been praying and then eating potatoes and gravy, and ham and cabbage with the Crucifix on the wall. So what? You know what they used to holler at me when they were beating me up? *God's little lamb.* That was my nickname."

Red-green, white-green, from the billiard balls new figurations emerged like so many signals. Then were swiftly scattered. Leaving naught behind. Music with no melody, painting without likeness, quadrilaterals, rectangles, rhombs, endlessly multiplied. Clicking billiard balls caroming from green cushions.

"And later I tried another way. I locked the door at home, piled furniture in front of it, whatever I could find, boxes, mattresses, odds and ends. Until they told the police, who came to get the boy who was playing hookey. They surrounded the house and hollered, 'Come out of there, you devil.' But I wouldn't come out and so they broke the door down, shoved the furniture to one side and then they had me. They took me off to school, to be thrashed again, pushed into the gutter again and again made fun of with that *God's little lamb*. *Feed my lambs*—but I was one lamb they didn't feed, if I ever was His to begin with. No use, Doctor. The wind blows, the snow falls, the trees turn green, the leaves fall—they go right on eating potatoes and gravy, ham and cabbage.

Then, of course, sometimes my mother was at home, drunk and dirty, smelling of death, giving off the stink of decay, screaming, *'whywhywhy!'* She yelled it more times than all the *Lord have mercy on us'es* in all the priest's prayers put together. Used to drive me crazy when she hollered *'whywhywhy'* like that for hours at a time. I ran away in the rain, a God's little lamb soaked to the skin, hungry, mud sticking to my shoes, all over me. I got plastered with wet mud from head to toe, hiding down there in the beetfields. But I'd rather be down in the mucky beet rows, letting the rain pour on me, than listen to that awful *whywhywhy*. Then, sooner or later, someone or other would take pity on me and bring me back home, or back to school, back to that hole called Denklingen. So then they walloped me again and called me *God's little lamb,* and my mother kept on with her *whywhywhy* rosary, so I ran away again, and again someone took pity on me, and this time they took me to a child-welfare center. No one knew me there, none of the kids and none of the grown-ups, but I hadn't been two days in the center before they were calling me *God's little lamb* the same as before, and I was afraid, even though they didn't beat me. They laughed at me, because there were so many words I didn't know. The word 'breakfast,' for instance. All I knew was 'eat'—whenever anything was there, whenever I found anything. But when I looked at the bulletin board and saw 'Breakfast: butter, 30 grams; bread, 200 grams; marmalade, 50 grams; coffee and milk,' I asked someone 'What's breakfast?' They all surrounded me, the grown-ups, too, laughing and saying, 'Don't you know what breakfast is? You've never had breakfast?' 'No,' I said. 'How about the Bible,' one of the grown-ups said, 'haven't you ever read the word breakfast there?' And then the other grown-up said to him, 'Are you sure the word breakfast's in the Bible?' 'No,' he said, 'but somewhere, in some reading or other, or at home, he must have heard the word breakfast at least once. After all, pretty soon he'll be thirteen, and savages aren't that bad, it just goes to show how poorly people speak today.' I didn't know, either, there'd been a war a little while before, and they asked me if I'd ever been in a cemetery where it said 'Fallen' on the gravestones, the way we Germans say it when we mean 'Killed in Battle.' I told them, yes, I'd seen 'Fallen.' Then what did I think 'Fallen' meant? I said I imagined that the people buried there had died from falling down. That made them laugh louder than they had at 'breakfast.' Then they gave us history lessons, from the earliest times on down, but soon I was fourteen, Doctor, and the hotel manager came to the center and we—all of the fourteen-year-olds—had to line up in the hall outside the rector's office, and the rector came out with the hotel manager. They walked past us, looking us over, and then both said, as if they had only one mouth between them, 'We're looking for some boys to go into hotel *service*. We need boys who will know how to *serve*.' But the only one they picked was me. I had to put my things in a box right away. Then I came up here with the manager, and in the car he said to me, 'All I hope is you never find out how much your looks are worth. You're the purest God's little lamb I ever laid eyes on, that's for a fact.' I was afraid, Doctor. I still am. I'm always thinking they're going to beat me."

"Do they beat you?"

"No, never. But what I'd like to know is what that war was like. I had to leave school before they could tell me about it. Do you know about the war?"

"Yes."

"Were you in it?"

"I was."

"What did you do?"

"I was a demolition expert, Hugo. That mean anything to you?"

"Demolition?"

"Blowing things up."

"Yes, I've seen them blowing up rocks in the quarry behind Denklingen."

"That's exactly what I did, Hugo, only I didn't blow up rocks, I blew up houses and churches. You're the first one I ever mentioned it to, except my wife, but she died a long time ago, so no one knows but you, not even my parents or my children. I'm an architect, as you know, and by rights I should be putting houses up. But I've never put any up, only blown them down. And the same goes for churches, too, which I used to draw on nice soft drawing paper when I was a boy, always dreaming that some day I'd build real ones like them. But I never did build any. When I went into the army, in my record they found a reference to a doctoral thesis I'd written on a problem in statics. Statics, Hugo, is the study of the equilibrium of forces, of stress and strain in supporting structures. Without statics you can't even build an African hut. And the opposite of statics is dynamics. Sounds like dynamite, the way it's used in demolition, and matter of fact it is tied in with dynamite. For the rest of the war I was all dynamite. I know a little something about statics, Hugo, and something about dynamics, too. But about dynamite I know a whole lot. I've read every book on it in existence from cover to cover. If you want to smash something, all you need is know where to place the charge and how strong it has to be. I happened to know that, boy, so I demolished. I blew up bridges and apartment blocks, churches and railroad bridges, villas and crossroads. They gave me medals for doing it. I was promoted from second lieutenant to first, from that to captain, and they gave me special leave and citations because I knew how to destroy things so well. By the end of the war I was attached to a general who had only one thought in his head: 'Field of fire.' Do you know what a field of fire is? You don't?"

Faehmel put the billiard cue to his shoulder like a rifle and aimed out through the window at St. Severin's tower. "Look," he said. "If I wanted to fire at the bridge, over there behind St. Severin's, the church would be lying in my field of fire. So, St. Severin's would have to be demolished, here, now, right off the bat. And, believe me, Hugo, I'd have blown St. Severin's to smithereens, even though I knew my general was crazy as a two-cent watch, even though I knew that 'field of fire' was complete nonsense. Why was it nonsense? If you're up in the air, you understand, you don't need a field of fire. And even the simplest general must have realized somewhere along the line that the airplane had been invented. But my general was off his rocker and the only idea in his one-track mind was 'field of fire.' Therefore, I gave him a field of fire. I had a good team working with me, physicists and architects, and whatever stood in our way we demolished. Our last job was something really big, something colossal, an entire system of huge and very solid buildings. A church, stables, monks' cells, an administration block, a whole farm-stead. An entire abbey, Hugo. It lay exactly between two armies, one German, the other American. I provided the German army with a field of fire, even though to tell the truth it needed one like a hole in the head. Out there ahead of me the walls went toppling down. The animals bellowed in the stables and the barns, the monks cursed me out. But nothing would stop me. I blew up the whole of St. Anthony's Abbey in Kissa Valley, just three days before the war ended. Very carefully and correctly. You know me, my boy—always just so!"

He lowered his cue, which he had been holding all along zeroed in on an imaginary target, returned it to a crooked finger and struck the cue ball. Whitely it rolled over green, and bounced in a wild zigzag from one green cushion to another.

St. Severin's muffled bells gave out the time. But when, *when* did eleven strike?

"Boy, go and see what all that commotion is at the door."

He played another ball. Red-green. Letting the balls come to rest, he put his cue down.

"The manager would like to know if you'd be so kind as to speak with a Dr. Nettlinger?"

"How about you? Would *you* speak with a Dr. Nettlinger?"

"No, I wouldn't."

"Show me how to get out of here without using that door."

"You can go through the dining room, Doctor, then you'll come out onto Modest Street."

"Goodbye, Hugo. See you tomorrow."

"Goodbye, Doctor."

They were setting the tables for lunch, a ballet of waiters, a ballet of busboys, pushing tea wagons from table to table in a precisely determined order, laying out silver, changing vases of flowers. White carnations in slender vases were replaced by modest violets in round ones, marmalade dishes by wine glasses, round for red wine, slender for white. Only exception was the sheep-lady's milk, which in the crystal carafe looked gray.

Faehmel threaded his way among the tables with a light step. Pushing aside the violet curtain, he went down the stairs and presently was standing across the way from the tower of St. Severin's.

four

Leonore's step soothed him. Carefully she went about the studio, opened cupboard doors, lifted lids of chests, untied packages, unrolled drawings. She seldom came to the window where he was to disturb him, only if the document had no date, the plan no name. He had always liked order, but never lived up to it. Leonore, she would take care of that for him. She was laying out piles of plans and papers, letters and old accounts, on the floor of the big studio, according to date. After fifty years the floor, as she worked, still shook from the heavy stamping of the presses below. 1907, '08, '09, '10—the stacks of material were visibly getting bigger with the century's advance. 1909 was bigger than 1908, 1910 than 1909. Leonore was laying bare the curve of his life's activities, trained as she was in precision.

"Yes," he said, "just ask me whenever you want, child. That one? That's the hospital in Weidenhammer. Built it in 1924, dedicated in September." In her neat handwriting she wrote "1924–9" on the margin of the plan.

The stacks from the 1914–1918 war years were meager:

three, four plans; a country house for the general, a hunting lodge for the lord mayor, a St. Sebastian chapel for the Rifle Club. Furlough assignments, costing precious days. To get to see his children he had built castles for the generals free of charge.

"No, Leonore, that one was in 1935. A Franciscan convent. Modern? Of course I've built modern things, too."

The view framed by the big studio window had always seemed like a kaleidoscope to him. The sky changed color, the trees in the courtyard went from gray to black to green, the flowers in the roof gardens bloomed and turned sere. Children played on the leaded sheet-metal roofs, grew up, had children themselves, whereupon their parents became grandparents. Only the profile of the roofs remained constant, that and the bridge, the mountains visible on the horizon on clear days. That is, remained constant until the second war altered the line of the roofs, tearing out gaps through which on sunny days the silvery Rhine could be seen, on days of overcast the gray Rhine, and beyond, in the Old Harbor, the drawbridge. But now these gaps had long since been filled in, and again children played on the metaled roofs, and his granddaughter crossed the Kilbs' roof, schoolbooks in her hand, as fifty years before his wife had done. Or had his wife, Johanna, gone there on sunny afternoons to read Schiller's *Love and Intrigue?*

The phone rang and it was pleasant to have Leonore take up the receiver and listen to her voice as she answered the unknown caller. "The Cafe Kroner? I'll ask His Excellency."

"Wants to know how many people to expect this evening? Birthday party?" Would the fingers of one hand be enough to count them off? "Let me see. Two grandchildren, one son, myself—and you. May I have that pleasure, Leonore?"

Five of them, then. The fingers of one hand were enough.

"No, no champagne. Everything just the way it was ordered. Thank you, Leonore."

She probably thinks I'm a little dotty, but if I am, it's nothing new. I saw everything before it happened, knew exactly what

I wanted, knew I'd get it. Only thing I never knew, and still can't figure out to this day, is why I did it. Was it for money, fame, or simply because it amused me? What was it I was looking for, that Friday morning fifty-one years ago, September sixth, 1907, when I walked out of that railroad station over there? From the moment I set foot in the city I had my moves all figured out, an exact daily routine, the steps of a complicated dance all down to a tee—myself soloist and ballet master all in one. Cast and decor were there for the asking, not costing a penny.

I had only ten minutes left to dance my first routine. That is, walk across the station square, out by the Prince Heinrich Hotel, kitty-corner across Modest Street and into the Cafe Kroner. It was on my twenty-ninth birthday that I came to the city. A September morning. Cab horses were standing guard over their sleeping drivers. Hotel boys in the violet uniform of the Prince Heinrich were lugging suitcases in the wake of guests on the way to the railroad station. On bank buildings substantial iron gratings were being pushed up for the day, to land with a solid sound in their storage racks. Pigeons, news vendors. Uhlans, a troop of them, riding by the Prince Heinrich, with the captain waving at a woman in a rose-red hat, standing veiled on the balcony. She blew him a kiss. Hooves clattering on the cobbles, pennants and plumes fluttering in the morning wind, organ music coming out of the big open door of St. Severin's.

I was excited, took a street map out of my coat pocket, unfolded it and looked at the red semicircle I'd drawn around the railroad station. Five black crosses indicated the cathedral and the four adjacent churches. I looked up and tried to locate the four church spires through the morning haze. The fifth, St. Severin's, was no trouble. There it was in front of me; its enormous shadow made me shiver a little. I looked down at the map again. Right. A yellow cross indicated the house where I'd rented a studio and a living room for six months, paid in advance, 7 Modest Street, between St. Severin's and the Modest Gate. It had to be over there to the right, where a group of priests were just crossing the street. The semicircle I'd drawn around the station had a radius of one kilometer. Somewhere inside that red line lived the woman I would marry. I'd never met her, didn't know her name. All I knew was that I would take her out of one of those patrician houses my father had told me about. He'd served three years here, in the Uhlans, soaking up hatred, hatred for horses and officers. A sentiment I deferred to, without sharing it. I was always glad my father didn't live to see me become an officer myself—lieutenant in the Engineer Corps Reserves. I burst out laughing that morning fifty-one years ago. I laughed and laughed. I knew I'd take a wife from one of those houses, that she would be called Brodem or Cusenius, Kilb or Ferve. She would be twenty years old and now, right this very minute, she would be leaving morning Mass on her way home to put her prayerbook back in the hall closet. She would arrive at just the right moment to be kissed on the forehead by her father, on the way, rumbling bass and all, through the hall and out to the office. For breakfast she would eat bread and honey, drink one cup of coffee. 'No, no, Mother, no egg, please.' Then she would read off the dates of coming galas to her mother. Might she go to the University Ball? She might.

By the University Ball at the latest, on the sixth of January, I would know the one I wished to make my own, would dance with her. I would be good to her, love her, and she would bear me children, five, six, seven of them. They would marry and present me with grandchildren, five times, six, seven times seven. I saw my troop of grandchildren, and myself, an eighty-year-old patriarch, lording it over the clan I proposed to found. At birthday celebrations, funerals, weddings and silver weddings, christenings. Infants would be handed over to be held in my old arms. There would be great-grandchildren for me to love as I had loved the pretty young things my sons had married. These, meanwhile, I would invite to breakfast, give candy and flowers, paintings and eau de cologne. I could see it all as I stood there, ready to begin the dance.

I stared at the porter as he wheeled off my luggage in his cart to the house at 7 Modest Street, the padlocked hamper with my linen and my drawings, the little leather valise containing papers, documents and my money. My money—four hundred gold coins, net proceeds of twelve years' work, spent in country builders' field offices, working in the draughting rooms of second-rate architects, at workers' housing developments, industrial plants, churches, schools, clubhouses sketched out, planned, built. Money which represented construction estimates plowed through backwards and forwards, to the very last dry specification—'and the sacristy paneling shall be made of the best clear walnut, the best-grade hardware used.'

I know I laughed as I stood there, yet to this day for the life of me I don't really know why or what made me do it. But I can say I wasn't laughing out of pure joy in being young and alive. There was mockery and derision in it, even malice, yet just how much of each I've never been able to tell. I was thinking of the hard benches I'd sat on during evening classes, when I went to learn arithmetic, mathematics, drawing, the manual arts, and how I'd struggled to learn dancing and swimming. I laughed thinking of myself as a lieutenant in the Engineer Reserves, stationed with the 8th Battalion in Coblenz. At how I used to sit, in the city, at the famous Elbow of the Rhine, where two rivers come together, and there found the Mosel just as dirty as the greater stream. I had lived in twenty-three furnished rooms; I'd seduced landlords' daughters and been seduced by them myself. I saw myself slipping barefoot through moldy-smelling hallways to exchange caresses, including that supreme tenderness which again and again turned out to be a fraud. Lavender water and hair let down. Horrible living rooms where fruit never intended to be eaten grew old in bowls of greenish glass, where hard words such as brute, honor, innocence came my way and never a whiff of lavender water. Shuddering, I saw what the future had in store for me, saw it, not in the face of the ravished one, but in her mother's face. Truth of it was, I was not a brute; I had never promised a soul I'd marry her; and I didn't want to spend my life in living rooms where fruit never intended to be eaten grew old in green glass bowls.

Always more drawing. When I came back from night school I calculated and drew from half-past nine till midnight. Angels and trees, cloud shapes, churches and chapels, Gothic ones, Roman ones, Romanesque, Rococo and Early Victorian— and modern ones besides, if you please. I drew long-haired maidens with soulful faces hovering above doorways, their long hair sweeping down either side the door like a curtain, with the part in the hair drawn sharp, precisely in the middle above the doorway. And the landlords' daughters, during these laborious evening hours, brought me weak tea or weak lemonade, inviting me to intimacies which they thought of as daring. Meanwhile I drew on, especially detail, since I knew that this was what they—who were they, anyway, the 'they'?—would be most likely to go for: door handles, ornamental gratings, *Agni Dei,* pelicans, anchors and crosses entwined with hissing snakes rising up to strike but all in vain.

I always remembered the trick my last boss, Domgreve, had pulled, pulled only too often. His gimmick was to drop his rosary beads at the critical moment after we'd looked over the site. The pious peasants had proudly shown us the field intended for the new church, and afterwards the deacons, upright and bashful, in the back room of some village pub had announced their intention of going along with the project. It was at this juncture the rosary would somehow be drawn out with cigarettes, coin or watch, providentially dropped and picked up with an air of simulated confusion. That, at least, was something I could never laugh at.

"No, Leonore, that A on the folders and drawings and estimates doesn't mean Assignment, it means St. Anthony. St. Anthony's Abbey."

With a deft touch and a soft step she imposed order, the kind of organization he had always loved and had never been able to maintain. It had been too much, too many jobs, too much money.

I'm a little crazy now, and I was crazy then, in the railroad station square, fingering the loose coins in my coat pocket to see how much I had, checking on my drawing pad, the green box with my pencils in it, testing the set of my flowing velvet four-in-hand, feeling around the rim of my black artist's hat, and letting my hands move farther down, over the tails of my suit, the only good one to my name, left me by Uncle Marsil who'd died of consumption as a young teacher. By then Uncle Marsil's gravestone was already covered with moss, out there in Mees, where, when he was twenty years old, he beat time with his baton in the choir loft, drummed the rule of three into farm kids' heads and, in the dusk of evening, went out walking on the moors, dreaming of young girls' lips, of bread and wine and the fame he hoped to win with his neatly turned verses. Dreams dreamed on moorland paths, two years of dreaming, until blood gushed from his mouth and carried him off to the far shore, leaving behind a copybook filled with verses, a black suit for his godson, two gold coins. And, on the greenish curtain of the schoolroom, a bloodstain which his successor's wife could not take out. Also, a song, sung at their hungry teacher's grave by children's voices: 'Watchman, whither has the swallow flown?'

I took another look back at the station, at the ad by the turnstile gate to the trains, put there so recruits reporting for duty couldn't help but see it. It said 'I recommend to military personnel my genuine, long-established Standard Underwear, designed by Professor Gustav Jaeger. Also, my genuine Pallas Underwear, patented in all civilized countries, and my genuine Reform Underwear, designed by Dr. Lahmann.'

It was time to start the dance.

I walked across the streetcar tracks, past the Prince Heinrich Hotel, across Modest Street, hesitated a second in front of the Cafe Kroner. In the door glass, backed with taut green silk, I saw my own reflection. I was a slightly built young fellow, almost a shrimp, a cross between a young rabbi and a bohemian, hair black, clothes black, with a vaguely countrified look. I had another laugh, and went in. The waiters were just starting to put vases of white carnations on the tables, to straighten out menus bound in green leather. There they were, the waiters, in green aprons and short black jackets, with white shirts and white ties. Two young girls, one blonde and rosy, the other brunette and pale, were arranging cakes on the buffet, making little piles of biscuits, renewing the cream dressings and polishing the silver cake knives bright. Not a guest in sight, and inside all clean as a hospital before the superintendent makes his rounds. Light as a feather, a solo dancer, I threaded my way through the waiters' ballet. Here all was training and drill, fine, very fine. I liked the way the waiters flitted from table to table, the way they set down saltcellar and flower vase with an air, gave the menu a nudge to achieve what was obviously a special angle in respect of the saltcellar. The ash trays were snow-white porcelain with gold rims. Good. I liked that. All a delightful surprise. The city, so different from the holes I'd been stuck in up to now.

I went to the farthest left-hand corner, threw my hat on a chair, put down drawing pad and pencil box beside it, and sat down. The waiters were coming back from the kitchen, soundlessly pushing tea wagons ahead of them, distributing bottles of condiment, hanging up newspaper holders. I opened my drawing pad and read—for the hundredth time!—the newspaper clipping I'd stuck inside the cover: 'Open Competition: Construction of a Benedictine Abbey, to be located in the Kissa Valley, between the hamlets of Stehlinger's Grotto and Goerlinger's Lodge, at a distance of approximately two kilometers from the village of Kisslingen. All architects who consider themselves competent may participate. Entry forms obtainable from Dr. Kilb, solicitor, 7 Modest Street. Fee, 50 marks. Deadline for delivery of plans: noon, Monday, September 30, 1907.'

I went climbing about among heaps of mortar, piles of brand-new bricks which I checked to see how well they had been fired in the kiln. I climbed mountains of quarried basalt that I intended to use for framing doors and windows. The cuffs of my pants were muddy, my vest all splattered with lime. I lost my temper in the construction sheds and said violent things. Those mosaic stones I needed for the *Agnus Dei* over the main entrance, why hadn't they been delivered yet? Terrible arguments, scandal. Credits cut off then granted again. By Thursday afternoon master mechanics already were getting lined up outside my office, though their pay checks weren't due till Friday. At night, exhausted, I climbed aboard the overheated local in Kisslingen, sank back on the cushioned seats of the second-class compartment and was hauled through the darkness past miserable little beet-villages. Meanwhile the trainman, half asleep on his feet, called out the stations: Denklingen, Doderingen, Kohlbingen, Schaklingen. On the platforms mountains of beets were piled, ready for loading, gray in the dark like mountains of skulls. On we went, past beet-villages, beet-villages. At the station I fell into a cab and then, once I got home, fell again into my wife's arms, to be kissed, to have my work-strained eyes tenderly stroked, to have her run her fingers over the mortar stains decorating my sleeves. Over coffee, my head in her lap, I smoked the cigar I'd been longing for—a sixty-center—and told her all about the masons and their swearing. Not really bad when you got to know them. A little rough, maybe, a little on the Red side, but I knew how to get along with them. What you had to do was set them up with a case of beer now and then, kid along a little with them in their own lingo. And never grouse about anything to their face or they'd dump a whole load of mortar all over your feet, the way they did to the Archbishop's clerk of works, or maybe let a plank slip from way up on the scaffolding, the way they did to that government architect. The big beam smashed to smithereens right in front of him. 'Dearest, don't you suppose I know it's me who's dependent on them, not they on me? That goes wherever anything's being built, here or anywhere else. Of course they're Red, why shouldn't they be? The main thing is, can they swing a trowel and help me meet my deadline. When I take the commissioners up on the scaffolding, a friendly wink works wonders.'

'Good morning, sir. Breakfast?'

'Yes, please,' I said, but shook my head when the waiter started to give me the menu. Instead I raised my pencil and ticked off the items I wanted in the air, as if I'd eaten that kind of breakfast all my life.

'A pot of coffee, one with three cups, please. Toast, two slices of rye bread, with butter, marmalade, one boiled egg and paprika cheese.'

'Paprika cheese?'

'That's right, cream cheese with paprika.'

'Very good, sir.'

Without a sound he glided, the green ghost of a waiter, over the green carpet past green-covered tables to the kitchen counter, and the first ritual of my little performance promptly evolved. The supers were well rehearsed and I was a good director. 'Paprika cheese?' the cook inquired from behind the kitchen counter. 'That's right,' the waiter said, 'cream cheese with paprika.' 'Ask the gentleman how much paprika he wants on his cheese.'

When the waiter came back I'd begun to draw the front of the railroad station. I was just sketching in the window frames with firm strokes. He stood there, waiting, until I raised my head, took my pencil off the paper and put on a look of surprise.

'Permit me to ask, sir, how much paprika do you want on how much cheese?'

'A thimbleful of paprika thoroughly worked into forty-five grams of cheese. And listen, waiter, I'll be eating breakfast here tomorrow, the day after tomorrow, the day after that, in three weeks, three months, three years—you hear? And it will always be at the same time, around nine.'

'Very good, sir.'

That was how I wanted it, and that's how it worked out. Exactly. Later on many a time it used to scare me, the way my plans worked out so perfectly. Why, it wasn't more than a couple of days before I was 'the gentleman with the paprika cheese.' A week later it was 'the young artist who always comes to breakfast about nine.' And after three weeks it was 'Herr Faehmel, that young architect working on a big assignment.'

"Yes, yes, child, all that stuff has to do with St. Anthony's Abbey. The Abbey goes on for years, Leonore, decades, right up to the present. Repairs, additions, then, after 1945, reconstruction from the old plans. St. Anthony's is going to take up a whole shelf. Yes, you're right, we could use a ventilator around here. It certainly is hot today. No thank you, I don't want to sit down."

The kaleidoscopic window was framing the blue afternoon sky of September 6, 1958, and the outline of the rooftops, all gaps filled in. Teapots on gay tables in the roof gardens. Women on deck chairs, lazily sprawled in the sun. And the station below, swarming with returning vacationers. Could that be why his granddaughter, Ruth, had failed to show up? Had she gone off on a trip herself, putting aside *Love and Intrigue?* Carefully he dabbed at his brow with his handkerchief; heat or cold never had made much difference to him. Over there in the right-hand corner of the kaleidoscopic window the bronze Hohenzollern kings on their bronze steeds kept right on riding toward the west, as they had been doing for eight-and-forty years. Including that one there, his erstwhile commander-in-chief. You could see the fateful vanity of him, in the very way he held his head.

That pedestal—there was no monument on it then—I laughed as I drew it in the Cafe Kroner, while the waiter was serving me my paprika cheese. Point is, I've always felt sure about the future, so sure that to me the present has always seemed like the past fulfilled. So then, was this my first, my very first, breakfast in the Cafe Kroner? Or was it the three-thousandth? Only one thing could keep me from breakfast at nine every day at the Cafe Kroner—a *Higher Power*. In this case in the form of my commander-in-chief, when he called me to the colors, that fool you see down there still riding toward the west on his bronze warhorse. Paprika cheese? How about it? Was this the first time I was eating it, this peculiar reddish-white spread that didn't taste half as bad as it looked, which I'd invented, in order to add the important personal note to my planned Cafe Kroner breakfasts, aboard the Northern Express as it roared toward the city? Or was I pasting it onto my rye bread for the thirtieth time, while the waiter takes away the egg cup and pushes the marmalade over the tabletop? Out of my coat pocket I took the one and only instrument I could depend on, when taken by visions so sudden and precise, to remind me, in my maze of fantasy, of place, day and hour —my pocket diary. It was Friday, September 6, 1907. And this breakfast was indeed my first. Until today I had in fact never drunk real coffee, only the substitute kind made from malt. I'd never eaten an egg for breakfast, only oatmeal, brown bread and butter and a slice of sour pickle. But now the myth I had it in mind to propagate was about to take shape. Indeed, it was already on the way toward its goal when the cook's 'Paprika cheese?' echoed my order. What was this goal? The Public. All I had to do now was wait there, simply stick around until ten o'clock, half-past ten, drinking cognac with a bottle of mineral water until the cafe slowly filled up, sit there with my drawing pad on my knee, a cigar in my mouth and pencil in hand, drawing, drawing, while bankers with their worthy clients went by me to the conference room, followed by waiters carrying bottles of wine on green trays. While clerics came in with confraters from foreign parts, fresh from a round of sightseeing at St. Severin's and praising the city's beauties in broken Latin, English or Italian. While government officials gave notice of their high rank by taking time out for a ten-thirty office break to drink a kirsch and mocha. Then there were the ladies who came in from the produce market with cabbages and carrots, peas and plums in woven leather bags, showing off their housewifely training, proving how clever they were at squeezing bargains out of weary peasant women, then gobbling up a hundred times their savings in cakes and coffee, brandishing their coffee spoons like swords, getting indignant about the cavalry captain who—'on duty, too, did you ever. . . !'—had blown a kiss to a certain cheap flirt of a creature on a balcony, the same captain, by the way—'Oh, I can prove it, you can just bet on that!'—who'd left at half-past four that morning by the service entrance. A cavalry captain at the service entrance! For shame!

I looked them all over, my supporting cast, listened to what they were saying. I sketched rows of chairs, rows of tables and the ballet of the waiters, at twenty to eleven called for my check. It proved less than I'd expected. I'd made up my mind to make my debut 'generous, but not extravagant.' I'd read it somewhere, and figured it was a good formula. By the time I'd taken leave of the waiter and his bowing and scraping, and tipped him an extra fifty pfennigs for helping advance my legend, I suddenly felt tired. As I was leaving the cafe they gave me the once-over, not dreaming it was I who was the soloist in their little ballet. I walked the gauntlet straight as a ramrod, my step elastic, and gave them a real eyeful: an artist in a big black hat, a small, slightly built fellow about twenty-five years old to all appearances, with a vaguely countrified air, but full of confidence. Then another groschen for the boy holding the door open for my passage.

From there to here, 7 Modest Street, it was only a minute and a half. Apprentices, trucks, nuns. Life in the street. Up and down, down and up, like pistons in a ship's engines the presses went. Edification was being printed on white paper. The doorman tipped his cap. 'You're the architect, sir? Your luggage is upstairs already.' A tip passed into a reddened hand. 'Always at your service, lieutenant, sir.' A grin. 'That's right, two gentlemen have been here already. They want the lieutenant to join the local Reserve Officers Club.'

Once again the future unfolded before my eyes, more clearly than the present, while the present, at the very instant of its consummation, sank back into the somber void whence it had come. In my mind's eye I saw the shabby doorman surrounded by newspaper people and imagined the headlines: 'Young Architect Wins Open Competition against Celebrities of Profession.' Eagerly the doorman would give the journalists their news: 'Him? Gentlemen, nothing but work, work, work. Eight in the morning goes to Low Mass at St. Severin's, breakfast in the Cafe Kroner till ten-thirty, from ten-thirty till five stays up there in his studio, won't see a soul. Yes, he lives up there on pea soup—go ahead and laugh—cooks it himself. He has his old mother send the peas and pork, even the onions. From five to six, a walk around town. Six-thirty to seven-thirty, billiards in the Prince Heinrich or the Reserve Officers Club. Girls? None that I know of. Friday nights, gentlemen, eight till ten, choir practice with the Germania Glee Club.' The Cafe Kroner waiters, they would also make a killing on news tips. Paprika cheese? Very interesting! Draws even at breakfast, got drawing on the brain.

Later on, I often used to think back on the time I arrived. Again I heard the hooves clattering on the cobblestones, saw the bellboys lugging suitcases, saw the veiled lady in the rose-red hat, read the sign: 'Recommended for Military Personnel,' cocked an ear to hear my own laughter again. For whom was it intended, my laughter, what was it made of? For whom? I used to see them every morning when I crossed over here after Mass to pick up my mail and the newspaper: the troop of Uhlans, riding by to the cavalry practice-field at the north end of the city. Every morning I thought of my father's hatred for horses and officers, as the clattering hooves disappeared into the distance, on their way to ride to attack and to kick up more dust in patrol formation. The bugle calls brought tears to the eyes of veterans standing at the roadside, but I could think only of my father. The riders' hearts, and the doorman's, too, beat faster. Girls with dusters in their hands stiffened into living statues and let the morning breeze cool breasts just made to comfort weary heads. Meanwhile the doorman handed me Mother's parcel: peas, pork, onions and God bless you my boy. No, my heart did not beat faster to see the company riding away.

I wrote letters begging my mother not to come. I didn't want her included among my supers. She should come later, later, when the play was in production, the game really under way. She was small, slight and dark like myself, and she lived between cemetery and church. Her face and manner, as a matter of fact, would have fitted into the play only too well. She never wanted money, got along on one gold coin a month for soup and bread, with a groschen left over for the collection plate on Sunday and a penny weekdays. Come later, I wrote her, but it was already too late. She was buried next to Father, Charlotte, Mauritius. She never saw the Heinrich Faehmel, 7 Modest Street, whose address she wrote each week. I was afraid of the wisdom in her gaze, of the unexpected things she might say. Which is it going to be, money or honor, serve God or man? I was afraid of her catechistic questions, which answered themselves, merely by putting a period after them instead of the question mark. Just why I felt like that about her, I couldn't have said. When I went to church it wasn't really out of hypocrisy, not part of my act although she would have regarded it as such. My performance began in the Cafe Kroner and ended at ten-thirty, then resumed at five in the afternoon and wound up for good at ten P.M. It was easier to think of Father, while the Uhlans were finally dropping out of sight beyond the Modest Gate, when organ grinders were hobbling to the city outskirts to get there early enough to play for lonesome housewives and servant girls. *Oh, breaking heart at break of day!* Late in the afternoon they hobbled back to the city, this time to make a few pennies from people on their way home from work in melancholy mood. *Annemarie, Rosemarie,* etc. Meanwhile, over there Gretz was hanging up the wild boar outside his shop. Fresh, dark red boar blood dripped onto the asphalt. Pheasants and partridges hung round the boar, and rabbits. Delicate plumage and humble rabbit fur garlanded the mighty boar. Every morning Gretz hung up his dead animals, always with their wounds staring the public in the face, rabbit guts, gaping pigeon breasts, the boar's scooped-out belly between raw flanks. Blood, the public had to see it. This while Frau Gretz' pink hands arranged flaps of liver between little heaps of mushrooms, and piled up caviar on cubes of ice to glitter in front of giant hams. Lobsters, violet as hard-fired brick, crawled blindly, helplessly about, feeling their way in the shallow pound, waiting to be plucked forth by housewives' skillful hands, on the seventh, the ninth, the tenth of September, 1907. Only on Sundays, the eighth, fifteenth and twenty-second of September was Gretz' shopfront free of blood. And only during those years when a *Higher Power* was at work did I lose sight of Gretz' beasts. I saw them without fail for fifty-one years—see them right now, when, on this Saturday afternoon, the housewives' skillful hands come feeling for something special for the Sunday dinner.

"Yes, Leonore, you've read it right: First fee, 150,000 marks. No date? Must have been in 1908. Yes, I'm sure, August, 1908. You've never eaten wild boar? You haven't missed much, if you'll trust my taste. Never did like it. How about making some more coffee, wash down the dust. And buy some cakes, if you want. Nonsense, it won't make you fat, don't pay any attention to that hocus-pocus. Yes, that was 1913, a little house for Herr Kolger, the waiter at the Cafe Kroner. No, no fee for that."

How many breakfasts in the Cafe Kroner? Ten thousand? Twenty thousand? Never added them up, went there every day, take away the days I was balked by the *Higher Power*.

Remember watching the *Higher Power* come in. Over there on the roof of No. 8, hidden behind the pergola, I looked down into the street, and saw them marching toward the station, no end to them, singing the 'Watch on the Rhine' and shouting the name of that idiot you see still riding his bronze steed toward the west. They wore flowers in their caps, on their top hats and derbies, flowers in their buttonholes, and they carried Professor Gustav Jaeger's Standard Underwear in little packages under their arms. The noise they made surged up to me in waves. Why, even the whores down in the Kraemerzeile district had sent their pimps off to the recruiting station with particularly fine, warm underwear tucked under their arms. I tried to share the feelings of the ones down below, but no use. I felt empty and alone, a real stinker, not an atom of enthusiasm in me, and not knowing why. I'd simply never put my mind to such matters. I thought of my Engineer's uniform, smelling of mothballs. It still fitted me, though I'd had it made when I was twenty and meantime had grown to be thirty-six. All I hoped was I wouldn't have to put it on again. I wanted to keep on being the star, not become one of the supers. They'd gone off their rockers down there, singing their way to the station. The ones who didn't have to go were the ones being pitied. They felt victimized, not being able to go along. As for me, I was ready to be victimized in such manner, wouldn't mind it at all. Down below inside the house my mother-in-law was weeping, both her sons having ridden away with the very first contingent to the freight yard, where they were loading up the horses. Proud Uhlans, for whose sake my mother-in-law was shedding prideful tears. There I stood, behind the pergola, the wistaria still in bloom, and from down below heard my four-year-old son, singing 'Get your gun, on the run. . . .' What I should have done was go down and give him a good licking, in front of my proud mother-in-law. But I let him sing and play with the Uhlan helmet his uncle had given him. I let him trail his sword behind him and shout, 'Frenchy dead! Englishman dead! Rooshian dead!' I let myself be told by the garrison commandant, his voice low and nearly breaking, 'I deeply regret, Faehmel, we can't get along without you here, not yet; I'm sorry you can't do your bit out there. But the home front needs people, too, people just like you.'

Barracks, fortifications, military hospitals—I built them all. Nights, in my lieutenant's uniform, I inspected the guard at the bridge. Elderly storekeepers with a corporal's rating, banker privates, they saluted me diligently when I climbed the bridge steps, my flashlight revealing obscene drawings which youngsters had scratched into the red sandstone on their way home from a swim. The bridge steps smelled strong of puberty. There was a sign hanging somewhere, 'Michaelis, Coal, Coke, Briquettes,' with a finger pointing toward the place where Michaelis' wares might be obtained. I savored my irony, my superiority, when Sergeant Gretz reported to me: 'Bridge guard, one sergeant, six men. Nothing unusual to report.' This information I acknowledged with what I fancied to be a comic-opera salute, and said, 'At ease.' Then I wrote my name in the guard book, went home, hung sword and helmet in the closet, went into the living room to Johanna, laid my head in her lap, smoked my cigar and said not a word while she did the same. All she did was take the paté de foie gras back to Gretz, and when the Abbot of St. Anthony's sent us bread and honey and butter, parcel it out among the poor. I kept my mouth shut, went on having breakfast in the Cafe Kroner, the two thousand four hundredth with paprika cheese. I still gave the waiter a fifty-pfennig tip, though he didn't want to take it, insisted on paying me a fee for the house I'd designed for him.

It was Johanna who said right out what I'd been privately thinking. She wouldn't drink any champagne when we were invited to the garrison commandant's, wouldn't eat the jugged hare and refused every dance. She said it out loud: 'That fool of a Kaiser.' You'd have thought the Ice Age had come, there in the Wilhelmskuhle Casino. Then she said it once again, in the silence: 'That fool of a Kaiser.' They were all there, generals, colonels and majors, together with their wives, and me, of course, just promoted to first lieutenant and commissioned to build the fortifications. A young officer-candidate had the presence of mind to start the orchestra playing a waltz. I took

Johanna's arm and led her to the coach outside. Wonderful autumn evening. Gray columns of men marching out toward the suburban railroad station. Nothing out of the way to report.

Now a military tribunal. No one dared repeat what Johanna had said. Blasphemies of that nature were not even put into the record. His Majesty—a fool of a Kaiser. It was something no one would have dared put down on paper. With them it was always 'What your wife said'; on my side, 'What my wife said.' I didn't say what I should have, that is, that I agreed with her one hundred per cent. Instead I said, 'Pregnant, gentlemen, in two months she'll be having it. Lost two brothers, Captain Kilb of the Horse Guards and Cadet Kilb, both killed on the same day. A little daughter, too, lost her in 1909.' All along I knew I should have been saying, 'I agree with my wife, absolutely.' I knew that irony wasn't enough, and never would be.

"No, Leonore, don't unwrap that little package. What's inside has only sentimental value. Not much weight, but precious: one cork. Thanks for the coffee. Put the cup on the windowsill, please. I can see it's no use waiting for my grand-daughter—usually does her homework out in the roof garden about this time of day. I'm forgetting her vacation's not over yet. Look, from up here you can see right into your own office. I can just see you at your desk, your pretty hair."

Why did the cup suddenly tremble and clink, as if from the pounding of the presses? Was the lunch hour over? Were they working overtime, printing edification on white paper even on Saturday afternoons?

I felt that same trembling countless mornings when, propped on my elbows, I looked down into the street at that blonde head of hair passing by, its perfume familiar to me from morning Mass. In time the strong plain soap she used would deaden its brightness. Respectability was being used as a substitute for perfume. I used to follow behind her, after Mass, when she went past Gretz' shop at a quarter to nine and so into the house at No. 8. It was a yellow house, with a rather weathered sign at the door, with 'Dr. Kilb, Attorney-at-Law' in white letters on black wood. I watched her when I waited in the doorman's room for my newspaper. The light would fall on her, on her delicate face wrinkled with a frown of dedication to justice as she opened the office door, threw open the shutters, twirled the safe combination and opened the steel doors which seemed too heavy for her. Then she checked the contents of the safe and while she was doing this I could look right across Modest Street, it was so narrow, into the safe, and read, neatly printed on a card on the top safe drawer: 'St. Anthony Project.' Three large packages lay inside, protected by seals that looked like wounds. Only three of them, and every child knew the senders' names: Brehmockel, Grumpeter and Wollersein. Brehmockel, builder of thirty-seven Neo-Gothic churches, seventeen chapels and twenty-one monasteries and hospitals; Grumpeter, builder of only thirty-three Neo-Romanesque churches, twelve chapels and eighteen hospitals; and of course the third packet from Wollersein, who had built only nineteen churches, two chapels and four hospitals, but who, on the other hand, had a real cathedral to his credit. 'Read what's in the *Guardian* today?' the doorman asked, and above his calloused thumb I read the line it was pointing at: 'Deadline for St. Anthony's Project Today/ Have Our Young Architects No Spirit?' I laughed, rolled up my newspaper and went to breakfast in the Cafe Kroner. The waiter said 'Breakfast as usual for Herr Faehmel' through the kitchen counter opening, and it sounded like a liturgy, old as the hills, a rite performed for centuries. The usual buzz of voices around ten-thirty—housewives, priests, bankers. Out with my drawing pad and its lambs, serpents and pelicans. A fifty-pfennig tip for the waiter, ten-pfennig for the busboy. A grin from the doorman as I slipped his morning cigar into his hand and took my mail in return. Upstairs, I stood leaning here at the window, feeling the vibration of the presses in my elbows, watching the apprentice at the window down below in Kilb's office wielding a white folding rule. I opened the letter the doorman had given me. '. . . we are in a position to offer you the post of chief draughtsman immediately. If you so wish, you will be treated as a member of the family. A friendly reception by local society can be guaranteed. There would be no lack of social occasions. . . .' In this manner architects' delightful daughters were intimated, cozy picnics at the forest edge suggested, young men wearing round peasant hats tapping beer barrels, young women unpacking and handing around sandwiches. On freshly mown lawns a little dance might be ventured, while the mothers, anxiously tallying their daughters' years and charmed by the grace of it all, clapped their hands in time. Then off for a stroll through the woods, arm in arm, whereupon the young ladies would make sure to trip over the roots. As wooded distances imperceptibly lengthened, opportunities would offer for a kiss, on the wrist, the cheek, the shoulder. Then, wending our way homeward, through pleasant meadows in the dusk, the deer, no less, as if summoned for that very purpose, would peek out of the forest and come to the meadow's rim. And then, when songs had begun to ring out, and spread from coach to coach, time would be ripe for an interchange of whispers declaring that Amor had done his work. So homeward, the coaches carrying aching hearts, wounded souls.

To this proposal I wrote a civil answer: 'I shall be delighted to consider your kind offer again as soon as I have completed the private studies which will be detaining me some time longer in this city. . . .' I sealed the envelope, stuck on the stamp, went back to the windowsill and looked down into Modest Street. The folding rule, brandished by Kilb's office boy, flashed like a dagger. Two employees from the hotel were loading the boar onto a handcart. I would sample wild boar meat that evening, at the Germania Glee Club's stag party. I would have to listen to their jokes, and of course they would fail to note that I was laughing at them, not at what they said. Their jokes were as repulsive to me as their sauces, and up here at my window I laughed my laugh, as yet still not knowing whether it sprang from hatred or contempt. One thing only I knew: it was not a laugh of joy.

Gretz' young servant girl had placed white baskets full of mushrooms beside the boar. The cook in the Prince Heinrich was already weighing out the spices, kitchen help were grinding the knives, worried extra waiters were standing at home in front of their mirrors straightening their ties as they tried them on and asking their wives—the smell from worn trousers being pressed filling the kitchen—'Do you suppose I'll have to kiss the Bishop's ring if I have the lousy luck to wait on him?' Down below the apprentice was still wielding the folding rule. Eleven-fifteen. I brushed my black suit, made sure my velvet bow was knotted straight, put on my hat, drew out my pocket diary, no larger than a flat matchbox, and looked within: September 30, 1907, 11:30, Kilb's, deliver design. Ask for receipt.

Careful now! How often I'd rehearsed it all—down the stairs, across the street, down the corridor, into the reception room.

'I'd like to speak to the attorney personally.'

'What is it you want to see him about?'

'I'd like to submit a design. The St. Anthony Open Competition.'

Only the apprentice would look surprised, hold the folding rule still, look round and then, abashed, turn his face back to the street and to his legal forms, mindful of the office rule: 'Discretion, discretion!' In this office shabbiness was style. Portraits of legally learned ancestors hung on the walls, inkwells were eighty years old, the folding rule a hundred and fifty. Prodigious transactions were consummated here in silence. Here entire city districts changed hands, and marriage contracts were signed and sealed, contracts in which the bride's annual clothes allowance was larger than what a probate clerk would earn in five years. Here, too, however, the honest cobbler's 2000-mark mortgage was officially witnessed, here the doddering old pensioner deposited his will, leaving his bedside table to a favorite grandchild. The legal affairs of widows and orphans, of workers and millionaires were settled here in strictest confidence, in view of the proverb on the wall: 'Their right hand is full of bribes.' No reason, then, to look up when a young artist wearing a worn suit handed down to him by his uncle delivered a package, rolls of drawings wrapped in foolscap, or when he erroneously imagined the attorney himself should give the matter his personal attention. The head clerk sealed the package, the rolls of drawings, pressed the Kilbian emblem, a lamb with blood flowing from its breast, onto the hot sealing wax, while the blonde girl clerk of righteous aspect wrote out the receipt: 'Monday, September 30, 1907, 11:35 A.M. Herr Faehmel, architect, delivered into our custody. . . .' Had not a glimmer of recognition passed over her pale, friendly face as she held the receipt out to me? I was delighted by this unforeseen response, because it proved to me that time after all was something real. See, then, this day, this minute did truly exist. But it had not been me who had proved it, by my actually having gone downstairs from my studio, by having crossed the street, entered the corridor and the reception room. Nor had it been proved by the blood-red wound left by the seal. It had been proved by the blonde clerk's unexpected smile of kindness. She surveyed my worn suit and then, as I took the receipt from her hand, she whispered, 'Good luck, Herr Faehmel.' These were to be the only words within the past four and a half weeks which branded time, which reminded me that there were signs of reality in this game I had set in motion. Time, this incident revealed, was subject to outside intervention, and not entirely governed out of the privacy of my dreams, a world in which the future seemed like the present, the present like something that had happened centuries past, and that which had been became that which was yet to come. Time was more than a childhood thing, to which I could run for refuge as, when a little boy, I had run to my father's arms. My father, he had grown silent, years heaped up around him like layers of leaden stillness. Organ stops pulled out, High Masses accompanied by song, for first-class funerals song at length, rather less for second-class, no song at all for third-class ones. And now silence. So still that merely thinking about him oppressed my heart. He had milked cows, cut hay, threshed grain, until the chaff stuck like an insect cloud to his sweat-drenched face. He had waved the baton for the youth club, the union club, the rifle club and the Saint Cecilia Club. He never opened his mouth, never complained. He merely sang in church, cut beets, cooked potatoes for the pigs, played the organ, put on his black sacristan's coat, over that his white robe. No one in the village noticed that he never spoke, for whenever they saw him he was busy doing something. Two of his four children died of consumption and two lived on: Charlotte and myself. My mother was a gentle woman, the kind who love flowers and pretty curtains, who sing songs at their ironing and tell stories by the fireside in the evening. As for Father, he drudged on, built beds, filled sacks with straw and killed chickens, until Charlotte died. Now the Mass of the Angels, church all in white. The priest sang, but the sacristan did not respond, did not pull out the stops, made no organ chords. The priest chanted on alone. Still mute, the procession formed in front of the church to move off to the cemetery. Troubled, the priest asked, 'But Faehmel, my dear, good Faehmel, why didn't you sing?' For the first time ever I heard my father give voice to an emphatic utterance, and was startled to hear how hoarse it sounded, the same voice that could sing so softly in the organ loft. He said it low, with a growly undertone: 'No singing for third-class funerals.' Haze over the Lower Rhine, damp fog wraiths coiling and dancing across the beetfields, crows in the willows cawing like Mardi Gras rattles as the troubled priest read the graveside liturgy. Never again did Father conduct for the youth club, the union club, the rifle club, never again for the Saint Cecilia Club, and it was as if, with that first sentence I ever heard him utter—I was then sixteen, Charlotte died at twelve—it was as if with that first sentence he had found his voice. Now he talked more, about horses and officers, which he hated, and he said menacingly, 'Bad luck to you all, if you give me a first-class funeral.'

'Yes,' the blonde said to me again, 'I wish you the best.' Maybe I should have turned back the receipt then and there, asked for the sealed package, the rolls of drawings, and gone home. To marry the mayor's daughter or the contractor's daughter, build fire stations, little schools, churches and chapels, and dance with the hostess at country housewarmings while my wife danced with the host. Why challenge Brehmockel, Grumpeter and Wollersein, great names of church architecture? Why bother? I felt no ambition, money did not tempt me. I would never need to go hungry. I could always play skat with the priest, the pharmacist, the innkeeper, the mayor, go hunting wild boar, build 'something modern' for newly rich peasants—but the apprentice had already rushed from his windowsill to the office door and was holding it open for me. 'Thank you,' I said, went out through the entrance hall, crossed the street, climbed upstairs to the studio and leaned on the sill there, which was trembling from the pounding of the presses. That was on September 30, 1907, around 11:45 A.M.

"You're right, Leonore, the presses are a nuisance. How many cups they've smashed on me, when I wasn't careful. Go slow, child, take it easy. If you keep on working like that you'll have more sorted out in a week than I would in fifty years. No, thanks, no cake for me. You don't mind if I call you child, do you? No need to blush at flattery from an old man like me. I'm a monument, Leonore, and monuments will never harm you. Old fool that I am, I still go to the Cafe Kroner every morning and eat my paprika cheese, even though I've long since stopped liking it. I owe it to my contemporaries not to ruin my legend. I'll found an orphanage, a school, perhaps, provide for scholarships, and somewhere, someday, they'll cast me in bronze and unveil me. You've got to be there, Leonore, and have a good laugh. You can laugh so prettily, did you know? I can't any more, lost the knack of it. Yet I used to think a laugh was a useful weapon. It wasn't, really, just small deception of sorts. If you think you'd like it, I'll take you with me to the University Ball and introduce you as my niece. You'll drink champagne and dance and meet a young man who'll be good to you and love you. I'll set you up with a nice little dowry . . . yes, take a real good look at that up there, the over-all view of St. Anthony's, two by three meters it is. Been hanging here in the studio for fifty-one years. It was hanging up there when the roof was blown in, which accounts for those mould stains you see on it. My first big assignment, a colossal job; barely thirty, then, I had 'arrived.' "

And in 1917 I couldn't summon the nerve to do what Johanna did in my stead. When Heinrich was standing up there on the roof by the pergola, she tore that poem he had to learn by heart out of his hand. He was reciting it in his serious child's voice:

> 'Said Peter, guardian of Heaven's gate,
> I'll put the case to higher fate,
> And see, within a trice was back:
> Bluecher, sir, luck's a thing you do not lack!
> It's leave for you, with time no bar.
> (And saying this, flung Heaven's gate ajar.)
> Take off, old warrior, give 'em hell,
> And if God you need, let out a yell.'

At the time Robert wasn't yet two, and Otto not even born. I was on leave and for a long time had known clearly what I'd only sensed before: that irony wasn't enough, and never would be, that it was only an opiate for a few privileged ones, that I should be doing what Johanna did. I, in my captain's uniform, should have spoken to the boy. But I merely listened, as he went on reciting:

'And General Bluecher came below
To lead to victory, blow on blow;
With Hindenburg let's march along,
With Prussia's savior, fortress strong.
As long as German woods stand high,
As long as German banners fly,
As long as German tongue remains,
So long will live that name of names,
Chiseled in stone, in bronze indite.
For you, our hero, hearts beat bright—
Hindenburg! On to the fight!'

Johanna snatched the paper out of the boy's hand, tore it up and threw the bits down into the street. They fell like snow-flakes in front of Gretz' shop. No boar was hanging there in those days. The *Higher Power* reigned supreme.

It won't be enough for you to laugh, Leonore, when they unveil my statue. Spit on it, child—in my son Heinrich's name and for Otto, who was such a fine boy, and good, and because so fine and good, and so obedient, more of a stranger to me than anyone in this world. And spit on me for Edith's sake, the only truly gentle lamb of a person I ever saw. I loved her, mother of my grandchildren, my daughter-in-law, yet I couldn't help her, any more than I could help the carpenter's apprentice, whom I saw only twice, or the youngster I never saw at all who slipped messages from Robert—on bits of paper no bigger than penny candy wrappers—into our letter box, and for that crime was swallowed up in a concentration camp. Robert was always clever and cool and never ironic. Otto was different. He had a heart; yet suddenly he went over to the Beast and grew away from us. Yes, spit on my statue, Leonore, tell them I asked you to; I'll give it to you in writing, if you want, and have it notarized. You should have seen that apprentice; he made me understand the phrase: *Angels came and ministered to him;* they chopped off his head. You should have seen Edith and her brother, Schrella, whom I saw but once, the time Schrella came across our courtyard on his way up to see Robert. I was standing at my bedroom window and laid eyes on him for only a moment. But that was enough to make me afraid. You could see both disaster and salvation written on his face. Schrella—I never heard his Christian name—was like some holy sheriff, sticking invisible foreclosure notices on people's houses. I knew it might cost my son's life, still I let Schrella go across the courtyard, shoulders bent; the oldest of my two living sons, a gifted boy; Edith's brother foreclosed on him. Edith was different. She was so deep in the Bible she could make fun of it all, in a Biblical way. During the air raids she used to laugh with her children. She gave them Biblical names, Joseph and Ruth. Death held no terrors for her. But she never realized how much I mourned my dead children, Johanna and Heinrich. And she never knew that Otto, the stranger, died, too, the one dearest to me. He loved my studio and my drawings, used to drive with me to the building jobs and drink beer at housewarmings. He was the workmen's pet. He won't be coming to my birthday party tonight, Otto. How many guests have been invited? You can count the clan I founded on one hand: Robert, Joseph, Ruth, Johanna and of course myself. Leonore will sit in Johanna's place. But what shall I say to Joseph when he tells me, with boyish pride, how the reconstruction work at St. Anthony's is getting on? They'll be having a dedication at the end of October. The brothers are hoping to sing the Mass of the Advent in the new church. These old bones are getting shaky, Leonore. And they have not fed my lambs.

Yes, I ought to have given the receipt back, and broken the red seal and got rid of it; then I wouldn't have to be hanging around here waiting for my granddaughter, that pretty, pretty dark-haired nineteen-year-old. Same age now as Johanna was when I was standing here fifty-one years ago and saw her over there in the roof garden. I could make out the title of her book, *Love and Intrigue*. Could it be my Johanna who still reads *Love and Intrigue* over there today? Can she really be gone?

Might she not still be at lunch with Robert in The Lion? Did I run away from that confidential man-to-man talk among the reserve lieutenants, on the way giving the doorman his indispensable cigar, and come up here merely for the sake of being here? Merely to perch up here from ten-thirty to five? Just to climb upstairs past freshly printed piles of books and diocesan booklets? What were they printing then on Saturday afternoons on white paper? Edification, or election posters for all the people committed to the Beast? No matter, the walls quaked, the stairs shook, the women brought out stack after stack of printed matter and piled them up until they reached as far as the studio door. Meanwhile I lay here in the studio, practicing the art of simply being here. I felt myself being pulled along as if by the suck of a dark wind tunnel which would hurl me out toward where I could not tell. I was pulled down into the vortex of a primeval bitterness, saturated with the ancient futility of all things. I saw the children I would have, the wine I would drink, the hospitals and churches I would build. And with it all I heard the sound of the clods of earth that would fall on my coffin, muffled drum sounds dogging me. I heard the women singing, the ones who fed the presses, the folders, the packers, some voices bright, others dark, sweet or rough. They were singing a simple song out of happiness for the afternoon break from work in prospect. But to me it sounded like a funeral dirge. It evoked love in the dance hall, poignant moments of ecstasy by the cemetery wall, the grass smelling of autumn. In it I divined the joys of young motherhood presaging the tears of mothers grown old, and the melancholy of the orphan home, where a brave young girl resolved on staying pure. Yet the selfsame fate would befall her, too, in the dance hall, poignant ecstasy by the cemetery wall, the grass smelling of autumn. The women sang on, their voices like a well-wheel always dipping into the same even water. They were singing a dirge for me, while clods of earth tumbled onto my coffin. From under lowered lids I looked at the walls of my studio, which I'd tapestried with drawings.

Majestic, in the center, the pinkish photocopy, scale 1:200, of St. Anthony's Abbey. In the foreground the hamlet of Stehlinger's Grotto, with grazing cows, a freshly dug potato field, with smoke rising from a fire of burning vines. And then, in powerful basilican style, the Abbey itself, which I'd boldly modeled after the Romanesque cathedrals, with the cloister low, severe and somber, cells, refectory and library, figure of St. Anthony in the center of the cloister garth. Set off against the cloister the big quadrangle of farm buildings, granaries, barns, coach houses, own grist mill with bakery, a pretty residence for the steward, whose job it was also to take care of the visitors on pilgrimage. And there, under high trees, simple tables and chairs at which to eat a meal, with dry wine, cider or beer, before setting out on the journey back. On the horizon, another hamlet, Goerlinger's Place, was sketched in, with chapel, cemetery, four farms, grazing cows, and, to the right, rows of poplars marking the boundary of the tilled land where the working brothers would tend the vineyards, where cabbages and potatoes, vegetables and grain would grow, and where from the beehives delicious honey would be taken.

Delivered twenty minutes ago, against receipt: one design, with detailed drawings and a complete breakdown of costs. The numbers and positions had been marked in with a fine pen. I gazed at the plan as if the buildings were really there, as if I were seeing them through a window. There they were, the brothers, bent in toil, and the pilgrims, drinking cider. Meanwhile, down below, the women sang their dirge, longing for the time to quit work, voices bright and voices dark. I shut my eyes and sensed the cold that would close in around me fifty years later, by then a man of established position, surrounded by the swarm of life.

These four and a half weeks had been endlessly long. What I had done during that time had been like so much dreamwork foreordained. Now only the morning Mass remained, and the hours between ten-thirty and five. I longed for something unexpected, the kind of break that had come my way in the form of a brief smile and a 'Good luck, Herr Faehmel.' When I closed my eyes again time divided into bands like a spectrum: past, present, future. In fifty years my oldest grandson would be twenty-five and my sons as old as the solid citizens into whose hands I just delivered myself together with my design. I felt for the receipt. I had it, it was truly there. Tomorrow morning the jury would assemble, and realize the situation had changed. Now there was a fourth plan to take into account. Already factions had been formed. Two for Grumpeter, two for Brehmockel and one, the youngest, smallest and yet most important of the five, the Abbot, for Wollersein. The Abbot liked Romanesque. The going would get hot, since the two most corruptible jury members would bear down hardest on the artistic angle. Adjournment. That young upstart has sabotaged our scheme. Now it had dawned on them, to their dismay, that the Abbot obviously liked my design. Again and again he had stood in front of the drawing, sipping at his wine. It was a total organic unity, fitted to the landscape, and the utilitarian quality of the farm-building close stood out clearly in contrast to the severe quadrangle of cloister and cloister garth. Fountain, pilgrim's hostel, he liked all of it. He smiled. In such a place he would feel first among equals. He was already seeing himself moving about in the plan, as if it were his own property, presiding in the refectory, sitting in the chancel, visiting the sick brothers, going over to the steward's to taste the wine, to let the grain trickle through his fingers. Bread for his religious and for the poor, from grain harvested in his own fields. Yes, there, as an afterthought, the young architect had added a little room for the beggars, right by the door, with benches outside for summer, inside for winter a table and stove. 'Gentlemen, there's no doubt in my mind. I vote without reservation for the what's his name? . . . for the Faehmel design. And look at the cost, three hundred thousand marks less than the least expensive of the other three.' Dried sealing wax scattered in bits on the table, whereon the experts now banged their fists, initiating a great palaver. 'You've got to believe us, Father, they underestimate all the time. What will you do when he comes to us four weeks before the dedication and says he's run out of green stuff. In a project like this it's common to run over the estimate by half a million marks. Take our word on it, we've had plenty of experience. And what bank will go hock for a young man like him, absolutely unknown, no experience? What collateral has he got to show?' A great burst of laughter now beat on the young Abbot. 'Resources, according to his own declaration: eight thousand marks.' More palaver. The gentlemen took angry leave of each other. Not one had come to the Abbot's support. The hearing was adjourned for four weeks. Who had given the benefit of the deciding vote, per the statute, to this young country fellow with the close-cropped head? So that if a decision was made on the spot, rather than postponed for further reflection, it would have to be for him? And could not be against him?

Now the phones began to ring, perspiring messengers raced with special-delivery letters from Prime Minister to Archbishop, from Archbishop to the Theological Seminary, where the trusted consultant of the archiepiscopal see was all for Neo-Gothic. This gentleman, face lobster red, rushed to his waiting coach. Hooves clattered away over the cobblestones, wheels screeched around sharp curves. Now, tell me what's up? Faehmel? Never heard of him. His plan? Technically brilliant. And his estimates, Excellency, you've got to admit, convincing as far as we can see. But the style! Horrible! Over my dead body. Dead body? The Archbishop smiled. Artistic temperament, the professor, fiery fellow, too much feeling, too many flowing white locks. Dead body? Well, I wouldn't go quite that far.

Now inquiries in code flew from Grumpeter to Brehmockel, from Brehmockel to Wollersein. For a few days the celebrities, ordinarily sworn enemies, were as one. In cipher and cryptic phone calls they asked each other: 'Can cauliflower be had?'

Which meant: 'Are abbots venal?' The crushing answer: 'Cauliflower cannot be had.'

For four and a half weeks I had buried myself from sight. How peaceful my grave. Slowly the earth slid down, fitted itself nicely round and over me. Bemused by the chant of the women at work, it was better simply to do nothing. But now, when they opened my grave, lifted my coffin lid, I would act, I would have to act. I would be flung back into time, where every day would have a name and every hour a duty. Then the game would be played for keeps. No more getting my pea soup in my little kitchen at two o'clock. Even now I had quit bothering to warm it and was eating it cold. I had never cared much about food, or money or fame for that matter. I loved the game. I liked my cigar and longed for a wife, my wife. Would it be the one I saw over there in the roof garden, dark-haired, slender, pretty? Johanna Kilb? Tomorrow she would know my name. Was I longing for just anyone, or just for her? I had had my fill and more of nothing but men's company. They had all come to seem absurd to me, the good fellows and the bad, the ones who told the dirty jokes and the ones who listened to them. Billiard players, reserve lieutenants, singers, doormen and waiters—I was sick of them all. And when, around five or six in late afternoon, I had a chance to look into the women's faces as they streamed out past me from work through the print-shop door, I was glad. I loved the sensuousness in their faces, ever putting them into debt to their mortality. I would have liked to take one of them out dancing and have lain with her in fragrant autumn grass by the cemetery wall, my receipt torn up, the great game abandoned. These girls laughed and sang, liked to eat and drink. They could weep real tears, unlike the false she-goats who had tried to entice me, when I'd been a gentleman-lodger, into intimacies they fancied were daring. But on this last day the routines and the properties of the play still belonged to me, the supporting actors were still subject to my command. I had no hankering for cold pea soup and was too lazy to warm it. I wanted to play it out to the very end, the game I'd planned on dull afternoons in provincial towns, after I'd had my fill of examining mortar, passing expert judgment on stone, trueing up walls. Choosing the boredom of gloomy taverns in preference to the boredom of the office, there I began to sketch the Abbey on odd slips of paper.

From then on I was never free of the game. The drawings became bigger, my ideas more precise. Then, almost without noticing it, I suddenly found myself in the midst of the estimates. Calculation learned, drawing learned. If you please. I sent thirty gold marks to Kilb and the terms of the competition in due course were sent to me. One Sunday afternoon I paid a visit to Kisslingen. Flourishing fields of wheat, dark green beetfields and a forest where, one day, the Abbey would stand. I persisted in the game, studied my competitors, Brehmockel, Grumpeter, Wollersein, whose names were mentioned by their fellow-architects with respectful hatred. I inspected their buildings, churches, hospitals, chapels, Wollersein's cathedral, and I sensed, I could smell it in those cheerless structures, that the future was mine for the taking, like a country waiting to be conquered. Terra incognita where gold lay buried, ready to be dug up by anyone who took the trouble to work out a little strategy. I held the future in the palm of my hand. All I had to do was close my fist around it. I suddenly saw time as a force that was being allowed to go by the board by default, while for a pittance I was letting bunglers and hypocrites exploit the skill in my hands and the mathematics in my brain. I bought paper, pencils, tables, handbooks. It was all a game, and it would cost me nothing but time. Meanwhile time was there for the asking. Sundays were days to reconnoitre, to look over the terrain, explore the streets. Modest Street: in No. 7, there was a studio for rent; across the street, in No. 8, there was the office of the attorney who'd keep the competition entries in his safe. The frontiers were wide open. All I had to do was march in. And not until now, when

I was already deep inside the country and half in possession of it with the enemy still asleep, had I made my declaration of war. I looked for the receipt again. Still there.

The day after tomorrow the first visitor was to cross my studio threshold; the Abbot, young, brown-eyed and level-headed, not yet fully mature, but born to lead. 'How did you know that our Holy Father Benedict never intended that working brothers and contemplatives should be kept apart in the refectory?' He walked up and down, looking at the design again and again, and asked, 'Do you think you'll hold on to the end? You're sure you won't break down and prove those carpers right?' And, true enough, I was frightened by the challenge of my own design. It threatened to overwhelm me. I'd played the game, but never quite realized I might actually win. The mere reputation of having stood up to Brehmockel, Grumpeter and Wollersein, even if I had never won, would have been good enough for me. But actually to come out on top! I was panicky, but I said, 'Yes, I'll stick it out, Your Reverence.' He nodded, smiled and left.

About five I joined the throng of printery workers going home through the big gate, and went for my evening stroll, all according to plan. I saw veiled beauties on their way to rendezvous in carriages, lieutenants in the Cafe Fuhl drinking hard liquor to soft music. Every day I walked four kilometers, in one hour, always the same way at the same time. I meant to be seen, and seen at the same place at the same time, always. Shopgirls, bankers and jewelers, whores and cab drivers, store clerks, waiters and housewives, I intended that they should see me, and they did, from five to six, cigar in my mouth. Impudent, I know, but I'm an artist, pledged to nonconformity. A man like me is permitted to stand and listen to the organ-grinder, and make capital of the melancholy of the hours when work lets out. Permitted to frequent dream streets in the city of dreams. My supporting players had well-oiled joints. They were moved about by invisible threads, they opened their mouths when I cued them. Cold melody of billiard balls in the Prince Heinrich, white-green, red-green. Manikins were crooking their arms to stroke with the cue, to guide glasses of beer to their mouths, chalk up points, play runs, and amiably clap me on the shoulder, and say, Oh yes, Oh no, brilliant, bad luck. As the case might be. Meanwhile I could hear the sound of clods of earth falling on my coffin. Already Edith's dying scream was lying in wait for me, and waiting, too, the blond carpenter's boy's last look at the prison walls, in the gray of dawn.

I drove with my wife and children out to the Kissa Valley, proudly showed them the work of my youth, visited the Abbot, grown older now, in his face detected the wear and tear of the years I could not see in my own. Coffee in the guest room, cakes baked with the brothers' own flour, plums they had picked themselves, and cream from their own cows. My sons were allowed to walk through the cloister while my wife and her giggling daughters had to wait outside. Four sons, three daughters, seven children who were to present me with seven times seven grandchildren. The Abbot smiled at me: 'What's more, we're more or less neighbors now.' Yes, I had bought the two farmsteads, Stehlinger's Grotto and Goerlinger's Place. "What, Leonore, the Cafe Kroner again? No, I explicitly told them, no champagne. I hate champagne. Now, quit for the day, child, please. And will you order me a taxi, for two o'clock? It can wait down there by the big door and perhaps I can take you a little way. No, I'm not going through Blessenfeld. Yes, we can clean up that much more, if you want to."

He turned away from the kaleidoscopic window and glanced into the studio, where the great St. Anthony design was still hanging on the wall. The air was full of dust, raised, careful as she was, by the young woman's busy hands. Assiduously she was cleaning out the steel cabinets, now holding out to him a stack of banknotes which had become valueless thirty years ago, now, shaking her head, bringing out another package of bills grown worthless ten years back, and counting out the unfamiliar things, carefully, onto the drawing board: ten, twenty, eighty, a hundred—all told twelve hundred and twenty marks.

"Into the fire with them, Leonore. Or give them to the kids in the street. What good are they. Nothing but jumbo receipts for the swindle that started thirty-five years ago and cropped up again twenty-five years later. Money's never meant much to me, yet they all thought I was greedy for it. They were way off the mark there. When I started to play the big game it wasn't money I was after. And it wasn't until I'd made money and therefore become popular that it dawned on me I'd had the makings of popularity all along. I was efficient, friendly and simple, an artist and a reserve officer. I'd arrived, I was rich and yet was still the 'young man who'd come up from nothing,' something which I never denied. Yet it wasn't for money or fame that I worked out an algebra of the future and turned X, Y and Z into farmhouses, bank accounts, power. Which I gave away again and again, only to have them come back to me twofold. A slight and smiling David, I never lost, never gained a pound. My 1897 lieutenant's uniform would fit me even today. No matter, the unpredictable that I longed for came to pass, and when it came, it hit me hard: my wife's love and my daughter Johanna's death. She was a real Kilb, a year and a half old when she went. I looked into her child's eyes, as into my silent father's eyes. I saw age-old wisdom in their dark depths, which already seemed to know death. Scarlet fever blossomed out on her body like a frightful weed, spread to the hips, ran down to the feet. Fever seethed in her and death grew in her, white as snow, grew like a mould beneath the bloom of red, grew, and burst forth black at the nostrils. The unpredictable I'd yearned for came, and came like a curse and lay in wait in that dreadful house. Now dissension arose, fierce arguments with the pastor at St. Severin's, with my in-laws, my brothers- and sisters-in-law, because I forbade all singing at the Requiem Mass. No matter, I wouldn't give in, I had my way. But I was filled with fear when I heard Johanna whispering 'Christ' during the Requiem."

I never uttered the name of Christ, and hardly dared think it, even though I knew all the time it had me in its power. Nothing had been able to kill the Word in me, the word 'Christ' that Johanna whispered. Not Domgreve's rosary, nor the sour virtues of husband-hunting landlords' daughters had been able to do it. Nor the trade in sixteenth-century confessionals, sold at private auctions for exorbitant prices, the profit from which Domgreve spent in Locarno on cheap sins. Nor yet the dismal moral failures of hypocritical priests—I myself had seen how they meanly seduced fallen girls. Not even my father's unspoken hardness had been able to do it, not even endless passages through wind tunnels of primeval bitterness and futility when, on the future's icy seas, loneliness around me like a great lifebelt, I drew strength from my laugh. The Word lived on. I was David, the little man with the sling, and Daniel, the little man in the lion's den, and I was ready to accept the unpredictability I had longed for: Johanna's death on September 3, 1910. That day, too, the Uhlans rode over the cobbles. Milkmaids, baker boys, clerics with fluttering robes, all was as usual that morning, and the boar hung as usual in front of Gretz' shop. The shabby melancholy of the family doctor who'd been issuing birth and death certificates to the Kilbs for forty years, all as usual. There it was as always, the scuffed leather bag, in it the instruments he used to disguise his futility. He drew the covers up over the disfigured body, but I drew them down again. I wanted to see how Lazarus had looked, and to see the eyes so like my father's, eyes which the child had wanted to keep for only a year and a half. In the next bedroom Heinrich was crying. The bells of St. Severin's shattered time into shards as it tolled for nine o'clock Mass. Had she lived, little Johanna would now have been fifty years old.

"War bonds, Leonore? I didn't buy them. They were left to me by my father-in-law. Throw them into the fire along with the banknotes. Two medals? Yes, of course, I built siege trenches, I bored tunnels, set up artillery emplacements, faced barrages, dragged the wounded out of the field of fire. Second-class, first-class, bring them here, Leonore, let's have them. We'll throw them into the roof gutter. Let the muck in the gutter bury them. Otto found them once when he was rummaging around in the cabinets while I was at my drawing board. I saw the fateful gleam in his eyes too late. He'd seen them, and the respect he felt for me took on added dimension. Too late. But at least let's get rid of them now, so Joseph won't find them some day among the things I'll leave behind."

Only a faint tinkle as he let the medals slide down the sloping roof. The medals tipped over as they fell from the roof into the gutter, and lay with their dull side uppermost.

"Why so shocked, child? They're mine, and I can do what I want with them. Too late, and yet maybe not entirely. Let's hope it'll rain soon and the dirt will be washed down off the roof. A belated salute to my father's memory. Down with the honor of our fathers and our grandfathers and our great-grandfathers."

I felt strong enough for the task, though I was not. I read the algebra of the future in my formulas, which resolved themselves into forms. Abbots and archbishops, generals and waiters, all belonged to my cast, my team, all played on my side. I alone was the featured player, even when, Friday evenings with the choir at the Germania Glee Club, I was singing: *'What glitters there in forest sun?'* I sang it well, I had learned it from Father. But suppressed laughter lurked in my baritone phrasings. The conductor, as he beat time with his baton, never suspected he was obeying my baton. Meanwhile I was invited to social functions of an obligatory nature, offered assignments, laughingly slapped on the back. 'Sociability, young fellow, it's the spice of life.' Gray-haired members of the club sourly inquired about my background and my prospects. But all I did was sing, from seven-thirty to ten, and not a minute longer. The legend had to be ready before the scandal broke. Cauliflower cannot be had.

I roamed in thought up the Kissa Valley with my wife and children, and imagined how the youngsters would try to catch trout. We would stroll through vineyards and fields of wheat, through beetfields and patches of wooded land, drink beer and lemonade at Denklingen station. Yet in fact I knew I had handed in my design and received the receipt only an hour before. Loneliness still held me round like a giant lifebelt. I was still swimming in a sea of time, sinking with the swell into troughs, crossing oceans of past and present, pressing on, aways saved from going down by my solitude. Into the future's icy cold I went, taking my laughter with me for iron rations, subsistence which I partook of only sparingly. Coming out of this reverie, I rubbed my eyes, drank a glass of water, ate a slice of bread and walked to the window, with my cigar. And there she was, strolling in the roof garden, visible every so often through a gap in the pergola as she looked down over the ledge to the street, where she saw what I was seeing, too: apprentices, trucks, nuns, life in the thoroughfare. She was twenty, her name was Johanna and she was reading *Love and Intrigue*. I knew her father, the Glee Club's booming bass. His voice to me did not seem to go with his office air of dignity, it lacked the ring of discretion which was drummed into the apprentices. It was a voice that had in it the timbre of secret sins, the kind that give you the creeps. Was he already aware that I wanted to marry his only daughter? That we were exchanging a smile now and then on quiet afternoons? That I was already thinking ardent thoughts about her, as if we were legitimately engaged? She was pale, her hair was dark. I would have her wear dresses of willow green. Green would suit her well. I'd already picked out frocks and hats for her in Hermine

Horuschka's shop window during my afternoon walks, when, come rain, wind or sun, I passed the place at twenty to five. I would set her free from conventionality, the properness that was lacking in her father's voice. I'd buy her marvelous hats, large as cartwheels, made of rough green straw. I had no desire to be her lord and master. I wanted to love her and I would not wait much longer. Some Sunday morning, armed with flowers, I would drive up in a carriage around half-past eleven, when they had finished eating breakfast after High Mass and were drinking brandy in the smoking room. I've come to ask for your daughter's hand. Every afternoon, I let her see me, here at the studio window. I bowed, we exchanged a smile and I moved back again into shadow. And then moved forward again a little, to let her know she was still being watched. I couldn't bring myself to lurk up here like a spider in his net. I couldn't bear to see her without her seeing me; there were some things you just didn't do.

The next morning she would know who I was. Scandal. She would laugh, and a year later she'd be brushing dried mortar from my pants legs. She would still be doing it when I was forty, fifty, sixty. She would be a charming old lady at my side. I finally made my decision on September 30, 1907, at three-thirty in the afternoon.

"Yes, Leonore, pay it for me. Take the money out of the cash box over there, and give the girl two marks for herself, yes, two marks. A pullover and skirt from Hermine Horuschka for my granddaughter Ruth, expecting her back today. Green suits her well. What a pity girls today don't wear hats, I've always got such a kick out of buying hats. You've called for the taxi? Thank you, Leonore. Aren't you ready to quit yet? Well, whenever you want. Of course it's curiosity, too, a little, isn't it? Don't blush. Yes, I'd like another coffee. I should have found out when the holidays ended. But is Ruth back, do you think? My son hasn't said anything? He won't have forgotten the invitation to my birthday party, will he? I've left orders for the doorman downstairs to take flowers and telegrams, presents and cards, tip all the messengers two marks apiece and say I've left town. Pick out the prettiest bunch or two for yourself and take them home with you. And if you'd like, you're welcome to spend the afternoon here."

This time the freshly filled cup of coffee did not tremble. Apparently they had stopped printing edification or election posters on white paper. In the kaleidoscope the scene was as always. Kilb's roof garden across the way was deserted. The nasturtiums on the pergola were drooping. Outline of rooftops, with mountains in the background and, above, a brilliant sky. In this same kaleidoscope I saw my wife, later my children, and my parents-in-law, when, now and then, I went up to the studio, to peer over the shoulders of my hard-working young architectural assistants, to check their calculations, set their deadlines. Actual work meant no more to me than art. Others could do it just as well as I could, and I paid them well for it. I could never understand the fanatics who sacrificed themselves to what they called "art." I did what I could for them, gave them work, but as for understanding them, I never could. Though I passed for an artist, and was admired as such, craftsmanship was all I knew. That villa I built for Gralduke, was it not daring, modern? It was, all right. Even my artistic colleagues admired and praised it. Yet I'd designed and built it without being conscious of art at all. Maybe they took it all too seriously because they knew so much about it. Yes they built horrible boxes which I knew, the minute I laid eyes on them, would be eyesores ten years later. Then every once in a while I'd roll up my sleeves and stand here in front of my drawing board and design an administration building for some public welfare society or other and make it so welfarish and public that I astonished the fools who took me for a money-grubbing, success-crazy hayseed. Why, even today I'm not ashamed of that administration building. Is that art? Perhaps I created the thing without knowing just what I was doing. Anyway, I never could take the word "art" seriously, any more than I did my three celebrated competitors, when they got so angry with me. Good God, why not make a little game of it? Do the Goliaths of the world always have to be so humorless? Well, they believed in art, and I didn't, and they felt their honor had been smirched by an upstart. As far as that goes, we all have to make a start somewhere, don't we? I just laughed in their faces. I'd jockeyed them into a position where I'd win even if I lost, and if I won, my victory would be a triumph.

I almost felt sorry for them as we climbed the museum steps. I made sure I walked in the ceremonial way to which these touchy gentlemen had been so long accustomed. It was the way you walked when you went up cathedral steps behind queens and bishops, the pace at which monuments are unveiled, a measured intensity, not too slow, not too fast, fraught with a self-conscious dignity that just naturally wasn't in me. If I'd had my way, I'd have raced up the stone steps like a puppy, past the statues of Roman legionaries, with their broken fasces, their swords and lances that might have been so many torches, past the statues of Caesars and the facsimiles of Roman children's graves, to the first floor and the committee room, between the Low Countries and the Nazarene exhibits. All bourgeois gravity. There should have been a ruffle of drums somewhere in the background. Altar steps and scaffold steps were climbed that way, and tribunal steps, when you're about to have a medal hung around your neck, or your death sentence pronounced. An amateur theatrical idea of ceremonial solemnity. But the gentlemen walking with me were no amateurs, not Brehmockel, Grumpeter and Wollersein.

Museum attendants in full-dress uniform were standing self-consciously in front of the Rembrandts, the Van Dycks and Overbecks. And at the marble balustrade, in the darkness of the hallway before the committee room, there stood Meeser, holding the silver tray with glasses of cognac ready to pour us a drink before we were told the jury's verdict. Meeser grinned at me. We hadn't agreed on any sign, but mightn't he do a little something along this line for me now? A nod, a shake of the head? Yes or no? But nothing was forthcoming. Brehmockel was whispering to Wollersein and Grumpeter had got to talking with Meeser. Now he pressed a silver coin into Meeser's thick hand, a hand which I'd hated even as a child. I'd served early Mass with him for a year. With him I'd listened to the mutterings of old peasant women in the background, stubbornly praying over their rosaries in response to the liturgy. Smell of hay, milk and stable warmth, while Meeser and I bowed our heads in unison, allowing the guilt of unspoken sins to beat at our breasts during the *mea culpa, mea culpa, mea maxima culpa.* And when the priest mounted the altar steps, Meeser's hand, the same hand now tightly clutching Wollersein's silver coin, would make an obscene gesture. And into this same hand were now entrusted the keys to the city museum, to Holbein and Hals, Lochner and Leibl.

None of them said a word to me. They left me leaning on the balustrade, left me to the cold marble. I looked down into the inner courtyard where a bronze burgomaster, inflexibly self-important, held out his belly to the centuries, where a marble Maecenas held eyelids lowered over froggy eyes, in a vain attempt to appear profound. Empty the statues' eyes like the eyes of marble-cold Roman women whose voyeurist parties reflected the passions of a dying culture. Meeser shuffled over to his friends, Brehmockel, Grumpeter and Wollersein, the three standing together in a huddle. The December sky was clear and cold above the courtyard. Outside, early evening drunks were bawling at each other, cabs were rolling toward the theaters, behind mignonette-green veils, gentle-faced women were looking forward to *La Traviata.* I stood there like a leper whose touch spells death, between Meeser and the three offended gentlemen, longing for my strict daily routine, where I alone was puppeteer, and alone decided what should exist, what should not, and the while propagated my legend. Here

I was no longer running the show. Now all was becoming scandal, rumor. An abbot in my studio. Building contractors sending me hampers of food, gold watches in red velvet cases. One writing to me: '. . . and rest assured I would not refuse you my daughter's hand.' *Their right hand is full of bribes.*

I would accept none of these things, not as much as a single brick. I like the Abbot very much. Had I really, just for a fleeting instant, thought of using Domgreve's trick on him? I went red with shame at the very thought, for toying with the idea even for a second. I loved Kilb's daughter, Johanna, and I loved the Abbot. By rights I should have taken a cab to Johanna's house, got there about eleven-thirty, presented my bouquet of flowers and said, 'I've come to ask for your daughter's hand.' In which case Johanna would have come out and joined us, her eyes twinkling, and not merely breathing her yes of consent, but saying it right out. I was still taking my walk from five till six, still singing Fridays at the Glee Club, still playing billiards in the Reserve Officers Club, though the twinkle in Johanna's eyes (as I imagined it) encouraged me to draw more recklessly on my stores of laughter.

Slowly I slid along the cold marble balustrade toward the three offended ones, and put my empty cognac glass back on the tray. Would they retreat from the leper? They did not give way before me. Were they expecting some sort of humble gambit on my part? 'May I introduce myself? I'm Faehmel.' Good God, didn't everyone have to make a start somewhere? Hadn't Grumpeter, as a young Swiss, milked cows for the Count of Telm and spread cow manure over the fragrant earth, before he discovered his architectural vocation? Leprosy, too, was curable, curable on the shores of Lago Maggiore, in the Monusio Gardens. Even the leprosy of respectable building contractors, was it not curable? Contractors who bought up Romanesque churches to tear down for salvage, together with their respective contents, their pews and ancient madonnas, and who then, with these same respective contents, decorated the salons of the newly rich and the landed gentry;

who sold confessional boxes in which humble peasants had whispered their sins for three hundred years for use in a whore's parlor. In hunting lodges, in Bad Ems, leprosy was indeed curable.

The deadly earnest faces of the offended ones stiffened as the committee-room door opened. An indistinct dark form took on shape and color. Members of the jury were stepping into the hall. Hubrich, professor of the history of art at the Theological Faculty. Only over my dead body. In this light, and in his black robe, he looked like a city councillor in a Rembrandt painting. Hubrich went to the tray, took a glass of cognac. I heard him heave a heavy sigh. Sweeping past the three offended gentlemen, who tried to crowd up to him, he moved away toward the end of the hall. The severity of his priestly garb was tempered by a white scarf. The blond locks falling like a child's over his collar heightened the impression which Hubrich deliberately tried to create. That is, of looking like an artist. He could be imagined with his wood-carver's burin bent over a block of wood, or with a delicate paintbrush dipped in gilt, humbly at work painting the hair of a madonna, or prophets' beards, or adding a droll twist to the tail of Tobias' little doggy. Softly Hubrich's feet glided over the linoleum. Wearily he nodded to the three offended ones, and then proceeded through the gloom of the hall toward Rembrandt and Van Dyck. On these narrow shoulders rested the responsibility for churches, hospitals and homes in which for many centuries to come nuns and widows, orphans and charity patients, fallen women and the mentally defective would all have to suffer the kitchen stink of generations long gone. Gloomy halls and cheerless façades which heavy mosaics made even more cheerless than the architect's design had contemplated. There he went, the preceptor and *arbiter architecturae ecclesiasticae,* a man who, with pathetic zeal and the conceit of blind conviction, had been pleading the cause of Neo-Gothic for forty years. When still a schoolboy, trotting home through the desolate suburbs of his industrial home town, taking with him his schoolboy honors, and en route observing the smoking chimney stacks and the blackened house fronts, he must have made up his mind then and there to make people happy, and leave a mark behind on this earth. This he would do, a reddish mark, of brick façades growing ever sadder with the passage of the years, in their niches morose saints staring at the future with implacable dejection.

Meeser was dutifully holding out the tray now to the second member of the jury, cognac for Krohl. Jovial, claret-colored face. A cigar-smoker. Meat-gorger who'd stayed slim. Irreplaceable master builder of St. Severin's. Pigeon droppings, engine steam, chemically poisoned clouds from the eastern suburbs, biting wet winds from the western suburbs, southern sun, northern cold, all natural and industrial atmospheric forces guaranteed him and his successors a lifetime in office. Being forty-five years old, he still had twenty more years for the things he really loved: eating, drinking, cigars, horses and women, the special kind you run into near stables, or on fox hunts—hard-limbed Amazons with a mannish smell. I had studied my adversary. Krohl hid his absolute indifference toward architectural problems behind an exquisite, almost Chinese politeness, an air of piety picked up from bishops. Krohl's movements brought to mind memorial dedications. He also knew a couple of very good jokes, which he gave different inflections, always in a certain order of succession. And since he had learned Handke's *Handbook of Architecture* by heart as a twenty-two-year-old, and at that time decided to make the most of this effort the rest of his life, when he needed a few architectural references he always cited 'the immortal Handke.' At plan-judging sessions he pleaded shamelessly for the project whose author had given him the biggest bribe, but switched to the favorite as soon as he saw his man had no chance. For he preferred saying 'Ja' to 'Nein,' on the grounds that a Ja has only two letters whereas a Nein has four, and beyond this the terrific disadvantage of not being pronounceable with tongue and palate alone, but of requiring a displacement backward almost to the roots of the nose. Moreover, a Nein had to be uttered with an expression of firmness, whereas a Ja required no such effort. So then, Krohl sighed, too, and likewise shook his head, avoided the three aggrieved ones, and went to the corner of the corridor where the Nazarenes were.

For a second only the table with the green felt top was visible in the rectangle of light made by the frame of the door, and on it a carafe, ash trays and clouds of blue smoke from Krohl's cigar above. Stillness within, not even a whisper audible. Death sentences hung in the air. For Hubrich it was a question of honor or shame, and the latter he had vowed as a dogged fifth-former never to have come on his head. A question of the dreadful humiliation of having to admit to the Archbishop that he had failed. 'Well, how about the corpse, Hubrich?' that humorous prince of the church would say. 'Where shall we bury you?' As for Krohl, for him it was a matter of a villa on Lake Como promised to him by Brehmockel.

A murmur arose among the rows of attendants and Meeser hissed for silence. Schwebringer came out the door, a small man, as slightly built as myself, and not only supposed to be incorruptible, but actually so. He had on threadbare breeches, darned stockings. His close-cropped head was darkish, a smile in his Corinthian eyes. Schwebringer represented Money; he controlled the funds which had built the Nation. He stood for the industrialists and the king, also for the shopkeeper's assist-ant who had contributed a ten-pfennig piece and the little old lady who had given thirty pfennigs. Schwebringer would make credit available, check over the bills, with a sour look on his face okay advances. He was a convert and the baroque was his secret architectural passion. He loved hovering angels, gilded choir stalls, curved prayer stools, whitely lacquered pulpits, incense and the singing of boy choirs. Schwebringer was power. Bank syndicates belonged to him as surely as the railroad crossing gate to its tender. He regulated rates of ex-change, ran steel mills. With his hard, dark Corinthian eyes he looked as if he had tried all the laxatives on the market without finding one that worked, as if he were waiting for someone to come along and invent a true and really helpful means of jarring his bowels loose. He took the cognac without leaving a tip on the tray. There he stood, only a couple of steps away, for all the world like a professional cyclist down on his luck, with his breeches, his darned stockings. Then suddenly he glanced my way, smiled, put down his empty cognac glass, and went to the Dutch corner, whither Hubrich had also vanished. Nor did he, Schwebringer, deign to say a word to the three aggrieved ones.

Whispering became audible in the committee room; the Abbot was evidently talking to Gralduke. But only the green-topped table, the ash trays, the carafe were visible. Conflict hung in the air. The panel of judges seemed to be still at odds.

Gralduke came out, took two glasses from Meeser's tray, stood there hesitantly a second and looked in Krohl's direction. Gralduke was large, of powerful build, correct in manner, as one might have told from the bags under his eyes. Gralduke represented the Law. He kept watch over the juristic correctness of the judgmental proceedings, took charge of protocol. Gralduke had almost become a monk. For two years he had sung Gregorian liturgies and still liked them. But he had returned to the world to marry a girl who was as pretty as a picture, by whom he had five daughters, all pretty as pictures. Now he lorded it as provincial governor. He had had preserves of land established, fields, meadows and woodlots released, in laborious detail, from land registry office complications, and had had to disencumber miserable little ponds of special fishing rights, realize on mortgages, set banks and insurance people's minds at rest.

Slowly the meeting in the committee room resumed. A wave of the Abbot's slender hand commanded Meeser's presence, whereupon Meeser disappeared for half a minute, reappeared, raised his voice and called down the corridor, 'I'm instructed to tell the gentlemen of the panel that the recess is over.' First to come from the Dutch corner was Schwebringer, all by himself. Quickly he went into the room. Hubrich was the last, looking pale, stricken to death, shaking his head as he went by the three aggrieved ones. Meeser shut the door after him, looked at his tray, at the freshly emptied cognac glasses, scornfully jingled his poor take in tips. I went up to him and threw him a thaler on the tray. It rang hard and loud and the three aggrieved ones looked up with a start. Meeser grinned, put his finger to his cap in thanks and whispered, 'And you're only a sexton's son, and he off his rocker at that!'

For a long time now there had been no sound of hackney carriages going by. *La Traviata* had started. The attendants, forming a lane, stood stiffly by, amid legionaries and matrons, and broken temple columns. An uproar broke like a wave of heat into the cold evening. Newspapermen had run by the first attendant and already the second was helplessly raising an arm, while the third looked toward Meeser, who was hissing a command to be quiet. A young reporter who had whisked past Meeser came up to me, wiped his nose on his sleeve and said, 'All yours! It's in the bag!' Two dignified art magazine editors, bearded, black-hatted and all hollowed out by the pathos of soulful verse, waited in the background and held the less worthy masses in check, that is, a bespectacled girl and a haggard socialist. Until the Abbot quickly opened the door, came to me breathlessly like a young man, put his arms around me, while a voice cried, 'Faehmel, Faehmel!'

Noise from below could be heard in the office. Ten minutes after the window ledge had stopped trembling, laughing working girls left through the big gate, bearing proud sensuousness into the evening hours of after-work. Into the warm fall day, with the grass by the cemetery wall sweetly smelling. Today Gretz had not sold his wild boar, dark and dry its bloody snout. Over there, kaleidoscopically framed, the roof garden: the white table, the green wooden bench, the pergola with the tired nasturtiums. Would Joseph's children, Ruth's children, come and go there, reading *Love and Intrigue*? Had he ever seen Robert over there, ever? Never. That one either stuck in his room working or practiced in the garden. A roof garden was too small for his kind of sport: rounders, the hundred-meter dash.

I was always a little afraid of him, always looking for the unexpected with him, and I wasn't even surprised when the man with the sloping shoulders came to pick him up. If I'd only known the name of the youngster who threw Robert's little messages into our letter box. I never found out what it was, and even Johanna was never able to get it out of Droescher. The memorial they will set up for me really should go to the boy. I never did get around to showing Nettlinger the door or forbidding that Vacano to go to Otto's room. They brought the *Host of the Beast* into my house, they changed the boy I loved into a stranger, the same little fellow I used to take to the construction jobs with me and up on the scaffolding. Taxi? Taxi? Was it the year 1936 taxi, the one I took Johanna in to The Anchor at the Upper Harbor? Or the 1942 taxi, when I took her to the asylum? Or the 1951 one, that I rode in with Joseph to Kisslingen, to show him the building site where he, my grandson, Robert's and Edith's son, was to work for me? The Abbey destroyed, a desolate heap of stone and dust and mortar. Brehmockel, Grumpeter and Wollersein would certainly have exulted over the sight. But I did not exult when I first saw the piles of ruins in the year 1945. I walked around reflecting more calmly, plain to see, than they had expected. Had they anticipated tears? Indignation? 'We'll find out who did it!' 'Why?' I asked, 'let them go their way in peace.' I would have given two hundred abbeys if I could have had Edith back, Otto, or the anonymous young fellow who threw the little notes into our letter box and had ⌐ dearly for it. And even if the exchange had not h I at least was glad to have paid the price: ⌐ the 'work of my youth.' I offered it up for the young fellow and the carpenter's app I knew it would do them no good. Fo⌐

this pile of ruins belong to the *unforeseen* that I had longed for so keenly? The monks were amazed at my smiles, and I by their indignation.

"The taxi? Coming right away, Leonore. Think over my invitation. Seven o'clock at the Cafe Kroner, birthday celebration. There won't be any champagne. I hate champagne. Take the flowers down at the porter's place along with you when you go, the boxes of cigars and the congratulatory telegrams. And, my child, don't forget to spit on my monument."

It was election placards that were being printed in overtime. Stacks of them blocked the corridor, the stairway, and were piled up right to his door, each bundle with an identifying sample stuck on the outside of it. All of them smiled at him, well-dressed samples indeed, the worsted of their suits recognizable even on the placards. Bourgeois earnestness and bourgeois smiles besought confidence and trust. Young ones and old ones, yet to him the young seemed more frightful than the old. He declined with a little nod the doorman's invitation to come in and look over the beautiful flowers that had come for him, to open the telegrams and the presents. He got into the taxi, the driver holding the door open for him, and quietly said, "To Denklingen, please, the hospital."

five

Blue sky, a whitewashed wall, alongside which the poplars, like ladder rungs, led down and away to the outer yard, where a sanatorium attendant was shoveling leaf mold into the compost pit. The wall was too high, the rungs too far apart. He would need four or five steps to cover each intervening space. Watch out! Why did the yellow bus have to travel so close to the wall, creeping along like a beetle? Today it had brought only one passenger—him. But was it really he? Who? If only he could climb the poplar ladder, go hand over hand from rung to rung. But no. Always upright and unbending, never lowering himself, that was the way it had to be with him. Only when he knelt in a pew, or at a starting line, did he abandon his upright stance. Was it he? Or who?

On the trees in the garden, in Blessenfeld Park, there had been neatly painted signs, saying: 25, 50, 75, 100. He had knelt at the starting line, to himself muttered, 'On your mark . . . get set . . . go!' Then sprinted off, slowed down, went back and read off the time from his stopwatch. Again he knelt down at the starting line, murmured the starting signal to himself, dashed away, this time lengthening out the trial stretch just a little. Often it was a long time before he even got past the 25-meter mark, still longer before he reached the 50 and eventually ran the entire course right to the 100 mark. Then he entered his time in his notebook: 11:2. It was like a fugue, precise, exciting, yet marred by intervals of intense boredom, yawning eternities on summer afternoons in the garden, or in the Blessenfeld Park. Start, return, start, a minimal increase, then back to the starting point once more. And when he had sat down beside her, to evaluate and comment on the figures in his notebook, and reflect on his system, it had been at once exciting and a bore. His training had smelled of fanaticism. The strong, slender boy's body gave off the serious sweaty smell of those who know nothing as yet of love. Her brothers, Bruno and Friedrich, had smelled like that, too, when they got off their bikes, heads full of times and distances, and went into the garden to try and relax their fanatical leg muscles by means of fanatical compensating exercises. Father had also smelled like that when he swelled out his chest at choir practice, when breathing had become a kind of sport in itself, and singing had lost all its pleasure. Bourgeois earnestness, mustache-framed, had taken its place. Seriously they had sung and seriously had ridden their bicycles, and their leg muscles, chest muscles, mouth muscles, all had been serious. On their cramped legs, cramped cheeks, hideous purple blotches had appeared. They'd stood for hours on end on cold fall nights to shoot hares hiding among the cabbage stalks. And only at dawn, at long last, had the hares taken pity on straining human muscles and taken off zigzag through a hail of shot. *Whywhy-why?* Where was he now, the one who carried that secret laughter inside him, hidden spring in hidden clockwork, which lightened the unbearable pressure, eased the strain? He, the only one who had never partaken of the *Host of the Beast?* Laughter behind the pergola, *Love and Intrigue;* she was leaning over the parapet, watching him come out by the printery gate, and go, light of step, toward the Cafe Kroner. He carried that secret laughter inside him like a spring. Was he her quarry, or she his?

Careful, careful! Why always so upright, so unbending? One false step and you'll topple into blue infinity, or be dashed to pieces on the concrete walls of the compost pit. Dead leaves won't cushion the impact, the granite side of the steps won't be any pillow. Was it he? Who, then? Huperts, the sanatorium attendant, was standing meekly at the door. Would the visitor like tea, coffee, wine or cognac? Let me think; Friedrich would have come on horseback. He would never have come by the yellow bus, crawling alongside the wall like a beetle. And Bruno, he'd always had his stick with him, when he came. He beat time with it, till time was dead, chopped up time, slashed it into bits. Or snipped it into pieces with his playing cards, which he flung in the face of time like blades, night after night, day after day. Friedrich would have come on horseback, Bruno never without his stick. No cognac for Friedrich, no wine for Bruno now. They were dead, those foolish Uhlans, had ridden into machine-gun fire at Erby le Huette, believing they could fulfill bourgeois virtue through bourgeois vice, meet the obligations of piety with obscenities. Actually, naked dancers on clubhouse tables did not offend respectable ancestors as much as one might have thought, these ancestors having been in fact much less respectable than they looked in their gallery portraits. Cognac and wine struck off the list of drinks forever, my dear Huperts. Then, how about beer? Otto's gait was not so elastic. His was a marching step, drumming en-em-y, en-em-y on the hallway tiles and en-em-y on the pavement, all the way down Modest Street. He, Otto, had gone over to the Beast very early. Or had his brother, when he was dying, passed on the name 'Hindenburg' to Otto? Fourteen days after Heinrich's death, Otto had been born, to die at Kiev. No use fooling myself any more, Huperts. Bruno and Friedrich, Otto and Edith, Johanna and Heinrich, all dead.

Nor will my visitor be wanting coffee, either, Huperts. He is no longer the one whose secret laugh I could hear in his every step. He's older. For him, tea, fresh and strong, Huperts, with milk but no sugar, for my upright and unbending son, Robert, the one who always fed on secrets. Even now he's carrying one around with him, locked in his breast. They beat and furrowed his back, but he didn't bend, didn't give up his secret, didn't give my cousin George away, the one who'd mixed gunpowder for him in the Huns' apothecary. He swung himself down between the two ladders and like Icarus hung poised with outstretched arms at the doorway. He'd never land in the compost pit or be smashed to smithereens on the granite. Tea, my dear Huperts, fresh and strong, with milk but no sugar. And cigarettes, please, for my archangel. He brings me somber messages that smack of blood, messages of rebellion and revenge. They've killed the blond boy. He ran the hundred meters in 10:9. Whenever I saw him, and I saw him only twice, he was laughing. He mended the little lock on my jewel box for me with his clever hands, something the carpenters and locksmiths had been trying to do, but couldn't, for forty years. He just picked the thing up and it worked again. He was no archangel, just an angel, name was Ferdi. He was blond and fool enough to think he could use firecrackers against the ones who'd eaten the *Host of the Beast*. He didn't drink tea or wine, beer, coffee or cognac, just put his mouth to the water tap and laughed. If he were still alive, he'd get me a gun. Either he or that other one, a dark angel that one, the one who didn't know how to laugh, Edith's brother. They called him Schrella, he was the kind you never call by his given name. Ferdi would have done it. He'd have ransomed me out of this crazy-house where they've stuck me, done it, he would have, with a gun. But here I am, doomed and damned. It takes giant ladders to reach the world. My son, see, is climbing down one to me.

"Good afternoon, Robert, you do like tea, don't you. Don't flinch when I kiss you on the cheek. You look like a man, a man of forty; you're getting gray at the temples and you're wearing narrow trousers and a sky-blue waistcoat. Isn't that too conspicuous? But perhaps it's good to go around disguised as a middle-aged gentleman. You look like the kind of office boss people would like to hear cough, just once anyway, but who's too refined to permit himself such a thing as cough. Forgive me if I laugh. How clever the barbers are today. That gray hair looks real, and the stubble on your chin like a man's who has to shave twice a day but does it only once. Clever. Only the red scar hasn't changed. They'll know by that, anyway. But maybe there's a remedy for that, too?

No, you needn't worry, they didn't touch me, they left the whip hanging on the wall, just asked, 'When did you see him last?' And I told the truth: 'In the morning, when he went to catch the streetcar to go to school.'

'But he never arrived at school.'

I didn't say a word.

'Has he tried to get in touch with you at all?'

The truth again. 'No.'

You'd left too plain a trail, Robert. A woman from the barracks district near Baggerloch brought me a book with your name and home address on it. Ovid, gray-green hard cover with chicken muck on it. And your school text was found five kilometers away. The box-office girl from a movie house brought it to me, with one page missing. She came into the office pretending to be a client and Joseph showed her in to me.

A week later they asked me again: 'Have you been in touch with him at all?' And I said, 'No.' Later on, the one who'd been to the house so often, Nettlinger, he came, too. He said, 'For your own sake, tell the truth.' But I had; only now I knew you had gotten away from them.

Nothing from you for months on end, son. Then Edith came, and said, 'I'm expecting a child.' I was terrified when she said, 'The Lord has blessed me.' Her voice filled me with fear. Forgive me, but I've never liked mystics. The girl was pregnant and alone. Father under arrest, brother disappeared, you gone, and on top of that they had held her in custody and questioned her for fourteen days. No, they didn't lay a hand on her. How easily the few lambs had been scattered, and now only one, Edith, remained. I took her in. Children, the Lord was certainly pleased with your foolishness. But you might at least have killed him with your homemade bomb; now he's become chief of police. God preserve us from martyrs who live to tell the tale. Gym teacher, chief of police; goes riding through the city on his big white horse, leads the beggar raids personally. Why didn't you at least kill him? With a bullet through the head. Firecrackers don't kill, my boy. You should have come to me. Death's made of metal. Copper cartridges, lead, cast iron, shrapnel—they bring death, whining and wailing, raining on the roof at night and rattling on the pergola. Fluttering like wild birds: *the wild geese rush through the night,* and dive down on the lambs. Edith is dead. I had her certified insane. Three authorities wrote out their opinions in elegantly unreadable writing on white parchment with an impressive letterhead. That saved Edith from them. Forgive me for laughing. Such a lamb she was. Her first child at seventeen, the second at nineteen and always so know-it-all. The Lord has done this, the Lord has done that, the Lord has given, the Lord has taken away. The Lord, the Lord! She never realized the Lord is our brother, and that among brothers you can laugh sometimes and feel at ease, even if you can't among Lords and Masters. As for myself, I had not realized that wild geese preyed on lambs; I'd always thought they were peaceful, plant-eating birds. Edith lay there as if our family coat-of-arms had come alive, a lamb with the blood flowing out of her breast. Though in her case there were no martyrs or cardinals, hermits, knights or saints standing around in adoration. And there she was, dead. Try and smile, my boy. I tried to myself, but couldn't manage it, least of all with Heinrich. He played with you and hung sabres on you and put helmets on your head, and made you into a Franceman or

Rooshian or Englandman, and sang—that quiet boy—*got to get a gun, get a gun.* And when he was dying he whispered that horrible password to me, that Beast's name, 'Hindenburg.' He wanted to learn that poem by heart, he was such an obedient little boy, but I tore up the piece of paper and scattered the pieces like snowflakes into Modest Street.

But drink your tea, Robert, it'll get cold. Here are the cigarettes, come closer. I must talk very softly. No one must hear us, Father least of all. He's a child, he has no idea how bad the world is, and few the pure in heart. He's one of them. A quiet man, no blemishes on his pure heart. Listen, you can save me. I've got to get a gun, get a gun and you must get one for me. I could easily shoot him from the roof garden. There are three hundred and fifty holes in the pergola. I can take a long, careful aim as he turns the corner at the Prince Heinrich Hotel on his white horse. You have to take a deep breath, I've read all about it, aim and squeeze the trigger. I've tried it out with Bruno's cane. When he turns the corner I'll have two and a half minutes, but whether I'll be able to fire the other bullet, too, I don't know. There'll be a lot of confusion when he falls off his horse, and I won't be calm enough to take a deep breath, aim and squeeze the trigger a second time. I've got to make up my mind, the gym teacher or that Nettlinger. He ate my bread and drank my tea and Father always called him "a bright boy." Now just see what a bright boy he turned out to be. He ripped the lambs to shreds and beat you and Schrella with barbed-wire whips. Ferdi paid too high a price for what he got out of it, burning a gym teacher's feet and breaking a dresser mirror. Not powder and wadding, my boy, powder and metal. . . .

Here, son, drink your tea, then. Don't you like it? Are the cigarettes too stale? Forgive me, I never had much to do with them. You look so handsome like that, with gray at your temples and fortyish, like a born attorney. It makes me laugh, just to think you could ever look like that. How smart the barbers are today.

Don't be so serious. It'll pass, we'll take trips out to Kiss-lingen again. Grandparents, children, grandchildren, the whole tribe, and your son will try to catch trout with his hands. We'll eat the brothers' wonderful bread and drink their wine and listen to Vespers: *Rorate coeli desuper et nubes plurant justum.* Advent. Snow on the mountains, ice on the brooks. Choose your season, boy. But Advent will please Edith the most. She has the smell of Advent about her, she hasn't realized that meantime the Lord has come, as a brother. The brothers' singing will gladden her adventist heart, and gladden that dim church your father built, St. Anthony's in the Kissa Valley, between two farmsteads, Stehlinger's Grotto and Goerlinger's Place.

I wasn't quite twenty-two when the Abbey was consecrated, I'd only finished reading *Love and Intrigue* a little while before. I still had a little girlish laughter left in my throat. In my green velvet dress from Hermine Horuschka's I looked like a girl just come from her dancing class. No longer a girl, not quite a woman, like someone who'd been seduced, rather than married, in my white collar and black hat. I was with child already, and always on the verge of tears. The Cardinal whispered to me, 'You should have stayed at home, dear lady, I do hope you'll be able to last it out.' I did last it out, I wanted to be there. When they opened the church doors and began the consecration rites, I was frightened. My little David, your father, had turned awfully pale, and I thought, now he's lost his laugh. They're killing it with all their cere-mony. He's too small and too young for this; hasn't got enough mannish seriousness in his muscles. I knew I looked sweet with my green dress and my dark eyes and my snow-white collar. I'd made up my mind always to remember it was all a game. And I had to laugh, thinking how the German teacher had said, 'I'll test you and see if you can get an A.' But I didn't get an A, for I was thinking about him all the time. I called him David, the little man with the sling, the sad eyes and the laugh hidden deep inside. I loved him, every day waited for the moment when he'd appear at the big studio window, and I used to watch him when he left the printery door. I sneaked into choir practice at the Glee Club and watched him, to see if his chest expanded and contracted like the others in that show-offy, manly way, and could see by his face he wasn't one of them. I had Bruno smuggle me into the Prince Heinrich when the Reserve Officers Club met for billiards, and watched him, the way he crooked and uncrooked his arm, struck the ball and sent white-green, red-green flying, and found out about that deeply hidden laugh. No, he never put the *Host of the Beast* to his lips. I was afraid he wasn't going to pass the last, the very last and hardest test of all, the Dress Inspection they gave on that fool of a Kaiser's birthday in January, a march to the monument on the bridge, parade past the hotel where the general would be standing on the balcony. How would he look, marching past down there, decked out with history, heavy with destiny, while the trumpets and drums were sounding and the bugles blowing for the charge? I was afraid and worried he might look ridiculous. Ridiculous was the one thing I didn't want him to be. They should never laugh at him, always he at them. And I did see him do the goose-step. Heavens, you should have seen him. As if with every step he was stepping on a Kaiser's head.

Later on I often saw him in uniform. You could tell time by the promotions: two years, first lieutenant; two more years, captain. I took his sword and humbled it. I used it to scrape muck from behind the moldings, rust off the iron benches in the garden, dug holes for my plants with it. It was too awkward for peeling potatoes.

Swords should be flung down and trampled on, and so should privileges, my boy. It's all they're good for, corruption that they are. *Their right hand is full of bribes.* Eat what everybody eats, read what everybody reads, wear the clothes everybody wears, then you'll come nearest to the truth. Noblesse oblige, obliges you to eat sawdust when everyone else is eating it, to read patriotic rubbish in the local paper instead of magazines for cultivated people. No, don't touch any of it, Robert —Gretz' patés, or the Abbot's butter and honey, his pieces of gold and his jugged hare, *whywhywhy,* when others haven't any. Let the unprivileged eat their honey and butter in peace, it doesn't corrupt their stomach and brain. But not you, Robert; you must eat this dirt-poor bread. Tears of truth will well up in your eyes; wear shabby clothes, and be free.

I've used privilege only once, one single time; you must forgive me for it. I couldn't bear it any longer. I had to go to Droescher to get amnesty for you. It was just too much for us —Father, myself, Edith and your son just born. We found your messages in the letter box, tiny little bits of paper no bigger than cough-drop wrappings. The first came four months after you'd disappeared: 'Don't worry, I'm studying hard in Amsterdam. Love to Mother. Robert.' The second came seven days later: 'I need money. Wrap it in a newspaper and give it to a man called Groll, waiter in The Anchor at the Upper Harbor. Love to Mother, Robert.'

We took the money there. The waiter named Groll served us beer and lemonade without saying a word, took the package and wouldn't take a tip, all without a word. He didn't seem to see us or even hear our questions.

We stuck your little messages in a notebook. For a long time none came and then they came more often. 'Received money all right: 2, 4 and 6. Love to Mother. Robert.' Then all at once Otto wasn't Otto any more. A terrible miracle had happened. He was Otto, yet he wasn't, any more. He brought Nettlinger and the gym teacher home with him. Otto. I understood what it means when they say there was only a husk of a man left. Otto now was only the husk of the real Otto, and the husk had suddenly taken on a new content. He'd not merely tasted the *Host of the Beast,* he'd been inoculated with it. They'd sucked out his old blood and pumped new in. There was murder in his eyes, and fearfully I hid the slips of paper.

For months on end no notes came. I crawled over the tiles in the hallway, examining every crack, every inch of the cold floor, took the moldings away and scraped out the dirt, fearing the little balls of paper might have fallen behind them, or have been blown there by the wind. During the night I unscrewed the letter box from the wall and took it to pieces. Nothing. Otto came in, pushed me against the wall when he opened the door, stepped on my fingers and laughed. Months on end I found nothing. I used to stand the whole night long behind the bedroom curtains, waiting for dawn, watching the street and the front door, running downstairs when I saw the newspaper boy. Nothing. I looked through the paper bags with rolls from the baker's in them. I was very careful when I poured the milk into a saucepan, when I took off labels. Nothing. And in the evening we went to The Anchor, pushed our way past uniforms to the farthermost corner where Groll was the waiter, but he kept mum, didn't seem to recognize us. Only after we'd sat there for months waiting night after night did he write on the edge of a beer coaster: 'Careful. I don't know a thing.' Then he spilled beer on it, smudged it all into one big inkstain and brought fresh beer for which he wouldn't take any money. Groll, the waiter in The Anchor. He was young, had a narrow face.

We didn't know, of course, that the boy who had put the little slips of paper into our letter box had long since been arrested, that we were being watched, and that Groll had not been picked up yet only because they were hoping he might begin to talk to us. Who, at the time, understood the higher mathematics of their murderousness? Groll, the boy with the slips of paper, both of them gone, vanished, and you, Robert, you won't get me a gun and release me from this dungeon of the damned.

We gave up going to The Anchor. No news for five months. I couldn't stand it any longer, for the first time in my life used privilege and went to Droescher, Dr. Emil, Council President. I'd been to school with his sister and to dancing school with him. We'd gone on picnics together, loaded barrels of beer onto the coaches, unpacked ham sandwiches at the forest edge, danced country waltzes on the new-mown lawns, and my father had arranged for his father to be elected to the University League, although Droescher's father had never been to the university. All a lot of nonsense, Robert, don't take any stock in that sort of thing when anything serious is at stake. I used to call Droescher 'Em,' short for Emil; it was thought chic at the time. And now, thirty years later, I had myself announced to him. I'd put on my gray suit, and wore a violet veil over my gray hat, and black laced shoes. He ushered me in from the waiting room himself, kissed my hand and said, 'Oh, Johanna, call me Em just once again.' And I said, 'Em, I've got to know where the boy is. I'm sure you people know.' Robert, it was as if the Ice Age had set in. I saw right away he knew all about it, and could feel how he was becoming formal, quite sharp. His lips, thickened by his passion for red wine, became thin with fear. He took a quick look around, shook his head and whispered to me, 'What your son did was a terrible thing. But on top of that it was politically stupid.' And I said, 'I can tell from looking at you what being politically clever leads to.' I was on the point of leaving, but he stopped me, and said, 'My God, should we all hang ourselves?' And I said, 'All of *you,* yes.' 'Do be reasonable,' he said. 'Things like this are the police commissioner's business. And you know what he did to him.' 'Yes,' I said, 'I know what he did to him. Nothing. That's the pity—nothing. All he ever did was win for him every game of rounders for five years on end.' At this the coward bit his lips and said, 'Sports—let me see—you can always do something about sports.'

At that stage, Robert, we didn't have any idea that merely raising your hand could cost you your life. Vacano had a Polish prisoner of war sentenced to death because the prisoner lifted his hand to him—just lifted his hand—hadn't actually struck him.

And then one morning I found a slip of paper on my breakfast tray from Otto. 'I need money, too—12—you can give it to me in cash.' I went over to the studio and took 12,000 marks from the safe—they were there all ready, in case we got any more messages from you—and threw Otto the wad onto the breakfast table. I was thinking of going to Amsterdam and telling you not to send any more messages, they might cost someone his life. But now you're here at last. I'd have gone mad if they hadn't pardoned you. Stay here. Does it really matter where you live, in a world where just raising your hand once may cost you your life? You know the conditions Droescher was given when he negotiated for you: no political activity, and into the army immediately after your examinations. I've already arranged for you to repeat your finals and Klaehm the statistician will coach you and save you as many semesters as he can. Must you really study? Very well, as you wish. Statistics? Why that? Very well, do as you want. Edith's glad. Will you go up to her? Go ahead! Quickly, now, don't you want to see your son? I've given her your room. She's waiting for you. Go on, now.

He went upstairs in the sanatorium, past brown cupboards and through silent corridors, up under the roof where a loft housed the hot water tank. It smelled of cigarettes up here, smoked by attendants on the sly, of damp bed linen, hung up to dry on the tank. The silence was oppressive. It came up the stairwell as through a chimney. He peered through the skylight down the poplar-lined drive leading to the bus stop. Neat flower beds, the greenhouse, the marble fountain, and, to the right of the wall, the chapel. It looked like an idyll, smelled like one, was one. Cows were grazing inside the electrified fence, pigs which themselves would become slops emptied out of guggly pails into the trough grunted in the garbage. The highway outside the sanatorium walls seemed to run off into an infinity of silence.

How many times had he stood at this station in the loft, to which again and again she sent him so that her rememberings might be precisely retraced and fulfilled. Now he was standing there as the twenty-two-year-old Robert, come back home and resolved on silence. He had had to go and greet Edith and their son, Joseph. Edith and Joseph; both had been strangers to him, mother and son; and they both had felt embarrassed, when he entered the room, Edith more so than he. Had they ever called each other by their first names, he and Edith?

When they'd gone that time to Schrella's after the game of rounders, she'd set food on the table, potatoes and some indefinable gravy, and green salad. Later she'd poured some weak tea for him, and those days he'd hated weak tea, had had his ideas about the woman he would marry, and one of them was that she would know how to make a good cup of tea. Quite obviously Edith didn't, yet he had known he would pull her into the bushes when they came out of the Cafe Zons and went through Blessenfeld Park on the way home. She was blonde, she seemed only sixteen, yet had no teenage giggliness about her. There was no false expectation of happiness in her eyes, eyes which let him into her nature at once. When she said grace at table, 'Lord, Lord,' he'd thought, 'we should be eating with our fingers.' He'd felt stupid, holding a fork in his hand, and the spoon felt strange. For the first time he'd understood what eating was: to appease hunger, no more. Only kings and beggars ate with their fingers. They hadn't said a word to each other as they walked down Gruffel Street, through Blessenfeld and the park into the Cafe Zons. And he had been afraid, holding her hand and swearing never to put the *Host of the Beast* to his lips. What foolishness. Yet he had been afraid, as if he were taking part in some solemn consecration. As they walked back again through the park, he'd taken Edith's hand, held her back, let Schrella go on ahead, had watched Schrella's dark gray silhouette disappear into the evening sky as he was drawing Edith into the bushes. She had offered no resistance and had not laughed as the ancient knowledge of how the thing should be done flowed into his hands, filled his mouth and arms. All he had remembered of it was her blonde hair, shining from the summer rain, a wreath of silvery raindrops on her eyebrows, like the skeleton of some delicate sea creature found on a rust-colored shore, the lines around her mouth puckering the skin into little cloud shapes as she whispered against his chest, 'They'll kill you, Robert!' So, they had used each other's first names, then, there in the park among the bushes, and again the following afternoon in that hotel of assignation. He had pulled Edith along by the wrist, holding her close to him, had gone through the city like a blind man, following a divining rod, instinctively finding the way and the right building. In a package under his arm he had carried the gunpowder for Ferdi, whom he would meet that same evening. He had found out she could even smile, looking into the mirror, the cheapest one the woman who ran the place had been able to find in the dime store, smile as she, too, discovered her own ancient knowledge. And he knew, even then, that the package on the windowsill contained a folly which had to be committed, since reason led to nothing in a world where lifting your hand to someone could cost you your life. Edith's smile had done wonders for her face, little used to smiling as it was. When they'd gone downstairs and into the woman's flat, he'd been amazed at how little she'd charged for the room. He had paid one mark, fifty, and the woman had refused the fifty-pfennig tip he'd tried to give her. 'Oh no, sir, no, I don't take tips, I'm an independent woman.'

So he *had* called her by her first name, she who sat in his room at home, with the child in her lap. Joseph. He had taken the child from her lap and held him a minute, awkwardly, then laid him on the bed. And again the ancient knowledge had flowed into him, into his hands, mouth, arms. She had never learned how to make tea, not even later on, when they were living in their own apartment—doll's furniture—after he'd come back from the university or was home on leave, a noncom in the Engineers. Meanwhile he had got himself trained as a demolition expert, later trained demolition squads himself, implanting formulas which contained exactly what he wanted: dust and rubble and revenge for Ferdi Progulske, for the waiter called Groll and the boy who had slipped his messages into the letter box. Edith. Edith with her mesh shopping bag and book of discount stamps, Edith leafing through the cook book, giving the child his bottle, settling little Ruth at her breast. Young father, young mother. She had come to meet him at the barracks gate with the baby carriage, and they had strolled along by the riverbank, across rounders fields and football fields, at high water and low water, had sat on stiles while Joseph played in the sand by the river, and Ruth made her first attempts to walk. For two years he had played the husband game. But he had never thought of himself as a husband, even when he had hung his coat and hat in the closet more than seven hundred times, had taken off his jacket and sat down at the table with Joseph on his lap while Edith was saying grace ... 'Lord. ...' Main thing had been, no privileges, no extravagances. Dr. Robert Faehmel, sergeant in the Engineers, mathematically gifted, eating pea soup while the neighbors were listening to the *Host of the Beast* as it was being broadcast over the radio. Off duty until reveille, then back to the barracks with the first streetcar, after Edith's kiss at the door and the curious sensation of having done her wrong again, a little blonde standing there in her red dressing gown, holding Joseph's hand, with Ruth in the baby carriage. No political activity, they'd said. Had he ever been politically active? And now his youthful folly had been pardoned. He had become one of the most talented officer-candidates. He had been fascinated by thickheadedness, because thickheads retained routine method. He had drummed demolition formulas into their brains, sowed dust and ruin. 'No mail from Alfred?' He had never known at first whom she was referring to, had forgotten her name had been Schrella, too. Time could be read off in promotions: half a year, lance corporal; half a year, corporal; half a year, sergeant; and still another half-year, lieutenant. And presently the dull gray completely joyless hordes had moved out and to the station. No flowers, no laughing on the way, no smile from the Kaiser for them. They had had none of the bravado of peace too long diked up. An irritable mass, but apathetically submissive. And so he and Edith had abandoned the doll's house in which they had played at marriage, and at the station had renewed their vow never to worship the Beast.

Was it the damp bed linen or the dampness of the walls that made him shiver? Now he was permitted to leave the station at which his mother had posted him. Caption: 'Edith, Joseph.' He trod out his cigarette on the floor, went downstairs, hesitantly worked the door handle, and suddenly remembered his mother, as she had looked standing at the telephone. Smiling, she had signed him to be silent as she said into the mouthpiece, 'I'm so very glad, Father, you can marry the two of them on Sunday. We've got the papers here and the civil marriage will be taken care of tomorrow.' Had he really heard the priestly voice reply, or had it been a dream? 'Yes, my dear Mrs. Faehmel, I shall be very glad when this embarrassment is out of the way.'

Edith had not worn a white dress and had refused to leave Joseph at home. She had held Joseph in her arms while the priest asked for the two yeses, and the organ played. And he hadn't worn black. No point in getting all dressed up. No champagne. Father hated champagne. And the bride's father, whom he had seen only once, had disappeared without a trace; also no sign of the bride's brother. Been wanted for attempted murder, even though he would have nothing to do with the package of gunpowder, and actually had tried to prevent the affair.

His mother had hung up the receiver, come toward him and had laid her hands on his shoulders, saying, 'Isn't the little boy sweet! You must adopt him immediately after the marriage, and I've remembered him in my will. Here, have some more tea. I know you must have drunk good tea in Holland. Don't be afraid, Edith will be a good wife, and soon you'll have passed your exams. I'll furnish an apartment for you, and don't forget you can always smile to yourself when you have to go into the army. Keep quiet, and remember this: in a world where raising your hand to someone can cost you your life, there's no more room for such feelings. I'll fix up an apartment for you. Father will be glad. He's gone out to St. Anthony's—as if he'll find any solace there. *How weary these old bones,* my boy. They've killed your father's secret laugh, the spring has snapped. It wasn't made to stand this sort of tension. There's no use in your using fine words like tyrant any more. Father just got to the point where he couldn't bear being penned up in his studio, and what's left of the old Otto was giving him nightmares. You should see what you can do about making up with Otto. Please, please try. Go now, please.'

Attempts to smooth things over with Otto. He'd made many such moves, climbing stairs, knocking on doors. That thickset young man had not even seemed like a stranger to him, the eyes had not even looked at him with a stranger's regard. Behind that pale, wide forehead had been the will to power in its simplest form, power over timid schoolmates, over passersby who had failed to salute the flag. Power which could have been a touching thing, had it been confined to suburban sports centers or street corners and made a matter of three marks won at a boxing match, of a gaily dressed girl taken to the movies by the winner and kissed in a doorway. But there had been nothing moving about Otto as there had been at times about Nettlinger. Otto's power had not been used to win boxing bouts or brightly dressed girls. In his brain power had become a formula, stripped of utility and freed of instinct, almost hateless, and exercised automatically, blow by blow.

'Brother' was a great word, a mighty word, echoing Hölderlin. Yet even death, it had seemed, was not enough to invest the word 'brother' with meaning when the death had been Otto's death. Not even the news of Otto's death had brought reconciliation. *Killed at Kiev!* What a ring it might have had

—a ring of tragedy, of greatness and brotherliness. It could have been as moving, taking his age into account, as a grave-stone inscription: Killed at Kiev, Aged Twenty-Five. But it had had no ring to it, and to no avail his attempts to effect a reconciliation after the event, as before. You two are brothers, after all, he had been told. And so they were, according to the registry office and the midwife's deposition. Had they really been strangers, perhaps he might have been able to feel the emotion and grandeur of it, but strangers they had not been. He had seen Otto eating and drinking, tea, coffee, beer. But Otto had not eaten the same bread as he had, drunk the milk or coffee he had drunk. And worse still with the words they had exchanged. When Otto said 'bread,' it had sounded less familiar to his ears than the expression 'du pain,' when he had heard it the first time not knowing it stood for bread. They were sons of the same mother and father, had been born in the same house and grown up in it together. There they had eaten, drunk and wept, breathed the same air and taken the same way to school, and laughed and played together. He had called Otto 'Junior,' had felt his brother's arm around his neck, felt for him in his fear of mathematics, helped him, boned with him day after day to dispel the fear, had managed it, too, really had succeeded in taking away his brother's fear. Now, suddenly, after he had been away for two years, only the husk of Otto was left. Not even strange any more. Not even the pathos of the word. It just didn't go, it didn't fit, sounded wrong when he thought of Otto, and for the first time he'd understood Edith's phrase about taking the *Host of the Beast*. Otto would have handed his own mother over to the hangman, if the hangman had wanted her.

When, on one of his conciliatory missions, he had actually climbed the stairs, opened Otto's door and gone in, Otto had turned round and said, 'What's the use?' Otto had been right. What was the use? They were not even strangers, knew each other perfectly, knew how one disliked oranges, how the other preferred beer to milk, how one smoked little cigars rather than cigarettes, how the other put his bookmark in his prayer-book.

He had not been surprised to see Old Wobbly and Nettlinger going up to Otto's room, or Otto meeting them in the hall, and it had horrified him when it occurred to him that they were both more familiar to him than his own brother. Even murderers were not murderers all the time, not at every hour of the day and night. Murderers, like railroad men, checked in and out of work, went home, relaxed. These two were a jovial pair, clapped him on the shoulder, and Nettlinger had said, 'Come on, now, wasn't I the one who let you get away?' They'd sent Ferdi to his death, and Groll, and Schrella's father and the boy who'd brought the messages, dispatched them to where you vanished without a trace. But now—let's forget it, boy! Don't spoil the game. No hard feelings. Sergeant in the Engineers, demolition expert, married, an apartment, book of discount stamps, two kids. 'You needn't ever worry about your wife, nothing will happen to her as long as I'm around.'

'Well,' his mother had said, 'have you talked with Otto? No use? I knew it, but you have to keep trying, again and again. Come here, quietly, I want to tell you something. I think he has a curse on him, bewitched, if you prefer to say it that way, and there's only one way to set him free. I've *got to get a gun, get a gun.* "Mine is the vengeance," saith the Lord, but why shouldn't I be the Lord's instrument?'

She had gone to the window and taken her brother's walking stick from the corner between the window and curtain, the brother who had died forty-three years before. She had raised the stick to her shoulder like a gun and aimed, taking a bead on Old Wobbly and Nettlinger. They were riding by outside, one on a white horse, the other on a bay. The moving stick had precisely indicated the tempo of the passing horses, as if timed by a stopwatch. They came round the corner by the hotel, into Modest Street and rode along to the Modest Gate, which presently cut off the view. Then she had lowered the stick. 'I have two and a half minutes,' that is, take a deep breath, aim, squeeze. Her dream's fabric was tear-proof, nowhere could the finespun lie be rent. She put the walking stick back into the corner.

"I'm going to do it, Robert, I shall be the instrument of the Lord. I've got patience, time doesn't touch me at all. You shouldn't use powder and wadding, but powder and lead. I'll have revenge for the word, the last ever to leave my son's innocent lips: 'Hindenburg.' The Word he bequeathed to this earth, I must wipe it out. Do we bring children into the world to die at the age of seven whispering 'Hindenburg!'? I'd thrown the bits of torn-up poem down into the street, and he was such an obedient little fellow he begged me to write a copy for him, but I refused, I didn't want that madness to cross his lips. In his delirium he tried to put the lines together, and I put my hands over my ears, but listened to him just the same through my fingers. 'If God you need, let out a yell.' I tried to force him out of the fever, to shake him awake, and get him to look me in the eye and feel my hands and hear my voice, but he went right on: 'As long as German woods stand high/ As long as German banners fly/ As long as German tongue remains/ So long will live that name of names!' It almost killed me, the way he still put emphasis on the 'that' in his fever. I gathered all his toys together, and took yours, too, leaving you to howl, and I piled all of them on the blankets in front of him. But he never came back to me, and he never looked at me again, Heinrich, Heinrich. I screamed and prayed and whispered, but he kept on staring into fever-land, where there was only a single line ready waiting for him: 'Hindenburg! On to the fight!' He started to say it, and the last word I heard from his mouth was 'Hindenburg.'
I have to have revenge for the mouth of my seven-year-old son, Robert, don't you understand? Revenge on those who go riding past our house to the Hindenburg monument. Shiny wreaths, with gold bows, and black and violet ones, will be

carried behind them. Always I've thought, won't he ever die? Will we have to have him dished up to us on postage stamps for all eternity, that ancient Beast whose name was the very last word my son ever uttered to me. Are you now going to get me a gun?

I'll take you at your word. It needn't be today, or tomorrow, just sometime soon. I've learned to be patient. Don't you remember your brother Heinrich? When he died you were getting on for two. We had a dog called Brom at the time— have you forgotten?—he was so old and wise that he turned the pain you two caused him not into meanness, but into sadness. You two held on to his tail and had him drag both of you through the room. Have you forgotten? You threw the flowers you should have laid on Heinrich's grave out of the carriage window; we'd left you in front of the cemetery, and later you were allowed to hold the reins from up on the coachman's box. They were made of cracked black leather. You see, Robert, you do remember. Dog, reins, brother—and soldiers, soldiers, endless soldiers too many to count. Have you forgotten? They came up Modest Street and swung round in front of the hotel and then down to the railroad station, dragging their cannon behind them. Father held your arm, and said, 'The war's over.'

A billion marks for a chocolate bar, then two billion for a single candy drop, a cannon for half a loaf of bread, a horse for an apple. Always more. And then not even a half-groschen for the cheapest bar of soap. Nothing good could come of it, Robert, and they didn't want it to. They kept coming in through the Modest Gate, and turning, all tired out, toward the station. Steadily, steadily, they carried the great Beast's name before them: Hindenburg. He made sure there was order, down to his last breath. Is he really dead, Robert? I can't believe it, 'Chiseled in stone, in bronze indite. Hindenburg!' He looked like national unity itself, with his buffalo-cheeks on the stamps. I tell you, he'll have us back at the same old stand, he'll show us what political reason leads to, and money reason—a horse for an apple, and a billion marks for a piece of candy, then not even half a groschen for a cake of soap, and always everything in an orderly fashion. I've seen and heard how they carried his name around in front of them. Dumb as the earth, deaf as a tree, and making sure all the time there was order. Respectable, respectable; honor and loyalty, iron and steel, money and a distressed agriculture. Careful, my boy, in the misty fields and the rustling forests, careful, that's where they'll be consecrating the *Host of the Beast*.

Don't think I'm crazy, I know exactly where we are. In Denklingen. You can see the road out there, between the trees running along the blue wall, to where the yellow buses crawl by like beetles. They brought me here because I let your children go hungry, after the last lamb had been killed by the fluttering birds. It's war, you can tell time by the promotions. You were a second lieutenant when you went away, and after two years a first lieutenant. Are you a captain yet? This time you won't do it in less than four years; then you'll be a major. Forgive me if I laugh. Don't carry the thing too far, with your formulas in your head, don't lose patience and don't accept any favors. We aren't going to eat a crumb more than we get on the ration cards. Edith is agreeable to that. Eat what everybody eats, wear what everybody wears, read what everybody reads. Don't take the extra butter, the extra clothes, the extra poem which dishes up the Beast in a more elegant fashion. *Their right hand is full of bribes,* bribe money in a variety of coins. I didn't want to have your children take any favors, either, so they might have the taste of truth on their lips, but they took me away from them. It's called a sanatorium; you're allowed to be crazy here without being beaten. They don't splash cold water over your body and they won't put you in a straitjacket without your relatives' consent. I do hope you won't let them put me in one. I can even go out when I want, for I'm harmless, completely harmless, son. But I don't want to go out, I don't want to know what time it is, or have to feel every day that his secret laughter has been killed and that the hidden spring within the hidden wheels has snapped. All at once, you know, he began to take himself seriously. Became pompous, I tell you. Whole mountains of stone went up, entire forests of lumber were cut down and concrete, concrete, you could have filled Lake Boden with it all. They try and forget themselves in building things, it's like opium. You'd never believe all the things an architect like that can put together in forty years—I used to brush the mortar spots off his pants and plaster splashes from his hat, and he used to lay his head on my lap and smoke his cigar. And we chanted our 'Do you remember?' litany, remember 1907, 1914, 1921, 1935—and the answer was always a building—or a death. 'Remember how Mother died, how Father died, and Johanna and Heinrich. Remember how I built St. Anthony's, St. Servatius', St. Boniface's and St. Modestus', the viaduct between Heiligenfeld and Blessenfeld, the monastery for the White Friars, the Brown Friars, convalescent homes for the Sisters of Mercy,' and every answer rang in my ears like a 'Lord have mercy on us'! Building after building, death after death. He began to chase after his own legend, imprisoned in a liturgy of self. Breakfast every morning in the Cafe Kroner, when he would rather have been eating breakfast with us, coffee half milk, rolls and butter. He didn't at all like soft-boiled eggs and toast and that disgusting paprika cheese, but he began to believe he did. I was frightened. He began to get angry when he didn't get a big assignment, where before he'd simply been glad when he got one. Do you understand? It's a complicated mathematics, as you move toward the fifties and sixties, with the choice of either emptying your bladder on your own monument or gazing up at it in awe. No more twinkling eyes. You were eighteen, then, and Otto was sixteen. And I was scared. I'd stood up there in the pergola like a sharp-eyed watchful bird, had carried you both in my arms, first as babies at my breast, then as children, then held your hands, or you'd stood beside me, already taller than I was, and I watched how time went marching by below. Time boiled up, struck and we were paying a billion marks for a single piece of candy and then didn't have three pfennigs for a roll. The savior's name, I didn't even want to hear it, but they hoisted the Beast onto their shoulders regardless, stuck him in stamps on their letters and repeated the litany: respectable, respectable; honor and loyalty, beaten yet not beaten. Order. Dumb as the earth, deaf as a tree, and down there in Father's office Josephine drew him across her damp sponge and stuck him, in all colors, on the letters. And your father, my little David, slept through it all. He didn't wake up until you'd disappeared, when he saw how a package of money could cost a life. One's own money, wrapped in newspaper and passed from hand to hand. When his other son had suddenly become the husk of a son. Loyalty, honor and respectability—then he saw it. I warned him about Gretz, but he said, 'He's harmless.' 'Of course,' I said, 'but you'll see what harmless people are capable of. Gretz is the kind who'd betray his own mother.' And my own clairvoyance frightened me when Gretz actually did betray his own mother. He did, Robert, he betrayed his own mother to the police. Just because the old woman kept on saying, 'It's a sin and a shame.' She didn't say any more than that, just that one phrase, until one day her son said, 'I can't stand it any more, it's against my principles.' They dragged the old woman away and stuck her in an old people's home, and certified her insane, to save her life, but as it turned out this precisely caused her death. They gave her an injection. Didn't you know the old woman? She used to throw the empty mushroom baskets over the wall to you, and you took them apart and used the reeds to build huts. When it had been raining a long while they turned a dirty brown, then you let them dry and I let you burn them. Have you forgotten that now? The old woman whom Gretz betrayed, his own mother? Of course, he still stands behind the counter, fondling his flaps of calf liver. They came to fetch Edith, too, but I wouldn't let them have her; I ground my teeth and screamed at them and they gave in. I kept Edith until the fluttering bird killed her. I tried to keep him off, too;

I heard his rushing wings as he dived down and I knew he was bringing death. He smashed his way in through the hall windows, triumphantly. I held up my hands to ward him off, but he flew between them. Forgive me, I couldn't save the lamb, and remember, Robert, you promised to get me a gun. Don't forget. Watch out when you climb ladders, my boy. Come here, let me kiss you, and forgive me for laughing. How clever the barbers are these days!"

He climbed bolt upright up the ladder, treading into the gray infinity between the rungs, while David climbed down to him from above. A slight man. All his life long he could have worn the same suits he'd bought for himself when he was young. Watch out! Why do you two have to stop up there half-way up, why can't you at least sit down on the rungs, if you have to talk to each other, instead of standing up straight like that. Were they really putting their arms around each other, did the son really have his arm around his father's shoulders, the father's around his son's?

Coffee, Huperts, strong and hot with a lot of sugar; he likes it strong and sweet in the afternoon, my lord and master, and weak in the mornings. He's coming out of that gray infinity into which the upright and unbending one is disappearing, with his long strides. My husband and my son are brave, coming here to see me in this dungeon of the damned. My son twice a week, my husband only once. He brings Saturday with him, he carries a diary in his eyes. With him I cannot hope to say it's the barber makes him look like that. He's eighty; it's his birthday today, and it will be solemnly celebrated in the Cafe Kroner. Without champagne. He always did hate it and I never knew why.

Once upon a time you dreamt of having a tremendous party on your birthday. Seven times seven grandchildren, great-grandchildren, too, and daughters-in-law and great-nephews and great-nieces by marriage. You've always felt a little like Abraham, founder of a mighty clan; you used to picture yourself with your twenty-ninth great-grandchild in your arms when you were dreaming of the future.

Increase and multiply. It will be a sad feast. Only one son, then the blond grandson and the dark-haired granddaughter Edith gave you; and the mother of the clan in dungeon with a curse on it, accessible only by infinitely long ladders with giant rungs.

"Come in, and welcome, old David, still with your young man's waistline. But spare me the diary in your eyes. I'm sailing along on the little diary page, marked May 31, 1942. Have pity on me, beloved, don't burn my little paper boat made of that folded diary page, don't spill me into the sea of sixteen years forever gone. Do you still remember? *Victory is won, not given.* Woe to all those who don't take the *Host of the Beast.* And of course you know that sacraments have the terrible quality of not being subject to the finite. And so they hungered, and the bread was not multiplied for them, nor the fish, and the *Host of the Lamb* did not still their hunger, while that of the Beast offered nourishment in plenty. They'd never learned how to reckon: a billion marks for a piece of candy, a horse for an apple, and then not even three pfennigs for a roll. And everything always in order, everything always respectable, honorable, loyal. Give it up, David, why carry the world around on your back? Be merciful, get the diary out of your eyes and let the other fellow make history. The Cafe Kroner is a safer bet for you. Some day a monument—a little bronze one—will show you with a roll of drawings in your hand, small, slender and smiling, something between a bohemian and a young rabbi, with that indefinable country air. You've seen where political reason leads —would you want to take my political unreason away from me?

You called down to me from your studio window: 'Don't worry, I'll love you, there'll be none of those dreadful things your school friends tell you about, the things that are supposed to happen on wedding nights. Don't believe a word of what those fools tell you, we'll laugh when it gets to that point, truly, I promise you, only you've got to wait a little, a couple of weeks, a month at the most, until I can buy the bunch of flowers, hire the carriage and ride up to call at your house. We'll travel, see the world, and you'll give me children, five, six, seven, and they'll give me grandchildren, five times, six times, seven times seven. You'll never notice that I'm a working man. I'll spare you the manly sweat and the muscle-bound, uniformed seriousness. Everything comes easy to me, I've learned it, I've studied a little, got my sweating over and done with. I'm no artist, don't fool yourself about that. I won't be able to give you the demonic, sham or genuine, in any shape or fashion, and what your school friends make into hair-raising stories will never happen to us in the bedroom, but out in the open air, so you can see the sky over you and have grass and leaves falling on your face, and smell the autumn evening, and not feel you're doing some disgusting gymnastic exercise that you have to go through. You will smell the autumn grass; we'll stretch out on the sand by the riverbank, between the willows, just above the high-tide mark. Bull-rushes, a couple of old shoe-polish cans, a cork, a rosary bead dropped overboard by a barge-woman, a message in a lemonade bottle. In the air the smell from ships' funnels, the rattle of anchor chains. We won't make all blood and serious-ness. Though naturally there'll be some blood and seriousness.'

And the cork I picked up with my naked toes and offered you as a souvenir. I picked it up and gave it to you, because you'd spared me the bedroom, the gloomy chamber of horrors hinted at in novels, schoolgirl gossip and nunnish warnings. Willow boughs hung down to my forehead, silvery-green leaves about my eyes, which were dark and shining. The steamers hooted; they called to me that I wasn't a virgin any more. Twilight, an autumn evening, anchor chains long since let down, seamen and barge-women coming ashore over swaying gangplanks, and I already longing for what a few hours before I'd feared. Though a few tears came into my eyes when I thought how I wasn't living up to my ancestors, who would have been ashamed to turn duty into pleasure. You stuck willow leaves on my brow and on the tear-stains, down by the riverbank, where my feet stirred the reeds, moved the bottles with their holidaymakers' greetings to local inhabitants. Where did all those shoe-polish cans come from; were they for the shiny boots of seamen ready to go ashore, for the barge-women's black shopping bags, and, yes, surely for the shiny-peaked caps glimmering in the twilight as we sat in Trischler's cafe, later on, on the red chairs? I was amazed at the loveliness of that young woman's hands, the one who brought us fried fish and lettuce so green it hurt my eyes. And wine. That young woman's hands, the same one who, twenty-eight years later, bathed my son's mutilated back with wine. You ought not to have yelled at Trischler when he called up and told us about Robert's accident. High tide, high tide, I was always tempted to throw myself in and let myself be carried out to the gray horizon. Come in, welcome, but don't kiss me; don't burn my little boat. Here's some coffee, sweet and hot, afternoon coffee, strong and black, and here are some cigars. Sixty-centers, Huperts got them for me. Change the focus of your eyes, old man, I'm not blind, just crazy and perfectly well able to read the date on the calendar down the hall. It's September 6, 1958. Blind I'm not and I know I can't put down your appearance to the barber's skill. Get in the game, lengthen the focus of your eyes, and don't tell me the same stories over and over about your stunning blond grandson with his mother's heart and his father's brains who's representing you in the reconstruction of the Abbey. Has he graduated yet? Is he going to study statics? Is he taking his on-the-job training? Forgive me if I laugh. I never could take building seriously. Concentrated baked dust, dust transformed into a building. An optical illusion, fata morgana, doomed to be reduced to rubble. *Victory is won, not given.* I read it in the paper this morning before they took me away. 'A wave of jubilation arose—they drank in the words, full of trusting faith—and over and over again the enthusiastic rejoicing welled up.' Do you want me to read it for you in the local paper?

I promised Edith, the lamb, that your flock of grandchildren —not seven times seven, but two times one, one times two— would have no privileges. They would never take the *Host of the Beast,* and never learn that poem for school.

> *Praise every blow that fate doth strike,*
> *Since pain makes kindred souls alike.*

You read too many newspapers with a national circulation; you let them serve up the *Host of the Beast* sweet or sour, baked or fried, in God only knows what kind of sauce. You read too many fancy newspapers; here, in the local sheet you can have the real, genuine muck of every day, unadulterated and unalloyed, and as well-meant as ever you could wish. The other ones, your national newspapers, are not well-intentioned at all, they're nothing but cowards, but here, everything's meant well. No privileges, if you please, no coddling. Look here, this bit is aimed at me: 'Mothers of the Fallen ... And though you are the people's holy ones/ Your souls cry out to your lost sons. ...' I'm one of the people's holy ones, and my soul cries out, my son has been killed: Otto Faehmel. Respectable, respectable. Honor and Loyalty. He denounced us to the police, and suddenly was the mere husk of a son. No special consideration, no privileges. They did go easy on the Abbot, naturally; he did have a taste of their sacrament, of respectability, orderliness and honor. They celebrated it, monks with flaming torches, up there on the hill with a view of the lovely Kissa Valley. A new age began, an age of sacrifice, of pain, and so once again they had their pfennigs for rolls of bread and their half-groschen for cakes of soap. The Abbot was astonished at Robert's refusal to take part in the celebration. They rode up the hill on big horses steaming from the effort, and lit their fires. Solstice time. They let Otto light the bonfire; he shoved the flaming torch in among the twigs, singing, with the selfsame voice that had sung the *rorate coeli* so wonderfully, singing what I want to keep away from my grandson's lips. *How weary these old bones*—aren't yours trembly yet, old man?

Come, put your head in my lap, light yourself a cigar, here's the coffee right by your hand. Close your eyes, shutters down, all done, diary obliterated. We'll say our do-you-remember prayer and remember the years when we lived out there in Blessenfeld, where the evenings smelled of people taking their leisure, stuffing themselves at fish-fries, at sugared-doughnut shops and ice cream carts. Blessed are those who are allowed to eat with their fingers; I never could as long as I lived at home. You used to let me. The hurdy-gurdies droned away and the merry-go-rounds squealed round and round and I smelled and heard and felt that only the transient has permanence. You got me out of that dreadful house where they all had huddled for four hundred years, trying in vain to free themselves. When they sat down in the garden to drink wine, I used to sit up there in the roof garden, during the summer evenings. Evenings for men, evenings for women, and in the women's shrill laughter I could hear what I heard in their husbands' raucous laughter: despair. When the wine loosened their tongues and freed them of tabus, when the smell of the summer night let them out of their prisons of hypocrisy, it all came out into the open. They were neither rich enough nor poor enough to find out that only the transient is permanent. And I longed for the ephemeral, though I'd been brought up for permanent things, marriage, loyalty, honor, the bedroom where only duty lay, not pleasure. Seriousness, buildings, dust changed into structures, and in my ears a sound like the call-note of the murmuring river at high tide: *whywhywhy?* I didn't want any part of their despair, or to feed on gloomy legacy handed down from generation to generation. I longed for the airy white *Host of the Lamb* and tried, during the *mea culpa, mea culpa, mea maxima culpa,* to beat the ancient heritage of power and darkness out of my breast. I laid my prayerbook down in the hall when I came home from Mass, getting there just in time to receive Father's morning kiss. Then his rumbling bass went away across the courtyard to the office. I was fifteen, sixteen, seventeen, eighteen and I could see the hard, waiting look in my mother's eyes. She had been thrown to the wolves. Should I, then, be spared the same fate? The wolves were growing up, into beer-drinkers wearing peaked caps, both the attractive and the less attractive ones. I looked at their hands and their eyes and had the awful curse laid on me of knowing how they'd look at forty, at sixty, with purple veins in their skin and never smelling of good times after work. Men, responsibility. Obeying the law, imparting a sense of history to children, counting money and resolved on political reason, all were doomed to partake of the *Host of the Beast,* like my brothers. They were young in years only, and only one thing—death—promised them glory, would give them greatness and enfold them in veils of myth. Time was nothing but a means of bringing them closer to death. They sniffed out its trail, liked what they smelt. For they smelled of it themselves; it lurked in the eyes of the men to whom I would be thrown. Wearers of caps, guarders of the law. One thing only was forbidden: to want to live and play. Do you understand me, old man? Play was a deadly sin. Not sport, they put up with that, it kept you lively, made you graceful, pretty, and stimulated their wolfish appetite. Dolls' houses: good, they were all for housewifely and motherly instincts. Dancing: that was good, too, part of the marriage market. But if I wanted to dance just to please myself, up in my room in my petticoat, that was a sin, because it wasn't a duty. I could let the wearers of caps paw me as much as they wanted at a dance, in the hallway shadow, or after a picnic in the country, or in forest shadow put up with their less ambitious caresses. After all, we're not prudes. And I prayed for him, the one who would set me free and save me from death in the wolves' lair. I prayed for that while I put the white *Sacrament* to my lips and saw you over there at your studio window.

If you only knew how I loved you, if you had any idea, you'd never open your eyes like that and greet me with your diary look and want to tell me how my grandchildren have grown since then, how they ask for me and haven't forgotten me. No, I don't want to see them. I know they love me and I know there's one way to give the murderers the slip—be certified insane. But what if I'd gone the way Gretz' mother did? What then? It was a stroke of luck with me, pure luck in a world where a gesture can cost a life, and being certified insane can save you or kill you. I don't as yet want to give back the years I've swallowed; I don't want to see Joseph as a twenty-two-year-old with mortar spots on his pants' legs and plaster stains on his jacket, a stunning young man swinging his folding rule with a roll of drawings under his arm. I don't want to see nineteen-year-old Edith reading her *Love and Intrigue*. Shut your eyes, old David, snap your diary shut—and there, there's your coffee.

I really am scared, believe me, I'm not lying. Let my little boat go sailing on, don't be a wanton boy and sink it. It's a wicked world and the pure in heart are so few. Robert humors me, too, and obediently goes to each station as I send him. From 1917 to 1942—not one step farther; he goes in his upright and unbending German way. I know how homesick he was and how unhappy, playing billiards and boning over formulas in a foreign land; he had come back not just for Edith's sake. He's a German, reads Hölderlin and has never let the *Host of the Beast* touch his lips. But he's no lamb. He's a shepherd. I only wish I knew just what he did in the war. But he never talks about it. An architect who's never built a house, never had a smitch of plaster stain on his pants' legs. No, impeccable and correct, an architect of the writing desk, with no enthusiasm for housewarming parties. But what has happened to the other son, Otto? *Killed at Kiev.* He came from our own flesh and blood, yet where did he come from, where did he go? Was he really like your father? Did you ever see Otto with a girl? I do so wish I knew something about him.

I know he liked beer, didn't like sour pickles, and I know how his hands moved when he combed his hair or put on his overcoat. He denounced us to the police and joined the army—even before he'd finished school—and wrote us postcards of deadly irony: 'I'm well, hope you are too, need 3.' Otto never once came home on leave. Where did he go? What detective could supply that information? I know his regimental number, his field post office number and his successive ranks: first lieutenant, major, lieutenant-colonel Faehmel. And the final blow in figures again, a date: Killed, 12,I.1942. With my own eyes I saw him knock down people in the street because they didn't salute the flag. He raised his hands and knocked them down, and would have knocked me down, too, if I hadn't turned quickly into the other street. How did he ever get into our house? I can't even cling to the foolish hope he might have been the wrong baby. He was born right in our own house fourteen days after Heinrich died, up in the bedroom on a gloomy October day in 1917. He looked like your father.

Quiet, old man, don't talk, don't open your eyes, don't show your eighty years. *Memento quia pulvis es et in pulverem revertis,* as we are quite clearly told. Dust the mortar leaves behind, dust of mortgage papers, of deeds of houses and estates. Then a statue in a peaceful suburb where children as they play will ask, 'Who was that man?'

As a young mother, radiant and gay, I walked through Blessenfeld Park, and I knew then that the peevish old pensioners scolding the children for being noisy were only scolding someone who some day would also sit where they were, and in turn scold other noisy children, who in their turn would soon enough be irritable pensioners. I had two children of my own, one for each hand, four and six years old, then six and eight, then eight and ten, while the carefully painted signs were hung out in the garden, 25, 50, 75, 100. The black numbers on the white enameled metal always made me think of the numbers of streetcar stops. In the evening, your head on my lap and the coffee cup within easy reach—we were waiting for happiness. But in vain. And in the railroad cars, the hotels, we never found it either. A stranger went walking about in our house, bearing our name, drinking our milk, eating our bread and using our money, to buy chocolate in kindergarten, later schoolbooks.

Take me back to the riverbank, so my naked feet can play at the high-tide mark, play to the steamers' hooting and the smell of smoke, back to the cafe where the woman serves the guests with lovely hands; be quiet, old man, don't cry, I'm just living in inner emigration, and you've got a son and two grandchildren, perhaps they'll present you with great-grandchildren soon. It is not up to me to come back to you again, and fold myself a new paper boat every day from a diary page, and sail blithely on till midnight—September 6, 1958, that's the future, the German future; I read it myself in the local paper:

'A View of the German Future, 1958: The twenty-one-year-old Sgt. Morgner has become the thirty-six-year-old Farmer Morgner. He stands on the bank of the Volga. Work done, he smokes a well-earned pipe, one of his blond children in his arms, lost in contemplation of his wife milking the last cow. German milk on the banks of the Volga. . . .'

You don't want to hear any more! Good, then leave me alone with the future. I don't want to know how it is as the present. Aren't they standing on the banks of the Volga? Don't cry, old man, pay the ransom and I'll come back from the bewitched castle. *Got to get a gun, get a gun.*

Careful when you climb up that ladder. Take the cigar out of your mouth, you're not thirty any more, you might have a dizzy spell. Family party in the Cafe Kroner tonight? I may be there. Happy birthday. Forgive me if I laugh. Johanna would have been forty-eight and Heinrich forty-seven. They took their future with them. Don't weep, old man, you wanted to play the game. Careful when you climb the ladder."

six

The black and yellow bus stopped at the road leading into the village, swung toward Doderingen from the highway, and Robert saw his father emerge from the cloud of dust left in the wake of the bus. The old man came into the light as if out of a great damp of fog, spry as ever, undaunted by the sweltering afternoon. He turned into the main street and went along by The Swan. At the front steps, young village idlers gathered and stared at him. Fifteen- and sixteen-year-olds, probably the very ones who had lain in wait for Hugo when he came out of school, and beaten him up in muffled side streets and dark stable stalls, and called him *Holy Lamb*.

The old man walked on past the mayor's office, and past the war memorial, where tired box-trees, out of sour earth, were offering up their leaves in memory of the dead of three wars. He stopped at the cemetery wall, took out his handkerchief, dabbed at his forehead, folded the handkerchief again, smoothed his coat and went on, and Robert saw the modish curve described at every step by his right trouser leg, its dark blue inner lining visible a fleeting instant before his foot landed back on the ground, to rise again in that modish curve. Robert glanced at the station clock—twenty to four; the train wasn't due till ten past four. Half an hour. As far as he could remember, he had never before been alone with his father that long. He had hoped the visit to the sanatorium would last longer, and relieve him of the necessity for a father-son conversation. The Denklingen station bar was the least appropriate place of all for a meeting for which his father had been hoping perhaps for twenty or thirty years. A conversation with a mature son, no longer a child to be held by the hand, brought along on trips to the seashore, offered cake and ice cream. Good-night kisses, good-morning kisses, questions about homework and words of worldly wisdom, honesty the best policy, trust in the Lord. Recipient of pocket money. Smiling pride in ribbons and medals won, in good report cards. Self-conscious discussions of architecture. Excursions to St. Anthony's Abbey. Not a word when he had to flee, not a word when he reappeared. Oppressive meals had been eaten, in company with Otto, who made even talk of the weather impossible. Meat carved with silver knives, gravy ladled out with silver spoons. Mother stiff as a rabbit facing a snake and the old man staring out of the window, crumbling bread and vacantly raising a spoon to his mouth, and Edith's hands trembling, while Otto, only one to do justice to the food, contemptuously took the largest morsels of meat. Father's one-time favorite, Otto, always ready for trips and excursions and extravagances, a happy child with a happy future. Now and then he had said cheerfully, 'You can always throw me out.' No one had said a word. After meals Robert had gone over to the studio with Father, had sat there drawing and playing around with formulas in the great empty room where draughting boards for five architects were still set up. Empty. While the old man wearily put on his smock, rummaged among rolls of drawings and again and again stopped in front of the plan of St. Anthony's. Later on he had gone out for a walk, to have a coffee and visit old colleagues and old enemies. In houses where he had been a welcome guest for forty years, the Ice Age had broken out, in some houses because of one son, in others because of the other. And yet the old man had a cheerful disposition, born to lead a gay life and drink wine and coffee, and regard every pretty girl he saw in a railway carriage as a prospective daughter-in-law. He would often go out for hours walking with Edith, as she pushed the baby carriage. He had little to do and had been happy when he could inspect a hospital he'd built, plan annexes for it, or ride out to St. Anthony's and see to the repairs on a wall. He felt Robert resented him, Robert that he was resented.

But now he had grown up. He himself was the father of grown-up children, a man who had suffered the blows of fate, through the death of his wife. Who had emigrated and come back home; who had been to war, been betrayed and tortured. Independent, with a fully recognizable position: 'Dr. Robert Faehmel. Architectural Estimates. Closed Afternoons.' Finally able to play an equal part in conversation.

"Another beer, sir?" the proprietor asked from the bar; he sponged beer froth off the nickeled dramboard, took two plates with meat balls and mustard from under the refrigerated glass shelf and carried them over to the young couple sitting in the corner, tired and hot after their walk in the country.

"Yes, please," said Robert, "another beer." He pushed the curtain aside. His father turned down to the right, passed by the cemetery gate, crossed the road and stopped at the stationmaster's garden, glancing at the violet-colored asters, just come into bloom. He was clearly hesitating.

"No," Robert said toward the counter, "*two* beers, please, and ten Virginia cigarettes."

The American officer had sat at that table where the young couple was sitting now, his close-cropped blond hair heightening the impression of youth, his blue eyes radiating confidence, confidence in a future wherein everything would be explainable. It was scaled down into squares, whose scale was the only question remaining to be clarified—1 : 1 or 1 : 3,000,000? On the table, beneath the officer's fingers toying with a slender pencil, had lain an ordinance survey map of the Kisslingen region.

The table had not changed during these thirteen years. The initials J.D., carved by an idle schoolboy were still there, on the table leg to the right where now the young man scraped his dusty sandals. Nor had the tablecloths changed, red-and-white check ones, or the chairs of clear beechwood, built to last. They had survived two world wars and accommodated the buttocks of waiting peasants for seventy years. Only new addition was the refrigerated glass shelf on top of the bar, where crisp meat balls, cold cuts and deviled eggs were waiting for the hungry or the bored.

"Here you are, sir, two beers and ten cigarettes."

"Thank you."

Not even the pictures on the wall had changed. A bird's-eye view of St. Anthony's Abbey, evidently taken from Cossack's Hill, with a trusty plate camera and a black cloth. There they were, the cloister garth and refectory, the mighty church, the farm buildings. Beside it hung a faded color print. Sweethearts at the field's edge. Ears of grain, cornflowers, a mud-yellow country road dried by the sun. The village beauty had her boy friend's head in her lap, and was tickling his ear with a blade of grass.

'You misunderstand me, Captain. What we'd all like to know is, *why* you did it. Are you listening? We know about the scorched-earth policy—leave nothing but rubble and dead bodies behind for the enemy, isn't that so? But I don't believe you did it to carry out that order. You are—pardon me—too intelligent for that. But then why, why did you blow up the Abbey? In its way it was an historical and artistic monument of the first rank. Now that the fighting here is over and, as our prisoner, you'll hardly have an opportunity to tell the other side what our intentions were, I may as well tell you that our commanding officer would have agreed to postpone the advance for two or even three days, rather than harm the Abbey in any way. Why then did you blow the Abbey sky-high, when it so obviously made no sense whatever, either tactically or strategically? You didn't slow down our advance, you hurried it up. Smoke?'

'Yes. Thank you.'

The cigarette, a Virginia, had tasted strong and spicy.

'I hope you understand what I'm getting at. Please, do say something. I see we're practically the same age, you're twenty-nine, I'm twenty-seven. Can't you understand that I should like to know your motives? Or are you afraid of consequences of letting the truth be known—of what we might do, or your own people?'

But even if he had said why, it wouldn't have been why any more. In black and white, on the record, it would have been least true: that he had waited through five years of war for that moment, the moment when the Abbey would be his booty, lying there like a gift of God. He had wanted to erect a monument of dust and rubble for those who had not been historical monuments and whom no one had thought to spare. Edith, killed by a piece of shrapnel; Ferdi, would-be assassin condemned by process of law; the boy who had pushed the tiny slips of paper with his messages into the letter box; Schrella's father, who had disappeared; Schrella himself, who had to live so far away from the land where Hölderlin had lived; Groll, the waiter in The Anchor; and the many others who had gone marching off, singing *How weary, weary these old bones*. No one would be called to account for them, no one had taught them any better. Dynamite, a few formulas, that had been his chance to erect monuments. And a demolition squad whose precision work had made it famous: Schrit, Hochbret, Kanders. 'We know perfectly well you could not take your superior officer seriously—General Otto Kösters; our army psychiatrists have unanimously—and if you only knew how hard it is to achieve unanimity among American army psychiatrists—they have unanimously certified him insane and not responsible for his actions. Therefore, that responsibility falls on you, Captain, since you are quite clearly not insane, and also, let me tell you in confidence, deeply incriminated by your own comrades' depositions. I don't want to question you about your political convictions. I've already heard too many protestations of innocence and frankly they bore me. I've already told my men that in this fair land we'll find only five or six, or at the outside nine, guilty ones and will have to ask ourselves just against whom we fought this war: against a lot of downright sensible, nice, intelligent, even cultivated people—please answer my question! Why, why did you do it?'

Now the young girl was sitting in the American officer's place, eating her meat ball, sipping her beer and giggling. On the horizon he could see the slender, dark gray tower of St. Severin's, undamaged.

Ought he to have said he found the respect for artistic and historical monuments no less touching than the mistake of expecting beasts, instead of nice, understanding people? A monument for Edith and Ferdi, for Schrella and his father, for Groll and the boy who'd pushed his bits of paper into the letter box, for Anton the Pole who had raised his hand against Vacano and been murdered as a result, and for the many others who had sung *How weary, weary these old bones,* and never been taught any better. A monument for the lambs no one had fed.

If she were going to catch the train, his daughter should now be walking past the portals of St. Severin's to the station, with her green beret on her dark hair, in her pink sweater, flushed and happy at meeting father, brother and grandfather for afternoon coffee at St. Anthony's, before the great birthday party that evening.
Father was standing outside in the shade, in front of the board, studying the times of departure. His narrow face was

ruddy, an amiable old man, kind and generous, one who had never tasted the *Host of the Beast,* who had not grown bitter with age. Did he know who had blown up the Abbey? Would he ever find out? And how could he ever explain it to his son Joseph? Better to be silent than to put these thoughts and feelings on record, for analysis by the psychologists.

He had not been able to explain it to the friendly young man either who had looked at him, shaking his head, pushing the opened pack of cigarettes across the table. He took the pack, said thank you and stuck it in his pocket, then plucked the Iron Cross from his chest, and pushed it across the table to the young man. The red-and-white check tablecloth crimped up, and he smoothed it as the young man flushed.

'No, no,' said Robert, 'forgive my clumsiness; I don't want to hurt your feelings, but I feel I should offer you this as a souvenir, a souvenir of the man who blew up St. Anthony's Abbey and got this medal for it. Who blew it up in spite of knowing the general was mad, and in spite of knowing its demolition had no tactical or strategical importance whatsoever. I shall be glad to keep these cigarettes—may I ask you to consider that we have, as contemporaries, merely exchanged gifts?'

Perhaps he had done it because he remembered the half-dozen monks who had celebrated the solstice by riding up Cossack's Hill and, as the fire raged up, started intoning *How weary, weary these old bones.* Otto had lit the fire and he himself had stood nearby, with his little blond curly-headed son Joseph in his arms, the child clapping his little hands with joy at the flames. And Edith beside him had pressed his right hand. Perhaps because he had not even found Otto a stranger, in this world where a lift of a hand might cost a life. The village youths from Doderingen, Schlackringen, Kisslingen and Denklingen had gathered round the solstice fire; the heated faces of the young men and women had shone wildly in the flames that Otto had been allowed to light, and all of them had sung, the pious monks, digging their spurs into the flanks of their pious farm horses, intoning along with the rest: *How weary, weary these old bones.* They had gone back down the hill with torches in their hands, chanting. Should he tell the young man he'd done it because they hadn't obeyed the injunction, *Shepherd my Lambs,* and that he felt no trace of regret. Aloud, he said, 'Perhaps it was for the fun of it, just a game.'

'Funny kind of fun you have here, funny kind of game. After all, you're an architect.'

'No. I do stress and strain estimates.'

'Well, there's hardly any difference.'

'Demolition,' he said, 'is merely stress and strain in reverse. They're complementary, so to speak.'

'I'm sorry,' said the young man, 'I was always weak in math.'

'And I always found it a pure delight.'

'I'm beginning to take a personal interest in your case. When you refer to your love of mathematics, do you mean you took a certain professional interest in the demolition?'

'Perhaps. Naturally an analyst is highly interested in knowing which forces are required to undo the laws of statics. You must admit it was a perfect demolition.'

'But do you seriously maintain that this so-to-speak abstract interest played some part in it?'

'Yes.'

'I don't think I can avoid a political investigation after all. I must point out to you it will be senseless to make false statements. We have all the documents needed to check on what you say.'

It had been only then that it occurred to him that his own father had built the Abbey thirty-five years before; they had been told it and had it confirmed for them so often that it seemed no longer true. And he had feared the young man would discover this fact, and then believe he had hit on the explanation: Oedipus complex. Perhaps it was better to say he had done it because they had not shepherded the lambs, thus providing tangible reasons to judge him crazy. But he had merely gazed through the window at St. Severin's slender tower, as at a prey which had got away, while the young man asked him questions, all of which he was able to answer without hesitation with a no. .

The young girl pushed her empty plate away from her, took the young man's plate and, holding both forks poised an instant in her right hand, with her left hand put his plate on hers. And then, on the top plate, the two forks. After which she put her right hand, free now, on the young man's forearm and smiled into his eyes.

'So you didn't belong to any organization? You read Hölderlin? Good. I may have to have you brought in once more tomorrow morning.'
Firm in compassion the eternal heart.

When his father walked into the bar, Robert flushed, went up to the old man, took the heavy hat out of his hand and said, "I forgot to congratulate you on your birthday, Father. Forgive me. I've ordered a beer for you. I hope it's still fresh enough, if not. . . ."
"Thank you," said his father, "thanks for the birthday wishes, and the beer will do; I don't like it too cold." The old man put his hand on Robert's arm, and Robert, blushing, remembered the intimate gesture they had exchanged on the street in front of the sanatorium. There, he had suddenly felt a need to put his arm round his father's shoulders, and his father had returned the gesture while they made their arrangement to meet at Denklingen station.
"Come on," said Robert, "let's sit down; we still have twenty-five minutes."
They raised their glasses, nodded to each other, and drank.
"Cigar, Father?"
"No thank you. By the way, did you know the train schedules have hardly changed in fifty years? Even the announce-

ment board with its enamel plates is still the same. On some of them the enamel is only chipped a little bit."

"The chairs and tables and the pictures on the wall," said Robert, "are all the same as they used to be, when we used to walk over here from Kisslingen on summer evenings and wait for the train."

"Yes," said his father, "nothing has changed. Did you call up Ruth? Will she be coming? It's so long since I've seen her."

"Yes, she's coming. I expect she's already sitting in the train."

"We can be in Kisslingen shortly after half-past four, have some coffee and cake, and easily get back home by seven. You are coming to the party?"

"Of course, Father, did you think we wouldn't?"

"No, but I was wondering whether to let it go, cancel it—but perhaps it's better not to, for the children's sake; and I've made so many preparations for today."

The old man lowered his eyes to the red-and-white check tablecloth, and drew circles on it with his beer glass; Robert marveled at the smooth skin on his hands, child's hands which had kept their innocence. His father raised his eyes again and looked Robert in the face.

"I was thinking of Ruth and Joseph. You know Joseph has a girl, don't you?"

"No."

The old man looked down again and let the beer glass go on circling.

"I'd always hoped my two properties out here might be something like a second home to you, but you all always preferred living in the city, even Edith—it seems Joseph is the first who might fulfill my dream. Strange you all still think he takes after Edith and not after us. And yet he looks so like Heinrich it sometimes scares me, when I see your son; Heinrich, as he might have been—do you remember him?"

Our dog was called Brom; and I held the coach-horse reins, made of black leather. All cracked. Got to get a gun, get a gun. Hindenburg.

"Yes, I remember him."

"He gave me back the farmhouse I made him a present of. Whom am I going to give it to now? Joseph or Ruth? You? Would you like it? Own cows and meadows, milk separators and beet-cutting machines? Tractors and hay tedders? Shall I deed it to the monastery? I bought both properties with my first fee; I was twenty-nine when I built the Abbey, and you can't imagine what it means to a young man to get such an assignment. A sensation. That's not only why I travel out there so often, to remember the future which meanwhile has long since become the past. I always thought of becoming sort of a farmer in my old age. But I haven't, only an old fool playing blind man's buff with his wife. We take turns closing our eyes, changing old times like the slides in that apparatus that throws pictures on the wall. If you please, let's have 1928. Two fine sons holding mother's hand, one thirteen, the other eleven. Father close by, cigar in mouth, smiling. In the background, the Eiffel Tower—or is it the Engelsburg or the Brandenburg Gate perhaps—pick your own backdrop; maybe the breakers at Ostend, or St. Severin's tower, or the lemonade stalls in Blessenfeld Park? No, of course it's St. Anthony's Abbey, you'll find it in the snapshot album, at all seasons, only the fashions change. Your mother in a large hat or a small one, with short or long hair, in a full skirt or a tight one, and her children three and five, five and seven years old; then there appears a stranger young and blonde, with one child in her arms and another held by the hand, the children one and three years old. Do you know, I loved Edith more than I could have loved a daughter. I could never believe she'd ever really had a mother and father—and a brother. She was an emissary of the Lord and while she lived with us I could think and pray His name again without blushing—what message did she bring you? Revenge for the lambs? I hope you carried out the mission loyally, without the false considerations I always had, without keeping your superiority feelings fresh in a refrigerator of irony, as I always did. Did she really have that brother? Is he alive? Does he exist?"

Drawing circles with his beer glass, he stared at the red-and-white check tablecloth, very slightly raised his head.

"Tell me, does he really exist? He was your friend, wasn't he. I saw him once. I was standing at the bedroom window and I saw him walk across the courtyard to your room. I've never forgotten him, and often thought about him, even though I can hardly have seen him for more than ten or twenty seconds. He scared me, like a dark angel. Does he really exist?"

"Yes."

"Is he alive?"

"Yes. You are afraid of him?"

"Yes. Of you too. Didn't you know? I don't want to know what mission Edith gave you, only, did you carry it out?"

"Yes."

"Good. You're surprised I was scared of you—and still am, a little. I laughed at your childish plots, but the laughter stuck in my throat when I read they had killed that boy. He might have been Edith's brother, but later on I knew it had been almost human to kill a boy who after all had thrown a bomb and scorched a gym teacher's feet—but the boy who pushed your slips of paper through our letter box, the Pole who raised his hand against the gym teacher, even an uncalled-for glance, certain kind of hair, certain shape of nose were enough, and the time came when it took even less. The father's or grandmother's birth certificate was enough. I'd lived on my laughter through the years, but that nourishment ran out, no new batch available, Robert. So I opened the refrigerator door and let my irony turn sour, then threw it out like the disgusting leftovers of something which once might have been worth something. I had thought I loved and understood your mother, but really it wasn't till then that I really understood and loved her, and understood you others, too, and loved you. Later only I quite saw it all; I was well set up when the war ended, building commissioner for the entire district. Peace, I thought, all over, a new life—when one day the British commanding officer came to apologize to me, so to speak, for having bombed the Honorius Church and destroyed the twelfth-century crucifixion group. He didn't apologize for Edith, only for a twelfth-century crucifixion panel. 'Sorry.' I laughed again for the first time in ten years, but it wasn't good laughter, Robert—and I resigned my office. Building commissioner? What for? When I would have given all the crucifixions down the centuries to see Edith's smile once again and feel her hand on my arm? What did the Lord's pictures mean to me, compared to His emissary's real smile? As for the boy who brought your scraps of paper—I never saw his face or learned his name—I would have given St. Severin's and known it would have been a ridiculous price to pay, like giving a medal to someone who's saved a life. Have you ever seen Edith's smile again, or the smile of that carpenter's apprentice? Just a hint of it? Robert, Robert!"

He let go of the beer glass and set his arms on the table.

"Have you ever seen it?" He murmured the question, head bent low.

"I've seen it," said Robert, "on the face of a hotel boy called Hugo—I'll show him to you."

"I'll give that boy the farm Heinrich couldn't take. Write me his name and address on the coaster. All the most important messages are sent on beer mats. And let me know as soon as you hear anything of Edith's brother. Is he alive?"

"Yes. Are you still afraid of him?"

"I am. Terrible thing was, there was nothing at all touching about him. I knew when I saw him crossing the courtyard that he was strong, and that everything he did wasn't being done for reasons that would carry weight with other people. Because he was poor or rich, ugly or handsome, because his mother had or hadn't beaten him. All the reasons why anyone does anything, either building churches or murdering women, being a good teacher or a bad organist. With him I knew that none of these reasons would explain anything. At that time I could still laugh, but I couldn't find a single crack in him where my laughter might have got through. It scared me, as if a dark angel had come walking across our courtyard, God's deputy sheriff come to take you into custody. That's what he did to you, seized your person. But there was nothing moving about him. Even when I heard they'd beaten him and intended to kill him, I wasn't moved. . . ."

"Your Excellency! I've only now recognized you; I'm so glad to see you well. It must be years since you were here."

"Ah, it's you, Mull? And your mother, is she still living?"

"No, Your Excellency, we had to lay her to rest. It was a huge funeral. She'd had a full life; seven children, thirty-six grandchildren and eleven great-grandchildren, a full life. Will you gentlemen do me the honor of drinking to my mother's memory?"

"But gladly, my dear Mull—she was a wonderful woman."

The old man got to his feet, and Robert stood up too as the proprietor went to the bar and ran the glasses full of beer. The station clock said ten past four. Two farmers were waiting at the counter, wearily pushing meat balls smeared with mustard into their mouths, drinking copious gulps of beer. The proprietor came back to the table, with red face and moist eyes, transferred the glasses of beer from tray to table and picked his own glass up.

"To your mother's memory, Mull," said old Faehmel.

They raised their glasses, nodded to each other, drank and put them down again.

"Did you know," the old man said, "that your mother gave me credit fifty years ago, when I came over here hungry and thirsty from Kisslingen. The railway tracks were being repaired at the time, and it was nothing for me to walk four kilometers. To your health, Mull, and to your mother. This is my son; haven't you ever met him?"

"Faehmel—how do you do."

"Mull—a pleasure."

"Every child here knows *you*, Excellency, everyone knows you built our Abbey, and many a grandmother can still tell stories about you; about the times you ordered whole truckloads of beer for the bricklayers, and danced a solo at the builders' party. Here's to you, your Excellency."

They emptied their glasses standing. Robert, his empty glass in his hand, stared after the proprietor as he went back to his bar, pushed the young couple's plates through the hatch, then worked out the bill with the young man. His father was tugging him by the coat.

"Come on," the old man said, "sit down, we've still got another ten minutes. They're splendid people, their hearts are in the right place."

"And you're not afraid of them, are you, Father?"

The old man looked his son full in the eyes, his narrow, still-smooth face unsmiling.

Robert continued: "These were the people who tormented Hugo—perhaps one of them was even Ferdi's hangman!"

"While you were away and we were waiting for news of you I was scared of everyone—but scared of Mull? Now? Are *you* scared of him?"

"Whenever I meet anyone I ask myself whether I'd want to be handed over to him, and there aren't many I'd say yes to."

"And were you handed over to Edith's brother?"

"No. We shared a room in Holland, shared everything we had. Half the day we played billiards, the other half we studied; he German, I mathematics. I wasn't handed over to him, but I would hand myself over to him any time—to you, too, Father." Robert took the cigarette out of his mouth. "I'd like to give you something for your eightieth birthday, Father—to prove, well, perhaps you know what I'd like to prove to you?"

"I know," said the old man, laying his hand on his son's arm, "you needn't tell me."

Some tears of remorse I'd like to give you, but I can't force them out, I still look at St. Severin's tower as at a quarry which got away from me. It was a shame it had to be your early work, the great prize, the first great gamble. And so well built, solid masonry, its statics irreproachable; had to requisition two truckloads of high explosive, and went round chalking my figures and formulas on the walls, on the columns and buttresses, on the great picture of the Last Supper, between the feet of St. John and St. Peter. I knew the Abbey so well, you'd explained it to me so often as a child, as a boy, as a young man. I chalked my figures on the wall, while the Abbot, the only one who'd stayed there, dogged me wherever I went, appealing to my reason, to my religion. Lucky he was a new abbot who didn't know me. He appealed to my conscience—in vain. He didn't know me as a weekend visitor eating trout, as the master builder's son, as the nature-pure-honey-eating, butter-on-country-bread-spreading master builder's son, and while he was staring at me as if I were crazy, I whispered to him, *How weary, weary these old bones.* I was twenty-nine, exactly the age you were when you built the Abbey, and now I am stalking the prey sticking up against the far horizon, gray, slender St. Severin's. But I was taken prisoner and the young man interrogated me, here in Denklingen station, over at the table that's empty now.

"What are you thinking about?" asked the old man.

"About St. Anthony's; it's been such a long time since I was there."

"Are you looking forward to going up?"

"I'm looking forward to Joseph, it's such a long time since I've seen him."

"I'm rather proud of him," the old man said, "he's so outgoing and quick, and he'll be a fine architect one day. A bit too strict with the workmen, a bit impatient, but I don't expect patience from a twenty-two-year-old. And now he has a deadline to beat—the monks are so eager to sing the Liturgy for Advent in the new church. We'll all be invited to the consecration, of course."

"Is the Abbot still there?"

"Which one?"

"Gregor."

"No. He died in forty-seven. He couldn't get over the Abbey being destroyed."

"And you, could you get over it?"

"When I heard it had been destroyed, the news hit me hard, but when I went out there and saw the rubble, with the monks in a state and wanting to set up a commission to find the culprit, I advised them not to. I didn't want to wreak any revenge for a building, and I was afraid they might in fact find the culprit and he would apologize to me. I still had the frightful echo of the Englishman's 'Sorry' in my ears. And, after all, buildings can be rebuilt. Yes, Robert, I got over it. You won't believe it, but I had never had too much feeling for buildings I designed and put up. I liked them on paper, I had a certain passion for the work, but I was never an artist, you understand, and I knew I wasn't. I still had my plans, of course, when they offered me the job of reconstruction. A great opportunity for your boy to get some practical training, learn coordination, take off the rough edges of his impatience—shouldn't we go to the train?"

"Four minutes to go, Father. We can go out onto the platform."

Robert stood up, made a sign toward the bar and reached for his wallet, but the proprietor came round from behind, went past Robert, laid his hand smilingly on the old man's shoulder and said, "No, no, Your Excellency, you're my guests, I wouldn't think of anything else, for the sake of my mother's memory."

Outside it was still hot. Streamers of smoke from the train were already visible over Doderingen.

"Have you got tickets?" the old man asked.

"Yes," said Robert, looking toward the train as it came over the rise behind Doderingen, as if down on to them out of the clear blue sky. The train was old, black and picturesque; the station master came out of his office, a weekend smile on his face.

"Here, Father, here," called Ruth, in her green beret and fluffy pink pullover, waving her arms. She stretched her hands out to her grandfather, helped him up onto the step, embraced him and pushed him carefully through the open carriage door, then pulled her father up and kissed him on the cheek.

"I'm glad," she said, "really awfully glad about St. Anthony's and this evening."

The station master blew his whistle and waved for the train to pull away.

seven

As they walked up to the counter Nettlinger took the cigar out of his mouth and nodded encouragingly to Schrella. The window was slid up from the inside; a guard leaned out with an inventory and asked, "Are you the prisoner Schrella?"

"Yes," said Schrella.

As the guard took the objects from a box he called them out and laid them on the counter.

"One pocket watch, nickel, without chain."

"One change purse, black leather, contents: five English shillings, thirty Belgian francs, ten German marks and eighty pfennigs."

"One tie, color green."

"One ballpoint pen, no trademark, color gray."

"Two handkerchiefs, white."

"One trenchcoat."

"One hat, color black."

"One razor, trademark Gillette."

"Six cigarettes, trademark Belga."

"You kept your shirt, underwear, soap and toothbrush,

didn't you? Please sign here and confirm with your signature that none of your personal property is missing."

Schrella put on his coat, stuck his worldly possessions in his pocket, signed and dated the inventory: September 6, 1958, 4:10 P.M.

"All right," said the guard, and pulled the window down.

Nettlinger reinserted the cigar in his mouth and tapped Schrella's shoulder. "Come on," he said, "this way out. Or do you want to go back in the pokey? Perhaps you'd better put your tie on now."

Schrella put a cigarette in his mouth, straightened his spectacles, turned up his shirt collar and put on his tie. He gave a start as Nettlinger suddenly held a cigarette lighter in front of his nose.

"Yes," said Nettlinger, "it's that way with every prisoner, high or low, guilty or innocent, poor or rich, political or criminal. First of all a cigarette."

Schrella inhaled the cigarette smoke deeply, and looked over his glasses at Nettlinger, while he tied his tie and turned his collar down again.

"You've had a lot of experience in such things, have you?"

"Haven't you?" asked Nettlinger. "Come on, I'm afraid I can't spare you the Superintendent's farewell."

Schrella put his hat on, took the cigarette out of his mouth and followed Nettlinger, who was holding open the courtyard door for him. The Superintendent was standing at the head of the line by the counter window, whence notes of permission for Sunday visits were issued. The Superintendent was big, not smartly but very respectably dressed. The way he walked and gestured as he came toward Nettlinger and Schrella unmistakably bespoke a civilian.

"I hope," he said to Nettlinger, "that it all went off to your satisfaction—quickly and efficiently."

"Thank you," Nettlinger said, "it was really fast."

"Fine," said the Superintendent. He turned to face Schrella: "You will forgive me if I say a few words to you in farewell, even though you belonged to my"—he laughed—"my protégés for only one day, and even though you were put by mistake in the punishment- instead of the detention-block. Look," he said, pointing to the inner prison door, "beyond that door a second door awaits you, and beyond that second door, something wonderful, the thing we value the most—freedom. Whether it was right or not right to have you tabbed a suspicious character, within my hospitable walls"—he laughed again—"you've had a taste of the opposite of freedom. All of us, of course, are nothing but prisoners, prisoners of the body, and will be till the day when our soul is freed and rises up to its Creator. Just the same, within my hospitable walls, imprisonment is not just symbolical. I leave you to your freedom, Herr Schrella. . . ."

Schrella, embarrassed, put out his hand, then quickly withdrew it as he saw from the Superintendent's face that handshaking was clearly not included in the formalities. Schrella remained silent in his embarrassment, transferring his cigarette from his right to his left hand, and blinked at Nettlinger.

Those courtyard walls and the sky above them were the last things on this earth which Ferdi's eyes had seen, and perhaps the last human voice he had heard had been the Superintendent's voice, in that same courtyard, a space sufficiently confined to be quite filled by the aroma from Nettlinger's cigar, concerning which the Superintendent's sniffing nose said: By God, you've always known a good cigar, I'll give you credit for that.

Nettlinger left the cigar in his mouth. "You might have spared yourself the farewell spiel. Well, thanks and so long."

He took Schrella by his shoulders, shoved him toward the inner door, which opened in front of them, Nettlinger always slowly shoving Schrella in the direction of the outer door. Schrella stopped, gave his papers to the official, who compared them minutely, nodded and opened the door.

"So there you are," said Nettlinger. "Freedom. My car's over there. Where can I give you a lift?"

Schrella crossed the street beside Nettlinger, and hesitated as the chauffeur held the car door open for him.

"Go on," said Nettlinger, "get in."

Schrella took off his hat, got into the car, sat down, leaned back and watched Nettlinger get in and sit down beside him.

"Where would you like to go?"

"To the station," said Schrella.

"Do you have any baggage there?"

"No."

"Are you thinking of leaving this hospitable city already?" asked Nettlinger. He bent forward and called to the chauffeur, "To Central Station."

"No," said Schrella, "I wasn't thinking of leaving this hospitable city yet. Were you able to get in touch with Robert?"

"No," said Nettlinger, "he is keeping out of sight. I've been trying to contact him all day, but he's very elusive. I nearly caught him in the Prince Heinrich Hotel, but he vanished through a side exit. I've had some highly embarrassing experiences because of him."

"You've never run into him before either?"

"No," said Nettlinger, "not once. He stays strictly by himself."

The car stopped at a traffic signal. Schrella took off his spectacles, wiped them with his handkerchief and leaned over toward the window.

"You must find it strange," said Nettlinger, "to be back in Germany again after such a long time and under such circumstances. You won't recognize it."

"I recognize it," said Schrella, "more or less the way you recognize a woman you loved when she was a girl, and see again twenty years later. Grown rather fat. Glands working overtime. Obviously married to not only a rich but a hardworking man. Villa on the edge of town, a car, rings on her fingers. Under such circumstances early love unavoidably leads to irony."

"Pictures like that are somewhat distorted, of course," said Nettlinger.

"They're pictures," said Schrella, "and maybe if you had three thousand of them you'd see a scintilla of the truth."

"I doubt whether you've got things in focus. Twenty-four hours in the country, of which twenty-three in prison."

"You wouldn't believe how much you can learn in prison about a country. In your prisons the most common offense is fraud. But self-deception is unfortunately not regarded as a crime. Perhaps you didn't know I've spent four of the past twenty-four years in prison?"

The car inched forward in the long line of cars which had piled up behind the traffic signals.

"No," said Nettlinger, "I wasn't aware of that. In Holland?"

"Yes," said Schrella, "and in England."

"What did you do?"

"Emotionally disturbed conduct due to disappointed love. But nothing idealistic in it. I was battling something real."

"Care to go into it?" asked Nettlinger.

"No," said Schrella, "you wouldn't understand and you'd take it for a compliment.

"I threatened a Dutch politician because he said all Germans should be killed—a highly popular politician. Then the Germans freed me when they occupied Holland, thinking I was some kind of a martyr for Germany. However, they found my name on their list of wanted persons, and I fled from their love to England. There I threatened an English politician because he said all Germans should be killed and only their works of art saved—a highly popular politician. But soon they let me out on probation, thinking my feelings should be respected, feelings I hadn't felt at all when threatening the politician—thus one gets locked up because of a misunderstanding, and because of a misunderstanding one is set free."

Nettlinger laughed. "If you collect pictures, let me contribute one. How about this one? Ruthless political hatred among schoolmates. Persecution, interrogation, flight and hate enough to kill. But twenty-two years later, the returning refugee rescued from jail by, of all people, the persecutor, the monster. Doesn't that picture deserve a place in your collection, too?"

"It isn't a picture," said Schrella, "it's an anecdote, one which has the drawback of being true—but if I translated it into abstract image and interpreted it for you, you'd hardly be flattered."

"It certainly is strange," Nettlinger said softly, taking the cigar out of his mouth, "that I should be pleading for understanding, but believe me, when I read your name on the Wanted List and checked the report and learned they really had arrested you at the frontier, I didn't hesitate an instant to get everything going for your release."

"I'd be sorry if you thought I doubted the sincerity of your motives and feelings," Schrella said. "I don't even doubt your remorse, but pictures—since you asked me to put the anecdote in my collection—involve an abstract idea, namely the part you played then, and the part you play today. The parts—forgive me—are the same, because then the way to keep me harmless was to lock me up, whereas today the way to keep me harmless is to set me free. I'm afraid that's why Robert, who has more of an abstract mind than I have, doesn't care to meet you. I hope you understand me—even at that time I never doubted the sincerity of your personal motives and feelings; you can't understand, don't even try; you didn't play your part knowingly—you'd be a cynic or a criminal—and you're neither."

"Now I really don't know if you're paying me compliments, or the opposite."

"Something of both," Schrella said, laughing.

"Perhaps you don't know what I did for your sister."

"Did you protect Edith?"

"Yes. Vacano wanted to have her arrested. He put her name on the list again and again, and again and again I took it off."

"Your good deeds," said Schrella, "are almost more terrible than your bad ones."

"And you're more merciless than God. He forgives the sins of the repentant."

"We're not God and can't any more measure up to His mercy than to His omniscience."

Nettlinger leaned back, shaking his head. Schrella took a cigarette from his pocket, put it in his mouth and again was startled as Nettlinger's lighter suddenly clicked in front of his nose and the clean light-blue flame nearly singed his lashes. 'And your politeness,' he thought, 'is worse than your rudeness ever was. Your always wanting to be Johnny-on-the-spot is the same now as it always was. It was that way when you threw the ball in my face. It's the same now when you offer me a light for my cigarette in an annoying way.'

"When can Robert be reached?" he asked.

"Probably not until Monday; I couldn't find out where he's spending the weekend. And his father and daughter are away, too. You might try his apartment this evening, or tomorrow morning at nine-thirty in the Prince Heinrich Hotel. He always plays billiards there between nine-thirty and eleven. I hope they weren't too rough on you in prison?"

"No," said Schrella. "Everything according to Hoyle."

"Let me know if you need money. You won't get far with what you've got."

"I think it'll last till Monday. I'll get some then."

The line of cars grew longer and wider on the way to the station. Schrella tried to open the window; after an unsuccessful struggle with the handle Nettlinger leaned across him and wound the window down.

"I'm afraid," he said, "the air coming in is no better than the air in here already."

"Thank you," said Schrella. He looked at Nettlinger, transferred his cigarette from left hand to right, and right to left again. "Tell me," he said, "the ball Robert hit that time—was it ever found? Do you remember?"

"Yes," said Nettlinger, "of course I do; I remember very well, there was so much talk about it afterwards. They never found the ball. They looked for it that evening till late into the night and even the following day, in spite of its being a Sunday. They couldn't get over it. Later on someone claimed it had only been a trick of Robert's and he hadn't hit the ball at all, only faked the noise of the strike and hidden the ball somehow."

"But they all saw the ball go in the air, though—or didn't they?"

"Of course, no one believed the business about hiding the ball. Others said it must have landed in the brewery yard in a beer truck standing there. You may remember a truck came out soon after."

"That was before, long before Robert hit the ball," said Schrella.

"I think you're mistaken," said Nettlinger.

"No, no," said Schrella, "I was standing there waiting and watching everything carefully; the truck came out before Robert hit the ball."

"All right, then," said Nettlinger. "In any case, they never found the ball. Here's the station. Won't you really let me help you?"

"No, thank you, I don't need anything."

"May I at least invite you to have a meal with me?"

"Fine," said Schrella, "let's go and have a meal."

The chauffeur held the door open and Schrella got out first, waiting, hands in pockets, for Nettlinger, who took his brief case from the seat, buttoned his overcoat and said to the chauffeur, "Call for me at the Prince Heinrich Hotel towards half-past five, please." The chauffeur touched his cap, and got back into the driver's seat.

Schrella, with his spectacles, sloping shoulders, strange, smiling mouth, blond hair not yet grown thin, with only a light silver sheen and still combed straight back. The same gesture, when he wiped sweat off his face and put his handkerchief back in his pocket. Schrella seemed unchanged, hardly grown older at all, a couple of years or so.

"Why did you come back?" asked Nettlinger quietly.

Schrella looked at him, blinking, the way he had always done, teeth biting into his lower lip; cigarette in his right hand, hat in his left. He looked long at Nettlinger, and waited, waited still in vain for what, during more than twenty years, he had longed for: hatred. For the tangible thing he had always wanted, striking someone in the face or kicking them in the arse, and shouting, 'Bastard, you miserable bastard.' He had always envied people who were capable of such simple feelings, yet he could not strike the round, self-consciously smiling face, or give the man's backside a kick. A leg stuck out on the school's step so he would go crashing down and drive the bow of his glasses into his ear lobe; waylaid on the way home, dragged into doorways and beaten up; he and Robert beaten with barbed whips; given the third degree. There he was, guilty of Ferdi's death—and of protecting Edith and setting Robert free.

He looked away from Nettlinger to the station square, teeming with people. Sun, weekend, taxis waiting and ice cream vendors, hotel boys in violet uniforms lugging suitcases this way behind guests. St. Severin's majestic gray façade, the Prince Heinrich Hotel, the Cafe Kroner. He gave a start, as Nettlinger suddenly ran off and plunged into the crowd, waving and calling, "Hello, there, Miss Ruth!" then came back, shaking his head.

"Did you see that girl?" he asked, "the one with the green beret and the pink pullover? She's strikingly pretty—Robert's daughter. I couldn't catch her. She could have told us where to find him. Pity—did you see her?"

"No," said Schrella softly. "Edith's daughter."

"Of course," said Nettlinger, "your niece. Hell—let's go and eat."

He walked along over the station square, crossed the street, Schrella following him, to the Prince Heinrich Hotel; a bellboy in a violet uniform held the door open for them. It swung back again in their wake, into its felt-lined frame.

"By the window?" asked Jochen. "Certainly. Not too much sun? Then the east side. Hugo, make sure the gentlemen are given a place on the east side. Not at all." Tips gratefully accepted here. One mark is a round and honorable coin, tips the soul of the profession, and *I did win after all,* my friend, you didn't get to see him. What's that, please, does Dr. Faehmel play billiards on Sundays too? Schrella? For heaven's sake! This time I needn't look at the red card. "Good God, Mr. Schrella, you'll forgive an old man a free way of talking at this quiet time of day! I knew your father well, very well; yes, he worked with us for a year, he did; that was the year they held the German Athletics and Sports Festival; do you actually remember it? Of course, you must have been round about ten or eleven by then. Here's my hand, it's a privilege to shake hands with you. My God, they'll forgive me a few feelings which as it were don't go with my job. I'm old enough to get away with that. He was a serious man, your father, a man of dignity. He never took any back talk from anyone, good God no, but when anybody was nice to him he was like a lamb. I've often thought about your father. Forgive me for opening old wounds—I clean forgot, good heavens; what a blessing those pigs have no more say over here. But be careful, Mr. Schrella, watch out; sometimes I think: *they did win after all.* Careful. Don't trust this state of affairs—and forgive an old man a few off-the-cuff feelings and remarks. Hugo, the very best table for the gentlemen on the east side, the very best. No, Mr. Schrella, Dr. Faehmel doesn't play billiards on Sundays, no, never on Sundays. He'll be very glad, you were childhood friends, weren't you, had a lot in common? Don't think everybody forgets. If he should show up here for any reason, I'll let you know, if you'll leave your address here with me. I'll send you a message or a telegram. Or call you up, if you like. We do anything for our customers, you know."

Hugo remained expressionless. Guests to be recognized only on their initiative. Shouting in the billiard room? Discretion. A barbed-wire whip? No, uncalled-for intimacies and conjectures should be avoided. Discretion the watchword of the profession. The menu? Here, please, gentlemen. Do the gentlemen like their table? East wall, window seats, not too much sun? Overlooking St. Severin's and the East Chancel, early Romanesque, eleventh or twelfth century, built by the Holy Duke Heinrich the Fierce. Yes, gentlemen, hot meals all day long. Every dish on the menu served from 12 A.M. to 12 P.M. The best à la carte? You're celebrating a reunion? A brief confidential smile befitting such confidential information; only don't think; Schrella, Nettlinger, Faehmel; no conjectures; scars on the back? Yes, the waiter's coming now and he'll take your order.

"Will you have a martini, too?" asked Nettlinger.

"Yes, please," said Schrella. He gave the boy his coat and hat, passed his hands through his hair and sat down. There were only a few guests in the room, in the corner at the back, murmuring softly to one another. Gentle laughter, underscored by the clink of glasses. Champagne.

Schrella took the martini from the tray the waiter proffered him and waited until Nettlinger had taken his, then raised his glass, nodded to Nettlinger and drank. Nettlinger seemed to have aged in an incongruous way. Schrella remembered Nettlinger as a stunning blond youth whose brutal mouth had always retained a hint of good nature. Who had effortlessly been able to do four and a half feet in the high jump and run the hundred meter in 11.5 seconds. A brutal, good-natured winner, but clearly, Schrella thought, winning hasn't made you happy. Poor education, poor nutrition and no style. Probably eats too much. Already half bald, the sentimentality of age already in the moist eyes. Nettlinger, tightening his mouth professionally, bent over the menu, his white cuffs sliding back to reveal a gold wrist watch, on his third finger a wedding ring. Good God, thought Schrella, even if he hadn't done all he did, Robert would have little desire to go out drinking beer with him or take his children out to Nettlinger's suburban villa for family badminton games.

"May I make a suggestion?" asked Nettlinger.

"Please," said Schrella, "by all means."

"Here then," said Nettlinger, "there's excellent smoked salmon as hors d'oeuvre, followed by chicken with *pommes frites* and salad. And I propose we don't decide on the dessert till afterwards. With me, you know, an appetite for dessert only develops during the meal; then I trust my instinct to tell me whether I should have cheese, a cake, an ice cream or an omelette. I'm only sure of one thing in the beginning—coffee." Nettlinger's voice sounded as if he had taken a course on *How to Become a Gourmet*. He still could not bear to interrupt the well-rehearsed ritual, and was murmuring to Schrella, *"Entre-côte à deux,* blue trout, veal *médaillon."*

Schrella watched Nettlinger's finger solemnly go down the list of dishes, stopping at certain items—a smack of the lips, a headshake, indecision—"I always weaken when I read *poularde."* Schrella lit himself a cigarette, glad to have avoided Nettlinger's lighter this time. He sipped at his martini again and let his eyes follow Nettlinger's index finger, which had arrived at the desserts. Their confounded thoroughness, he thought, ruins your appetite even for something good and sensible like roast chicken; they just have to do everything better, and they are evidently well on the way to topping even the Italians and the French in the art of epicurean indulgence.

"Please," he said, "I'll stick to chicken."

"And smoked salmon?"

"No, thank you."

"You're missing something really tasty there. And you must be hungry as a horse."

"I am," said Schrella, "but I'll make up on the dessert."

"Up to you."

The waiter brought another two martinis on a tray that must have cost more than a night's lodging. Nettlinger took one glass from the tray, passed it to Schrella, took his own, leaned forward and said, "Here's to your special health and prosperity."

Schrella said, "Thank you," nodded and drank. "One thing still isn't clear to me," he said. "How was it they arrested me right off at the frontier?"

"By rotten luck your name was still on the Wanted List. Attempted murder comes under the statute of limitations after twenty years, and you ought to have been struck off two years ago."

"Attempted murder?" asked Schrella.

"Yes, what you tried with Vacano comes under that heading."

"You know very well I had no part in it; I never even approved of that business."

"So much the better, then," said Nettlinger. "If that's the case there won't be any difficulty at all getting your name definitively struck off the Wanted List. All I could do was vouch for you and arrange for your provisional release. I couldn't have the entry annulled. Now the rest will be merely a matter of form. Do you mind if I begin my soup?"

"Not at all," said Schrella.

He looked away toward the station while Nettlinger ladled his soup from the silver bowl. The pale yellow lumps of marrow in the soup undoubtedy came from the noblest breed of cattle which had ever grazed on German pastures; the smoked salmon on the tray gleamed golden between the green lettuce leaves, the toast was gently browned and silvery drops of water clung to the pats of butter. Yet the sight of Nettlinger eating caused Schrella to fight down a wretched feeling of compassion. He had always thought of eating as an act of great brotherliness, in humble or in grand hotels a feast of love. Having to eat alone had always seemed to him like a curse, and the sight of men eating alone, in waiting rooms and breakfast rooms and the countless boardinghouses in which he had lived, had always been for him a vision of damnation. He had always sought company at meals, sitting for preference near a woman. Just the few words exchanged as he broke a roll of bread, the smile across the soup plate, the objects passed from hand to hand, made the purely biological operation bearable and pleasurable. Men like Nettlinger, whom he had watched in infinite number, reminded him of men condemned, and their meals, of hangmen's meals. Though they knew and observed the customary table manners, they ate without ceremony, in deadly seriousness which murdered their pea soup or their *poularde*. And furthermore felt obliged to note the price of every mouthful they ate. He looked away from Nettlinger toward the station again, reading the huge banner which hung above the entrance: *Welcome to our Homecomers.*

"Tell me," he said, "would you describe me as a Homecomer?"

Raising his eyelids as if emerging from the depths of grief, Nettlinger looked up from the slice of toast on which he was spreading butter.

"That depends," he said. "Are you in fact still a German citizen?"

"No," said Schrella, "I'm stateless."

"Pity," said Nettlinger, bending over his slice of toast again, spearing a morsel of smoked salmon from the dish and laying it on. "If you could manage to prove you had to flee not for criminal but political reasons, you could collect a pretty handsome restitution payment. Would you like me to check into the legal position?"

"No," said Schrella. He leaned forward as Nettlinger pushed back the salmon dish. "Are you going to let some of that marvelous salmon go back?"

"Of course," said Nettlinger. "But really you can't. . . ."

He looked round, shocked, as Schrella took a slice of toast from the plate and, with his fingers, some salmon from the silver dish and laid it on the toast. ". . . you really can't. . . ."

"You haven't any idea of all the things one can do in such a distinguished hotel as this. My father was actually a waiter in these sacred halls. They wouldn't bat an eyelid if you chose to eat your pea soup with your fingers, in spite of its being unnatural and impracticable. But the Unnatural and the Impracticable precisely would cause the least of sensations here, hence the high prices; it's the price of waiters who don't bat their eyelids; but eating bread with your fingers and laying fish on it with your fingers—that is neither unnatural nor impracticable."

Smiling, he took the final sliver of salmon from the dish, separated the slices of toast again and slid the fish between them. Nettlinger was watching him angrily.

"Probably," Schrella said, "you feel very much like killing me now, not from the same motives as in the past, I must admit, but the intention is the same. Now listen to what the son of a waiter has to tell you: a really well-bred man never submits to the waiters' tyranny, and among the waiters, of course, are some who think as well-bred people do."

He ate his sandwich, while the waiter, aided by a busboy, prepared for the main course, setting up complicated constructions on little tables to keep it warm, distributing cutlery and plates, clearing away the dirty dishes; wine arrived for Nettlinger and beer for Schrella. Nettlinger tasted his wine. "Just a shade too warm," he said.

Schrella let them serve his chicken, potatoes and salad, toasted Nettlinger with his glass of beer and watched how the waiter poured the rich, dark-brown gravy over Nettlinger's portion of sirloin.

"By the way, is Vacano still alive?"

"Of course," said Nettlinger, "he's only just fifty-eight, and —you'll doubtless find the word strange in my mouth—he's one of the incorrigible ones."

"Oh," asked Schrella, "how am I to interpret that? Can there really be incorrigible Germans?"

"Well, he is faithful to the same traditions he followed in 1935."

"Hindenburg and the rest? Respectability, loyalty, honor and so on?"

"Exactly. Hindenburg could be the caption for him."

"And the caption for you?"

Nettlinger looked up from his plate, holding his fork firmly in the piece of meat he had just cut off. "If only you could understand me," he said. "I'm a democrat. A democrat by conviction."

He lowered his head to the piece of sirloin again, raised up the fork with the meat speared on it and thrust it into his mouth, touched his lips with his serviette and then, shaking his head, reached for his wine glass.

"What became of Trischler?" asked Schrella.

"Trischler? I can't say I remember him."

"Old Trischler who lived down in the Lower Harbor, where they broke up ships later on. Can't you remember Alois either? He was in our class."

"Oh," said Nettlinger, taking some celery from the dish. "Now I remember. We looked for Alois for weeks without finding him, and Vacano himself interrogated old Trischler, but he got nothing out of him, nothing at all out of him or his wife."

"You don't know whether they are still alive?"

"No. But that district down there was bombed a lot. If you want, I'll see you get down there. Good God," he said softly, "what's going on now, what are you doing?"

"I'd like to go," said Schrella. "Excuse me, but I've got to get out of here now."

He stood up, drank down his beer standing, made a sign to the waiter and, as the latter came noiselessly up to them, indicated the silver platter on which three pieces of roast chicken were still simmering over the spirit flame, in gently spluttering fat.

"Would you please have them wrapped for me," said Schrella, "so the fat doesn't leak out?"

"Certainly," said the waiter. He took the platter off the flame and had begun to go when he turned back again and asked, "The potatoes too, sir—and perhaps a little salad?"

"No, thank you," Schrella said, smiling, "the French fries go soft and the lettuce loses flavor." He looked into the gray-haired waiter's well-groomed face for a trace of irony, but none was there.

Nettlinger looked up angrily from his plate. "All right," he said, "you want to get back at me. I can understand that. But do you have to do it this way?"

"Would you prefer me to kill you?"

Nettlinger made no reply.

"In any case, it's not revenge," Schrella said, "I just have to get out of here, I can't stand it any longer, and I'd have kicked myself for the rest of my life if I'd let that chicken go back. Perhaps you can blame my instinct for economy; if I were sure they permitted the waiters and busboys to eat up leftovers, I'd have left it—but I know they don't allow it here."

He thanked the boy who had brought his coat and helped him on with it, took his hat, sat down again and asked, "Do you know Mr. Faehmel?"

"Yes," said Hugo.

"Do you know his phone number, too?"

"Yes."

"Would you do me a favor and call him up every half-hour, and when he answers tell him a Mr. Schrella would like to see him?"

"Yes."

"I'm not sure there's a phone booth where I'm going, or I'd do it myself. Did you get my name?"

"Schrella," said Hugo.

"Right. I'll ask for you at about half-past six. What's your name?"

"Hugo."

"Thank you very much, Hugo."

He stood up, looked down at Nettlinger, who was taking another slice of sirloin from the dish. "I'm sorry," Schrella said, "that you see revenge in such a harmless act. I wasn't thinking of getting even for a single instant, but perhaps you will understand that I'd like to go now. Matter of fact, I don't want to spend much time in this hospitable city and I still have several matters to deal with. May I perhaps remind you once more of the Wanted List?"

"I'm available to you at any time, of course, officially or unofficially, as you wish."

Schrella took the neatly packed white carton from the waiter's hand and gave him a tip.

"The fat won't leak out, sir," said the waiter. "It's all wrapped in cellophane in our special picnic carton."

"Goodbye," said Schrella.

Nettlinger raised his head slightly and said, "Goodbye."

"Yes," Jochen was saying, "certainly, and then you'll see the sign post: 'To the Roman Children's Graves.' It's open till nine and lit at dark, Madam. Not at all, thank you very much." He came out from behind the desk and hobbled up to Schrella as the boy was opening the door for him.

"Mr. Schrella," he said quietly, "I'll do everything I can to find out how Dr. Faehmel may be reached. In the meanwhile I've learned one thing from the Cafe Kroner. There's a family party there at seven in honor of old Mr. Faehmel, and you'll certainly meet him there."

"Thank you," said Schrella, "thank you kindly," and he knew no tip was called for in this case. He smiled at the old man, and walked through the door, which swung softly back into its felt-lined frame.

eight

The entire width of the autobahn was barricaded by massive signboards. The bridge that had spanned the river at this point had been destroyed, its ramps blown clean off. Rusty wire cables hung down in tatters from the pylons. Signboards ten feet high announced what lay in wait behind them: DEATH. A skull and crossbones, menacing, ten times life size, painted in dazzling white on jet black, made the same announcement graphically to those for whom the word was not enough.

Assiduous students from the driving schools practiced their gear-changing along that dead stretch, grew familiar with speed and ground their gears, backing to the left, backing to the right. And neatly clad men and women, relaxing after work, would stroll along the roadway leading past the golf course and between the small garden plots, and peer at the ramps and the menacing signboards, behind which, seeming to mock at death, the modest little construction workers' huts lay hidden; behind DEATH, blue fumes rising up from the stoves where the night watchmen were warming their lunches, toasting bread and lighting their pipes with splinters of wood. The steps, of bombastic design, had survived destruction and now, on the warm summer evenings, served as seats for weary strollers; from a height of sixty feet, they could watch the progress of work. Divers in yellow suits slid down into the waters, guided the crane hooks to segments of iron or blocks of concrete, and the cranes hauled up the dripping catch and loaded it onto barges. High on the scaffolding and on swaying catwalks, up in crow's nests fixed to the pylons, workmen severed the torn steel girders, their oxyacetylene lamps giving off blue flashes as they cut out twisted rivets and sheared away the remains of tattered cables. In the river, the columns with their transverse buttresses stood like giant empty gates framing acres of blue nothingness. Sirens signaled "Waterway clear," "Waterway blocked," green and red lights went on and off, as the barges carried coal and wood here and there, there and here.

Green river, cheerfulness, soft banks with their willow trees, gaily colored boats, blue flashes from the welding torches. Wiry men and wiry women, serious-faced, carrying golf clubs, went walking over the immaculate turf, behind their golf balls, for eighteen holes. Smoke rose up from the allotments, where bean shoots and pea shoots and discarded stakes were being burned, making sweet-smelling clouds in the sky, like primitive cave paintings, balled together in baroque shapes, then dissolving, against the clear, gray afternoon sky, into tormented figures until a rush of wind mangled them again and swept them away to the horizon. Children went roller skating on the rough-surfaced parking edge, fell down, cut their arms and knees and showed their scratches and abrasions to their startled mothers, extracting promises of lemonade and ice cream. Hands entwined, loving couples went wandering down to the willow trees, where the high-tide mark had long ago been bleached away, where the reed stalks stood and corks and bottles and shoe-polish cans were littered. Barge-men climbed up their swaying gangways onto land, women appeared with shopping baskets on their arms, self-confidence in their eyes; the washing flapped in the evening wind on the spotless barges; green pants, red blouses, snow-white bed linen against the fresh, jet-black tar, gleaming like Japanese lacquer. Parts of the bridge were being hauled from the water, covered in slime and seaweed. In the background the slender gray silhouette of St. Severin's, and in the Cafe Bellevue the exhausted waitress announced: "The cream cake's sold out," wiped the sweat from her broad face and fumbled in her leather purse for change. "Only raisin cake left—no, the ice cream's sold out too."

Joseph held out his hand and she counted the change into it. He put the coins into his trouser pocket and the note into his shirt pocket, then turned to Marianne and with outstretched fingers combed the pieces of reed out of her dark hair and brushed the sand off her green sweater.

"You were so happy about the party," she said. "What's the matter?"

"Nothing's the matter," he said.

"But I feel there is. Is it something else?"

"Yes."

"Don't you want to tell me?"

"Later," he said. "Maybe not till years from now, maybe soon. I don't know."

"Is it anything to do with us?"

"No."

"Really not?"

"No."

"With you?"

"Yes."

"Then it has to do with us."

Joseph smiled. "Of course, since I have to do with you."

"Is it something bad?"

"Yes."

"Is it anything to do with your work?"

"Yes. Give me your comb, but don't turn round. I can't get the fine sand out with my hands."

She took the comb from her handbag and passed it over her shoulder to him; he held her hand for an instant.

"I've always noticed how in the evenings after the workmen have gone you walk along by the big heaps of brand-new stone, and just touch some of them—and I've noticed that yesterday and the day before you didn't do so; I know your hands well. And you left so early this morning."

"I went to get a present for Grandfather."

"You didn't leave early because of the present. Where did you go?"

"I was in town," he said, "the picture frame still wasn't ready, and I had to wait for it. You know the photo, don't you, the one with Mother holding my hand, Ruth in her arms and Grandfather standing behind us? I had it enlarged; I know he's going to like it."

And then I went to Modest Street and waited till Father came out of his office. Tall and straight, and I followed him to the hotel. I waited half an hour in front of the hotel, but he didn't come out and I didn't want to go in and ask for him. I only wanted to see him, and I did see him. A well-groomed gentleman in the prime of life.

He let Marianne go, put the comb in his trouser pocket, laid his hand on her shoulder and said, "Please, don't turn round, one can talk better this way."

"Lie better, you mean," she said.

"Perhaps," he said, "or better still, keep back some things." Looking past her ear he could look over the parapet of the cafe terrace and into the river, and he envied the workman hanging in a basket from the pylon, more than a hundred feet high, branding blue flashes on the air with his welder's torch. Sirens howled and an ice cream vendor went along by the hedge below the cafe, calling, "Ice cream, ice cream," then stopped and smoothed ice cream into crumbly wafers. In the background, St. Severin's gray silhouette.

"It must be something very bad," said Marianne.

"Yes," he said, "it's fairly bad—but maybe not. It's not certain yet."

"Bad inside or outside?"

"Inside," he said. "Anyway I gave Klubringer my notice this afternoon. Don't turn round or I won't say another word."

He moved his hands from her shoulders to her head and held it firmly facing the bridge.

"What will your grandfather say about your giving notice? He was so proud of you, he lapped up every nice thing Klubringer said about you like honey. And the Abbey means so much to him. You shouldn't tell him today."

"They'll have told him already, before he meets us. You know he's coming to St. Anthony's with Father; afternoon coffee before the big birthday party."

"Yes," she said.

"I'm sorry about Grandfather. You know that I like him. He'll certainly be coming out this afternoon, after he's visited Grandmother; anyway, for the time being I can't look at another brick or smell any more mortar."

"Only for the time being?"

"Yes."

"And what will your father say?"

"Oh," he said quickly, "he'll only regret it for Grandfather's sake. He's never been interested in the creative side of architecture, only in the formulas. Wait, don't turn round."

"So it's something to do with your father, I feel it. I'm so excited about seeing him at last; I've already talked to him a few times on the phone. I think I'm going to like him."

"You'll like him. You'll see him this evening at the latest."

"Do I have to go with you to the birthday party?"

"Absolutely. You can't imagine how glad Grandfather will be—and he particularly invited you."

She tried to free her head, but he laughed, held her fast and said, "Stop, we can talk much better this way."

"And lie."

"No—leave unspoken," he said.

"Do you love your father?"

"Yes. Especially since I learned how young he still is."

"You didn't know how old he was?"

"No. I always thought he was fifty or fifty-five—funny, isn't it, I was never interested in his exact age, and I was really shocked when I received my birth certificate yesterday and found out that Father is only just forty-three. It's young, isn't it?"

"Yes," she said, "and you're twenty-two."

"Yes, and until I was two years old I wasn't called Faehmel, but Schrella. Funny name, isn't it?"

"Are you angry with him because of that?"

"I'm not angry with him."

"Then what has he done, for you suddenly to lose all desire to go on building?"

"I don't understand what you mean."

"All right—but why didn't he ever visit you at St. Anthony's?"

"He's obviously not interested in building jobs, and perhaps they went out to St. Anthony's too much as children, you see? Sunday walks you go on with your parents—when you're grown up you only do them again when you definitely feel a need to take a repeat course in Melancholy I."

"Did you ever go on Sunday walks with your parents?"

"Not often, mostly with Mother and my grandparents, but when Father came home on leave he went along with us."

"To St. Anthony's?"

"There too."

"Well, I still don't understand why he never came out to see you."

"He simply doesn't like construction jobs. He's a little

strange, maybe. Sometimes when I come home unexpectedly, he's sitting at the desk in the living room, scribbling formulas on the margins of blueprints—he has a large collection of them—but I think you'll like him."

"You've never shown me a picture of him."

"I haven't any recent ones. There's something touchingly old-fashioned about him, in his clothes and his manners. Correct, charming—much more old-fashioned than Grandfather!"

"I'm so curious about him. Can I turn round now?"

"Yes."

He let go of her head and tried to laugh as she suddenly turned, but his forced smile faded before her round, light gray eyes.

"Why won't you tell me?"

"Because I don't yet understand it myself. As soon as I've understood it I'll tell you. But that could be a long time. Shall we go?"

"Yes," she said, "let's go. Your grandfather will soon be there, don't keep him waiting. If they tell him before he sees you, it would be bad for him—and please promise me you won't drive up to that frightful signboard and stop at the last moment."

"As it happens," he said, "I'd thought of driving through it and crashing down the workers' huts and over the open ramp as if from the deck of a ship and plunging away into the water with the car. . . ."

"Then you don't like me."

"Goodness," he said, "it's only a game."

He helped Marianne up and they went down the steps leading to the riverbank.

"I'm really sorry," Joseph said on the steps, "that Grandfather has to find out today of all days, on his eightieth birthday."

"Can't you spare him?"

"The facts, no—but notification of them, yes, if they haven't already told him."

He unlocked the car, got in, opened the door for Marianne from inside, and put his arm round her shoulders as she sat down beside him.

"Now listen," he said, "it's really quite simple; this stretch is exactly two and eight tenths miles. I need one thousand feet to get up to seventy-five miles an hour—another one thousand to brake, and that's allowing for a generous margin. That leaves just a little over two and four tenths miles, and for that I need exactly two minutes. All you have to do is look at the watch and tell me when the two minutes are up and I have to start braking. Understand? I'd like to see just once what this car can really do."

"It's awfully dangerous," she said.

"If I could actually get up to a hundred ten I'd only need twenty seconds—but then the braking distance would be greater too."

"Please don't," she said.

"Are you scared?"

"Yes."

"All right, I'll let it go. But can I at least get her up to fifty?"

"All right, if it means so much to you."

"At that speed you don't need to look at the watch, I can drive by sight and go over the braking distance afterwards, you see? I'd simply like to know whether the speedometer is accurate."

He started up, drove slowly through the narrow streets of the resort town, quickly past the golf-course hedge and stopped where the road led onto the autobahn.

"Listen," he said, "at fifty I need exactly three minutes; it's really quite safe, but if you're scared get out here and wait for me."

"No, I'm certainly not going to let you drive alone."

"It's really the last time," he said, "perhaps by tomorrow I won't be around here any more and I won't have an opportunity like this anywhere else."

"But you could try it out much better on an open stretch."

"No, it's precisely the necessity of stopping at the sign-board which fascinates me." He kissed her on the cheek. "Do you know what I'm going to do?"

"No."

"I'm going to drive at twenty-five."

She smiled as he started off, but nonetheless she watched the speedometer.

"Now," he said, as they went by the five-mile marker, "keep an eye on your watch and take the time we use to get to the seven-mile marker. I'm driving at exactly twenty-five."

Far ahead, like bars slid in front of the huge gates, she could see the signboards. At first only the size of hurdles, they grew larger and larger, continually and oppressively. What had looked like a black spider materialized into a pair of crossbones, and what had appeared to be a curious knob became a skull, rising up as the word rose up, and rushing down on her, seeming nearly to touch the radiator. DEATH, and the speedometer needle flickering between 70 and 80, children on roller skates, men and women, no longer relaxed, went flying past, their arms raised in warning, their voices shrill; they looked like vultures flapping their wings.

"Joseph," she said quietly, "are you really all there?"

"Of course," he said, smiling, "and I know exactly where I am"; he was looking fixedly at DEATH. "Don't worry."

Shortly before quitting time the foreman of the demolition company had called him into the refectory, where a pile of debris was waiting to be shoveled onto a conveyor belt and thence conveyed to a truck. Damp remnants of brick and cement and indefinable rubble had formed sticky lumps. As the pile grew smaller, damp appeared on the walls, first in a dark and then in a light patch. And behind the patch were shades of red, blue and gold, traces of a fresco which the foreman thought were valuable, a Last Supper, blotched by the mildew: gold of the chalice, white of the Host, the face of Christ, light-skinned with a dark beard, St. John's brown hair and, "Here, look here, Mr. Faehmel, here's the dark leather of Judas' purse." The foreman carefully wiped away the white patch with a dry cloth, and reverently exposed the picture: a damask tablecloth, the twelve disciples. Feet became visible, edges of the tablecloth, and the tiled floor of the room where the Last Supper had taken place. Joseph smiled and laid his hand on the foreman's shoulder. "It's a good thing you called me; of course the fresco has to be saved. Have everything cleared away and dried out before anything's done with it." He wanted to go, tea had already been poured, it was on the table with bread, butter and herrings; Friday evening, you could always tell by the fish. Marianne had already left Stehlinger's farm on her way to meet him for a walk; and there, just before he finally turned away, he saw the XYZX written down in the corner of the picture, had seen it hundreds of times, being helped at his mathematics homework, Father's X, his Y, his Z; here he saw it again, about the hole that had been blown in the cellar roof, between the feet of St. John and St. Peter. The refectory columns shattered, the supporting vault destroyed, leaving the remains of the wall and the picture of the Last Supper; XYZX. "Anything wrong, Mr. Faehmel?" asked the foreman, touching him on the shoulder. "You look kind of pale—or is it just love?" "Only love," he said, "only love, nothing to worry about, and thank you very much for calling me." The tea had lost its flavor, and so had the bread and butter and herrings. Friday, you could tell it by the fish. Even his cigarette had lost its flavor. He went through all the buildings and round the Abbey chapel into the pilgrims' lodge, looking in all the places where the statically significant points must have been, but he only found one more, one single little X in the guest-house cellar. His handwriting was unmistakable, as unmistakable as his face, his walk, as his smile and the austere grace of his movements when he poured wine or passed bread across the table. His little X. Dr. Robert Faehmel. Architectural Estimates.

"Please, please," said Marianne, "wake up!"

"I am awake," he said, and let up on the accelerator, put his left foot on the clutch, his right on the brake and pressed down. Screeching and skidding, the car slid right up to the great DEATH, raising dust as the brakes squealed and excited strollers hurried toward them with arms raised, gesticulating, and a tired night watchman appeared with his coffeepot in his hand, between DEATH and the crossbones.

"Oh God," said Marianne, "why do you have to scare me like that!"

"Forgive me," he said gently, "please forgive me, I simply got carried away." He turned the car rapidly and drove off before anyone could gather round, and did the couple of miles or so at a leisurely pace, steering with one hand and holding the other round Marianne's shoulders, past the golf course where wiry women beside their wiry men struggled toward the sixteenth, seventeenth, eighteenth hole.

"Forgive me," he said, "I really won't do it again," and he turned off the autobahn and drove along between pleasant fields, by the edge of the quiet woods.

XYZ, they were the same letters he had detected on the neat blueprints of postcard size which his father played with in the evenings, like playing cards. Publisher's House at edge of forest—XxX; Annex for Co-operative Welfare Society—YxY; Teacher's house on riverbank—just Y. Between the feet of St. John and St. Peter.

He drove slowly on between fields where the fat beets were already pressing their way up beneath great, green leaves. Behind the stubble fields and meadows they could already see Cossack's Hill.

"Why won't you tell me?" asked Marianne.

"Because I don't understand it myself yet, because I can't yet believe it's true. Perhaps it's only a ridiculous dream. Maybe I'll be able to explain it to you later, but maybe never."

"But don't you want to be an architect?"

"No."

"Is that why you drove up to the signboards like that?"

"Perhaps," he said.

"I've always hated people who don't know what money is," said Marianne, "people who drive around like crazy in cars, up to signboards with DEATH written on them, who upset people without any reason at all and spoil their well-earned walk after work."

"I had a reason for driving like crazy up to the signboard." He slowed down, stopped at a sandy path on the edge of Cossack's Hill, and parked the car under low-hanging pine branches.

"What do you want here?" she asked.

"Come on," he said, "let's walk a bit more."

"It'll be too late," she said, "your grandfather's sure to come on the four-thirty train. It's four-twenty already."

Joseph got out and walked a few paces up the hill, held one hand in front of his eyes and looked toward Denklingen.

"Yes," he called out, "I can see the train coming from Doderingen, the same old puff-puff as when I was a child, and the same time too. Come on, they'll wait a quarter of an hour, all right."

He went back to the car, drew Marianne from her seat and up the sandy path. They sat down in a clearing. Joseph pointed to the plain, following the train with his finger as it went through beet fields and between meadows and fields of stubble up to Kisslingen.

"You can't imagine," he said, "how well I know those villages. How often we came out on that train. After Mother died we were almost always in Stehlingen or Goerlingen, and I went to school in Kisslingen. In the evening we ran to the train to meet Grandfather coming from the city, to that train there; look, now it's leaving Denklingen. Funny, I always had the feeling we were poor. While Mother was alive and Grandmother lived with us we had less to eat than the other children we knew, and I was never allowed to wear good clothes, only cut-down things—and we had to look on while she gave away the good things to strangers, and the bread and butter and honey from the Abbey and the estates; we had to eat imitation honey."

"Didn't you hate your grandmother?"

"No, and I don't know myself why I didn't hate her for such foolishness. Perhaps because Grandfather took us to his studio with him, and gave us good things on the sly. He took us to the Cafe Kroner too, and fed us up to the neck. He used to say, 'It's a big thing that Mother and Grandmother are doing, very big—but I don't know whether you're big enough yet for that kind of bigness.' "

"Did he really say that?"

"Yes," Joseph laughed. "When Mother died and Grandmother was taken away we were alone with Grandfather, and then we had enough to eat. We were almost always in Stehlingen during the last years of the war. I heard them blow up the Abbey one night. We were in Stehlingen, crouching in the kitchen, and the farmers from the neighborhood were cursing the German general who had given the demolition order, and they were murmuring to themselves, *whywhywhy*. Father came to visit me a few days later, in an American car escorted by an American officer, and was allowed to stay with us for three hours. He brought us chocolate, and it scared us, that sticky, dark-brown stuff; we'd never eaten it before and would only eat it then after Mrs. Kloschgrabe, the caretaker's wife, had tasted it first. Father brought coffee for Mrs. Kloschgrabe, and she said to him, 'You needn't worry, Doctor, we are looking after the children as if they were our own,' and she said, 'What a shame they blew up the Abbey like that, so near to the end of the war,' and he said, 'Yes, it's a shame, but perhaps it was God's will,' and Mrs. Kloschgrabe said, 'There are some who do the Devil's will as well,' and Father laughed, and the American officer laughed, too. Father was kind to us, and for the first time I saw him cry, when he had to leave us again; I hadn't believed he could cry. He'd never said much or showed his feelings. Even when he had to go back from leave and we went to the station with him, he never cried. We all cried, Mother and Grandmother, Grandfather and us, but he, never—there," said Joseph, pointing to the streamer of smoke from the train, "they've just got to Kisslingen."

"Now he's going to go into the Abbey and find out what you ought to have told him yourself."

I wiped away the letters chalked between St. John and St. Peter's feet, and the little X in the guest-house cellar. He would never find it, and never find out, never find out from me.

"For three days," he said, "the front was spread out between Denklingen and the city, and in the evenings we prayed with Mrs. Kloschgrabe for Grandfather's safety. Then one evening he came back from the city, pale and sad as I'd never seen him before, and walked through the rubble of the Abbey with us, mumbling what the peasants were mumbling, what Grandmother had always muttered in the air-raid shelter, *whywhywhy.*"

"How happy he must be that you're helping to rebuild the Abbey."

"Yes," said Joseph, "but I can't prolong that happiness. And don't ask me why."

He kissed her, drew her hair behind her ears and with outspread fingers combed out the pine needles and the grains of sand.

"Soon Father came out of prison and took us into the city, even though Grandfather protested and said it would be better for us not to grow up among the rubble, but Father said, 'I can't live in the country, and I want the children with me now, I hardly know them.' We didn't know him either and at first we were scared of him, and we sensed that Grandfather was scared of him, too. We were living at the time in Grandfather's studio, for our house was unlivable, and there was a huge plan of the city hanging on the studio wall. All that had been destroyed was marked on it in heavy black chalk, and when we did our homework at Grandfather's draughting table we often listened when Father and Grandfather and other men were standing in front of the map. They often used to quarrel, for Father always said, 'Away with it—blow it up,' and drew an X over the black spot, and the others would say, 'For God's sake, we can't do that,' and Father said, 'Do it, before people come back into the city—there's no one living there now so you needn't worry, tear it all down.' And the others said, 'But there are the remains of a lintel from the sixteenth century, and there's still part of a chapel from the twelfth,' and Father threw his black chalk down and said, 'All right, do as you wish, but let me tell you, you'll regret it—do as you wish, but then do it without me.' And they said, 'But my dear Faehmel, you're our best demolition expert, you can't leave us in the lurch,' and Father said, 'But I am leaving you in the lurch if I have to worry about every chicken-run from the time of the Romans. Walls are walls as far as I'm concerned, and believe you me there are good ones and bad ones. Away with all the rubbish. Blow it up and make some breathing space.' When they'd gone, Grandfather laughed and said, 'My God, you really ought to understand their feelings,' and Father laughed. 'I do understand their feelings, but I don't respect them.' And then he said, 'Come on, children, we're going to buy some chocolate,' and he took us to the black market, bought cigarettes for himself and chocolate for us, and we crept into gloomy, half-destroyed doorways with him, and climbed up stairways, because he also wanted to buy cigars for Grandfather. He always bought, but never sold. When we got bread or butter from Stehlingen or Goerlingen we always had to take his share to school with us, and he let us give it to anyone we wanted; and once we bought some butter we had given away, bought it back on the black market. Mrs. Kloschgrabe's note was still on it; she had written, 'Sorry, only a kilo for you this week.' But Father only laughed and said, 'Oh well, people need money for cigarettes too.' The Mayor came again and Father said to him, 'I've found some four-teenth-century fingernail dirt in the rubble of the Franciscan Monastery. Don't laugh. It's demonstrably fourteenth-century since it's mixed with some fiber, the remains of a woolen yarn *demonstrably* produced only in our city during the fourteenth century. An absolutely unique historical relic, Mr. Mayor.' And the Mayor said, 'Really Mr. Faehmel, you're going too far,' and Father said, 'I'll go farther, Mr. Mayor.' Ruth laughed; she was sitting beside me scribbling her sums in her exercise book; she laughed aloud, and Father came over to her, kissed her on the forehead and said, 'Yes, it is a joke, sweetheart,' and I was jealous because he'd never yet kissed me on the forehead. We loved him, Marianne, but we were still a little scared of him, when he stood there with his black chalk in front of the city plan and said, 'Blow it up—get rid of it.' He was always strict where my homework was con-cerned. He used to say to me, 'There are only two possibilities: either know nothing or everything. Your mother knew nothing, I don't think she even finished elementary school, and yet I would never have married anyone else, so make up your own mind.' We loved him, Marianne, and when I realize he can't have been much more than thirty at the time, I can't believe it, for I always looked on him as being much older, even though he didn't look old at all. He even joked at times, which he doesn't do any more today. When we all crawled out of bed in the mornings he would already be standing at the window, shaving, and used to call to us, 'The war's over, kids,' although the war had been over at least four or five years by then."

"We ought to go now," said Marianne, "we can't keep them waiting such a time."

"Don't worry, let them wait," he said. "I still want to know all about what they did to you, little lamb. I hardly know anything about you."

"Little lamb?" she said. "What made you say that?"

"It just came to me," he said. "Tell me what they did to you. It always makes me laugh when I hear the Doderingen accent in your voice. It doesn't go with you, and all I know is that you went to school there but that you weren't born there, and that you help Mrs. Kloschgrabe with the baking and cooking and ironing."

She drew his head down onto her lap, covered his eyes and said, "To me? Do you really want to know what they did to me? They threw bombs at me and didn't hit me, although the bombs were so big and I so small. The people in the air-raid shelter put tidbits in my mouth and the bombs fell and didn't hit me; I only heard how they exploded, and the shrapnel whizzed through the night like fluttering birds, and someone in the air-raid shelter sang, 'The wild geese rush through the night.' My father was big, very dark and handsome; he wore a brown uniform with a lot of gold on it, and a kind of sword at his belt that glittered silver. He fired a bullet into his mouth, and I don't know if you've ever seen anyone who's fired a bullet into his mouth? No, I suppose not. Then thank God you've been spared the sight. He lay there on the carpet, the blood flowing over the Turkish colors, over the Smyrna pattern—genuine Smyrna, my dear. My mother, however, she was big and blonde and wore a blue uniform with a smart little hat, but no sword at her hip. And I had a small brother, much smaller than I was, and blond, and my small brother dangled in the doorway with a rope round his neck, and I laughed, and went on laughing while my mother put a rope noose round my neck too, murmuring to herself, *He ordered me to,* but then a man came in, without any uniform or gold braid or sword; he only had a pistol in his hand which he pointed at my mother, and wrenched me out of her hands, while I cried because I had the noose round my neck already and wanted to play the game they had let my little brother play up there, the *He ordered me to* game, but the man put his hand over my mouth, dragged me downstairs, took the noose off my neck and lifted me into a truck. . . ."

Joseph tried to take her hands away from his eyes, but she held them fast and asked, "Don't you want to hear any more?"

"Yes," he said.

"Then you must let me hold your eyes shut and you can give me a cigarette."

"Here in the woods?"

"Yes, here in the woods."

"Take one out of my shirt pocket."

He felt her unbuttoning his shirt pocket and taking out the cigarettes and matches, while her right hand held his eyes shut.

"I'm giving you one too," she said, "here in the woods. At that time I was exactly five years old and so sweet that they even pampered me in the truck, sticking tidbits in my mouth and washing me with nice soap when the truck stopped. And they fired on us with cannon and machine guns but they didn't hit us. We drove for a long time, I don't know how long but certainly for two weeks; and when we stopped, the man who had interrupted the *He ordered me to* game took me with him, rolled me in a blanket and laid me down beside him, in the hay and in the straw and sometimes in a bed, and said, 'Call me Father, go on,' but I couldn't say Father, I had always called the man in the fine uniform Daddy, but I learned to say 'Father.' I said it to the man who had interrupted the game, for thirteen years. I got a bed, a blanket and a mother; she was strict and loved me, and I lived nine years in a nice neat house. When I went to school the priest said, 'Look what we've got here, we've got a real natural genuine little heathen-child,' and all the other children, none of whom were heathens, laughed and the priest said, 'But we'll very soon make a little child of Christ out of our little heathen-child, out of our good little lamb.' And so they made me into a little child of Christ. And the little lamb was good and happy, played ring-around-the-rosy and hopscotch and later on played skip-rope and basketball and loved her parents very much. Then one day in school a few tears were shed, a few speeches were made and some allusion to *a new threshold of life,* and little lamb was apprenticed to a dressmaker and learned to use needle and thread very well, and learned from her mother how to polish and bake and cook, and everyone in the village said, 'She'll marry a prince one day, she won't settle for less than a prince,' but one day a very large and very black car drove into the village, and the bearded man at the wheel stopped in the village square and from inside the car asked them, 'Can you tell me where the Schmitzes live, please?' and they said, 'There's a whole lot of Schmitzes here, which ones do you mean?' and the man said, 'The ones that have the adopted child,' and they said, 'Yes, that's the Edward Schmitzes, they live back there, look, just behind the smithy, the house with the box tree in front of it.' And the man said, 'Thank you,' and the car drove on, but they followed him since it was only fifty steps at the most from the village square to Edward Schmitz's. I was sitting in the kitchen cleaning lettuce; I loved doing that, cutting off the leaves, throwing the bad ones away and the good ones into the colander, where they lay so green and fresh, and Mother was saying to me, 'You mustn't let it upset you, Marianne, boys are that way—when they get to thirteen or fourteen, or sometimes even at twelve, they start behaving like that, it's nature, and nature isn't easy to control.' And I said, 'I'm not upset about that.' 'About what, then?' my mother asked. I said, 'I was thinking about my brother, the way he hung there, and I laughed without knowing at all how frightful it was—and he hadn't even been baptized.' And before my mother could answer me, the door opened— we hadn't heard any knocking—and I recognized her straightaway. She was still big and blonde and wore a smart little hat, only she wasn't wearing the blue uniform any more. She came up to me at once, opening her arms and saying, 'You must be my Marianne—can't you feel it in your blood?' I held the knife still for a moment, then trimmed clean the next lettuce leaf and said, 'No, I can't feel it in my blood.' 'I'm your mother,' she said. 'No,' I said. 'She's my mother, there. My name is Marianne Schmitz.' I paused a moment, then said, '*He ordered me to*—and you tied the noose round my neck, Madam.' That was something I'd learned from the dressmaker —address women like that with 'Madam.'

She screamed and cried and tried to put her arms round me, but I held the knife in front of me, point forward. She went on talking about schooling and studies, screamed and cried, but I ran out through the back door into the garden, and across the field to the priest, and told him all about it. He said, 'She is your mother, Nature's rights are Nature's rights; and until you're of age, she has a right to you. It's bad business.' And I said, 'Didn't she give up her rights when she played that *He ordered me to* game?' And he said, 'You're a smart little thing. Remember that argument.' I remembered it and brought it out every time they talked about feeling it in the blood, and I kept on saying, 'I don't feel it in my blood, I simply don't feel it.' They said, 'It's inconceivable, cynicism like that is unnatural.' 'Yes,' I said. '*He ordered me to*—that was unnatural.' They said, 'But that's more than ten years ago, and she's sorry for it.' And I said, 'There are some things you can't be sorry for.' 'Do you,' they asked me, 'intend to be harder than God in His judgment?' 'No,' I said, 'I'm not God, and that's why I can't be as forgiving as He is.' So, I stayed with my parents. But there was one thing I couldn't prevent. My name wasn't Marianne Schmitz any more, but Marianne Droste, and I felt as if something had been cut out of me.—I still think of my little brother," she said softly, "who had to play the *He ordered me to* game—and do you still believe there's something worse, so bad that you can't tell me about it?"

"No, no," he said, "Marianne Schmitz, I'll tell you about it."

She took her hand away from his eyes, and he straightened up and looked at her; she was trying not to smile.

"Your father really can't have done anything as bad as that," she said.

"No," he said, "it wasn't as bad as that, but it was bad enough."

"Come on," she said, "tell me about it in the car, it's almost five o'clock and they'll be waiting now; if I had a grandfather I wouldn't keep him waiting, and if I had one like yours I'd do everything for him."

"And for my father?" he asked.

"I don't know him yet," she said. "Come on. And don't keep it back, tell him as soon as you have an opportunity. Come on."

She pulled him up, and he put his arm round her shoulders as they went back to the car.

nine

The young bank clerk looked up pityingly as Schrella pushed his five English shillings and thirty Belgian francs across the marble counter.

"Is that all?"

"Yes," said Schrella, "that's all."

The young clerk set his adding machine in motion, and peevishly cranked the handle—even the small number of cranks he had to make expressed contempt—jotted a few figures on a form and pushed a five-mark note, four groschen and three pfennigs across the counter.

"Next, please."

"Blessenfeld," asked Schrella quietly, "can you tell me if No. 11 still goes there?"

"Does No. 11 still go to Blessenfeld? This isn't the streetcar information office," said the young clerk, "and in any case I really don't know."

"Thank you," said Schrella, sliding the money into his pocket. He made way at the window for a man who pushed a bundle of Swiss francs across the counter. And heard the handle of the adding machine respectfully begin to make a large number of respectful turns.

'Politeness is really the most effective form of contempt,' he thought.

The railroad station. Summer. Sun. Gaiety. Weekend. Hotel bellboys lugging suitcases toward the platforms. A young woman was holding up a sign: "Travelers to Lourdes assemble here." Newspaper vendors, flower stalls, youngsters with brightly colored beach towels under their arms.

Schrella walked across the square, stood on the traffic island and studied the streetcar schedule. No. 11 still did go to Blessenfeld. There it was, waiting at the red traffic light between the Prince Heinrich Hotel and the chancel of St. Severin's. Then it moved along, stopped, emptied and Schrella joined the line of people waiting to pay at the conductor's box. He sat down, took off his hat, wiped the sweat from his eyebrows, dried the lenses of his spectacles and waited in vain, as the car began to move, for feelings to come to him. Nothing. As a schoolboy, he'd gone back and forth on No. 11 four thousand times, his fingers stained with ink, listening to the other children's silly chatter which had always been a source of appalling embarrassment to him; conic sections, the pluperfect, Barbarossa's beard which went on growing and growing through the table, *Love and Intrigue,* Livy, Ovid bound in gray-green cardboard, and the farther from the city the streetcar went, on its way to Blessenfeld, the quieter grew the chatter. At the edge of the old town, those with the most educated voices had got off, splitting up amid the wide, gloomy streets of substantial houses. Those with the next-best-educated voices got off at the edge of the new town, splitting up amid narrower streets of less substantial houses. Only two or three remained who went all the way to Blessenfeld, which had the least substantial buildings of all. And as the streetcar rocked on past allotment gardens and gravel pits to Blessenfeld, conversation returned to normal. 'Is your father on strike too? They're giving four and a half per cent discount at Gressigmann's. Margarine is five pfennigs cheaper.' There was the park, with the green of summer long since trampled flat, and the sandy strip around the wading pool stirred up by thousands of children's feet and covered with litter, paper and bottle tops. And there Gruffel Street, where the junk dealers' lots were continually filled to overflowing with scrap metal, rags, paper and bottles; where a lemonade stall had been opened up in the midst of wretched poverty, an attempt by a skinny unemployed laborer to set up as a trader. And, before long, he'd got fat and his stall was decked out with chrome and plate glass, and glittering automats had been installed. Getting hog-fat on pfennigs, getting bossy though only a few months before he'd been forced to obsequiously lower the price of a lemonade by two pfennigs, meanwhile whispering anxiously, 'But don't tell anyone else.'

No feelings would come to him as he went rocking on in No. 11 through the old town, the new town, past allotment gardens and gravel pits to Blessenfeld. He had heard the names of the stops four thousand times: Boisserée Street, North Park, Blessischer Station, Inner Ring. They sounded strange, the names, as if out of dreams which others had dreamed and vainly tried to let him share; they sounded like calls for help in a heavy fog, while the almost empty streetcar went on toward the end of the line in the afternoon summer sun.

There on the corner of Park Line and the Inner Ring had stood the stall in which his mother had attempted to set up a fish-fry business, but had been undone by her compassionate heart. 'How can I refuse those hungry kids a bit of fried fish when they see me frying it? How can I?' And Father said, 'Of course you can't, but we must close down the stall, there's no more credit, the dealers won't deliver any more.' Mother had dipped the fillets of fish in egg and breadcrumbs, then let them fry in hot oil while she heaped one, two or three spoonfuls of potato salad on the paper plates. Mother's heart had not remained *firm against compassion*. Tears had welled out of her blue eyes and the neighbors whispered, 'She's crying her heart out.' She ate no more, drank no more, and her plump, full-blooded body changed into a thin, anemic one and nothing remained of the pretty barmaid everyone had loved at the station bar. Now she did nothing but whisper *Lord, Lord,* paging through dog-eared sectarian prayer books that foretold the end of the world, while out on the streets the red flags fluttered in the dusty wind and other people bore Hindenburg's head on placards through the streets. Screaming and violence and shooting, and piping and drumming. When she died, Mother had looked like a girl, anemic and thin. Asters on the grave and a thin wooden cross: Edith Schrella, 1896–1932. Her soul had been sobbed out, and her body mingled with the earth in the Northern Cemetery.

"End of the line, sir," announced the conductor. He climbed out of his box, lit a cigarette butt and walked up front. "Sorry, we don't go any further."

"Thank you." He'd climbed in and climbed out at the No. 11 terminus four thousand times. The rusty rails went on and lost themselves among barracks and old excavations. Thirty years before, there had once been a projected extension of the tram service there. Now, lemonade stalls: chromium, plate glass, glittering automats and orderly rows of chocolate bars.

"A lemonade, please."

The green concoction in a spotless glass tasted of sweet woodruff.

"If you don't mind, sir, put the paper in the basket, please. Taste all right?"

"Yes, thank you." The two chicken legs were still warm, and the tender breast was crispy, baked in the very best quality fat, all preserved in the cellophane pack clipped tight with Special Picnic Insulating Clips.

"That smells pretty good. Want another lemonade with it?"

"No, thank you. But I'll have six cigarettes, please."

He could still recognize, in the plump proprietress, the gentle, pretty girl she once had been. Those blue, childlike eyes, during their First Communion lessons, had moved the romantic chaplain to adjectives such as "angelic" and "innocent," and now they had grown hard and businesslike.

"That'll be ninety pfennigs, please."

"Thank you."

The No. 11 in which he had arrived was ringing its bell for departure. But he hesitated too long, and found himself imprisoned in Blessenfeld for another twelve minutes. He smoked and slowly drank the rest of his lemonade, trying to recall, through that pink and stony face, the name of the young girl she once had been—a blonde, flying through the park with windblown hair, shouting and singing, and enticing boys into dark doorways, after the resemblance to an angel had become a thing of the past; teasing hoarse declarations of love from them, while her brother, no less blond, no less angelic, made vain attempts to summon the street boys to noble deeds; a carpenter's apprentice and a hundred-meter runner, beheaded at dawn for a piece of folly.

"Please," said Schrella, "I'll have another lemonade after all." He stared at the immaculate parting in the plump woman's hair as she bent to hold the glass below the tap of the balloon. Her brother had been the angelic Ferdi. Her own name later on had been hoarsely whispered from youth to youth, from mouth to mouth like a certain password to Paradise. Erika Progulske would help you get rid of your need and *she won't take a thing for it,* because she likes it.

"Do we know each other?" She smiled and set the glass of lemonade on the counter.

"No," he said, smiling back, "I don't think so."

Don't encourage the frozen memory to thaw; such frostflowers would only turn into dull dirty water and run down the pane. Evoke nothing, never expect to bring back childhood's austerity of feeling in adult souls grown soft; you'll just find out that now *she takes something for it.* Careful, just don't start talking.

"Yes. Thirty pfennigs. Thank you." Ferdi Progulske's sister

looked at him with professional friendliness. You gave me relief, too, and *took nothing for it,* not even the bar of chocolate gone soft in my pocket, although it wasn't meant as payment, only as a present, but you wouldn't take it. And you set me free with the compassion of your mouth and hands. I hope you didn't tell Ferdi; part of compassion is discretion, and secrets once turned into words may become deadly. I hope he didn't know, when he saw the sky for the last time, that morning in July. I was the only one he found in Gruffel Street, prepared for noble deeds; Edith didn't yet count, she'd only turned twelve and the wisdom in her heart wasn't apparent as yet.

"Don't we really know each other?"

"No, I'm sure we don't."

You'd accept my present today; your heart has stayed firm, but not in compassion. Already, a few weeks later, you had lost the innocence of childish sin; you'd already made up your mind it was better to get rid of pity, decided you weren't going to be a weeping blonde slut and sob your soul away. No, we don't know each other, we really don't. We won't be thawing out any icicles. Thank you, Goodbye.

There at the corner was still the Blesseneck where Father had been a waiter. Beer, *schnapps,* meat balls, beer, *schnapps,* meat balls, all served with an expression in which mildness and doggedness mingled in a kind of unity, the face of a dreamer to whom it was a matter of indifference whether he served beer, *schnapps* and meat balls in the Blesseneck or lobsters and champagne in the Prince Heinrich or the kind of breakfasts of beer and chops or chocolate and cherry brandy which the whores ate after a night at the Upper Harbor. Father had brought home traces of those sticky breakfasts on his cuffs, brought good tips home, but had not brought home what other fathers brought, after-work good spirits, which could be translated into shouting and teasing, into protestations of love or tears of reconciliation. Always that dogged mildness in his face, a lost angel who hid Ferdi under the taproom table, where the police found him, between the beer pipes. And who, when he knew he was going to die, kept his smile; the sticky stuff was washed out of his cuffs and the waiter's white shirt starched so it was stiff and shining; they came for him only the next morning, as he was going off to work with his sandwiches and his patent leather shoes under his arm. He got into their car *and was not seen again.* No white cross, no flowers for the waiter Alfred Schrella. Not even *shot while attempting to escape—was simply not seen again.*

Edith had ironed and starched, polished the extra pair of black shoes, cleaned the white ties, while I studied, playfully studied—Ovid and conic sections, the thoughts and deeds of Henry the First and Henry the Second and Tacitus, and William the First's and William the Second's thoughts and deeds. Kleist, and spherical trigonometry. Talented, talented, quite unusually talented, a worker's child who had to learn exactly what the others had to learn, in face of four thousand times more obstacles, and dedicated furthermore to noble deeds. I even allowed myself one additional, personal pleasure: *Hölderlin.*

Seven more minutes till the next No. 11 leaves. Here's No. 17 Gruffel Street, redecorated; a car parked in front, green, and a bicycle, red, and two scooters, dirty. He had pressed that bell eighteen thousand times, on the pale, yellowish brass button which his thumb could still feel. Where Schrella once had been, there now was Tressel. Where Schmitz had been, was Humann now. New names. One alone had remained—Fruhl, lending cups of sugar, cups of flour, cups of vinegar and eggcupsful of salad oil, how many cups, how many egg cups, and at what high interest. Mrs. Fruhl would always fill the cups and egg cups half full only, making a mark at the door frame, where she had written in S, F, V, O, only rubbing out that mark with her thumb when she had received full cups and full egg cups in return. Then she'd whispered, 'My God, what fatheads!'—whispered it through the doorways, in shops and to her friends when they gathered to air their old-wives' gynecology, over eggnogs and potato salad. She'd taken the

Host of the Beast very early and had forced her husband and her daughter to swallow it as well, and in the hall she sang, *How weary, weary these old bones.* Nothing, not a bit of feeling, only the skin of his thumb touching that pale yellow brass button felt something resembling emotion.

"Are you looking for someone?"

"Yes," he said, "the Schrellas; don't they live here any more?"

"No," the girl said, "I'd know if they lived here."

She was rosy-cheeked and delightful, balancing on her little swaying scooter and propping herself up against the wall of the building.

"No, they never lived here." Off she went, scampering wildly across the sidewalk, and across the gutter, shouting, "Anyone here know the Schrellas?" He trembled for fear someone would call out yes, and he should have to go over and greet them, and exchange memories: Yes, Ferdi, they got him . . . your father, they got him . . . and Edith, what a fine marriage . . . but the little red-cheeked girl was racing round without success, swerving boldly on her dirty scooter and shouting, from group to group, into open windows, "Anyone here know the Schrellas?" She came back, her face flushed, turned smartly and stopped in front of him. "No sir, no one here knows them."

"Thank you," he said, smiling. "Would you like a groschen?"

"Yes"; she rushed gaily away to the lemonade stall.

"I've sinned, I've sinned greatly," he softly muttered to himself as he walked back to the terminus; "I've had woodruff-lemonade from Gruffel Street with chicken from the Prince Heinrich. I've left undisturbed the memories and not thawed out the frost-flowers. I didn't want to see recognition light up in Erika Progulske's eyes, or hear Ferdi's name from her lips. The only memory celebrated was in the skin at the end of my thumb, when it recognized the pale, yellow, brass bell-push."

It was like running the gauntlet, the eyes so clearly watching him, from the edge of the street, from windows and doorways, while they took the summer sun after the day's work. Would anybody recognize his spectacles or his walk, or the close set of his eyes; would anyone recognize the much-mocked student of Hölderlin, beneath his foreign overcoat, he at whom they had shouted their song of derision, 'Schrella, Schrella, Schrella, he's a poem-reading fella.'

He anxiously wiped the sweat away, took his hat off and stopped, looking back from the corner down Gruffel Street. No one had followed him. A couple of young fellows were sitting on their motorcycles, bending slightly forward and whispering love-talk to the girls standing beside them. Here and there on a window ledge beer bottles caught the afternoon sun. There, across the street, was the house where the angel had been born and raised. The brass doorbell might still be there, where Ferdi's thumb had pressed it fifteen thousand times. The front of the building was green, and there was a gleaming array in the chemist's shop window, with toothpaste advertisements, exactly underneath the window from which Ferdi had so often leaned down.

There was the path through the park, the path from which Robert had drawn Edith into the bushes one evening in July, twenty-three years before. Now there were retired men sitting bent over on the benches, swapping jokes and sniffing different brands of tobacco, peevishly observing that the children playing round them were being badly brought up. And short-tempered mothers were calling a bitter fate down upon their disobedient brood, invoking a terrible future: *The atom'll come and get you.* And young people were coming back from confession, as yet undecided whether to abandon their state of grace on the spot or wait until the next morning.

One more minute still remained before the next No. 11 left. The rusty tracks had been running for thirty years now toward an empty future. Now Ferdi's sister was pouring green lemonade into a clean glass. The motorman was ringing for his passengers. The weary conductor stubbed out his cigarette, straightened his leather satchel, got in behind his cabin and rang the bell, and far back where the rusty rails ended an old woman began breaking into a run.

"To Central Station," said Schrella, "with a Harbor transfer."

"Forty-five pfennigs."

Less substantial buildings, more substantial houses, very substantial houses. Transfer, yes, it was No. 16 that still went to the harbor.

Building material, coal dumps, loading ramps. And from the ramp of the old weighhouse he could read it: "Michaelis, Coal, Coke, Briquettes."

A couple more minutes, around a corner, and he'd be able to complete his remembering. Mrs. Trischler's hands would have withstood time, like the old man's eyes and Alois' photo on the wall. Beer bottles, bundles of onions, tomatoes, bread and tobacco; ships at anchor, swaying gangways down which rolls of sailcloth were carried; giant pupa-shaped vessels would be ready to sail on down the Rhine to the North Sea fog.

Silence lay on the place. Fresh piles of coal were heaped up behind Michaelis' fence, and there were mountains of bright red bricks in the construction-materials yard; nightwatchmen's shuffling feet behind fences and sheds only made the silence greater.

Schrella smiled, leaned over the rusty railing, turned, and got a start. He had not known about the new bridge, nor had Nettlinger told him about it. It swung out, wide, over the old harbor basin, and the dark green pillars stood exactly where Trischler's house had been. Shadows from the bridge were cast out in front where the old tughouse had stood, and the huge, open steel gates rising up out of the water framed blue nothingness.

Father had preferred most of all working in Trischler's tavern, serving the seamen and their wives in the beer garden during the long summer evenings, while Alois, Edith and he went fishing in the old harbor basin. Eternity of a child's time-scale, infinity otherwise encountered only in verse. On the other side of the river the bells of St. Severin's had chimed, chiming peace and confidence into the evening, while Edith traced the bobfly's jerky motion in the air, her hips, her arms and her entire body dancing to the bobbing rhythm; and the fish had not even bitten once.

Father had served yellow beer with white foam, radiating more mildness than doggedness in his face, smilingly refusing every tip because *all men are brothers.* He called it out in the summer evening: brother, brother. Smiles appeared on the seamen's thoughtful faces, and pretty women with confidence in their eyes shook their heads at so much childlike pathos, but clapped their applause nonetheless, brothers and sisters.

Schrella came slowly down from the balustrade and walked along by the harbor basin, where rusty boats and pontoons awaited the junk dealer. He plunged deep into the greenish shadow under the bridge and saw, in the middle of the water, industrious cranes loading bits of the old bridge onto barges, where the groaning scrap iron was crushed beneath the weight of more scrap iron descending on it. He came on the pretentious stairs going up onto the bridge, and felt, walking up them, how the wide steps enforced a solemn pace. With ghostly confidence the neat and empty autobahn rose up toward the river and the bridge, where the signboards stopped confidence short with their giant skull and crossbones, black on white. The way west was barred by signboards reading DEATH, DEATH, while across the endless expanse of shining beet leaves an empty road led out to the east.

Schrella walked on, slipping through between DEATH and the skull and crossbones, past the construction workers' huts, and pacified a nightwatchman who had raised his arms angrily, only to drop them again, appeased by Schrella's smile. Schrella walked on farther, to the edge of the old bridge where rusty reinforcement rods, with lumps of concrete still dangling from them, testified by their fifteen years of unbroken survival to the quality of German steel. Behind the empty steel gates, over on the other side of the water, the autobahn resumed its way again, past the golf course and into the endless expanse of glimmering beet leaves.

The Cafe Bellevue. The promenade. On the right, the playing fields, rounders, rounders. The ball that Robert hit, and then the balls they had struck with their cues in Dutch drinking places, red-green, white-green, the monotonous music of the balls sounded almost Gregorian, and the figures formed by the balls were like some strict poetry, endlessly conjured up to the power of three on the green felt. Never a taste of the *Host of the Beast,* always blindly putting up with the injury inflicted; *Feed my lambs* on suburban fields, where rounders was played, in streets like Gruffel Street and Modest Street, in English suburban streets and behind prison walls. *Feed my lambs* wherever you can find them, even when they haven't anything better to do than read Hölderlin or Trakl, nothing better for fifteen years than write on blackboards 'I bind, I bound, I have bound, I shall bind, I had bound, I shall have bound,' while Nettlinger's children played badminton on well-kept lawns—'The English are really best at that'—while his pretty wife, well-groomed, well-groomed, very well-groomed, called to him from the terrace, where he reclined in his pretty deck chair, 'Would you like a drop of gin in your lemonade?' and he called back, 'Yes, a good, big one!' and his wife, letting out a little giggle of delight at such a witty man, poured him a good big drop of gin in his lemonade and went outside and sat down beside him, in the second deck chair, no less pretty than the first, and passed expert judgment on her oldest daughter's movement at play. Just a shade too thin perhaps, a shade too bony, the pretty face a shade too serious. And now she laid the racket down, exhausted, and went to sit at Daddy's feet, at Mummy's feet, by the edge of the lawn—'Now don't go and catch cold, darling'—and asked, oh so seriously, 'Daddy, tell me, what does it mean, exactly, democracy?' And that was the perfect moment for Daddy to grow solemn, and set down his glass of lemonade, and take the cigar out of his mouth—'Ernst-Rudolf, that makes five today'—and explain to her, 'Democracy. . . .' No, no, I'll not be asking you officially or privately to clarify my legal status. I *don't take anything for it,* I swore the childish oath in the Cafe Zons; I swore to uphold the nobility of defenselessness. Let my legal position remain unclear. Perhaps Robert has clarified it already with dynamite. Wonder whether Robert's learned to laugh in the meanwhile, or at least to smile. Always serious, never got over Ferdi's death. He froze his thoughts of vengeance into formulas and carried them about, lightest of luggage, in his brain, carried them with him for six years, exact formulas, through the sergeants' mess and the officers' mess, without laughing once, whereas Ferdi when they arrested him smiled, that angel from the suburbs, from the hovels of a Gruffel Street. And only a square inch or so of skin on the tip of his thumb had consecrated his memory. A gym teacher's scorched feet. The last lamb killed by a piece of shrapnel. Father *was not seen again,* not even *shot while attempting to escape.* And never again a trace of the ball that Robert hit.

Schrella flicked his cigarette butt into the river, stood up and began sauntering back, slipped through once more between DEATH and the crossbones, nodded to the apprehensive nightwatchman, and then with a last glance back at the Cafe Bellevue went down along the neat and empty autobahn toward the horizon where the beet leaves were glimmering in the summer light. Streetcar No. 16 ought to cross the highway somewhere. One ticket to the station, forty-five pfennigs, including one transfer. He thought longingly of a room in a hotel. He loved the casual aspect of being "at home" in that way, the anonymity of shabby rooms, interchangeable one with another. The icicles of memory would never thaw in rooms like that. Stateless and homeless and in the morning an indifferent breakfast served by a sleepy waiter, his cuffs not quite clean, his shirt front showing no sign of the ardor which Mother had bestowed on such articles. And if the waiter were over sixty, might one not dare ask: 'Did you once have a colleague called Schrella?'

Farther on, along the empty, tidy road, through the glimmering beet-leaf sea, for luggage only his hands in his pockets and his small change strewn along the way, for Hänsel and Gretel. Postcards formed the only bearable contact with that life which still went on, after Edith and Father and Ferdi had died. 'Dear Robert, I am well, hoping you are the same. Regards to the niece I have never met, to my nephew and your father.' Twenty-four words, too many words. Compress the text: 'Am well, hope you are too, regards to Ruth, Joseph, your father.' Twelve words. Say the same using half as many. Why now come back, shake hands and go a whole week without conjugating: I bind, I bound, I have bound; and find Nettlinger unchanged and Gruffel Street unchanged? Mrs. Trischler's hands were missing.

A sky of beet leaves, as if grown over with silvery-green plumage. Down below, the No. 16 was rocking through an underpass. Forty-five pfennigs. Everything more expensive. Nettlinger would doubtless not yet have reached the end of his elucidation of democracy, his voice grown mellow in the late afternoon light, when his daughter would have gone and got the rug from the living-room couch—Yugoslav, or Danish or Finnish, lovely colors, in any case—and laid it over her father's shoulders and kneeled down again, to listen devotedly while in the kitchen her mother . . . 'Yes, please do stay out there, my dears, it's such a lovely afternoon and so quiet and peaceful . . .' was preparing tasty finger sandwiches and mixing a colorful salad.

Imagining Nettlinger produced a more exact picture than the meeting with him, than his way of conveying slices of sirloin to his mouth and drinking the best, the best, the very best wine with it, lost already in meditation on whether cheese or ice cream or cake or an omelette would most fittingly top the meal. 'One thing, gentlemen,' the former legation secretary who gave the course on *How to Become a Gourmet,* had said 'you must add one thing to what you have learned, a breath, just a breath of originality.'

He had written it on the blackboard in England: 'He should have been killed.' Had played the xylophone of language for fifteen years: I live, I lived, I have lived, I had lived, I shall live. Shall I live? He had never understood how there were people who were bored with grammar. He is killed, he was killed, he has been killed, he will be killed. Who will kill him? *Mine is the vengeance,* said the Lord.

"End of the line, sir, Central Station."

The crowd was as big as ever. Which ones were coming, which going? Why didn't they all stay home? When did the train for Ostend leave? Or perhaps to Italy or France. There would have to be someone in those places, too, who would want to learn about I live, I lived, I have lived; he will be killed. And who will kill him?

A room? What price did he have in mind? A cheap one? The young woman's friendliness perceptibly declined, as she ran her pretty finger down the list. Obviously a sin in this country to ask the price. *Always the best—the dearest is the cheapest:* an error, pretty child, the cheapest's the cheapest, in point of fact; just let your pretty finger slide down to the bottom row on that list. 'Pension Moderne.' Seven marks. Without breakfast. "No thank you, I know the way to Modest Street, really, I know No. 16, it's right by the Modest Gate."

As he turned the corner he nearly walked into the wild boar, stepped startled back from the dark-gray animal's massive form and almost went past Robert's house. Memory, here, was in no danger. He had been here only once. Modest Street, No. 8. He stopped in front of the shiny brass nameplate and read: "Dr. Robert Faehmel. Architectural Estimates. Closed Afternoons," and as he pressed the bell, trembled. That which he had not personally witnessed, which had been played with props other than those he knew, had always hit him harder. Edith had died behind this door, and in this house her children had been born, and Robert lived there now. He realized from the sound of the bell ringing inside that no one would open, and heard the ringing of the bell mingling with that of the telephone. The bellboy in the Prince Heinrich Hotel had kept his word. I'll tip him well when we play billiards there.

The Pension Moderne was only four buildings farther on. Home at last. No cooking smells in the tiny hall, happily. Fresh bed linen for a tired body. "Yes, thank you, I'll find it." "Second floor, third door on the left, careful on the stairs, sir, the carpet rods are loose in a few places; some guests have such bad manners. You don't want to be waked in the morning? One more thing, please. Would you pay in advance, or is there more luggage on the way? No? Then eight marks five pfennigs, if you please, service included. Sorry I have to take such precautions, sir, you'd never believe how many bums there are in the world; it makes you distrust respectable people, that's the way it is, and some of them even manage to take out the sheets wound round them, and cut up the pillowcases into handkerchiefs. If you only knew some of the things we see. No receipt? So much the better; they tax me to death as it is. You're probably expecting a visit from your wife, aren't you, I'll send her up, don't you worry. . . ."

ten

His fear had been unfounded: memory did not become feeling, remained formula. It did not disintegrate into bliss or grief and did not strike fear in the heart. The heart was not involved. There he had stood, in the evening twilight, between the guest house and the Abbey, where now stood the heap of violet, hard-fired bricks. And beside him had stood General Otto Kösters, whose feeble-mindedness had been coined into a single formula: field of fire. Captain Faehmel, First Lieutenant Schrit, and the two cadet officers, Kanders and Hochbret. Their faces deadly serious, they had convinced Field-of-Fire Otto that it was imperative not to be inconsistent, even when confronted by such venerable buildings; and when other officers lodged a protest, when tearful murderers spoke soulfully up in defense of cultural heritage which had to be saved, when one of them would utter the evil phrase 'high treason'—no one could argue so sharply, so fluently or logically as Schrit, who put the case for demolition to the General in these persuasive words: 'And if undertaken only as an example, to show we still believe in victory, General, such painful sacrifice would make quite clear to the people and the army that we still do believe in victory,' and back came the old, proverbial answer: 'I have made my decision; blow it up, gentlemen. With victory at stake, we may spare not even our own sacred cultural monuments. Go to it, then, gentlemen.' All saluted and clicked their heels.

Had he ever been twenty-nine, ever been a captain, ever stood on that spot with Field-of-Fire Otto? Where now the new Abbot was smiling and welcoming his father:

"We're so glad, Your Excellency, it's such a pleasure to have you visit us again; I'm very happy to meet your son. And Joseph is almost an old friend of ours already, aren't you, Joseph? The fortunes of our Abbey have always been linked with the fortunes of the Faehmel family—and Joseph has even, if I may inject a personal note—Joseph has even been struck by Cupid's arrow in these precincts. Look, Doctor Faehmel, nowadays young people don't even blush when you talk about such things; Miss Ruth and Miss Marianne, I'm sorry, I have to exclude you from the tour."

The young girls giggled. Hadn't Mother and Josephine and even Edith giggled on that same spot when they were excluded from the tour? All you had to do in the snapshot albums was replace the heads and change the styles.

"Yes, we've already moved into the cloister," said the Abbot. "This is the apple of our eye, the library—round here, please, the infirmary, unoccupied at present, I'm glad to say. . . ."

Never had he here gone from point to point with his chalk, writing his secret combinations of XYZ on the walls, the code for nothingness which only Schrit, Hochbret and Kanders knew how to decipher. Smell of mortar, smell of fresh paint, freshly planed wood.

"Yes, this here was saved from destruction thanks to your grandson's—your son's alertness. The picture of the Last Supper, here in the Refectory. We know perfectly well it's no great work of art—you'll forgive me that observation, Your Excellency—but even the work of this school of painters is beginning to be rare, and we've always felt a responsibility to tradition. I must admit that even today I'm delighted by these painters' fidelity to detail—look here, how lovingly and carefully he has painted the feet of St. John and St. Peter, here the feet of an old man, there the feet of a young man. Accuracy of detail."

No, no one had sung *How weary, weary these old bones* in this place. No solstitial fire. Only a dream. A distinguished gentleman in his early forties, the son of a distinguished father, the father of a vigorous, very intelligent son who was smilingly making the rounds with the rest even though the whole undertaking seemed to bore him very much. Whenever he turned to Joseph he saw only a friendly, somewhat tired smile on his face.

"As you know, not even the farm buildings were spared. We rebuilt them first since it seemed they were the practical requisites for a successful new start. Here's the cow barn. We milk with electricity, of course. You're smiling—I'm quite sure our Holy Father Benedict would have had no objections to electrical milking. May I offer you some refreshment? A token of welcome—our celebrated bread and butter and honey. You may not be aware that every Abbot, when he dies or retires, leaves this word with his successor: Don't forget the Faehmel family. You really do belong to our cloister family—oh, there are the young ladies again. Of course, here they're allowed again."

Bread and butter, wine and honey on simple wooden boards; Joseph had one arm round his sister, and the other round Marianne. A blond head between the two dark heads.

"You'll do us the honor of coming to the consecration? The Chancellor and the Cabinet have accepted, a few foreign dignitaries will be there, and it would be a great pleasure for us to be able to welcome all the Faehmel family as our guests. My official speech will be made not in the spirit of indictment but of reconciliation; of reconciliation also with those powers who, in their blind passion, destroyed our home. But not, of course, reconciliation with those destructive powers which once again are threatening our culture. May I, then, extend our invitation to you, here and now, with our sincere hope that you will do us this honor?"

'I won't come to the consecration,' thought Robert, 'for I'm not reconciled. Not reconciled with the powers guilty of Ferdi's death, or with the ones that caused Edith to die and St. Severin's to be spared. I'm not reconciled, not reconciled either to myself or to the spirit of reconciliation which you in your official speech will proclaim. Blind passion did not destroy your home, hatred destroyed it, which was not blind and does not as yet repent. Should I confess it was I who did it? I'd have to inflict pain on my father, although he is not guilty, and perhaps on my son, although he is not guilty either, and on you, Reverend Father, although you, too, are not guilty; just who is guilty, then? I am not reconciled to a world in which a gesture or a word misunderstood can cost a life.' And aloud he said, "Thank you very much, Reverend Father, it will give me great pleasure to attend your ceremony."

'I won't come, Reverend Father,' thought the old man, 'for I'd only stand here as a monument to myself, not as what I am: an old man who this very morning gave his secretary the assignment to spit on his monument. Don't be shocked, Reverend Father; I'm not reconciled with my son Otto who was my son no longer, only my son's husk, and I can't celebrate my reconciliation to a building, even if I did build it myself. We shan't be missed at the solemnities. The Chancellor, the Cabinet members, the foreign dignitaries and the high ecclesiastical dignitaries will undoubtedly fill the gap in worthy style. Was it you, Robert, and were you afraid to tell me? It was your look and the way you acted during the tour that told me so. Well, it doesn't affect me—perhaps you were thinking of that boy whose name I never learned, the one who pushed your little slips of paper through our letter box—and of the waiter called Groll, and the lambs no one shepherded, not even we. So let's not celebrate any reconciliation. Sorry, Reverend

Father, you'll have to make the best of it, you won't miss us. Hang up a plaque: Built by Heinrich Faehmel in 1908, in his twenty-ninth year; destroyed by Robert Faehmel, in 1945, in his twenty-ninth year—and what will you do, Joseph, when you're thirty? Will you take over your father's architectural estimates office? Will you build or destroy—formulas are more effective than mortar. Strengthen your heart with hymns, Reverend Father, and consider carefully whether you are truly reconciled to the spirit which destroyed the monastery.'

"Thank you very much, Reverend Father, it will give us great pleasure to attend your ceremony," said the old man.

Cool air was already rising from the meadows and lowlands, and the dry beet leaves were becoming damp and dark, promising riches. Behind the steering wheel to the left was Joseph's blond head, and to the right the dark heads of the two girls. The car glided quietly toward the city; was someone out there singing the song, "We've harvested the wheat"? It couldn't be true, any more than St. Severin's slender tower on the horizon; Marianne was the first to speak:

"Aren't you going through Doderingen?"

"No, Grandfather wanted to drive through Denklingen."

"I thought we were going the shortest way to town?"

"If we get to town at six, it'll be early enough," said Ruth. "We don't need more than an hour to change."

The young people's voices sounded muffled, like people buried in underground caverns whispering hopeful words to each other: Look, there's light. You're mistaken. No, really, I can see light. Where? But can't you hear them tapping, it's the rescue team. I don't hear a thing.

It's wrong to get formulas free, put secrets into words, transpose memories into feeling. Feelings can even kill such good hard things as love and hate. Had there really been a captain called Robert Faehmel, who knew the jargon of the casino so well, did all the right things so perfectly, so dutifully invited the senior officer's wife to dance, was so good at proposing toasts in his incisive voice: I give you a toast, in honor of our beloved German people. Champagne, ordnance. Billiards. Red-green, white-green. White-green. And one evening someone was standing opposite him, holding the billiard cue in his hand, smiling and saying, 'Schrit, lieutenant, as you see, a demolition expert like yourself, Captain, defending Western Culture with dynamite.' Schrit had carried no mixed soul about in his breast; he had been able to wait and save his strength, hadn't needed again and again to remobilize heart and feeling, was not one to get drunk on tragedy. He had made a vow to blow up *only* German bridges and *only* German buildings, and not destroy so much as a pane of glass in whatever Russian hut. We waited and played billiards and never talked more than we had to—and finally we came upon it lying there in the spring sunshine, the great prey we had waited for so long: St. Anthony's. And on the horizon the prey that would escape us: St. Severin's.

"Don't drive so fast," Marianne said quietly.

"Sorry," said Joseph.

"Tell me, what are we doing here in Denklingen?"

"Grandfather wants to come here," said Joseph.

"No, Joseph," said Ruth, "don't drive into the avenue, didn't you see the signboard: 'Residents Only'? Or maybe you're one?"

The grand delegation, husband, son, grandchildren and granddaughter-in-law to be, got out at the bewitched castle.

"No, no," said Ruth, "I'm going to wait out here. Please let me."

In the evenings when I sit in the living room with Father, Grandmother could be there. I read and he drinks wine and fumbles in his card indexes, laying the postcard-size prints out in front of him, as if playing solitaire. Father, always correct, tie never loose, waistcoat never unbuttoned, never relaxing into paternal joviality. Restrained and solicitous. 'Do you need books, clothes, money for the journey? Aren't you bored, child? Would you rather go out? To the theater, to the cinema, out dancing? I'd be glad to take you. Or would you prefer to ask in your school friends for coffee again, up on the roof garden, now the weather's so fine?' And before going to bed, the evening walks, round the block, up Modest Street to the Modest Gate, then down Station Street to the station. 'Can you smell the far-off places, child?' And on through the underpass, past St. Severin's and the Prince Heinrich Hotel. 'Gretz has forgotten to wash the bloodstains off the pavement.' Boar's blood turned hard and black. 'It's half-past nine, child, time to go to bed now. Good night.' A kiss on the forehead. Always kind, always correct. 'Would you rather we hired a housekeeper, or aren't you tired of restaurant food yet? Frankly, I don't much like strangers in the house.' Breakfast. Tea, rolls, milk. A kiss on the forehead and, sometimes, in a very low voice, 'Child, child'—'What is it, Father?' 'Come on, we're going away.' 'What, now, right now?' 'Yes, let school be for today and tomorrow, we're not going far. Just to Amsterdam. It's a lovely city, child, and the people are quiet and very kind —you only have to get to know them.' 'Do you know them?' 'Yes, I know them. It's so nice walking along in the evenings by the canals.' 'Glass. Glass. Stillness. Do you hear how quiet the people are here? Nowhere are they as noisy as at home, always bawling and shouting and boasting. Would it bore you if I went and played billiards? Come along if it amuses you.'

I never understood the fascination with which old and young men alike watched him play, when he stood there, amidst the cigar smoke, a glass of beer near him on the edge of the table, and played billiards, billiards. Did they really use the familiar "thou" with him, or was it just a peculiarity of Dutch speech that it sounded like "thou" when they spoke to him? They did know his first name. They rolled the R of Robert like a hard piece of candy on the tongue. Silence. So much glass by the canals. My name is Ruth, half-orphan, my mother was twenty-four when she died. I was three, and when I think of her, I think of seventeen or of two thousand years. Twenty-four is a figure that doesn't suit her; it should rather be something under eighteen or over eighty. She always looked to me like Grandmother's sister. I know that big, well-guarded secret, that Grandmother's crazy, and I don't want to see her so long as she's like that. Her craziness is a lie, grief behind thick walls, I know it, I get drunk on it sometimes myself and swim away in a lie. The house at the rear, No. 8 Modest Street, inhabited by ghosts. *Love and Intrigue,* Grandfather built the monastery, Father blew it up, and Joseph has rebuilt it. All right with me; you'll be disappointed how little it upsets me. I saw them bringing the dead out of the cellars, and Joseph tried to convince me they were sick, and only being taken to the hospital, but does one simply throw the sick onto trucks like sacks? And I saw Krott, the teacher, sneaking into the classroom during recess and stealing Konrad Gretz's sandwiches out of his desk, and I saw Krott's face and was scared to death, and prayed, 'Please God don't let him find me here, please, please,' because I knew he would kill me if he found me. I was standing behind the blackboard looking for my barrette, and he could have seen my legs, but God had mercy and Krott didn't notice me. I saw his face, and I also saw how he bit into the bread, then went out. Anyone who has looked into faces like that doesn't get upset any more about blown-up abbeys. And then the scene afterwards, when Konrad Gretz discovered his loss and Krott exhorted us all to be honest: 'Now children, be honest. I'll give you a quarter of an hour, and the culprit will have to have owned up, or else'—eight minutes more, seven minutes more, six,—and I looked at him, and he caught my eye, and bore down on me, 'Ruth, Ruth,' he yelled. 'You? Was it you?' I shook my head and began to cry, because I was scared to death again. And he said, 'Good heavens, Ruth, tell the truth.' I wanted to say yes, but then he would have seen that I knew, and I shook my head through the tears; four more minutes, three, two, one, time. 'You're a bunch of damnable thieves, a gang of liars. For punishment you can write out "I must not steal" two hundred times.' You and your abbeys. I've had to keep more awful secrets than that and stuck out being scared to death. They threw them on the trucks like sacks.

Why did they have to treat that nice Abbot so coolly? What did he do, did he kill somebody or steal a sandwich from someone? Konrad Gretz had enough to eat, liver paté and herb-flavored butter on white bread. What devil suddenly possessed the teacher's gentle, reasonable face? Murder was crouched between his eyes and nose, nose and mouth, between his ears. They threw the bodies onto the trucks like sacks, and I enjoyed it when Father scoffed at the mayor in front of the big wall map, when he drew marks with his black chalk and said, 'Get rid of it, blow it up.' I love him; I don't love him any the less now that I know about it. Has Joseph at least left his cigarettes in the car? And I also saw how the man handed over his wedding ring for two cigarettes—how many would he have wanted for his daughter, and how many for his wife? The price list was written on his face: ten, twenty, he'd have been ready to discuss it. They're all ready to do business. I'm sorry, Father, but I still like the taste of the honey and bread and butter, even after I know who did it. We'll go on playing father and daughter. Precise as a ritual dance. After the refreshments, there should have come the walk up Cossack's Hill: Joseph, Marianne and me far ahead, and Grandfather behind, like every Saturday.

'Are you all right, Grandfather?'

'Yes, thank you.'

'Aren't we walking too fast?'

'No, don't worry, children. I wonder if I could sit down a little, or do you think it's too damp?'

'The sand's dry as dust, Grandfather, and it's still quite warm, don't worry, you can sit down; here, give me your arm.'

'Of course, Grandfather, light yourself a cigar; we'll see to it nothing happens.'

Luckily Joseph has left his cigarettes in the car, and the lighter works, too. Grandfather gave me such pretty dresses and sweaters, much prettier than those from Father whose taste is old-fashioned. Easy to see Grandfather understands something about girls and women. I don't want to understand Grandmother, I don't want to; her craziness is a lie. She wouldn't give us anything to eat, and I was glad when she'd gone and we were given more. Maybe you're right, maybe she was great and still is, but I don't want to know about greatness. One white-bread sandwich with liver paté and herb-flavored butter nearly cost me my life. Let her come back again and sit with us in the evenings, but please don't give her the key to the kitchen, please don't. I've seen hunger on the teacher's face and I'm scared of it. Dear God, always give them something to eat, always, so the horribleness won't ever come back on their faces. It's a harmless Mr. Krott who gets into his little car Sundays and drives his family out to St. Anthony's to attend High Mass. Today is how many Sundays after Pentecost, how many Sundays after Epiphany, after Easter? A dear man with a dear wife and two dear little children, 'Look, Ruth, hasn't our little Frankie grown?' 'Yes, Mr. Krott, your little Frankie's grown.' And I never think any more about my life hanging by a thread. No. And I also wrote out very nicely two hundred times, 'I must not steal.' And of course I don't say no when Konrad Gretz gives a party; they have wonderful paté de foie gras with herb-flavored butter and white bread, and when someone treads on your toes or spills your glass of wine they don't say, *'Entschuldigen Sie bitte,'* and they don't say, *'Excusez-moi,'* they say, 'Sorry.'

The grass by the roadside ditch is warm, and Joseph's cigarette has a spicy smell, and I still liked the taste of bread and honey after I learned it was Father who blew the Abbey sky-high; Denklingen is lovely back there in the evening sun. They ought to hurry, we'll need at least half an hour to change.

eleven

"Come on over here, General. Don't be embarrassed, they introduce all newcomers to me first. I'm the oldest inhabitant here, in this fine house. Why do you keep hacking away with your walking-stick at our garden soil that never did you any harm, and shaking your head all the time and muttering 'field of fire' at every wall, at the chapel, the hothouse—it's a nice phrase, by the way, 'field of fire.' Make way for bullets and shells. Oh, is it Otto? Kösters? No, no familiarities, name no names; and besides, the name Otto is already being used. So may I call you 'Field-of-Fire'? I can see from looking at you, and can hear from your voice, and smell on your breath, that you've not only tasted the *Host of the Beast,* you've lived on it. Regular diet with you. Listen, new one, tell me, are you a Catholic? Of course, I'd have been surprised if not. Can you serve at Mass? Of course, you were brought up by the Catholic Fathers. Forgive me if I laugh. We've been looking for a new altar boy here for three weeks. They decided Ballosch was cured and let him go. How would you like to make yourself useful a little bit? You're a pretty harmless lunatic, not violent, with your one and only tic of muttering 'field of fire' at every occasion, suitable and unsuitable. You'll surely be able to carry the Missal from the right to the left and the left to the right of the altar. You can manage a genuflection in front of the tabernacle, can't you? You're in splendid health, after all that's part of your profession; you can beat the *mea culpa, mea culpa, mea maxima culpa* on your breast and say the *kyrie eleison*. You see how useful an educated general brought up by Catholic priests can be. I'll tell the sanatorium priest to make you our new altar boy. All right with you, isn't it?

Thank you. You can tell right away when a man's a gentleman. No, round this way, please, this way to the hothouse, I just want to show you something, part of your stock-in-trade. And please, no uncalled-for gallantries; don't work off your dancing-class complexes on me, if you please. I'm seventy-one and you're seventy-three, so no hand-kissing, no senile flirtations, just lay off the nonsense. Now listen. See what's there behind that light green pane of glass? Yes, weapons; that's our good chief gardener's arsenal. It's used for shooting hare and partridge, crows and deer, because our chief gardener's a passionate hunter, and there between the guns and rifles lies such a pretty, handy, black object, a pistol. Now remember what you learned when you were a cadet, or a lieutenant, and tell me, is a thing like that really deadly dangerous, can you really kill somebody with it? Now don't turn pale on me, old warhorse; you've swallowed the *Host of the Beast* by the ton, and now when I ask you a couple of simple questions you turn weak. Don't start trembling, I know I'm a bit crazy, but I'm not going to stick the pistol into your seventy-three-year-old chest and save the State your pension. I've no intention of saving the State anything. I've asked you a clear, military question, so give me a clear, military answer: could that thing kill anybody? Yes? Good. At what range, for the greatest accuracy? Ten yards, twelve, at the very most twenty-five.

Good God, now, don't get so upset! What a timid old General you are! Report me? What's there to report? They've poured so much reporting into you, you can't get it out of your system, can you? Kiss my hand if you have to, but do hold your tongue, and there's a Mass early tomorrow morning, right? They've never had such a fine, handsome, white-haired, well-bred altar boy here before. Can't you take a little joke? I'm only interested in weapons the way you're interested in fields of fire. Don't you realize that one of the unwritten laws in this excellent institution is that we all let each other have our little hobbies? You've got yours, with your field-of-fire tic; be discreet, Field-of-Fire, remember your fine education —*and forward with Hindenburg, hurrah*—there you are, you like that, don't you, just a matter of choosing the right words —let's go round here, by the chapel; wouldn't you like to go in and have a look round the scene of your future operations? Quietly now, old man, you know what to do: hat off, right finger in the font, now the sign of the cross, that's fine, fine. Kneel down now, eyes on the sanctuary light, pray, say one *Ave Maria* and one *Pater Noster*—nice and soft. You can't beat a Catholic education. Stand up, finger in the font, sign of the cross, let the lady go first, hat on. Very nice, here we are again. What a lovely summer evening, lovely trees in the lovely park; there's a bench. *Forward with Hindenburg, hurrah,* you do like that, don't you? How do you like the other one, *got to get a gun, get a gun,* you like that one, too, do you? Let's stop joking, that joke was worn out in any case, *after* Verdun. They were the last knights—killed in battle, too many knights, too many lovers, all at once—too many well-brought-up young people. Have you ever thought of how much pedagogical sweat was wasted in the space of a few months? All in vain. How was it none of you ever had the idea of setting up a machine gun at the entrance of the trade schools and colleges, right after the exams, and shoot dead all those radiant successful graduates? You think that's exaggerated? Well, then let me say that the truth is pure exaggeration. I danced with the graduates of 1905, 1906 and 1907. They wore their caps, they drank their beer and I drank with them at their student parties—but more than half the students of those three years fell at Verdun. And how many do you think are left of all who graduated in 1935, or 1936 or 1937? Or in 1941 or 1942? Pick any year you like. And don't start shaking again—I'd never have thought an old General like you could be so nervous. No, don't do this; don't put your hands in mine—what's my name? Remember, you don't ask that kind of question here, no one here keeps visiting cards, we don't ask each other out for drinks and a chat; here, we call each other by our first names and no further questions. All of us here know that all men are brothers, even if they be hostile ones. Some have tasted of the *Host of the Lamb,* only a few of us of the *Host of the Beast,* and my name is *got to get a gun, get a gun,* and my Christian name is *forward with Hindenburg, hurrah.* Forget all your bourgeois prejudices for good, your conversational clichés; here the classless society rules. And stop complaining about losing the war. Good heavens, did you really lose two wars, one after the other? You could have lost seven for all of me. Stop your sniveling, I wouldn't give five cents for all the wars you lost; losing children is worse than losing wars. You can be an altar boy here in the Denklingen Sanatorium, it's a highly respectable occupation, and don't make speeches to me about the German future. I read about it in the newspapers: the German future is all pegged out. If you have to weep, don't blubber. So they've been unjust to you, too? Impaired your honor, yes, what's the use of honorableness when any stranger can make dents in it? But now relax, in this booby hatch they take care of you fine, in this place they go into it every time your soul lets out a squeak, all complexes respected here. Just a question of money: if you were poor, it would be cold water and a good thrashing, but here they cater to every one of your whims. They even let you go out, you can go and drink beer in Denklingen. All you have to do is holler, 'field of fire, field of fire for the second army, field of fire for the third army,' and someone or other will answer, 'Yessir, General.' Here we don't think of time as an indefinite continuous concept but rather as separate units which must not be related and become history. Do you understand? I quite believe you that you've seen my eyes before, in someone with a red scar on the bridge of his nose, but statements and associations like that aren't allowed here. With us, time is always *today*, Verdun is today and today Heinrich died and Otto fell, it's May 31, 1942, today, and today Heinrich whispered in my ear, '... *and forward with Hindenburg, hurrah.*' You knew Heinrich, you shook his hand, or rather he shook yours. Fine. But now we're going to get some work done. I can still remember which prayer was the hardest for an altar boy to learn. I learned it myself with my son Otto, when I had to hear him recite it: '*Suscipiat Dominus sacrificium de manibus tuis ad laudem et gloriam nominis sui*'—here comes the hardest part, old man—'*ad utilitatem quoque nostram, totiusque Ecclesiae suae sanctae*'—say it after me, old man—no, '*ad utilitatem,*' not '*utilatem*'—they all make that mistake—I'll write it down for you if you like, or you can look it up in a prayer book— goodbye now, Field-of-Fire, see you later, it's suppertime; *bon appétit.*"

She went along the wide, black paths by the chapel and back to the hothouse, and only the walls were there to witness her opening the door with the key and slipping quietly past the empty flowerpots and the flower beds into the chief gardener's office. She took the pistol from between the guns and rifles and opened her soft black leather handbag. The leather closed round the pistol, leaving ample room for the clasp to be snapped shut. And smiling, caressing the empty flowerpots, she left the hothouse and locked the door again behind her. And only the walls were there to witness her withdrawing the key and going slowly back along the wide, black paths to the house.

Huperts was laying the supper table in her room. Tea, bread, butter, cheese and ham. "You look wonderful, Madam."

"Really," she said, putting her handbag on the dressing

table and taking off her hat to release her dark hair; she smiled and asked, "Could the chief gardener possibly bring me a few flowers?"

"He's out," said Huperts, "he's off duty till tomorrow morning."

"And can't anyone but he go into the hothouse?"

"No, Madam, he's terribly particular about it."

"That means I'll have to wait till tomorrow evening—or I'll get myself some in Denklingen or Doderingen."

"Will you be going out, Madam?"

"Yes, probably, it's such a fine evening, and I suppose I may."

"Of course, of course you may—or should I telephone His Excellency, or Dr. Faehmel?"

"I'll do so myself, Huperts. Would you be kind enough to switch my telephone over to exchange—but for a long while, if you please?"

"Certainly, Madam, certainly."

When Huperts had gone she opened the window, threw the key to the hothouse out onto the compost pile, shut the window, poured herself some tea and milk, sat down and drew the telephone toward her. "Come on," she said quietly, "come on," and tried with her left hand to steady her trembling right hand, which was reaching out for the receiver. "Come on, come on," she said, "I'm ready with death in my handbag to return to life. None of them understood that this contact with cold metal would be all I'd need; all of them took *gun* wrong, I don't need rifles and cannon, a pistol will do as well. Come on, come on, tell me the time, little voice, tell me the time, are you still that same soft voice, is your number still the same?" She took the receiver in her left hand and listened to the buzz-buzz-buzz from exchange. "All Huperts has to do is press a button and there it is: time, the world, the present, the German future. I'm excited at seeing how it looks when I get out of the bewitched castle." With her right hand she dialed: one-

one-one, and heard the soft voice say: "At the signal, the time will be five-fifty-eight and forty seconds." Time flowed into her face and blanched it deathly white as the voice said, "Five-fifty-nine and ten—twenty—thirty—forty—fifty seconds." A harsh gong stroke. "Six o'clock precisely, September sixth, 1958," said the soft voice. Heinrich would have been forty-eight, Johanna forty-nine and Otto forty-one; Joseph was twenty-two, Ruth nineteen. And the voice said, "At the signal, the time will be six-one, precisely." Careful, or I'll really go crazy and the play will be in earnest, and I'll relapse into the eternal Today forever, never find the way in again and go running round and round outside the leafy walls, never finding the entrance. Time's visiting card, like a challenge to a duel—not to be accepted: September 6th, 1958, one minute and forty seconds past six o'clock, P.M. A fist full of vengeance has smashed my pocket mirror and left me only two fragments in which to see the deathly pallor in my face. I did hear that rumbling explosion, going on for hours, and heard the outraged people whispering, 'They've blown up our Abbey.' I heard the waiters and the doormen, the gardeners and the baker boys relaying the frightful news—which I don't find so frightful. Field of fire. A red scar on the bridge of his nose. Deep-blue eyes. Who can it be? Was it he? Who was it? I would have blown every abbey in the world sky-high to have Heinrich back again, to wake Johanna from the dead, and Ferdi, and the waiter called Groll, and Edith . . . and to be able to learn who Otto really was. *Killed at Kiev.* It sounds so stupid and smells of history. Come on, old man, let's cut out our game of blindman's buff, this holding my hands over your eyes. You're eighty today, and I'm seventy-one. And at a distance of ten to twelve yards anyone's pretty sure to hit a target squarely. Come to me, you years, you weeks and days, you hours and minutes, and which second, "six-two, and twenty seconds." I'm going to leave my paper boat and throw myself into the ocean. Deathly pallor. Perhaps I'll live through it. "Six-two and thirty seconds"; it sounds so urgent. Come on,

I haven't any time to lose, no seconds to waste, "Hello, Miss, quick, why don't you answer me, Miss, Miss, I need a taxi right away, it's very urgent, help me, please." Recording machines can't reply, I ought to have known it. Put the receiver down; take the receiver up and dial: one-one-two—were taxis still ordered from the same number? "This evening," said the soft voice, "Denklingen Theater will be showing that old-time film, 'The Moorland Castle Brothers.' Programs begin at six o'clock and eight-fifteen; Doderingen Theater is now offering you an opportunity to see that fine film, 'The Power of Love.' " Hush, hush, now, my little boat's gone—but I did learn to swim, didn't I, at the Blücher pool in 1905, wearing a black bathing suit with skirt and frills, diving off the three-foot board. Pull yourself together, deep breath, you know how to swim. What do you have to say on one-one-three, soft-voiced one: "And if you are expecting guests this evening, may we suggest this tasty and economical menu: a first course of Welsh rarebit with ham and cheese, followed by green peas and sour cream, a fluffy potato pudding, and a freshly grilled schnitzel"—"Operator, Operator"—Recording machines don't answer—"Your guests will appreciate you as a superb homemaker." She dialed again, one-one-four, and again the soft voice: ". . . so the camping equipment all packed, the picnic prepared, and don't forget to pull up your hand brake when you park on a slope. And now—a happy Sunday with your family."

I'll never make it. There's too much lost time to be made up, my face is getting paler all the time and even if my stony face doesn't dissolve into tears, all the time I've played truant with and denied is still in me like a hard lie. Mirror, Mirror, —jagged ·fragment of it—has my hair really gone white in the torture chambers of soft voices? One-one-five—a sleepy voice: "Hallo, Denklingen exchange, can I help you"—"Can you hear me, Miss? Can you hear me?" "Yes, I can hear you"—a laugh—"I want to put an urgent call through to the office of Faehmel, the architect, at 7 or 8 Modest Street, both addresses are listed under Faehmel, child, you don't mind if I call you child?"

"Not at all, Madam, not at all."

"It's very urgent."

Sound of turning pages.

"I have Mr. Heinrich Faehmel and Dr. Robert Faehmel —which number do you want, Madam?"

"Heinrich Faehmel."

"Hold the line, please."

Was the telephone still kept on the window sill, so that when he phoned he could look out onto the street and over to 8 Modest Street, where his children would be playing on the roof? And look down to Gretz' shop where the wild boar hung at the door? Was it really ringing there now? She heard the bell, far away, and the intervals between the rings seemed endless.

"Sorry, Madam, I'm afraid there's no answer."

"Would you please try the other number?"

"Certainly, Madam." Nothing, nothing, no answer.

"Then would you order me a taxi, please, child?"

"Certainly. Where are you?"

"At the Denklingen Sanatorium."

"At once, Madam."

"Yes, Huperts, clear the tea away, and the bread and cold meat as well. And I'd like to be alone, please. I'll see the taxi when it comes up the avenue. No, thank you, I don't need anything else. You aren't a recorded voice, are you? Oh, I didn't mean to offend you—it was only a joke. Thank you."

She felt cold. She could feel her face shriveling, a grandmother's face, wrinkled, tired, she could see it in the window-pane. No tears. Was time really creeping, silvery time, into her hair? I learned how to swim but I didn't realize how cold the water would be. Soft voices harassed me, drove the present into me. Grandmother with silvery hair, anger turned into wisdom, thoughts of revenge to forgiveness. Hatred candied over with wisdom. Old fingers clutched the handbag. Gold, brought with her from the bewitched castle, ransom gold.

Come get me, dearest, I'm coming back. I'll be your dear old white-haired wife, a good mother and a kindly grandmother who can be described to all your friends as particularly nice. She was sick, our grandmother, for years, but now she's well again, she's bringing a whole handbag full of gold with her.

What shall we eat this evening in the Cafe Kroner? Welsh rarebit with ham and cheese, green peas with sour cream, and a schnitzel—and will we shout 'Hosanna, David's bride, who has come home from the bewitched castle.' Gretz will come and pay his respects. His mother's murderer. He did not feel it in his blood, nor did Otto. When the gym teacher comes by the house on his white horse I'll shoot. It is no more than ten yards from the pergola to the street—on the diagonal it can't be much more than thirteen yards. I shall ask Robert to work it out for me exactly. At all events it is within the range of maximum accuracy. Field-of-Fire explained it to me and he ought to know, our white-haired altar boy. He'll start serving early tomorrow morning. Will he learn before then to say *'utilitatem'* and not *'utilatem'?* A red scar on the bridge of his nose—and so he did become a captain. That shows how long the war lasted. The windowpanes tinkled when yet another demolition charge exploded and in the morning there was dust on the window sill. I wrote 'Edith, Edith' in the layer of dust, with my fingers. I loved you more than if our blood had been the same. Where did you come from, Edith, tell me?

I'm getting more and more wizened. He'll be able to carry me with one hand, from the taxi into the Cafe Kroner. I'll be on the dot. It's six-six and thirty seconds at the most. My lipstick has been squashed by the black fist of revenge. And my poor old bones are trembling. I'm scared: how will they look, the ones my age? Will they be really the same as then, or only like what they were? And what about our golden wedding, old man, September, 1908, don't you remember,

September 13th? How do you intend to celebrate the golden wedding? Silver-haired the jubilee bride, silver-haired the jubilee bridegroom, and gathered all around them their countless flock of grandchildren, forgive me if I laugh, David. You were no Abraham, yet I feel a little of Rachel's laughter in me. Only a little, there's no room for a lot of it in me, just a nutshell of laughter and a handbag of gold, that's all I'm bringing with me. Still, my laughter may be small but powerful energies are hidden in it, more than in Robert's dynamite. . . .

Here you are all coming down the avenue much too solemnly, much too solemnly and slowly; there's Edith's son, far away in front, but that isn't Ruth at his side. She was three when I left, but I'd still recognize her if I met her at eighty. That isn't Ruth. People don't unlearn the way they use their hands. The tree is contained in the nutshell. How often did I see my mother in Ruth when she brushed the hair away from her forehead. Where is Ruth, she must forgive me —this one's a stranger, a pretty one. Oh, that's the womb that will bear you your great-grandchildren, old man. Will there be seven of them, seven times seven? Forgive me if I laugh, you're moving like heralds, slowly and much too solemnly. Have you come to get the jubilee bride? Here I am, ready, wizened like an old, old apple. You can carry me to the taxi on one hand, old man, but quickly: I haven't a second more to lose. Yes, the taxi's here already—you see how well I can coordinate. I learned that much at least as the wife of an architect—make way for the taxi now—there's Robert and the good-looking stranger lining up on the right, and there on the left the old man with his grandson; Robert, Robert, is this the place to put your hand on someone's shoulder? Do you need someone to hold you up? Come on, old man, come in, welcome—we want to celebrate and be merry! The time is ripe!

twelve

The desk clerk looked uneasily at the clock: it was past six already, Jochen had not appeared to relieve him, and the gentleman in Room 11 had now been asleep for twenty-one hours, with the card Please Do Not Disturb hanging on the door handle, and still no one as yet had sensed the silence of death behind the locked door. There had been no whispers, no chambermaids screaming. Dinnertime, dark suits, bright dresses. Much silver, candlelight, music. Mozart with the lobster cocktail, Wagner with the meat course, jazz for dessert.

Disaster lay in the air. Full of anxiety, the man looked at the clock, which was propelling the seconds much too slowly on toward the point where the disaster would erupt. Again and again the telephone: menu 1 to Room 12, menu 3 to Room 218, champagne to Room 14. The weekend adulterers were ordering the necessary stimulants. Five globetrotters were hanging about in the lobby, waiting for the bus to take them to the night plane. "Yes, Madam, first left, second right, third left—the Roman children's graves are illuminated evenings and you're allowed to take photographs." Grandma

Blessieck was drinking her port back in a corner. She had finally nabbed Hugo, who was reading to her from the local newspaper: "Purse-Snatcher Foiled. Yesterday, near the Memorial Field, a young man made an attempt to snatch an old woman's handbag, but the courageous grandmother succeeded in . . . Foreign Minister Dulles. . . ." "Nonsense, all nonsense," said Grandma Blessieck, "nothing political and nothing international, the local events are the only interesting ones"; and Hugo read, "City head honors deserving boxer. . . ."

Mockingly, time postponed disaster's eruption, while glasses softly tinkled, silver dishes were placed on the tables, and fine china plates began to vibrate to the noble music. The airlines coach driver was standing in the doorway, raising his hands, admonishing, warning, while the door swung softly back into its felt-lined frame behind him. The desk clerk nervously glanced at his notebook: "As of 6:30, reserve room for Mr. M., street side; 6:30, double room for Councillor Faehmel and wife, absolutely on street side; 7:00, pick up dog Kaessi in Room 114 for walk." The special fried eggs for that dreadful canine were just being taken up: yolk hard, white soft, and slices of sausage, crisply fried, and as usual the stinker would fastidiously turn up his nose at the meal. The gentleman in Room 11 had now been sleeping twenty-one hours and eighteen minutes.

"Yes, Madam, the fireworks begin half an hour after sundown, that is to say about half-past seven. The Fighting Veterans' parade about seven-fifteen. Sorry, I'm not in a position to tell you whether the Minister will be there." Hugo read on in his high school graduate voice: "And the city fathers presented to the deserving boxer not only the Key to the City but also the golden Marsilius Plaque, which is awarded only for particularly outstanding cultural accomplishments. The dignified ceremony closed with a gala banquet." The globetrotters were finally leaving the lobby. "Yes, gentlemen, the banquet for the Left Opposition party is in the Blue Room—no, for the Right Opposition party in the Yellow Room. There are signs marking the way, sir." Who belonged to the Left, who to the Right? You couldn't tell by looking at them. Jochen would have been better at such a job. When it came to labeling people, his instinct was infallible. He could spot the real gentleman in a shabby suit or the upstart in a tailor-made. He would have known how to distinguish between the Left and the Right Opposition, though otherwise you couldn't tell them apart even to their menus. Oh, there's still another banquet: the board of directors of the Co-operative Welfare Society. "The Red Room, sir." Their faces were all the same, and they would all eat lobster cocktail as hors d'oeuvre, the Left, the Right and the board of directors; all would have Mozart for the hors d'oeuvres, Wagner for the main course and the taste of rich sauces, and jazz for dessert. "Yes, sir, in the Red Room." Jochen's instinct was infallible in social matters, but failed him beyond that. When the shepherd priestess came onto the scene for the first time, it had been Jochen who'd whispered: 'Careful, that's real upper class.' And when the small, pale young woman appeared, with her long unruly hair and only a handbag and pocketbook under her arm, Jochen whispered: 'Hustler.' And I said: 'She does it with anyone, but *takes nothing for it,* so she's not a whore,' and Jochen said, 'She does it with anyone, *and takes something for it.'* And Jochen was right. Jochen, however, has no instinct for disaster; for when the blonde came in, glamorous with her thirteen suitcases, I said to him as she got into the lift: 'Do you want to bet we won't see her alive again?' And Jochen said, 'Don't be ridiculous, she's only skipped out on her husband for a couple of days.' And who was right? I was! Sleeping tablets and a Do Not Disturb notice in front of the door. She slept twenty-four hours, and then the whispering started: 'Dead, someone dead in Room 118.' It's a fine thing when the murder squad arrive around three in the afternoon, and around five a body's dragged out of the hotel, a fine thing.

Now, how's that for a buffalo-face! A trunk with a diplomatic air, two hundred pounds, a dachshund-waddle—and look at the suit on the man. This one fairly reeked of importance, kept in the background while two less significant birds stalked over to the desk. Mr. M.'s room, please. "Oh, yes, Room 211. Hugo, come here, take the gentlemen upstairs." And six hundredweight swathed in English woolens soundlessly glided upward.

"Jochen, Jochen, good God, where've you been all this time?"

"Excuse me," said Jochen, "you know I'm almost never late. And I wanted to be on time especially tonight when your wife and children are waiting for you. But when it comes to choosing between you or my pigeons, well, I'm not so sure. And when I send six of them off on a trip, I want six back, but only five were on time, you understand; the sixth came in ten minutes late and completely exhausted, poor creature. Go on, now, if you still want to get a good seat for the fireworks. Yes, all right, I see, Left Opposition in the Blue Room, Right Opposition in the Yellow Room, board of directors of the Co-operative Welfare Society in the Red Room. Well, all right, that's not bad for a weekend. Not nearly as tough as when the Stamp Collectors or the National Beer Brewers' Committee meet. Don't worry, I'll manage them okay, and I'll control my feelings, even though I'd just as soon warm the seat of the Left Opposition's pants, and spit into the hors d'oeuvres of the Right and the Co-operative Welfare Society—all right, don't get excited, we'll keep the old house flag a-flying. And I'll check up on your would-be suicides. Yes, Madam, Hugo to your room at nine o'clock for cards, certainly. Ah, Mr. M.'s already here? Don't like him, that Mr. M.; without even having seen him I hate his guts. Yes, sir, champagne to Room 211, and three Partagas Eminentes. By the smell of their cigars shall ye know them! Good God, here comes the entire Faehmel family."

Girl, oh girl, what's happened to you! When I saw you for the first time, at the Emperor's Parade in 1908, my heart beat faster. Even though I knew that little flowers like you didn't grow for the likes of us to pick. I took the red wine into the room where you were sitting with Papa and Mamma. Child, child, who ever would have thought you would grow into a downright grandma, all silver hair and wrinkles; I could carry you up into the room with one hand, and I'd do so if they'd let me. But they won't let me, old girl, too bad, you're still good-looking.

"Your Excellency, we've reserved Room 212 for you and your wife, pardon, for your wife and you. Any luggage at the station? No? Anything to be brought from your house? Nothing. Oh, only for two hours while the fireworks are on, and to watch the Veterans' parade. Of course there are seats for six people in the room, there's a large balcony, and if you wish we can have the beds pushed together. Not necessary? Hugo, Hugo, show the ladies and gentlemen to Room 212, and take a wine list with you. I'll send the young people up to your room. Of course, Doctor, the billiard room has been reserved for yourself and Mr. Schrella, and I'll see that Hugo is free for you. Yes, he's a good boy, he's spent half the afternoon hanging onto the telephone, dialing again and again; I don't think he'll ever forget your phone number or the Pension Moderne's as long as he lives. Why is the Fighting Veterans' League parading today? Some field marshal's birthday—the hero of Husenwald, I think; we'll get to hear that wonderful song, 'Fatherland, the ship of state groans in every timber.' Well, we'll let her groan, Doctor. What? Always has groaned? If you'll allow me to express a personal political opinion here, I'd say, 'Watch out if she ever groans again. Watch out!' "

"I've stood right here once before," she said quietly, "and watched you as you went marching by below, during the Emperor's Parade in January, 1908. It was imperial weather, dearest, a crackling frost, as they say in poems, I believe. And I was all aquiver to see if you'd stand up to the last and hardest of the tests: of how you would look to me in your uniform. The General stood on the next balcony and toasted Father,

Mother and me. You made out all right, old man—don't look at me so suspiciously, yes, suspiciously, you've never looked at me like that before—put your head in my lap, smoke your cigar and forgive me if I'm shaky. I'm scared. Did you see that boy's face? He might have been Edith's brother, mightn't he? I'm scared, and you must understand that I cannot go back into our apartment as yet, perhaps never again. I can't step back into the circle, I'm scared, much more than I was then. Obviously, you're all quite used to the faces. But I'm beginning to wish I were back among my poor old harmless lunatics. Are you all blind, then? So easily fooled? Don't you see they'd kill you all for less than a gesture, for less than a sandwich? You needn't even be dark-haired or blond any more, or show your grandmother's birth certificate. They'd kill you if they just didn't like your faces. Didn't you see the posters on the walls? Are you all blind? You just don't know any more where you are. I tell you, dearest, the whole pack of them have partaken of the *Host of the Beast*. Dumb as earth, deaf as a tree, and as terribly harmless as the Beast in his last incarnation. Respectable, respectable. I'm scared, old man— I've never felt such a stranger among people, not even in 1935 and not in 1942. Maybe I do need time, but even centuries wouldn't be enough to get me used to their faces. Respectable, respectable, without a trace of grief. What's a human being without grief? Give me another glass of wine and don't stare at my handbag so suspiciously. You all knew about the medicine but it's me who has to use it. You have a pure heart, with no idea how bad the world is, and today I want to ask you to make another great sacrifice: cancel the party in the Cafe Kroner, destroy that legend, don't ask your grandchildren to spit on your statue, simply make sure you never get one. You really never liked paprika cheese—let the waiters and kitchenmaids sit down at the banquet table and eat up your birthday dinner. We'll stay here on this balcony and enjoy the summer evening in the family circle, drinking wine and looking at the fireworks and watching the Fighting Veterans march past. What are they fighting against, anyway?

Shall I go and telephone the Kroner to cancel the dinner?"

Blue-uniformed men were already gathering at the big doors of St. Severin's, standing around in groups, smoking, carrying blue and red flags with great, black F.V.'s on them. The brass band began to rehearse "Fatherland, the ship of state groans in every timber." On the balconies, wine glasses clinked softly, champagne buckets echoed metallically, corks popped into the dark blue evening sky. The bells of St. Severin's chimed a quarter to seven, and three dark-suited men stepped onto the balcony of Room 211.

"Do you really believe they might be some use to us?" asked M.

"I'm certain," said the one.

"No doubt about it," said the other.

"But won't we antagonize more voters than we'll win by such a show of sympathy?" asked Mr. M.

"The Fighting Veterans' League is known as non-radical," said the one.

"You can't lose anything," said the other," and you're bound to win something."

"How many votes are involved? At best and at worst?"

"At best, around eighty thousand, at worst around fifty thousand. Make up your mind."

"I haven't made up my mind yet," said M. "I'm still waiting for K.'s instructions. Do you think up till now we've managed to escape the attention of the Press?"

"We have, Mr. M.," said the one.

"And the hotel personnel?"

"Absolutely discreet, Mr. M.," said the other. "Mr. K.'s instructions should come in soon."

"I don't like those guys," said Mr. M., "they *believe* in something."

"Eighty thousand votes ought to believe in something, Mr. M.," said the one.

Laughter. Clink of glasses. The phone.

"Yes, M. speaking. Have I got you right? Show sympathy? Right."

"Mr. K. has decided in the affirmative, gentlemen. Let's move our chairs and the table out onto the balcony."

"What will they think abroad?"

"They'll have the wrong ideas in any case."

Laughter, the clink of glasses.

"I'll go down to the leader of the parade and draw his attention to your balcony," said the one.

"No, no," said the old man, "I don't want to lie on your lap and I don't want to look up into the sky. Did you tell them in the Cafe Kroner to send Leonore here? She'll be disappointed. You don't know her, she's Robert's secretary, a dear child, she mustn't be done out of her party. I don't have a pure heart, and I know exactly how bad the world is; I feel like a stranger, more strange than when we used to go to The Anchor in the upper harbor and take the money to the waiter called Groll. They're getting into marching formation down there—it's a warm summer's evening, the laughter's echoing up here in the dusk—shall I help you, dearest? I suppose you don't know that you laid your handbag on my lap in the taxi. It's heavy, but not heavy enough—what do you intend to do, precisely, with that thing?"

"I want to shoot that fat man there on his white horse. Can you see him, do you still remember him?"

"Do you think I could ever forget him? He killed the laughter in me, and broke the hidden springs within the hidden wheels. He had that little blond fellow executed, Edith's father taken away, and Groll too, and the boy whose name we never learned. He taught me how lifting your hand could cost you your life. He made Otto into someone who was only Otto's husk—and in spite of all that, I wouldn't shoot him. I've often asked myself why I came to this city. To get rich? No, you know that. Because I loved you? No—since I hadn't yet met you and couldn't yet love you. Ambition? No. I think

I just wanted to laugh at them and tell them at the end: it wasn't really serious. Did I want children? Yes. I had them. Two died young and one fell in battle, and he was a stranger to me, stranger even than those young men picking up their flags down there. And the other son? How are you, Father? Well, and you? Well, thank you, Father. Can I do anything for you? No, thank you, I don't need anything. St. Anthony's Abbey? Forgive me if I laugh, dearest. Dust. It doesn't even arouse my sentimentality, much less my feelings. Would you like some more wine?"

"Yes, please."

I'll take my stand on Paragraph 51, dearest husband. The law is flexible—look down there, there's our old friend Nettlinger, clever enough not to appear in uniform, but just the same here to shake hands and slap people on the back and finger the flags. I'd rather shoot Nettlinger, if anyone—but perhaps I'll think it over and not shoot into that menagerie down there. My grandson's murderer is sitting nearby on the balcony, can you see him, in his dark suit, respectable, oh so respectable. That one thinks differently now, acts differently, plans differently; he's learned a little, speaks fluent French and English and understands Latin and Greek, and he's already put the bookmark in his prayer book for tomorrow. Fifteenth Sunday after Pentecost. He's just hollered 'What's the Introit?' into his wife's bedroom. I won't shoot fat-guts there on his white horse. I won't shoot into the menagerie—just a bit of a turn, and, at a range of six yards at the most, I can't miss. At seventy-one what else good can I accomplish? No tyrannicide for me, it'll be murder of respectability. Death will bring the great wonder back into his face; come, don't tremble, dearest, I want to pay the ransom money. And it gives me pleasure, to breathe deep, aim and fire—you needn't hold your ears, dearest, it doesn't bang louder than a balloon bursting. Vigil of the fifteenth Sunday after Pentecost. . . .

thirteen

One was blonde, the other brunette, both were slender, both smiling, and both were wearing becoming costumes of red-brown tweed, and both their pretty necks grew out of snow-white collars like flower stems. They spoke French and English, Flemish and Danish fluently, without a trace of accent, and fluently, without a trace of accent their German mother tongue. They knew some Latin, too, these pretty nuns of No-Order-at-All waiting in the employees' powder room behind the ticket office for visitors to gather in groups of twelve at the barrier. They ground out their cigarette butts with spike heels, and touched up their lipstick with a practiced sweep before they stepped outside, to ascertain the nationalities of the guided-tour addicts. Smilingly they asked after languages and countries of origin, and the tourists made their responses by solemnly raising their hands; seven spoke English, two Flemish, three German. Then the gay question as to who knew Latin. Hesitantly Ruth raised her hand. Only one? A trace of sadness appeared on the pretty face at such a scanty haul of humanists. Only one to appreciate her metrical exactitude when she quoted the epitaphs? Smiling and holding the long flashlight pointed downward like a sword, she walked ahead of them down the steps. It smelled of concrete and mortar, like a tomb, although a faint hum testified to the presence of an air-conditioning apparatus. Out came the English, Flemish and German, without a trace of accent, recounting the proportions of gray stone blocks and the width of Roman streets —and notice the second-century staircase—the fourth-century thermal baths—look, that's where some bored sentry scratched a kind of checkerboard on a sandstone block (What had the instructor said? 'Always emphasize the human element.')— here's where the Roman children played marbles—notice how perfectly the paving stones were fitted—that's a drain, Roman dishwater and Roman slops were emptied into that gray conduit—and the remains of a small, private Temple of Venus built for the Governor. The visitors' grins were lit up by the neon light. English grins and Flemish grins. Were the three young Germans really not grinning? How do you explain why the foundation was built so deep? Well, at the time when it was built the ground almost certainly was swampy, underground water leaked in from the river, went greenly gurgling about gray stones. Can you hear the curses of the German slaves? The sweat poured down over blond eyebrows, across fair faces, into the blond beards, and barbarian mouths swore an alliterative oath: 'From wounds Wotan will wage revenge on ruthless Romans, woe, woe, woe.' "Patience, ladies and gentlemen, just a few steps more. Here the remains of a law court, and now there they are, *The Roman children's graves.*"

('At this point,' the instructor had said, 'you should go ahead of the others into the vault and wait for the first wave of emotion to die down before you begin your explanations. It's purely a matter of instinct, girls, just how *long* you should keep the silence, it depends of course on what kind of a group it is. But whatever you do, don't let yourself be drawn into discussing the fact that actually they aren't Roman children's graves at all, merely tombstones which weren't even found on this particular spot.')

The tombstones were propped against the gray walls in a semicircle. Their first emotion having duly faded away, the visitors looked up in surprise. The deep blue night sky could be seen above the neon lights. And was that not an early star, or was it only the glitter of a golden or a silver button on the banister, winding smoothly upward through the light shaft in five spirals?

"There, at the first spiral—can you see the white cross-line in the concrete?—was the approximate level of the street in Roman times. At the second spiral—you can see the white cross-line in the concrete there too, can't you?—was the medieval level, and there, at the beginning of the third spiral, the level of the street today—no need to point out the white cross-line in the concrete—the present-day street level—and now, ladies and gentlemen, we'll proceed to the inscriptions."

Her face became stony, like a goddess's, and raising her arm a little she held the long flashlight aloft like a torch:

DURA QUIDEM FRANGIT PARVORUM MORTE PARENTES
CONDICIO RAPIDO PRAECIPITATA GRADU
SPES AETERNA TAMEN TRIBUET SOLACIA LUCTUS . . .

A quick smile at Ruth, the only one who could appreciate the original Latin; a tiny tug at the collar of her tweed jacket, to straighten it; and lowering the flashlight a little, she recited the translation:

> "Hard is fate, indeed, for parents
> When precipitously advening
> Death strikes down their little ones.
> But in grief for those of tender age
> Eternal hope gives balm.
> Six years, nine months thou wert,
> When this grave enfolded thee, Desideratus."

Grief seventeen centuries old came upon all the faces, seeped into all hearts, and even paralyzed the jaw muscles of the middle-aged Flemish gentleman, who let his lower mandible hang while his tongue swiftly thrust his chewing gum into a quiet pocket of his cheek. Marianne began sobbing and Joseph pressed her arm. Ruth put her hand on her shoulder as the ever-stony face of the guide went on quoting in Flemish:

"Hard is fate, indeed, for parents . . ."

A dangerous moment when one left the gloomy vaults to climb up again into light, air, the summer evening. When the age-old pain of death buried deep in the heart was mingled with the mysteries of Venus, and when lonely tourists spat out their chewing gum in front of the ticket office and tried to arrange a date in broken German: *Tanz im Hotel Prinz Heinrich; Spaziergang, Abendessen—a lonely feeling, Fräulein.* At this juncture the vestal virgin routine was indicated, no flirtatious openings permitted, all invitations refused. For display purposes only, please do not touch. No, sir, no, no —yet feeling the breath of corruption too, feeling sympathy for the sad foreigners who, shaking their heads, bore away, taking love's hunger with them, toward precincts where Venus reigned to this very day, and was not ashamed to name her price, being up on all exchange rates, in dollars, pounds, in guilders, francs and marks.

The cashier was tearing the tickets off the roll as if the little entrance led into a cinema; it hardly gave you time for a couple of drags in the powder room, a bite of sandwich, a gulp at the thermos flask. And then as always the difficult decision as to whether it was worth saving the cigarette butt or whether it would be better to kill it off with the spike heel. One more drag, yet another as the left hand began to fish in the handbag for the lipstick, while the heart defiantly resolved to break its vestal vows, while the cashier stuck his head in the doorway and said, "Come on, kid, there are two groups waiting already, make it snappy—the Roman children's graves are practically a box-office hit!" And she smiled and stepped out to the barrier to inquire about nationalities and mother tongues: four spoke English, one French, one Dutch and, this time, six Germans. Pointing the long flashlight downward like a sword she descended into the gloomy vaults, to describe the age-old cult of love and decipher the age-old pain of death.

Marianne was still crying when they went outside past the line of waiting people. The Germans, English and Dutch waiting there looked away from the girl's face, embarrassed. What were these painful secrets hidden down there in gloomy cellars? Who had ever heard of historical monuments eliciting tears? Such deep emotion for sixty pfennigs, seen on faces only very occasionally, after very bad or very good movies. Could stones actually move some people to tears, while others cold-bloodedly shoved fresh chewing gum into their mouths, greedily lit cigarettes and wound their flashlight cameras round ready for the next shot, eyes already on the lookout for the next target: gable-end of a fifteenth-century bourgeois dwelling, just opposite the entrance. Click, and the gable was immortalized on a chemical basis.

"Easy, easy, ladies and gentlemen," the cashier called out from his box. "In view of the extraordinary attendance we have decided to allow fifteen instead of twelve visitors to participate in each tour. Would the next three ladies and gentlemen please pass through—tickets sixty, catalogues one-twenty."

They were still walking past the waiting line, which had arranged itself all the way along the wall of the building to the corner of the street. Tears still showed on Marianne's face as she smiled at Joseph in response to the insistent pressure of his arm, and then at Ruth in gratitude for the hand on her shoulder.

"We'll have to hurry," said Ruth, "we've only ten minutes to go before seven o'clock and we oughtn't to keep them waiting."

"We'll be there in two minutes," said Joseph, "we're going to be on time. Mortar—even today I had to smell it—and concrete. By the way, did you know that they owe those discoveries down there to Father's zeal for demolition? When they were blowing up the old guardhouse, one of the vaults below collapsed and opened the way into those ruins and relics. Long live dynamite. Tell me, Ruth, what do you think of your new uncle? Do you feel it in your blood when you look at him?"

"No," said Ruth, "my blood tells me nothing, but I think he's nice. Rather dry, rather helpless—is he coming to live with us?"

"Probably," said Joseph. "Will we be living there too, Marianne?"

"Do you want to move into the city?"

"Yes," said Joseph, "I'm going to study statics and go into my father's honorable business. Don't you like the idea?"

They crossed a busy street and went on into a quieter one. Marianne stopped in front of a shop window, let go of Joseph's arm, eased off Ruth's hand and dabbed at her face with a handkerchief. Ruth brushed her hands over her hair and straightened her sweater.

"Are we dressed up enough?" she asked. "I wouldn't like to offend Grandfather."

"You're both elegant enough," said Joseph. "How do you like my plan, Marianne?"

"I care a great deal what you're going to do," she said, "I'm sure it'd be a good thing to study statics, but what are you going to do with it after you've learned?"

"Construction or demolition, I don't know yet," said Joseph.

"Dynamite will be out of date," said Ruth, "there must surely be better ways. Do you remember how happy Father was when he could still blow things up? He's only grown so

serious now that there's been nothing more to blow up. . . .
What do you think about him, Marianne? Do you like him?"

"Yes," said Marianne, "I like him a lot. I'd always imagined he would be worse than he is. Colder. And before I knew him I was almost afraid of him, but I think he's the last person one need be afraid of. You'll laugh but when I'm with him I feel protected."

Joseph and Ruth didn't laugh. They took Marianne in the middle and continued on. They stopped in front of the Cafe Kroner and the two girls looked themselves over once again in the glass door which was faced with green silk stretched across the inside. Once again they smoothed their hair until Joseph smiled and opened the door for them.

"Good heavens," said Ruth, "I'm so hungry. I'm sure Grandfather's ordered something good for us."

Mrs. Kroner was coming toward them, past the green-covered tables and over the length of green carpet, her arms raised; her silver hair was dishevelled, the expression on her face spelt disaster, her watery eyes were glistening and her voice shaking with unfeigned distress.

"Haven't you heard yet, then?" she asked.

"No," said Joseph, "what?"

"Something dreadful must have happened. Your grandmother has canceled the party—she rang up a few minutes ago. You are to go over to the Prince Heinrich, Room 212. I'm not only very worried, I'm very disappointed too, Mr. Faehmel; I'd even say hurt, if I didn't think there must be very important reasons for it. Because naturally we'd prepared a surprise for a client who's been a regular here for fifty, fifty-one years, we've made—well, I'm going to show it to you. And what am I going to say to the Press and the radio people; they were scheduled for around nine o'clock, after the private party—what am I going to say?"

"Didn't my grandmother tell you what the reason was?"

"Indisposition—am I to suppose it means the, er, chronic indisposition—on your grandmother's part?"

"We haven't heard anything about it," said Joseph. "Would you be kind enough to have the presents and flowers taken over?"

"Yes, certainly, but won't you at least come and take a look at my surprise?"

Marianne nudged him, Ruth smiled, and Joseph said, "Yes, we'd like to, Mrs. Kroner."

"I was just a young girl," said Mrs. Kroner, "just fourteen, when your grandfather came to this city, and I used to serve out here at the cake counter. Later on I learned to wait at table, just imagine how often I laid his breakfast for him—how often I took away his egg cup and set the marmalade in front of him, and when I bent over to take away the cheese dish I used to glance at his drawing pad. Heavens, you take an interest in your clients' lives, you mustn't think we business people are all callous—and do you think I've forgotten how he became famous overnight and got that great commission? Perhaps the customers think, one goes into the Cafe Kroner, orders something, pays and leaves; but after all, someone with a life like that does not cross your path without leaving an imprint. . . ."

"Of course, of course," said Joseph.

"Oh, I know what you're thinking, you're wishing the old gossip would leave you in peace, but would it be asking you too much to come and take one look at my surprise, and tell your grandfather I'd be very glad if he'd come over and see for himself? It's already been photographed for the newspaper."

They walked slowly after Mrs. Kroner, over the length of green carpet between the green-covered tables and stopped when she stopped, at the large, square table covered by a large linen cloth; the cloth concealed something which seemed to be of uneven height.

"It's lucky," said Mrs. Kroner, "that there are four of us; may I ask each of you to hold one corner in your hands and when I say 'up' all lift it up at the same time."

Marianne gently pushed Ruth to the unoccupied, left-hand

corner, and they each grasped an end of the cloth. "Up," said Mrs. Kroner, and they lifted the cloth up. The two girls stepped over and joined their corners and Mrs. Kroner carefully folded the cloth.

"Good heavens," said Marianne, "it's a miniature model of St. Anthony's."

"That's right," said Mrs. Kroner, "look here—we didn't even forget the mosaic above the main entrance—and there, there are the vineyards."

Not only was the model accurately scaled, it was also accurately colored. The church was dark, the farm buildings light, the pilgrim's lodge had a red roof and the refectory had its many-colored window.

"And it isn't made of icing sugar or marzipan," said Mrs. Kroner, "all of it is cake; our birthday present for His Excellency—the finest pastry. Don't you think your grandfather might come over and look at it here before we take it up to his studio?"

"Definitely," said Joseph, "he'll definitely come over and look at it. Meanwhile, let me thank you on his behalf. There must be serious reasons to cause him to cancel the party, and you'll understand. . . ."

"I quite understand that it's time you left—no, don't spread the cloth over it again, Miss, the television say they're coming."

"I'd like to do one thing," said Joseph, as they crossed the square in front of St. Severin's, "laugh or cry, but I can't do either."

"I know which I could do more easily," said Ruth. "Cry. But I'm not going to. Who are those people there? What's all the fuss about? What are they doing with those torches?"

There was a lot of noise, clopping of horses, whinnying, and imperious voices barking out orders to assemble. The brass instruments were warming up. A short, brittle sound, not especially loud, broke through the noise, something very foreign to it all.

"My God," said Marianne fearfully, "what was that?"

"That was a shot," said Joseph.

She was startled when she came through the city gate into Modest Street. The street was empty. No apprentices, no nuns, no life on the street. Only Mrs. Gretz' white smock there behind the counter, scrubbing, pink-armed, pushing around soapsuds with the scrubbing brush. The printers' door was locked fast, as if never again, in all eternity, would there be printed edification on white paper. The wild boar, its legs splayed out and the wound in its flank blackly encrusted, was being dragged slowly inside the shop. Gretz' red face showed how heavy the animal was. Only one of the three rings had been answered; not in No. 7, not in No. 8, only in the Cafe Kroner. "Dr. Faehmel. It's important." "He's not here. The party's canceled. Miss Leonore? You're expected in the Prince Heinrich Hotel." The messenger had rung insistently while she was sitting in the bath. The wild noise had boded no good. She had got out of the bath, thrown on her bathrobe, wound a towel round her damp hair, gone to the door and took in the special-delivery letter. Schrit had written the address with his yellow pencil, made a big crisscross on the envelope and, no doubt, sent his eighteen-year-old daughter chasing off with it to the post office on her bicycle. Urgent.

'Dear Miss Leonore, please try to reach Dr. Faehmel at once. The entire estimates for building project X-5 are wrong. Mr. Kanders, whom I have just telephoned, has moreover sent along the—incorrect—documents direct to the client, contrary to our usual practice. The matter is so urgent that if you do not let me know by 8 P.M. that something is being done about it, I will come in myself on the night express. I hardly need point out to you the scope and importance of project X-5. Yours sincerely, Schrit.'

She had already walked past the Prince Heinrich Hotel twice, and twice retraced her steps back into Modest Street, almost to Gretz' shop, and twice again turned back; she was scared of the row that would ensue. Saturday for him was a sacred day, and he would tolerate interruptions for personal matters only, but interruptions for business matters on Saturdays he would never put up with. The 'Stupid thing!' still rang in her ears. It wasn't seven yet, and Schrit could still be reached by phone in a few minutes. A good thing the old man had canceled the party. Seeing Robert Faehmel eating or drinking would have been desecration. She thought fearfully about building project X-5. This was no personal matter; nor was it a 'Publisher's house at edge of forest,' or a 'Teacher's house on river bank.' X-5—so secret she hardly dared think of it—was buried deep in the safe. She caught her breath; hadn't he spent nearly a quarter of an hour on the telephone discussing it with Kanders? She was scared.

Gretz was still tugging at the wild boar, and by fits and starts managed to get the mighty animal over the steps. A messenger with a huge basket of flowers was ringing at the door of the printing press. The janitor appeared, took the flower basket, and shut the door again. The messenger looked at the tip in the palm of his hand, disappointed. 'I'm going to tell him,' she thought, 'I'm going to tell that nice old man that his instructions to give every messenger a two-mark tip are clearly not being obeyed. That wasn't any silver shining in the messenger's hand, only dull old copper.'

Courage, Leonore, courage, grit your teeth, get hold of yourself and go into the hotel. But once again, she shrank back round the corner. A girl with a food hamper walked up to the door of the printing press. She too stared at the palm of her hand. 'That bastard of a janitor,' thought Leonore, 'I really will tell Mr. Faehmel.'

Still ten minutes to seven. She'd been invited to the Cafe Kroner but ordered to the Prince Heinrich, and she would arrive with a business message, exactly what he hated on his sacred Saturdays. Would he, in this exceptional instance, react differently? She shook her head as, with blind courage, she finally pushed the door open and felt with a shock that it was being held open from within.

Child, child, I might allow myself a personal observation in your case too. Just come closer, now. I hope the cause of your timidity lies not in the purpose but merely in the fact of your presence here. I've seen plenty of young girls come in here before but never one like you; you don't belong in this place, at the present moment there's only a single guest in the house to whom I would admit you and not allow myself a personal observation—Faehmel; I could be your grandfather and therefore you won't mind my personal comments. What do you want in this den of thieves? Leave a trail of breadcrumbs so you can find your way back. You've made a mistake, child. Whoever comes here professionally doesn't look like you, and whoever comes here privately, even less so. Come closer. "Dr. Faehmel? Yes. His secretary? Urgent—wait a moment, please. Miss, I'll have him called to the telephone . . . I hope the noise out there won't disturb you."

"Leonore? I'm glad Father invited you. And please excuse me for what I said this morning, will you, Leonore? My father's expecting you in Room 212. A letter from Mr. Schrit? All the calculations on the X-5 documents wrong? Yes, I'll look into it, I'll telephone Schrit. Anyway, thank you, Leonore. And I'll see you later."

She laid down the receiver, went across to Jochen and was about to ask the way to the Faehmels' room when a short, brittle sound that seemed very foreign, not especially loud, made her jump.

"Good God," she said, "what was that?"

"That was a pistol shot, child," said Jochen.

Red-green, white-green. Hugo was leaning against the white-lacquered door panel with his hands crossed behind his back. It seemed to him that the forms were less precise and the rhythm of the billard balls disrupted. But were the billiard balls not the same, and was the table not the same, of the finest make, kept in the finest condition? And had not Schrella's hand become even lighter and his touch even more accurate, when he struck out a form from the green void? Yet still it seemed to Hugo that the rhythm of the billiard balls had been disrupted, the precision of the figures lessened. Was it Schrella who had brought the perpetual present with him and broken the spell? This was here, it was today, it was six-forty-four on Saturday, September 6, 1958. Here you were not carried thirty years back, four ahead, forty back again and then flung into the present. This was the perpetual present, moved steadily on by the second hand, here, today, now, as the commotion from the dining room came crowding in. The bill, waiter, the bill. They were all clamoring to leave, to watch the fireworks, to get to the window, to see the parade. To go to the Roman children's graves. Are the flash bulb attachments in working order? Didn't you know that M meant Minister? Clever, isn't it? The bill, waiter, the bill.

The clocks did not chime in vain, and their hands did not move in vain. They piled up minute on minute and added them together into quarter-hours and half-hours, and the total would exactly account for the years and hours and seconds. And the question, 'Robert, where are you, Robert, where were you, Robert, where have you been?' did it not echo out in time to the rhythm of the balls? And did Robert not return the question with each stroke? 'Schrella, where are you, Schrella, where were you, Schrella, where have you been?' And was this game not a kind of prayer wheel? A litany struck out across the green felt with billiard balls and cues? *Whywhywhy* and *Lord have mercy on us, Lord have mercy on us!* Each time Schrella stepped back from the edge of the table he smiled and shook his head, as he turned over the figure formed by the balls to Robert.

Hugo involuntarily shook his head too, after each shot. The

spell had vanished, the precision diminished, the rhythm disrupted, while the clock so exactly answered the question of *when?* Six-fifty-one on September 6, 1958.

"Oh," said Robert, "let's quit, we're not in Amsterdam any longer."

"Yes," said Schrella, "you're right, let's quit. Do we still need the boy here?"

"Yes," Robert said, "I still need him, unless you'd rather go, Hugo? No? Please stay. Put the cues on the stand, put the balls away, and bring us something to drink—no, stay, son. I have something to show you. Look here, here's a whole bundle of papers. By affixing stamps and signatures they've been turned into documents. All they need is one more thing, Hugo. Your signature at the foot of this page—when you write it in, you'll be my son! Did you see my mother and father up there, when you took up the wine? They'll be your grandparents, Schrella will be your uncle, Ruth and Marianne your sisters and Joseph your brother. You'll be the son Edith was no longer able to give me. What will the old man say when I present him with a new grandson for his birthday—with Edith's smile on his face? Do I still need the boy, Schrella? Yes, we need him, and we'd be glad if he needed us. Better still—we're suffering from the want of him. . . . Listen, Hugo, we're in want of you. You can't be Ferdi's son, yet you have his spirit. Hush, boy, don't cry, go up to your room and read these through. Be careful when you go through the halls, careful, son!"

Schrella drew back the curtain and looked out onto the square. Robert offered him a cigarette and Schrella struck a light; they both began smoking.

"Haven't you left your hotel room yet?"

"No."

"Don't you want to live with us?"

"I don't know yet," said Schrella. "I'm afraid of houses you move into, then let yourself be convinced of the banal fact that life goes on and that you get used to anything in time. Ferdi would only be a memory, and my father only a dream. And yet they killed Ferdi, and his father vanished from here without a trace. They're not even remembered in the lists of any political organization, since they never belonged to any. They aren't even remembered in the Jewish memorial services, since they weren't Jews. Ferdi, perhaps, lives on at least in the court records. Only we two think of him, Robert, your parents and that old desk clerk down there—not even your children, any longer. I can't live in this city because it isn't alien enough for me. I was born here and went to school here. I tried to free Gruffel Street from their spell. I carried within me the word I never uttered, Robert, never even when I talked to you, the only one that I expect to do anything for this world— I won't even say it now. Perhaps I'll be able to say it to you at the station, when you take me to the train."

"Do you want to leave today?" asked Robert.

"No, no, not today; my hotel room's exactly right. Once I shut the door behind me, this city becomes as foreign as all the others. There I can imagine I must soon be getting ready to go out and give my language lessons somewhere, in a schoolroom perhaps, wiping the arithmetic homework off the blackboard and then chalking on it: 'I bind, I bound, I have bound, I shall bind, I had bound—you bind, you bound.' I love grammar the way I love poetry. Maybe you think I don't want to live here because this country seems to me to have no political future, but I'm more inclined to believe I couldn't live here because I always have been, and still am today, completely unpolitical." He pointed toward the square outside and laughed. "Those people down there aren't scaring me off. Yes, yes, I know the whole story, I see them all down there, Robert—Nettlinger, Vacano, and I'm not afraid because those people there exist but rather because the other kind do not exist. What kind? Those who think the word, sometimes, or perhaps whisper it. I once heard it from an old man in Hyde Park, Robert: 'If you believe in Him, why don't you obey His commands?' Silly, isn't it, and unrealistic, eh,

269

Robert? *Feed my lambs,* Robert—but all they do is breed wolves. What did you bring home from the war, Robert? Dynamite? It's a wonderful toy to play with, I understand your passion for it. Hate, for the world which had no room for Edith and Ferdi, no room for my father or for Groll or the lad whose name we never learned, or for the Pole who raised his hand to strike Vacano. And so you collect statistics the way others collect baroque madonnas, and file your formulas in card indexes, while even my nephew, Edith's son, is sick of the smell of mortar and out looking for the formula for the future somewhere else than in St. Anthony's patched-up walls. What's he going to find? Will you be able to give him that formula? Will he find it in the face of his new brother whose father you want to be? You're right, Robert, one can't *be* a father, one *becomes* a father. That feeling in the blood is false, the other feeling alone is true—that's the reason I never married, I didn't have the courage to rely on becoming a father; I couldn't have stood it if my children had grown as alien to me as Otto became to your parents. Even the memory of my own mother and father didn't give me courage enough, and you don't yet know what Joseph and Ruth will grow into one day, or of what host they'll partake—you can't even be sure of Edith's and your children; no, no, Robert, you'll understand if I don't leave my hotel room and move into the house where Otto lived and where Edith died. I couldn't stand seeing that letter box every day, where the boy used to put your messages—is it still the same old letter box?"

"No," said Robert, "the entire door's been replaced—it was riddled with shrapnel—only the pavement's the same— the same one he used to walk on."

"Do you remember that when you walk across it?"

"Yes," said Robert, "I remember it, and perhaps that's one of the reasons I collect stress and strain formulas—why didn't you come back earlier?"

"Because I was afraid the city might not be alien enough to me. Twenty-two years, however, cushion things pretty well.

And isn't there room enough for what we have to say to each other, Robert, on postcards? I'd enjoy living near you, Robert, but not here. I'm scared. And am I kidding myself, or aren't the people I've run into just as bad as those I left behind?"

"You probably aren't kidding yourself."

"What's become of people like Enders? Do you remember him—the redhead? He was nice, certainly wasn't a brute. What did people like him do during the war, and what are they doing today?"

"Perhaps you underestimate Enders; he wasn't merely nice, he—well, why not simply put it as Edith used to—he never tasted the Host of the Beast. Enders has become a priest. After the war he preached what to me were some unforgettable sermons. It would sound bad if I were to repeat his words, but when he said them they sounded good."

"What's he doing now?"

"They've stuck him in a village the trains don't even go to. And there he's preaching away over the heads of the peasants and the schoolchildren. They don't hate him, they simply don't understand him, they even honor him after their fashion, like a likable fool. Does he really tell them that all men are brothers? They know better, and secretly think: 'But isn't he a Communist?' Nothing else occurs to them—the list of stereotypes has dwindled, Schrella. No one would have had the idea of labeling your father a Communist. Not even Nettlinger was as stupid as that. Today they'd have no other category for your father. Enders would shepherd the lambs, but they only give him goats. He's an object of suspicion because he makes the Sermon on the Mount the subject of his sermons so often. Perhaps some day they'll discover it's an extraneous interpolation and have it struck out—we'll go and visit Enders, Schrella, and when we take the evening bus back to the railway station, we'll be taking more despair than comfort back. I'm closer to the moon than I am to that village—we'll give our compassion a workout and visit him, people ought to visit prisoners—but what made you mention Enders?"

"I was thinking about whom I'd like to see again. You forget that I had to disappear right from classes. But I'm afraid of meeting people since I've seen Ferdi's sister."

"You've seen Ferdi's sister?"

"Yes, she runs the lemonade stall at the No. 11 terminus. Haven't you ever been there?"

"No, I'm afraid I might find Gruffel Street strange now."

"It was more alien to me than any other street in the world —don't go there, Robert. Are the Trischlers really dead?"

"Yes," said Robert, "Alois, too. They went down with the *Anna Katharina*. They hadn't been living at the harbor for some while. When the bridge was built they had to leave, but they didn't go for living in a city apartment. They needed water and ships. Alois was going to take them to friends in Holland, on the *Anna Katharina*. The boat was bombed; Alois tried to get his parents out of the cabin but it was too late—the water was already rushing in from above, and they never got out. It took me a long time to find any trace of them."

"Where did you hear that?"

"In The Anchor; I used to go there every day and question all the boatmen—until I found one who knew what had happened to the *Anna Katharina*."

Schrella drew the curtains together again, walked over to the table and stubbed out his cigarette. Robert followed him.

"I believe," he said, "it's time we went up to my parents— or would you rather not come to the party?"

"No," said Schrella, "I'll come with you, but shouldn't we wait for the boy? Tell me, what are people like Schweugel doing now?"

"Are you really interested?"

"Yes. Why do you ask if I'm really interested?"

"Did you really think about Enders and Schweugel in your hotel rooms and boarding houses?"

"Yes, and about Grewe and Holten—they were the only ones who didn't join in when the others attacked me on my way home. Nor did Drischka. What are they doing? Are they still alive?"

"Holten's dead, killed in the war," said Robert, "but Schweugel's still alive. He's a writer. And when he phones in the evening or rings the front door bell I have Ruth say I'm not at home. I find being with him unbearable and unproductive. I simply get bored with him. He's always talking about bourgeois and non-bourgeois, and I suppose he thinks he's the latter. What's the use of it? It just doesn't interest me. But he's several times asked after you."

"I see. And what's become of Grewe?"

"He's a party member, but don't ask me which party—it doesn't matter anyway. And Drischka is making 'Drischka's Auto-Lions,' a patented article that brings him in a lot of money. Don't you know what an Auto-Lion is? Stick around a few days and you'll find out. Anybody who thinks well of himself keeps one of Drischka's lions in the back of his car, on the rear window ledge. And you'll hardly find a person in this country who doesn't think pretty well of himself. This has been drummed into all of them. They brought a great deal back home from the war, memories of pain and sacrifice, but today they just plain think about themselves—didn't you see the people down there in the foyer? They were going to three different banquets: one banquet for the Left Opposition, one banquet for the Co-operative Welfare Society, and one banquet for the Right Opposition—but you'd have to be a genius to know who was going to which banquet."

"Yes," said Schrella, "I was sitting down there waiting for you while the first guests were coming in. I heard some talk about an Opposition. The first arrivals were the harmless kind, the good old Joe Blows of democracy, the business small fry who aren't so bad when you get to know them, as they say. They were talking about different makes of cars and weekend villas, and telling each other the French Riviera was beginning to be fashionable precisely because it's so overcrowded, and that in spite of all forecasts to the contrary it was becoming the fashion among intellectuals to go on package tours. Is that what they call inverse snobbery in this country, or dialectics? You'll have to enlighten me on such matters. An English snob would say to you: 'For ten cigarettes I'd sell you my granny.' But here they actually would sell you their grandma, and for five cigarettes at that, since they take even their snobbism seriously. Later on they got talking about schools; some were for the Humanistic ones, some against, and so on. Well, all right. I listened because I'd have very much liked to hear something about their real problems. Again and again they whispered to each other reverently the name of the star they were waiting for this evening. Kretz—have you heard the name before?"

"Kretz," said Robert, "in a manner of speaking, is an Opposition celebrity."

"I kept on hearing the word 'Opposition,' but it wasn't clear, from what they were saying, what Opposition they were talking about."

"If they were waiting for Kretz they must have belonged to the Left Opposition."

"If I got it right, this Kretz is what they call a 'white hope.' "

"Yes," said Robert, "they're expecting a lot from him."

"I saw him," said Schrella, "he came last. If he's their white hope, I'd like to know what their despair would be like. I think if ever I wanted to knock anybody off, he'd be the one. Are all of you blind? He's clever and cultured, of course, he can quote Herodotus in the original, and to these little businessmen who'll never get over their education tick, this has the ring of heavenly music. But Robert, I hope you'd never leave your daughter or son alone with Kretz for one instant. He's such a snob he's forgotten what sex he belongs to. They're playing going to hell in a hand bucket, Robert, but they're not playing it well. All you need is a little slow music and you'll have a third-class funeral. . . ."

Schrella was interrupted by the phone ringing, and he followed Robert to the corner as he picked up the receiver.

"Leonore?" said Robert, "I'm glad Father invited you. And please excuse me for what I said this morning, will you, Leonore? My father's expecting you in Room 212. A letter from Mr. Schrit? All the calculations on the X-5 documents wrong? Yes, I'll look into it, I'll telephone Schrit. Anyway, thank you, Leonore. And I'll see you later."

Robert put down the receiver and turned back to Schrella. "I believe—" he said, but a very strange sound, not especially loud but short and brittle, interrupted him.

"Good God," said Schrella, "that was a shot!"

"Yes," said Robert, "that was a shot. I believe we ought to go upstairs now."

Hugo read: 'Declaration: claims waived by the undersigned: I hereby declare myself as having agreed that my son Hugo. . . .' Underneath was an important-looking stamp, and signatures, but the inner voice he had held in such fear remained silent. Which voice had ordered him to cover his mother's nakedness when she came home after her expeditions, and lay on the bed muttering that fatal litany, *whywhy-why*. He had felt compassion and covered her nakedness, and brought her something to drink, and—at the risk of being assaulted, beaten and called *Holy Lamb*—he had slipped into the shop and begged two cigarettes. Which voice ordered him to play canasta with *a thing like that should never have been born*. Warned him against going into the shepherd-priestess's room, and now inspired him to murmur the word to himself, "Father."

To lessen the fear which beset him, he spilled out other words after it, brother and sister, grandfather, grandmother and uncle, but those words did nothing to lessen his fear. He cast forth more words, dynamics and dynamite, billiards and correct, scars on the back, cognac and cigarettes, red-green, white-green, but the fear was not alleviated. Action perhaps might assuage it: and he opened the window and looked down at the murmuring crowd. Was their murmur menacing or friendly? Fireworks were exploding against the deep blue sky.

Claps of thunder from which giant flowers blossomed. Orange shafts of light, like searching fingers. Window down. He ran his hands over the violet uniform hanging on the coat hanger behind the door. He opened the door into the corridor, and sensed the excitement which had spread even up to his floor—someone in Room 211 had been seriously wounded! He heard a buzz of voices, steps here, steps there, steps going up, steps going down and again and again a police officer's penetrating voice saying: "Make way there, make way there!"

Make way! Away! Hugo was afraid, and he whispered the word, "Father." The manager had said, we'll miss you, do you have to go like this, so suddenly? And he hadn't said it out loud, only thought, yes, I have to, like this, suddenly, the time is ripe. And when Jochen had brought in the news of the attempted assassination, the manager had forgotten his surprise at Hugo's giving notice. The manager had received Jochen's news not with horror but with delight, not shaking his head sadly but rubbing his hands, 'None of you has any idea what this means. This kind of sensation can send a hotel zooming. It's the only way to hit the headlines. Murder isn't suicide, Jochen, and political murder isn't just any murder. If he isn't dead yet, we must act as if he will be soon. You've no idea what it means; at least we must get a "Life in Grave Danger" into the headlines. I want all phone calls put straight through to my line, so I can see to it we don't foul up this chance. Good God, don't all look at me like a bunch of sadsacks! Keep cool. What I want you to do is put on a look of restrained commiseration, like someone in mourning, but comforted by the coming legacy. Okay, boys, get to work. There's going to be an avalanche of wired reservations. M., of all people; you've no idea what this means. I only hope we don't get a suicide to cross us. Phone the gentleman in Room 11 right away. As far as I'm concerned he can get angry and leave—goddamn, the fireworks ought to have waked him up. Okay, boys, man the guns.'

'Father,' thought Hugo, 'you've got to come and get me, they won't let me through to Room 212.' Flashbulbs were popping in the gray, shadowy stairwell. The elevator was in the shaft, a square of light, bringing up guests to Rooms 213–226, who, because of the police barricade, had to ride up to the third floor and walk down the service stairs. The elevator door as it opened released a loud buzz of voices, dark suits and bright dresses, bewildered faces and petulant lips forming the words, "It's too much, really, it's scandalous." Hugo pushed his door shut. Too late; she'd detected him, had begun to hurry down the corridor toward his room. He had just managed to turn the key on the inside when the handle shook violently.

"Open the door, Hugo, come on, open the door," she said.

"No."

"I order you to."

"I stopped working for this hotel a quarter of an hour ago, Madam."

"Are you leaving?"

"Yes."

"Where are you going?"

"To my father's."

"Open the door, Hugo, open the door, I won't hurt you and I won't frighten you any more. You can't leave. I know you haven't got a father, I know very well you haven't. I need you, Hugo. You're the one they're waiting for, Hugo, and you know it. You'll see the whole world and they'll lie at your feet in the best hotels. You won't need to say anything, you'll only need to be there. Your face, Hugo—come on, open the door, you can't leave."

Her words were interrupted by shakes of the door handle, punctuating her voice's pleading flow.

". . . it's not for my sake, really, Hugo, forget all I've said and done. It was just despair made me do it—come now, Hugo, for their sake—they're waiting for you, you're our lamb. . . ."

The door handle shook again.

"What do you want here?" the woman outside asked.

"I'm looking for my son."

"Hugo's your son?"

"Yes. Open the door, Hugo."

For the first time he forgot to say 'please,' thought Hugo. He turned the key and opened the door.

"Come on, son, we're leaving."

"Yes, Father, I'm coming."

"You have no other bags or things?"

"No."

"Come on."

Hugo picked up his suitcase and was glad his father's back hid her face. He could still hear her sobbing on his way down the service stairs.

"Now stop your sobbing, children," said the old man. "She'll be coming back to stay with us. She'd be very upset to know we were letting the party spoil. After all, he wasn't fatally wounded, and I hope that look of great wonder will never leave his face again—a brittle, short noise like that can work wonders. Will you young women please see to all the presents and flowers. Leonore, you take over the flowers, Ruth the greeting cards, Marianne the presents. Order is half of life—I wonder what's the other half? I can't help it, children, I can't be sad. It's a great day, it gave me back my wife and presented me with a son—may I call you that, Schrella? Edith's brother—I've even acquired a grandson, eh, Hugo? I'm still not quite sure about calling you grandson; it's true you're my son's son, but somehow not my grandson, and what voice or feeling orders me not to call you grandson I'm unable to explain.

"Sit down, the girls will make us all sandwiches; children, help yourselves from the gift baskets, and don't disturb Leonore's orderly files. Each of you had better sit on a year's pile. Schrella, you take pile A, it's the highest, and, Robert, allow me to offer you 1910, it's the next highest. You'd better pick out one for yourself, Joseph, 1912 isn't bad. That's right, settle down, all of you. Let's drink first to Mr. M., may the wonder never go from his face—the second toast to my wife, God bless her. Schrella, would you be kind enough to see who's knocking at the door?

"A certain Mr. Gretz come to pay his respects? I do hope he isn't lugging the wild boar on his back. No? Thank God for that. My dear Schrella, would you please tell him I'm busy? Or do you consider this the time and place, Robert, to receive a certain Mr. Gretz? No? Thank you, Schrella. It's the time and place to forgo false neighborly feelings. One word out of the way can cost a life—old Mrs. Gretz had said, 'It's a sin and a shame.' Lifting your hand can cost a life, and a misconstrued wink of the eye. Yes, please, Hugo, pour out the wine—I hope you won't be offended if we appreciate your hard-earned professional skills, and make good use of them here among the family.

"Good, yes, put the large bouquets in front of the bird's-eye view of St. Anthony's, and the smaller ones beside them on the left and right, on the shelf for the rolls of drawings—you can take those off and throw them away, they're only there for decoration, they're empty—or does anyone here still intend to use that precious paper? Maybe you, Joseph! Why are you sitting on such an uncomfortable seat, you've picked 1941, that was a meager year, boy. 1945 would have been better, it rained assignments then, almost like 1909, except that I gave it up, the 'Sorry' part spoiled my desire for building. Ruth, stack the greeting card addresses on my drawing board; I'll have some thank-you notes printed and you must help me address them, then I'll get you something pretty at Hermine Horuschka's. How should they read? 'My most sincere thanks for your kind courtesy on the occasion of my eightieth birthday.' Perhaps I shall enclose an original drawing with each acknowledgment, what do you think, Joseph? A pelican or a serpent, a buffalo or a beast—Joseph, would you please go to the door this time, and see who else it is so late?

"Four of the staff at the Cafe Kroner? Bringing a present

you think I shouldn't refuse? Right, then have them come in."

They came in, two waiters and the two girls from the cake counter, carrying it carefully through the door, the rectangular board, far longer than wide and covered with a snow-white tablecloth. It startled the old man; were they bringing in a corpse? Was that point there, tautening the white cloth like a post, the nose? They were carrying it carefully, as if the corpse were a precious one. Absolute silence reigned. Leonore's hands froze around a bouquet, Ruth stood holding a gold-rimmed greeting card, and Marianne did not put her empty hamper down.

"No, no," said the old man softly, "please don't put it on the floor; children, bring those two drawing trestles."

Hugo and Joseph brought two trestles from the corner and set them up in the middle of the studio, on the years 1936 to 1939. Silence again as the two waiters and the two girls set the board on the trestles, went each to one corner, grasped each the edge of the tablecloth and, when the eldest waiter uttered a short, sharp "Up!" they raised the cloth.

The old man flushed deeply, sprang toward the cake model, raised his fists, like a drummer gathering strength for a furious beat, and it seemed for an instant as if he would smash the sugared edifice to smithereens, but he let his fists sink slowly, till his hands hung loose at his sides. With a soft laugh, he bowed first to the two girls, then to the two waiters, straightened, took out his wallet and tipped each of the four with a bill. "Would you," he said, "kindly thank Mrs. Kroner for me most sincerely, and tell her that unfortunately important events oblige me to cancel my breakfast—important events, as of tomorrow, no more breakfasts."

He waited till the waiters and the girls had gone, then cried, "Come on, children, get me a big knife and a cake plate."

He cut off the spire of the Abbey first, and passed the plate to Robert.

Catalog

If you are interested in a list of fine Paperback
books, covering a wide range of subjects
and interests, send your name and address,
requesting your free catalog, to:

McGraw-Hill Paperbacks
1221 Avenue of Americas
New York, N.Y. 10020